DAUGHTER
of a
THOUSAND
YEARS

DAUGHTER

❧ *of a* ❧

THOUSAND
YEARS

Amalia Carosella

LAKE UNION
PUBLISHING

Published by Lake Union Publishing, Seattle

www.apub.com

Amazon, the Amazon logo, and Lake Union Publishing are trademarks of Amazon.com, Inc., or its affiliates.

ISBN-13: 9781503941205
ISBN-10: 1503941205

Cover design by Rex Bonomelli

Printed in the United States of America

For Thor
(And of course, Adam)

CHAPTER ONE:
AD 998
FREYDÍS

I f I had stayed in Iceland, my days would have been filled with women's work. Shearing the sheep and washing their wool in barrels of boiling urine, combing the fibers, spinning and weaving, or at the least directing others to do the same, with a break in the late summer to rake hay beneath the hot sun until the back of my neck matched the red of my hair, and my skin and clothes were soaked with stinking sweat. And perhaps that wouldn't have been the worst thing, really, I couldn't help but think, if it meant I was not in my father's hall at Brattahlid, to be seen by that weakling, Thorvard.

"You'll want for nothing as his wife," my father said, as if that mattered to me at all. "And though he wishes to make his fortune here in Greenland through trade and by farming, you'll have the wealth of his family to support you, should you wish to return home to Iceland."

It was the morning after Thorvard's arrival from the small farm he'd claimed to the east, and my father had found me in the pasture, counting the sheep. It hadn't needed doing, exactly, but I couldn't stand the thought of remaining in the longhouse even a moment longer under Thorvard's lustful gaze.

"I don't want a husband," I said, and not for the first time. My feelings on that matter had been more than clear since I'd turned fourteen. Certainly I had not changed my mind in the five years since. "And I haven't any interest in returning to Iceland, either. Give me a ship, Father, and thirty men, and let me sail!"

"And where am I to find the lumber for your ship?" he demanded. "Half our ships were lost in the crossing. Thorbjörn's, too, along with all their wealth and supplies, and if not for the grace of the gods, he and Gudrid might have drowned as well. I don't dare risk those we have left for anything but necessity, even if the men would follow you."

I lifted my chin, my hand closing tight around the hilt of my belt knife, my temper flaring hot at the implied slight. "I am the daughter of Erik the Red, their chieftain! They would grant me the same respect they show you, if you would only command it."

"You're the daughter of Erik the Red, that's true enough," he said ruefully, for he had never shied from admitting to me the weakness we shared—both of us far too quick to anger, too willing to draw our swords, to be swept up in emotion before reason. It was why we lived in Greenland now. The murders for which he'd been punished had not been wholly my father's fault, but the chieftains at the Althing had ruled against him all the same, and he had been lucky to escape Iceland with his life. "You'd set them to fighting amongst themselves before the first night, the way you've been carrying on. A full fortnight, and they'd be slitting one another's throats trying to win your favors for themselves. No. If you want your ship and your crew, you can beg it of your husband, and let what comes of it be on his head, not mine."

"He's soft," I said, not quite able to keep the curl from my lip.

"And you're hard as iron," my father said, and then he met my eyes sidelong, his hand falling heavy on my shoulder. "He'll look the other way, Freydís, when it matters most. You'll be free to do as you will, to act as you must. I cannot say the same for any of the rest of them, with your brother's talk and Thjodhild clamoring for a church to be built for their White Christ."

My jaw locked at the reminder. Thjodhild, my father's wife and the mother of all three of his sons, had even gone so far as to refuse to share his bed so long as he denied her god, and my brother Leif encouraged her, encouraged all the women to do the same, for that matter. Their foolishness had served me well enough, until Leif and Thjodhild had learned I'd been *talking* with more than one of the men, and Thorvard had so conveniently arrived, looking for a wife.

"Better if the gods had left Leif to rot across the sea in his Vinland," I muttered.

My father grunted. "Marry Thorvard, buy your ship with his silver, and perhaps the gods will guide you on your way to Vinland instead. You'd be free enough there, too."

"I shouldn't have to sail away to a strange land to be free," I said.

"And I never wanted for you to live as I did, exiled from every land you called home. But I won't live forever, Freydís, and you know as well as I do that Greenland will be Leif's when I'm gone. He's proven himself time and again as a capable leader, and with the favor and support of that fool King Olaf behind him, the others will not wish to fight the tide. Not when Norway's friendship might be the difference between life and death after a hard winter."

Yes, I knew. Leif had brought word to us that King Olaf of Norway had taken the ships of men who might have sailed to Iceland, and onward still to us, in Greenland, holding them hostage until they accepted the White Christ. Olaf felt it was his duty to see us all baptized, though I could not understand why. His ancestors surely could not approve, to say nothing of the gods—gods I had no intention of forsaking, whether my brother Leif and King Olaf willed it or not.

"You truly believe Thorvard is the best choice?" I asked.

"Because he is weak," my father agreed. "And his weakness will serve you well, if you are shrewd. He's promised me he'll remain with you at Brattahlid for as long as you wish, and he owes no true loyalty to Leif. I cannot speak to his family in Iceland, but if what you truly desire is to sail, to find your own fortune on the seas, then it will not matter what they might think once you have the ship you desire."

And once I was married, Thjodhild and Leif would be satisfied for a time. Certainly they would have no right to grumble about who I *talked* to, for that would be Thorvard's trouble, not my father's or theirs. Not that my father had cared overmuch, one way or the other. He'd only laughed at Thjodhild's demands that he run off the men who came to visit in hopes of luring me to the privacy of a hayfield for a romp.

"Why should I wish to frighten them off, when a babe in her belly is the only chance you'll have of convincing her to marry?" he'd told her. "Let her have her fun, just the same as the boys, and at least no man will doubt she'll make a lusty wife."

Which was probably why Thorvard couldn't stop staring at me since he'd come, imagining the pleasure he'd find in my bed. Soft as he was, I doubted he'd return the favor beneath the blankets. But if my father spoke truly—and I'd never known him to measure a man wrong—perhaps my new husband could offer me more important things in exchange.

"Tell him I'll agree only if he'll promise me a ship come next spring."

My father chuckled. "Be fair, Freydís."

I wrinkled my nose. "Give him two years, then, to find one, but no longer."

"And you'll be wed this summer."

I sighed and gave in. "Yes. In exchange for the promise of a ship, I will marry him this summer."

Because if I could only find myself a ship, I was certain I could find my fortune. Unlike my brother, lucky as he'd been, I'd have more than the support of a king.

I'd have the blessings of the gods.

The next day dawned blue white, the mist blown off the ocean a milky blanket over the fjord, hanging heavy and damp over Brattahlid. I dressed warmly, too familiar with how the cold fog sucked the heat from a body, and with a dish of skyr and a cup of milk set out for the steep, rocky slope behind my father's farmhouse.

It was land that still belonged to the wilds, to the *landvættir* and the gods, who had cloaked so much of the heart of this island with glacial ice. Sometimes I wondered if it belonged to the Jotuns themselves, all frost and trouble, rather than the gods. I could not imagine the gods overlooking my brother's work against them, or his mother's, happening as it was in their backyard. But the Jotuns, what would those giants care? All the better for them at the end of days if our warriors no longer heeded Odin's call.

The horses stirred as I passed, the fog turning their familiar whickers to strange, otherworldly sounds. I ignored the chill that crept down my spine and continued on, sure of the path beneath my boots, even if I couldn't see my destination. The hard-packed earth, once well worn and grass-free, was beginning to sprout with weeds, and I kicked at them as I went by. Thjodhild had stopped making offerings to the friendly wights and had forbidden the rest of the women and slaves in her household from doing the same. But if I was to be married, I wouldn't go to my husband without the blessing of the landvættir, the ancestors, and the gods, no matter what Thjodhild might say.

And it wasn't as though she could stop me—a fact that clearly infuriated her. Not that my father's wife had ever had much affection for me to begin with, not even after my mother had died. Thjodhild hadn't wanted my father to bring me to Greenland at all, never mind to live beneath her roof, my presence a daily reminder that he had spent some not inconsiderable portion of his time during that first exile in Iceland dallying with my mother, rather than on the work of finding a new homestead for his wife and sons. Leif, Thorstein, and Thorvaldur were all fair-haired, like their mother, and could have been anyone's children, truly. But not me. There was no denying who my father was—we shared the same brilliant red hair, the same temper, the same slightly snubbed nose and hazel eyes. I was my father's daughter, the child of his heart, and Thjodhild would never forgive it.

I'd brought a piece of driftwood, tucked into my belt alongside my knife, and after I reached the boulder of the wights and spread out my offerings, I sat on a nearby stone and began the slow process of carving the runes I desired. Runes for protection from the sea and the sky, runes to beg blessing from the gods, runes for prosperity and riches, runes to keep poison from my wine.

Gods give me strength, give me courage and glory. Make me hard and unbreakable and wise.

Thor was my father's god, for whom he'd named two of his sons, and I carved his name into the brittle wood as well, promising the god a portion of my wealth, should I succeed in finding my fortune upon the seas. A sacrifice of nine goats, perhaps, to please him for the gift of his protection and aid. If he'd only hear me.

I squinted into the mist, hearing voices on the wind—not from the farmhouse, surely, which meant someone had come in search of me, or in search of something. I rose from my stone seat and moved carefully, as silently as I was able, to crouch behind the boulder. It was large enough to hide me in the fog, so long as I made no noise.

"He said he saw her come this way." And I recognized one of the voices now as my brother Thorstein's. This past autumn, he'd married the insufferably pious, well-bred, shipwrecked Gudrid, to whom

Thjodhild was constantly comparing me. Thorstein had bought her father's last ship—the one that had not cracked open like an egg upon the rocks—with the earnings from his share of the farm at Lysufjord in the North and intended to sail for Vinland before the week was out, with our brother Thorvaldur alongside. "She can't have meant to go anywhere else but to that old boulder in this fog."

Thorstein himself was not so insufferable as his wife, but rather the opposite, and I hated that he'd married her, thinking nothing of the baptism she'd asked of him in return for her hand. At least he hadn't abandoned the old gods the way Thorvaldur and Leif both had, just accepted the White Christ alongside the rest. Always the peacemaker, Thorstein, but even he hadn't been able to calm Thjodhild's ire when our father had refused her new faith.

"Freydís!" he called out. I wasn't so great a fool as to reveal myself before I knew who he'd brought with him so far from the house. "Freydís, it's only me and Thorvaldur."

I let out a breath and used my knife and my hands to quickly bury my driftwood at the base of the boulder. The good Christian Thorvaldur would give me grief for it, even if Thorstein wouldn't, and I hadn't the patience to listen to more of Leif's words from anyone's mouth.

"Ha!" Thorstein said when I appeared, stepping out from behind the boulder and retaking my seat upon the stone. "I knew you'd be here. Talking to the wights again?"

"Hiding from the man Father insists I marry, more like," I said easily, for it wasn't truly a lie. Thorvard would not stray so far as this from the house, and the last thing I'd wanted was to fend off his pawing hands all day long.

"He does seem an odd choice," Thorvaldur agreed, rising out of the mist like a god with his broad shoulders, looming height, and golden hair. Thorvaldur was no weakling, that was certain.

Thorstein sauntered over to the boulder, leaning one hip casually against it and blocking my offerings from our brother's sight before he might comment upon them. "You could have sailed with me, you know. You needn't have promised yourself to that sop Thorvard to find your fortunes upon the sea."

"Upon Gudrid's ship?"

"My ship," Thorstein said, stiffening.

"Yours and Gudrid's, then," I said. "And if you think she'd have had nothing to say about my sailing among your men—"

"Gudrid is a good and obedient wife," Thorstein said, a flash of iron in his words. "If I'd told her my sister meant to sail with us, she wouldn't have argued."

I snorted. Thorstein was so in love with his new bride he couldn't see her manipulations, but I did. A soft touch and a cow-eyed look, and my brother was clay in her hands, formed however she liked.

"It's because she's a Christian," Thorvaldur said, crossing his arms over his chest. "That's why Freydís doesn't like her, though she'd do better to follow her example than sneer."

"And why shouldn't I sneer when she looks down her nose at me?" I asked. "When you all do!"

"Not all of us, Freydís," Thorstein said, giving Thorvaldur a hard look. "But that's enough. We didn't come out here to fight over our faiths. Did we, brother?"

Thorvaldur half growled, but the tension bled out of his frame, his shoulders slumping slightly even as he looked away. "No."

"You shouldn't be forced to marry a man beneath you," Thorstein said. "Despite the rest of our differences, Thorvaldur and I both agree upon that. And if you truly are only marrying the man for a ship, we would rather offer you a place upon ours, instead, than see you bound for any length of time to an unfit husband."

I flushed, my pride pricked by their kindnesses. Of course Thorvaldur would be happy to offer me a place on his ship, beneath his command, where he might control me, and as for Thorstein, he would have no luck at all making peace with his wife if he brought me along.

"Do you truly think I would marry someone so unfit as that? That Father would encourage it?"

"Father is old," Thorvaldur said. "And this is not the first time he has refused all reason."

"You mean, because he rejects your faith, that he is a fool because he remains loyal to the old ways." I lifted my chin, glaring at him. "You know nothing of which you speak, Thorvaldur. It is not only for a ship that I've agreed to marry Thorvard, and whatever you believe, *I* still trust in my father's wisdom."

"Surely there are more suitable men," Thorstein said, cutting off Thorvaldur's anger before he could put it to words. "Men who will not be cowed by your temper. Men who would stand as your equal."

"Christian men," I said. "Men who would demand I change my loyalties and deny my gods."

"It does not have to be that way, Freydís," Thorstein said. "You need not give up your old ways completely to accept the White Christ. He is just another god, another power to turn to in times of trouble. Another strength to draw upon, should Thor or Odin, Freyr or Freyja refuse you their blessing."

"I am not so disloyal to the gods I am named for as you," I said. And my gaze shifted to Thorvaldur, then, his hands fists at his sides. "Either of you."

Thorstein sighed. "You are determined then, upon this course?"

"I am."

He shook his head. "Then may the gods grant you their favor. I only hope your reward for such loyalty is counted in blessings, not curses."

"I will count it in silver and gold," I promised. "You'll see."

"I hope, for your sake, that is true. Come along, Thorvaldur. It's clear our sister has no use for our counsel, and I will not disturb her prayers any longer. We have arrangements of our own to make, after all."

I watched them go, disappearing back into the mist, a cold wind swirling behind, chilling me through my cloak. Part of me wanted to run after them, but I willed my feet to remain where they were. They had turned their backs on me, on Father, and on our ancestors, not the other way around.

But I hated it all the same, this rift between us. All the fighting amongst ourselves.

My fingers found the hammer hanging from my neck. *Thor, protect them.*

Perhaps if I slipped Mjölnir into their purses, he'd make sure they came home again, safe.

CHAPTER TWO:
AD 2016
Emma

The spaghetti supper, a fund-raiser for the Catholic school rather than yet another event for my father's campaign, was almost a refreshing change of pace. Or it would have been, if it hadn't been in the parish center and if half the people already seated hadn't greeted me with "Oh, Emma, we haven't seen you in so long!" or "Does this mean we'll be seeing you at mass on Sunday?" or the more subtle "The church does so need young couples like the two of you." Exactly the comments and circumstances I'd been trying hard to avoid since I'd come home—and the reason I wouldn't have attended at all if David hadn't been so determined to bring me.

I forced a hundred smiles, my well-practiced fund-raiser game face firmly in place, and made noncommittal responses, mostly complimenting the women on how great they looked and agreeing that it was, in fact, wonderful to see them again. But I could feel David growing more and more uncomfortable beside me as we made our way to an empty stretch of table, even if he did his best to hide it behind hearty handshakes with his fellow Sons of Italy and some good-natured ribbing about who was making the meatballs (Mrs. DiAngelo, of course) and whose mother had the best sauce (pretty much everyone was a winner).

"Are your parents coming, Emma?" Mrs. DiAngelo asked, paying us the honor of delivering our plates of spaghetti and meatballs herself. "I know how busy your father is with his campaign, but he always does try to make time for the school."

"He'll be here a little bit later," I promised. "And my mother, too."

"Oh, good!" But her smile turned slightly anxious. "She isn't planning on trying to help in the kitchen, is she?"

My mother was an incredible cook, but she'd been universally banned from the kitchens at the church. Apparently her Icelandic heritage prevented her from understanding the finer points of Italian cuisine—or more honestly, nobody wanted their family recipe fussed with, no matter how well intentioned my mother's suggestions might have been.

"She said to tell you she was bringing bread and dessert, but she was sure that you had the kitchen well in hand without her."

"God bless her!" Mrs. DiAngelo said. "And just look at the two of you. Such a lovely couple. Your father must be so pleased. He must be hearing church bells by now."

"It hasn't even been a year yet, Mrs. DiAngelo," David said, laughing. It was forced and self-conscious, but I didn't think she noticed.

"Well." She beamed. "I'll just let the two of you eat while the food is still hot. Salads are on their way! Oil and vinegar?"

"Nothing better!" I agreed. To admit to a preference for ranch was practically social suicide—and one had to pick her battles when one hadn't stepped foot in a church since Easter and was hoping desperately to find a way to skip out on Christmas Eve mass.

"You aren't going to change your mind, are you?" David asked after Mrs. DiAngelo had disappeared back into the kitchen.

"About my salad dressing?"

The grim set to David's mouth didn't change at all. "About coming back to church."

I focused on my plate, twirling my spaghetti on my fork with way more concern than necessary for someone who was purposely wearing a red shirt to better hide any splashes or sauce stains.

"I've tried to be patient with you, Emma," he said when I didn't respond. "I think I've been incredibly understanding, all things considered, while you've worked through whatever rebellion this is. I haven't pressured you or made any demands—"

"Is this the part where you start?" I asked. "If I'd known all this time you were just being patient, waiting for me to get over my *rebellion*, I'd have been happy to set you straight long before now. This isn't a phase for me, and I think I was pretty honest about that from the beginning. I'm glad that going to mass and being so involved here does so much for you, and you know I don't have any objection to raising a family in the Church, but it just isn't my thing, personally."

His lips pressed into even thinner, more uncompromising lines. And I knew. I knew where this was going, and based on what he'd just said, everything that had just happened, I couldn't even be surprised. Not really. Mostly I was just tired.

"I don't think this is going to work," he said.

I sighed. "Maybe you're right."

And that was it.

But even if the rest of our meal was awkward and uncomfortable—because of course David didn't want to make a scene, and there was no way I was going to draw attention to myself, either, with my parents on their way and the campaign to consider—Mrs. DiAngelo's meatballs were, as always, pretty great.

Of all the things about being Catholic, I was pretty sure I was going to miss the food the most.

"I wasn't Catholic enough."

"What does that even mean?"

I shook my head, the whole mess of it still too fresh, too ridiculous. "When he asked me to go to church with his family at Easter, I didn't think it was going to turn into a whole . . . *thing*. Obviously I hadn't been in forever, because they changed half the wording of the prayers and I was on autopilot with the wrong script. Of course his mother noticed, and you should have seen the look she gave me. Needless to say, Easter dinner was *ice* cold. But I thought we were fine. We laughed about it after."

Sarah raised both eyebrows, peering at me over the rim of her coffee cup. "Are you sure it wasn't just you laughing about it?"

I sighed, leaning back in the booth. "I don't know. Honestly. After the way his mother was acting, I didn't have the heart to tell him how long it had been since I'd stepped foot in a church." I swirled my hot cocoa, dissolving some of the whipped cream while I waited for it to cool. "I guess it would have only been a matter of time, either way."

"You had to expect that, though," she said. "Right?"

There it was. I bit back a sarcastic response and forced myself to take a drink instead, savoring the silk of the chocolate on my tongue, letting the just-too-warm liquid burn the back of my throat. I loved Sarah, I did. We'd been friends practically since birth. But if I hadn't been Catholic enough for David, I would never be Christian enough for her, either. Which made this whole conversation just that much more frustrating. And if I hadn't told her, it would've been the same mess later, with a side of guilt for not trusting her to understand.

Of course she'd never admit that she didn't, in fact, understand. Since I'd been raised in an extremely Catholic family, sent to an even more Catholic school, and surrounded by Catholic and lapsed-Catholic friends—with the exception of Sarah, who had decided to jump ship for nondenominational Protestantism, and my mother's side of the family, who we never saw—there were very few people in my life who did. Which was fine, generally. Until times like this, when it wasn't.

But it was Saturday brunch, and you just didn't miss Saturday brunch with your best friend, no matter how awkward it was going to be when you had to confess that you'd been dumped by the first serious boyfriend you'd had in years. Because of religious differences that said best friend had predicted would be your downfall from pretty much the minute you'd started dating the guy.

It made me want to beat my head against the table. That was the proof of a best friendship, though, right? Best friends always brought the tough love, even if sometimes it fell a little on the misguided side.

"Not everyone needs to marry someone who believes exactly the same thing they do," I said, hoping it sounded mild and reasonable, and not like a critique of her life choices. Sarah had long since stopped even considering men who weren't at least Protestant, and she mostly preferred her particular congregation—which was why she was still single. "He didn't make a big deal about going to church when we started dating, and he knew up front that I wasn't really into it."

"There's a difference between not really being into it and not believing his god exists," Sarah said.

"I don't not believe that his god exists," I corrected her, and for the record, it was definitely ground we'd covered at least a million times before. Why people thought faith in one god necessitated the invalidation of all other gods was something I'd never understood—even when I was a good little Catholic girl. "I absolutely believe that God and Jesus are out there and that they're doing their thing with their flock. But religion isn't one size fits all. I tried square-pegging myself into that round hole for two decades. It doesn't work for me." I reached for the pendant tucked beneath my shirt, the symbol of my faith in a god that *she* didn't believe existed, but I stopped myself and returned my hand to my mug instead. "I just need to meet someone who can agree to disagree with me, that's all."

She made a soft noise, her lips pressing together in unvoiced frustration. The same frustration I felt, probably, from the other perspective. "All I'm saying is that you're going to have a hard time finding someone who this isn't going to be an issue for, okay? That's it. I'm not trying to start a fight, I'm just saying. And not just guys you're dating. People could take it the wrong way, and I just don't want you to get hurt, you know?"

"I understand," I said, forcing myself to smile, to take another deep breath and let it out slowly until I could be reasonably certain I wasn't going to *sound* annoyed. "But this is who I am now. I've never been happier or felt freer." This wasn't so different from how she felt about her faith. And it wasn't like I made a big deal out of it. People made assumptions, and I was happy to let them come around to the realization that they might have been wrong in their own time. Or never at all, if they preferred to live in ignorant bliss. "If that means I have to work a little harder to find someone who wants to be part of my life, or whatever, then that's a price I'm willing to pay."

"Emma—"

"I knew David wasn't going to be the one, anyway," I hurried to say, before she could ask me if I wouldn't consider just going to church with *her* one Sunday, because even if I didn't want to be Catholic, maybe I could still be some kind of Christian. I was tired of having that conversation. "Did I tell you he fell asleep during *Star Wars*?"

Her forehead creased. "What?"

"He fell asleep. In the theater. On opening night."

She laughed, a little hesitantly and maybe not all that sincerely, but she laughed. "Well, then I guess his days really were numbered, weren't they?"

"Let's just say I was having some serious doubts. It was the beginning of the relationship, so I wanted to give him a second chance, you know? Like maybe his cold medicine knocked him out and it was involuntary. But nope. Before all this not-Catholic-enough stuff went down, he admitted to me that he thought the Original Trilogy was boring. Because they weren't real people and it wasn't like it was something that could ever happen."

"No!"

The server slid Sarah's pancakes in front of her, and then my hash and eggs.

"And that wasn't the worst of it," I said.

"How could that not be the worst?" she asked, smiling more genuinely now.

"He doesn't like the Muppets, either. Not even *Sesame Street.*"

"How were you dating this man at all?"

I grabbed the ketchup, squirting it over my hash. "I think I was just taken in by the fact that he really seemed to adore me in the beginning. The lengths he went to in order to ask me out that first time were really impressive, and going so out of his way to visit me at school the last semester. Maybe I was tired of showing up at all those events alone, and getting those pats on the cheek and pitying remarks. Or worse, the offers to set me up with some bingo player's grandson."

"I'm sure that some of those bingo players' grandsons are worth the blind date," Sarah said, perfectly serious. "They're probably all good Italian boys, too."

And good Catholic boys, I was sure. The kind with statues of the Virgin Mary somewhere in the yard and antique crucifixes hanging over the bed. The kind who take their grandmother to church every Sunday and go to confession at least twice a year, which was all fine, until I was sitting here again, three weeks or three months down the road, after they found out I wasn't the good little Catholic girl my kindly relatives and family friends had made me out to be.

"Should I ask Auntie Christina to set one up for you?" I asked, sidestepping the implications, and the argument that would follow on its heels. "I'm sure she'd be just *thrilled*."

Sarah snorted. "I think I've had my fill of good Italian boys, thanks. But if your auntie Anja wants to send any of those Icelandic cousins my way . . ."

I laughed. "My agnostic Icelandic cousins, you mean?"

"The country is officially Protestant, with the Church of Iceland, isn't it?" Sarah said. "There's got to be one of them who goes to church."

My mother's side of the family all lived in Iceland, for the most part, but we'd gone to see them only a handful of times, when I was small, to bring Amma back to her family before she passed away. Auntie Anja, my mother's sister, was the only one I really knew well, from her visits once or twice a year. But there were plenty of pictures of very attractive family members I'd never met, and Sarah had been admiring them for years. Not that I blamed her. When we were boy-crazy teenagers, I'd admired them along with her.

"I'll place your order with Auntie Anja."

She'd promised to come for the holidays, even though New Year's Eve in Reykjavík was a thousand times more awesome than anything we did in New Hampshire. And for the first time, she was bringing her husband with her. A man Auntie Anja swore traced his lineage all the way back to none other than the Norse god of thunder, Thor.

I absolutely could not *wait* to meet him.

I trudged through the crisp, fresh fall of rainbow leaves, the gravel of the driveway crunching under my brown suede boots, and then hesitated at the door, taking a deep breath to fortify myself against what was waiting inside.

My house. My parents' house, I supposed, since May, when I'd graduated with my master's in history—women's history, but my father always glossed over my feminist leanings, even if his voting record was more for women's rights than against, and I'd gotten used to censoring the evidence for his political convenience. They'd kicked me out of my bedroom and into the guesthouse the minute I moved back, to grant me an illusion of success as an adjunct professor at the local community college, for whatever good it would do Dad's latest campaign.

My dad, Congressman Moretti.

Another reason why being not Catholic enough was a recurring problem in my life: when your father runs his campaign on conservative Christian family values, and you've spent the last decade realizing Christianity is an ill-fitting suit that you really don't want to keep putting on, it's not exactly something you can go public with. Or even semipublic anonymously on the Internet, for fear of what kind of PR bomb that would be if I were ever found out. In fact, I didn't really have any plans to tell my father I didn't share his particular beliefs at all. Of course he'd been thrilled that I'd been seeing David, because David was everything he wished I would be—everything he'd hoped that I'd become, now that I was home again.

He wasn't going to be happy it was over. And he was going to be even unhappier about the reason why.

Don't rock the boat, I reminded myself. I just had to keep on keeping on for the time being. While I was living under their roof, at least, and an easy potshot for the press who might want to smear my father's reputation.

I grasped the pendant, cool to the touch, squeezing it for courage, then dropped it beneath my shirt again and opened the door.

"Hello?"

"*Halló,* sweetheart," my mother called from the kitchen.

When they hosted big events, my parents hired a chef, but my mother never liked letting anyone else manhandle her pots and pans. Cooking was one of the ways she burned off the stress of a campaign season, as well as the noncampaign season, when Dad was in session and didn't make it back outside of the occasional weekend.

I kicked off my boots in the mudroom and followed her voice deeper into the house. She smiled and pressed a kiss to my cheek. "I thought you had plans with David tonight?"

"David's decided the congressman's daughter isn't quite the catch he was hoping for," I said, trying to keep my tone light. "I don't think we'll be seeing him again anytime soon."

"Oh dear," she said, frowning. "Your father will be disappointed to hear it, but I hope it wasn't anything too dramatic."

Too dramatic. My mother's euphemism for anything that might be a headline on a slow news day. I grimaced. "I don't think so. We just weren't quite on the same page. He wanted someone more serious, um, religiously. Easter and Christmas attendance wasn't going to cut it."

My mother pursed her lips, studying me with that cool, assessing look—the one that made me squirm even when I was completely innocent. Which I wasn't, not entirely. But David hadn't known anything about me that could hurt my father. I was always careful about that.

"You know it would be good for people to see you at mass a little more often," she said at last. "For the next few weeks, just in case."

I rolled my eyes. "I'm not going to start going to church just because David might tell someone who knows someone else who might tell another person's brother's dog that I'm a lapsed Catholic."

"For your father, not for them," she said, waving the David issue away and turning her attention back to her bubbling pot. "This campaign has been hard on him, and I know he'd appreciate having your support."

"He can have my support in other ways," I said. "But I'm not going to lie for him by pretending to be part of a faith community that isn't mine. Dad is good at what he does because he believes the things he says—he's honest in his politics and his beliefs. I'm not going to sully his campaign that way."

"You need *some* kind of community involvement, Emma. If not for the campaign or anyone else, then for yourself."

"I've been plenty involved," I said.

"With campaign events. Not anything else, outside of David's commitments. You think I haven't noticed? You go to work and then come home and hide yourself away every night."

"Would you rather I go out and get wasted Thursday through Saturday like Holly?"

"Holly volunteered everywhere, plus church every Sunday, even when she was fighting us tooth and nail in every other respect. And she's very involved in her church in California, too. Which you would know if you ever picked up the phone to call your sister."

On that count, I was definitely guilty. But it didn't mean I was going to roll over. "If I start involving myself, it's going to be the spaghetti supper all over again. People pointedly asking why they haven't seen me at church and me feeling entirely dishonest. I'm not going to do that to myself, Mamma. Not anymore."

She sighed, banging her wooden spoon against the heavy cast-iron pot. "Set the table, please, Emma. We're having leek, potato, and pancetta soup."

I accepted the dismissal for the mild rebuke it was meant to be and opened a cabinet, reaching for the bowls, perfectly content to let the entire matter drop. My mother was good at that.

"And set an extra place, if you wouldn't mind," she added as my fingers closed around the cool ceramic, my thumb slipping between the third and fourth dish. "Alexander is coming for dinner tonight."

My father's public relations director for his last two campaigns, Alex had been far enough ahead of me in school that we hadn't really had a lot of contact with one another until he'd started working for my dad.

One of the bright young local boys he'd taken under his wing—though why a congressman would hire a small-town PR guy, I didn't know. I guess Dad had thought it wouldn't matter, because he'd never been touched by any real scandals and he was always incredibly deliberate about the words that came out of his mouth. How Alex would cope if my father ever needed a real spin doctor wasn't something I wanted to find out.

I grabbed a fourth bowl, flashing it at my mother in acknowledgment. At least with Alex at the table, I wouldn't have to worry about Dad grilling me about the David situation. If I was careful, I could slip off to the guesthouse right after dessert, under the guise of politely walking Alex out, and leave Mom to break the news. Not to mention the fact that Alex wasn't exactly hard on the eyes—by this point I was pretty convinced that his young Marlon Brando meets Harrison Ford appeal was part of what made him good at his job. When he turned that smile on someone, it was like he'd just shared some incredible secret with them, and them alone.

My night was looking better and better.

CHAPTER THREE:
AD 998
FREYDÍS

We celebrated my marriage to Thorvard with a fine feast under a clear sky. More generous than Thjodhild would have liked, no question, but as chieftain, my father could hardly skimp on such things, and I knew he did not want Thorvard to think me a poor choice of bride, worth so little to my family that they would not even part with the food required to mark the occasion properly.

My new husband could not have missed the coldness of Leif's manner, or Thjodhild's, for all of that, and I'd barely exchanged a handful of words with Thorvaldur and Thorstein since our argument at the wights' boulder. Thorvaldur particularly had made it clear I should consider myself fortunate that he had waited to sail until after my wedding day. It was enough to make me reconsider the pendant I'd had made for him, four bronze hammers joined together at the hilts to form a cross, to keep him safe on his journey, and the same again for Thorstein, that it might not offend his wife. Gifts I had saved to give them before they sailed the following day.

"More wine, my love?" Thorvard asked, topping off my cup before I could answer. "Your father's offered us the use of the pit house for our wedding night, that we might have some peace and privacy."

I forced a smile to my lips. "My father is consideration itself."

"I wasn't certain he'd part with you at all, in truth," Thorvard said. "And your brothers—Thorstein and Thorvaldur—I won't deny I feared for my life that first night, after Erik announced our engagement."

My gaze shifted to Thorstein, a flush warming my cheeks. "Oh?"

"They are formidable men, no question," Thorvard said. "I can hardly believe my good fortune to have secured such a strong alliance. And your father is not at all what I expected. I never would have imagined he could be so charismatic, the way they speak of him in Iceland."

I stiffened, all the warmth of affection for my brothers washed away with the implications of my husband's words. "And how exactly do they speak of my father in Iceland?"

He laughed, but nervously, I thought, and that was as it should be. "I fear in Iceland your father is infamous for his temper. They say he was known to fly into rages as foul as any berserker. That he made enemies of his neighbors before he'd even finished cutting the turf for his house."

My eyes narrowed, and it took all my will not to throw my wine in his face. "Such a man could not entice more than thirty ships of men and women to follow him to Greenland. Such a man would not rule those same men and women, still, as their chieftain all these years later."

Thorvard cleared his throat. "No . . . no, you're right, of course. I simply did not know what to expect of him, that's all. Or of this settlement, for that matter, though you Greenlanders seem to have done well in carving your farms from the ice."

"Greenland was green before we came here, and it will be green still, long after we have left. Or do you mean to suggest that my father lied, as well?"

"I meant no disrespect, of course," Thorvard said, too quickly, and I knew that was precisely what he had meant to imply, for we'd all heard the joke that Erik the Red had named this land Greenland in order to deceive those ships of men and women into following him. That Greenland was nothing but snow and stone and ice, and the farmland was all buried beneath it. A cruel joke upon the Icelanders who were fool enough to take an outlawed man at his word.

But I swallowed my temper and turned away, that he wouldn't see my disgust. Fighting with my husband was no way to begin a marriage, and I had no intention of shaming my father before his guests. "My father is a good and generous man, loyal to the gods and to the men who follow him. Anything else that you've heard is a lie, and I will not have it so much as whispered in my hearing again."

"Of course," he said again. His favorite words, it seemed, as often as he repeated them. "Of course. Forgive me."

I didn't speak to him for the rest of the meal, my gaze wandering from face to face, friend to friend, before landing again upon my brother and his wife. Gudrid smiled up at Thorstein, and his eyes warmed, his hand covering hers upon his arm.

It cut me through, and I rose from the table, meaning to leave before I could see any more clearly just what I had given up in my stubbornness, my stupid pride. But my movements were too sudden, catching the attention of my father and his guests, and causing a rash of bawdy jokes to rise up from the men at the tables below. Thorvard rushed to stand as well, grinning along with them, and while I blinked the sting of tears from my eyes, I had no choice but to pretend that my actions were that of an eager bride impatient to bed her husband.

With the laughter of fools at my back, I let Thorvard lead me away.

Weak as my husband seemed to be, I could not imagine the night's obligations would take very long. Perhaps if I was lucky, he'd sleep like the dead after he was spent, and I would be spared any more of his talk.

I crept out of the pit house the following morning, stiff and sore and far from satisfied as I climbed the ladder and slipped and slid down the damp turf. My husband had been gifted with stamina, but not the wit to understand how best to make use of it, and I hadn't been in any mood to tutor him.

In truth, I did not think it would have mattered overmuch if I'd tried. Thorvard was the first man I had ever taken to my bed for any reason other than desire and mutual appreciation, and I hadn't cared for the hollowness of it all. How other women married so easily at their father's command, to a man they neither knew nor particularly cared for, I would never know.

My father's man, Thorhall, had readied my horse for me, as I'd asked of him the day before, but I winced at the thought of sitting astride, then grimaced outright when I had managed to find my seat. Worthless, three-legged Thorvard. My new husband might as well have had the world serpent stuffed down his pants. If only Thor had come down from his hall to slay the beast before I'd been forced to suffer his intrusion.

I rode anyway, cursing myself and Thorvard with every stride, for even as early as I'd risen, I hadn't the time to walk all the way if I meant to catch my brothers before they shoved off.

"Freydís!" Thorstein greeted me happily when I found him on the beach, doing one last check of the lines and the hull of his ship before he set sail. "I trust you slept well, and that your husband did not leave you disappointed after all the wine he drank with his dinner."

"Even soft, he would have been man enough to satisfy any woman." There was nothing else to do *but* boast, for I couldn't bring myself to admit my foolishness after the things I'd said, and I did not want Thorstein's last thought of me to be pitying. "Pray to the gods that Gudrid doesn't get a look at him, or she'll never be satisfied again by the likes of you."

Thorstein threw back his head and roared with laughter. "Thank the gods for that! There's much in a marriage that can be overlooked so long as he knows how to please you in bed."

"Mm," I said, hoping it sounded smug instead of smarting.

But I ought to have known I could not fool my brother for long, because his laughter faded at my response, his eyes narrowing and his good humor edged with concern instead. "You could sail with us still, Freydís. Say he was not fit and divorce him before you go. Father would have it all settled again and forgotten by the time we returned home."

I shifted my gaze to his ship instead, stepping forward to reach up and stroke the curve of the dragon-headed prow. "You don't mean to raid, do you?"

"Freydís—"

"Will you?"

He grunted, irritated by my stubbornness, no doubt, and I did not blame him, but I had not come to dry my tears on my brother's tunic. I'd come to see him off and wish him well on his voyage. To be certain that when he left, it was not with anger in his heart.

"The dragon head is meant to frighten the landvættir of Vinland away, that's all, that we might raid the land itself for its bounty without trouble or curse upon our heads."

I smiled. "She is surely fierce enough for that."

"And then some." Thorstein joined me, patting the dragon's long neck with a gloved hand. But he sighed, and I felt his gaze on me again. "Promise me you will not let your pride bring you to ruin, Freydís. You need not say anything more, and I will let it rest, but promise me that."

"The gods can hardly afford to see me ruined, for my pride or otherwise," I said. "But you needn't fear I'll get myself in trouble over the summer while you're away. I'll be kept too busy by my new husband, I'm certain, and Thjodhild and Leif are sure to keep a sharp eye upon me so long as I remain beneath our father's roof."

"And a good thing," he grumbled.

I threw my elbow into his ribs, and he grunted again, this time in surprise, and I turned to face him. "I promise I will not let my pride rule all, if that will please you. But you must promise me something in exchange. You and Thorvaldur, both."

"And what is that?" he asked, wary.

I pulled the twin bronze crosses from my belt pouch and held them out. "Wear these. That I might have some hope Thor will bring you home."

Thorstein laughed, accepting the gift. "And you wish me to lie to our brother as to the meaning behind such a thoughtful gift, I assume."

I shrugged. "Let him think what he wishes, and Gudrid, too. So long as you have the thunder god's protection, I'll sleep soundly at night. Leif said the waters were tricky, and I would not see the least insufferable of my brothers bewildered by the sea and lost."

Thorstein looped the leather thongs over his head, the two Thor's crosses clinking together where they hung against his chest. "I'll let Thorvaldur believe you made him a true cross, to make peace, and he'll be well pleased with the gift."

I threw myself into his arms, hugging him hard and tight, the bronze cold against my cheek. "May Thor protect you and keep you safe."

"And you, Freydís," he said into my hair. "Try not to let Leif and Thjodhild goad you, either."

I laughed and let him go, grabbing my horse's reins to keep from clinging to him like a child. He gave me a boost up on her back, and I turned from the shore. I had a husband to see to, after all, whether I liked it or not, and I would not let Thorstein see me weep. He'd never let me forget it if I did.

CHAPTER FOUR:
AD 2016
Emma

Your father said you were going to be staying local—teaching at the community college this fall?" Alex asked, and I realized belatedly the mistake I had made. Of course I wasn't going to be fading into the background of tonight's dinner. Alexander Stone was always quick to take advantage of an opportunity to get the facts directly, and by sitting down at the table, I'd unwittingly agreed to an interview. Or an interrogation.

Probably both.

"Just a little short stop of experience to decide whether or not I want to continue on and go for the PhD and a life in academia," I said. Just like I'd told everyone else, and likely the same words my father had used. Consistency was important, and I'd been raised with a background chorus of *stay on message*. "Fortunately they had an opening.

Medieval history isn't my favorite, but I'm looking forward to being able to touch on the Viking Age, at least."

My father frowned at my ad lib, but I ignored it. Alex was on our side, and I wasn't here to play politics anyway. I was here to eat and get out again as quickly as possible.

"So you're not settled on what your plans are, beyond this year?" Alex asked. "No five-year plan that we can sketch out if necessary, to create an illusion of momentum and success?"

I sighed, pushing my dish away and abandoning all hope of actually being able to enjoy my soup. "Could you ask that question with a little bit more condescension, Alex?"

Now my mother was scowling at me, too. "Don't be rude, Emma."

But Alex's lips twitched. "Would you like me to try?"

"It doesn't really sound like my idea of dinner entertainment, actually," I said, cutting my own glare back at my parents. "But then, I wasn't expecting to have to justify my life plan tonight, either."

"You'll have to forgive her, Alex," my mother said. "David's decided to make other plans rather suddenly, and Emma's obviously distraught."

"Mom!"

"Alex was bound to find out sooner or later anyway," my mother said, infernally calm.

"What's this about David, now?" my father asked, looking from my mother to me and back again.

I groaned, hiding my face in my hands. The back of my neck was burning, and my ears had gone hot with embarrassment. And frustration. And *intense* resentment that my love life had just become another data point in Alex's PR machine.

"We're no longer seeing one another," I said, dropping my hands and addressing my soup bowl. "It's not a big deal. We weren't together for that long, and it's not like it was some big blowout. We just both realized it wasn't quite the right fit, that's all."

"Well." Alex cleared his throat. "I think we can all agree that it's his loss."

I looked up, surprised at his sudden awkwardness. Alex, who always knew exactly what to say, hemming and hawing. He didn't meet my gaze, seeming to stare at the butter dish between me and my mother instead.

"I'm sorry," he said. "I really didn't mean to stir anything up."

"You don't think David is going to make this into something, do you?" my father asked.

I closed my eyes, not sure whether I was irritated or relieved that he'd jumped so quickly to his campaign concerns. "No, Dad."

"I'm sure it would hardly register with anyone even if he did," Alex said. "If we were talking about Holly, with her history, I'd maybe be a little bit more concerned, but your voters have always loved Emma, and she reads as honest and forthright no matter what she says."

I pressed my lips together to keep from grimacing and poked at my soup. It had cooled enough now to congeal at the top, and I scraped at the thicker skin with the back of my spoon. "I'll do my best to keep my head down until after the election," I said. "And you don't have to worry. I don't plan on doing any more dating while I'm under the microscope."

"I don't think anyone's saying you can't date, Emma," my mother said, clearly exasperated. "Honestly!"

"It's only that everything we do in these last few months is magnified," I said, repeating the refrain I'd heard over and over again growing up. "I know how it works, Mom. I do. And if I could have planned it, I would've made sure we split closer to Thanksgiving than Election Day, but it wasn't exactly my idea."

"You'd really have stayed with him until after the election if you'd known?" Alex asked.

I shot him another glare. "You think I don't know my obligations to the campaign by now?"

He recoiled, his face red. "That wasn't—" He swallowed. "Sorry. Not my business."

"Here I thought everything was your business," I grumbled.

"Emma, really," my father said. "I understand that you must be upset, but this kind of behavior—"

"It's okay, Joe," Alex said. "If I'd realized, I wouldn't have . . ."

"Poked the dragon?" I suggested when he seemed to hesitate over his words. "Begun an interrogation about my life plan? Deliberately invaded my privacy?"

"It's his job, Emma," my mother said. "You know that."

I took a deep breath, struggling to regather the shredded remains of my temper. "I know. I'm sorry, Alex. I just . . . I didn't know you were going to be here, and I wasn't exactly prepared for your questions."

"You really don't need to apologize," he said, so graciously that I wanted to punch him. "I understand how wearing all this can be. It was thoughtless of me to jump on you this way."

I forced a smile. "But if you didn't, how would I ever be prepared for guerilla attacks from reporters?"

He laughed. "I don't think the guerilla reporters would survive to tell their tales if they tried to jump you, anyway."

My father snorted. "Don't encourage her, Alex."

But it was more teasing than serious, and I felt another notch of tension slip away. It had been a long time since I'd been caught up in the mess of the last few months of campaigning. Long enough that I'd forgotten what it was like. The way every life event was dissected in those last weeks, teased for every last thread of goodwill that might be spun out to draw in voters.

The last time I'd been a part of it, I'd had a lot less to hide, and tonight's disastrous dinner made my stomach roil with doubts.

Maybe coming home had been a mistake.

The rest of dinner was quiet, mostly Alex discussing mailers and ad placement. My father was being challenged in his run by an even more conservative opponent, and the election wasn't quite as in the bag as my father would have liked. I helped my mother clear the table after the meal, and made coffee for Alex and my father to go along with the apple pie my mother had baked in an attempt to get ahead of the fruit that was already starting to fall from her trees. It wasn't going to be a really great year for the apples, but she always ended up with more than she could use and sent buckets to the local food banks.

I shooed my mother out of the kitchen with the pie and started cleaning up rather than joining them for dessert. Apple pie had never really been my favorite, and thinking I was going to be out with David, my mother had experimented with raisins, making it even less appealing to me. Raisins never belonged in any kind of dessert, as far as I was concerned.

"Thank you so much for the meal, Irena," Alex said, his chair groaning against the wood floor. If I leaned back from the sink, I could see the table through the broad archway—but it would be better for my escape if I pretended not to be listening. "It's always a pleasure."

"You'll have to come back next week, then," my mother said. "Joe keeps you so much to himself, and you know I like to stay informed."

He laughed. "When you put it like that, how can I refuse?"

"Emma," my mother called. "Stop playing Cinderella and come say good-bye."

"I wouldn't blame her if she'd had enough of me for one night," Alex said ruefully.

"Don't be silly," my mother said. "Emma!"

"Coming!" I dried my hands and made my way to the front of the house. *Playing Cinderella.* Please. Doing enough cleanup so I wouldn't feel guilty for cutting and running, more like, but that was for me to know and my mother to find out.

Dad and Alex were discussing their schedule for the coming week when I appeared. And plans for some nondenominational town hall event at the parish center on Thursday that my mother had made clear I was expected to attend, regardless of my disaffection. I kissed her on the cheek and shoved my feet into my boots. "Let me walk you out, Alex."

He blinked, glancing at my parents. "You really don't have to—"

"I'll sleep better tonight," I said, and slipped past him to give my dad a kiss, too. "Besides, I should get going and make sure I'm prepped for class on Monday."

My parents could hardly object to my gesture in front of Alex, I knew, and it wasn't like I was leaving my mother holding the bag on my breakup with David anymore. Instead, I got a murmured "Good night" in response to my "Thanks for dinner," and when the door closed again behind us, I grinned at Alex in triumph.

"Thanks for that."

"For what?" he asked.

"Helping me make my escape. You were the sheep fleece to my Odysseus act."

He lifted both eyebrows, stopping at his car. "I thought he was after the Golden Fleece."

"That was Jason and the Argonauts, actually. But on their way home from Troy, Odysseus and his men were captured by a Cyclops, and to escape, they blinded him, then strapped themselves to the undersides of the monster's sheep to slip by him when he let the flock out to graze."

"That's right," Alex said, smiling. "Wasn't there something about Odysseus going by the name No One, or Nobody, or something?"

"You know your Homer," I said, leaning against the side of his car. A shiny silver Prius. "Good for you."

"Now who sounds condescending?" he teased.

I flushed. "I really am sorry about dinner."

Alex shook his head, stuffing his hands into his pockets. "You don't have to apologize. I get it. Breakups are rough."

I made a face. "It wasn't David. I mean, I liked him when he wasn't patronizing me, but I'm not exactly going to be crying myself to sleep over him or anything. It's just . . . everything else. I forgot what it was like. The pressure to have it all completely together all the time. I guess being away at school kind of wrecked my tolerance. But you should probably know—it's because I wasn't willing to be David's good little Catholic wife, at his side every Sunday at mass, sharing his devotion. I feel like that's kind of relevant to Dad's whole conservative Christian values platform. Just in case it comes up anywhere."

He let out a breath, leaning against the car next to me. "You know, the more you talk, the more convinced I am that you're better off without this David guy."

I shrugged. "He was nice enough. Made a really impressive date for all Dad's functions, with his mother on the parish council and his dad on the school board. I mean, I never had to worry that he was going to go off message."

"That's not really a reason to stay in a relationship, though," he said, giving the leaves an idle kick. "And for the record, I don't think your dad would want you to stay with a guy who wasn't right for you just because he had an election coming down the pipe, either. No matter how close the race was."

"Hm." I pushed off from the car, straightening. Alex had deserved an apology, and I was glad to make peace, but that didn't mean I needed to overshare any further. He knew enough about my life and my family and my world already without my help. "Should I have my life plan spreadsheeted and ready for dinner next weekend?"

He smiled. "Just the major bullet points would be fine. But I promise not to jump straight into the interrogation this time."

I turned, walking backward away from his car toward the guesthouse. "I'll believe it when I see it."

He opened the driver's-side door, then hesitated, looking back up at me. "Hey, Emma?"

"Yeah?"

Alex drummed his fingers against the roof of the car, his lips pressed tight together for a moment as he stared at me just a little too intently.

"What's up?"

He forced a polite smile. "Just . . . good luck with your class."

"Um." I laughed, mostly because it was so strange. "Thanks, I guess. See you."

But even after I'd let myself into the guesthouse, his headlights flashing through the front window as he drove away, I couldn't help but feel like there'd been something a lot more serious on his mind. Something he'd thought better of bringing up at all.

CHAPTER FIVE:
AD 998
FREYDÍS

It was a long and miserable summer without Thorstein to keep the peace between us. Thjodhild still refused to allow my father into her bed, and Leif still stood firm and unyielding in support of his mother, pushing again and again for my father to accept baptism and name himself a Christian.

"Will they never stop?" I asked my father, for I had stuck to his side like a burr, unwilling to leave him to face their nagging alone. If I could say nothing more for my husband, at least he had not abandoned us, either.

My father stood still as stone on the rise, watching Leif and his followers cut turf for the church he had finally allowed them to build. "I fear they will only become more insistent now."

"But you've given them what they want. They have their church."

"Until I am Christian, Greenland is not Christian. No matter how many churches they build, these lands, my lands, still belong to the old gods, and King Olaf will be unhappy with my son's work. Leif will not be welcomed back to Norway, nor given the trade he desires, so long as Greenland defies the command of that fool king."

"But that cannot be Thjodhild's reasoning as well?"

"Can it not?" He snorted, tearing his gaze from the men to look at me at last. "Thjodhild is almost certain to outlive me, and Leif will inherit everything I've built here. It is in Thjodhild's interests to be certain Leif has the strength to keep it, and strength, as she and I both have reason to know after what became of us in Iceland, comes in no small part from the allies you can count upon in a conflict. The more powerful and influential the better. To have a king as your ally—no man in Greenland would act against Leif, so long as Olaf supported his claims. While Leif is protected, so is Thjodhild, and so are the rest of her sons."

I grimaced, seeing clearly the place I did not have in Thjodhild's future. "This is why you wanted me married. Even if it was only to Thorvard."

He looked away. "I ought not to have indulged you the way I did. Or perhaps I should have left you in Iceland to be raised by your grandparents after your mother was lost. Bringing you here, setting you beneath Thjodhild's nose . . . I fear I have done you no favors, Freydís."

"You have made me strong," I said. "That is favor enough, and the rest does not matter. Once I have my ship, I will be free to leave Thjodhild's foolishness behind. And Leif's as well."

"I do not think you can outsail the storm of the Christians, Dísa, no matter how fast your ship."

"But on the sea, there will be no law but my own. No one to tell me I must forget the old ways and embrace the new. I can explore, as you did, and find my own lands, my own place. And surely in Vinland it will not matter what gods I worship."

"It may matter to your men," my father warned. "And should the sea turn against you, and your men believe it is the work of your gods, they will not hesitate to act against you."

"Then I will sail only with those men that I trust, men who love the old gods, who honor their ancestors over the White Christ."

"Hope that you sail soon, then," my father said. "While such men still live among us."

I hugged myself against the cold wind gusting down from the ice. An ill wind, it seemed, and my own gaze went to the water, hoping for the glimpse of a sail. It would take Thorstein more than a week, according to Leif, to cross the strait to Vinland, and the same again to return. Most of a month spent just in sailing, and he had been gone only for two. Hardly enough time to gather the lumber or do any hunting at all for furs and ivory. But I wished he would hurry home.

"When you go, I will give you Thorhall," my father said. "He is not well liked, I know, but there is no one more loyal to me or to Thor himself. He'll serve you well, I think."

I let out a breath, touched by his offer. Thorhall had been with my father through every challenge he had faced, even following him into exile and outlawry not once, but twice. I could not imagine Erik the Red on this farm without Thorhall, dark and scarred, looming nearby, ready to serve his chieftain. Even now, he stood not far from us, holding the reins of our horses.

"Are you certain you can spare him, Father?"

He smiled at me, throwing an arm around my shoulders and drawing me against his side to press a kiss to the top of my head. "If it meant you were kept safe, I would spare even my sword arm for the rest of my days."

"Or pluck out your eye and give it up to the gods?" I teased.

My father grinned. "Are you certain you're worth so much as that?"

"You cannot tell me you value your eye more greatly than your sword arm!"

He laughed and mussed my hair before letting me go. "Go along, then, and make use of yourself. Or see to your husband, perhaps. Surely he deserves some small reward for being so steadfast." I must have made a face at his suggestion, for my father laughed again. "You can hardly blame him for wanting his payment, Freydís. He may be soft and weak, but he is not quite so dull-witted that he does not understand how he's been used."

"It does not mean I have to enjoy it," I said.

He grunted. "For both your sakes, I hope you learn to. That he learns how to please you, in one way or another. You're not a woman who will sit by if he doesn't."

But privately I wondered if the only way Thorvard might please me would be by looking the other way when I found another man I'd rather take to my bed.

Another month passed, the seas growing rough, and I spent my days upon the shore, a sharp eye on the horizon. Thorvard had accompanied me at first, like a dog at my heels. Likely he did not trust that I was not carrying on with one of the other men, but I did not care what he believed, so long as he did not stop me from going.

"If your brother Leif could make such a journey, I do not see why you should fear for Thorstein and Thorvaldur. Surely they sailed with the benefit of your brother's knowledge."

I said nothing in response, for I would not admit that as formidable as my brothers might be upon land, they had not Leif's experience upon the sea. Not to a man like Thorvard, who had sailed in trade far and often before he had married me.

"I would not have believed you could be moved by anything but anger if I did not see the proof of it myself," Thorvard said, stretching out in the grass beside my perch on the cliff. I could have taken to the beach instead, I supposed, but the vantage would have been far poorer. My husband folded his hands neatly behind his head, his eyes closed, perfectly relaxed. "I wonder if you will worry half so much for me when I set sail again."

"Of course I will worry," I said. "You'll have gone to fetch my ship."

He laughed, rolling to his side and reaching out to catch the hem of my tunic. "Come and lie down with me, Freydís."

I stepped away, crossing my arms over my chest. "I cannot see from the ground."

"There is nothing *to* see," he said, sitting up. "And I would pass the time in a more pleasant fashion."

"Then you're free to return to the farm and warm yourself by my father's fire," I said. "I'm more than capable of keeping watch on my own."

He fell silent, but I could feel his gaze on my back, and I knew that my father was not wrong about his wits. Perhaps he could not wield his sword, steel or otherwise, but Thorvard was no fool, much as I might have wished him to be.

I let out a breath, irritated with myself as much as him. My father had warned me I must be shrewd, but so far I had been only shrewish, and should Thorvard abandon me before I had my ship, all the unpleasantness I had suffered would be for nothing. Besides, he was not so terrible outside of our bed. He had never rebuked me before the men, nor stopped me from doing as I wished day after day. If he'd only learned what to do with his spear, or desired me less, I might have even been content instead of resentful.

"Forgive me, husband," I said. "It is my fear that speaks, not my heart. If Thorstein does not return to us soon—there is no one else who can reason with Leif and Thjodhild. He is Christian enough that they will listen when he speaks in support of our father, and loyal enough to the old ways, to our ancestors, that he will stand at our father's side against their foolishness."

Thorvard reached out a hand again, and this time I took it in my own, ignoring the churn of my stomach. "You need not fear that your father will stand alone," he said. "Perhaps I am not so well admired as your brothers, but Erik has been generous to me, and I will not forget his kindness. Nor will I forget that I am bound to him through his daughter, in marriage."

I swallowed, not so certain I cared for the meaning behind his words. He would support my father to repay him, but beyond that, his loyalty to my father rested upon our marriage, upon me. My brothers had spoken of divorce, that I might break from Thorvard easily enough, but it was just as true that he could break from me, should he find me too troublesome a wife. And if he did, my father would lose an ally he could not afford to do without. Not so long as Thorstein sailed the seas, and Leif and Thjodhild and King Olaf demanded we abandon our ways.

"Now come," he said, squeezing my hand. "Lie with me, and let us talk of other things. Happier things."

And what choice did I have, truly? Perhaps I had been the hard one when we started, but this trouble with Leif, impossible to hide from my husband once we had married, had shifted the once firm ground beneath our feet, gifting Thorvard a new position of strength. He knew I had the greater need of him—that my father had the greater need of him—than he had of either of us.

Thorstein had been right to worry when he left. For my pride had caught me, well and truly, and it would not be so easy to escape what it had wrought.

Not ruin, perhaps, so long as Thorvard remained sympathetic and tolerant of my ways. But trouble, all the same.

CHAPTER SIX:
AD 2016
Emma

Remember when you're reading *The Vinland Sagas*, these were written hundreds of years after the events they relate—after a tremendous cultural shift from a mostly pagan North to a primarily Christian worldview. Neither of these belief systems were particularly uniform, even if historians like to think about them that way. But when we're examining any text, we need to take into account the context in which it was written," I said, glancing quickly at the clock to make sure I wasn't quite out of time, no matter what the packing up of my back row of students might suggest. Some days they were more eager than others. "For example, the author of *The Saga of Erik the Red* can be traced back to a nunnery, and possibly even a descendent of Gudrid the Far-Traveler, which might account for the very sympathetic and pious illustration of her character, particularly in opposition to Freydís, Erik the Red's daughter, who behaves far less modestly."

It was the end of the second week of class, and we'd managed a solid overview of the early Middle Ages, from the collapse of the Roman Empire in the West through Charlemagne and the Carolingians, and into the Viking Age—my personal favorite, and one I hoped the class would embrace. Everyone loved Vikings. Or at least the romanticized idea of them, with all the raiding and pillaging. And they definitely had a lot of fun stories.

"So, what?" Ashley (center aisle, front row, gum snapper, but never late to class and always did the reading) interrupted. "You're saying that Gudrid couldn't actually have been a good Christian? That they made it up to make themselves look better?"

"I'm saying that we need to be mindful of the influences on the author which might have created bias or supported an agenda. And that we need to remember the world that Gudrid most likely lived in, under Erik the Red's pagan leadership, may not have been as traditionally or consistently Christian as the later generations wanted to believe, and certainly not as we know Christianity today.

"We don't know what Gudrid actually believed or who she actually was—but we do know that in the early years of conversion, Christianity was a more fluid concept. In Iceland, for example, though the country agreed to baptism and conversion in the year 1000, they also allowed people to continue worshipping their old gods, so long as they did so privately. Men and women who were baptized in circumstances like these were unlikely to have abandoned their old practices, rituals, and beliefs overnight."

"So you don't *believe* that Jesus could change their hearts and minds once they accepted him?" she demanded.

I forced myself to smile. "It isn't really about what I believe. But we should also take into consideration that the gods the pagans worshipped pre-Christianity were just as real to them as Jesus is to Christians today."

"Are you serious?" Ashley said, thoroughly disgusted, judging by the curl of her lip. "You're going to stand up there in a *history* class and try to tell me that those gods were as real as Jesus? That they *existed?*"

"That isn't—" I took a breath, steadying myself. My words needed to be deliberate, not emotional, no matter how personal it felt. "I'm saying that the people of the past believed in them, and when we're trying to study those people and their history, we shouldn't dismiss that."

"This is *garbage*," she said, and the rest of the class stopped their small movements of packing up, everyone's attention now riveted on the two of us. "Just like that *trash* about Charlemagne, blaming him for the raids by Vikings, because he was trying to convert his empire to Christianity. Every topic we've covered, you've had something bad to say about Christians, acting like they aren't the foundation of the western world—of our *country.*"

I bit my tongue on a sharp response, on any direct response at all, and fought to keep my voice perfectly level. "I'd be happy to discuss this with you one-on-one during office hours, Ashley."

"I don't think there's anything to discuss. It's clear where you stand. And probably the only reason you were hired at all is because you're Congressman Moretti's daughter."

There was always one. Always. In every class. Ever since I'd started college, straight through my master's program, and now again here. I should have expected it, I guess, planned for it somehow. But it wasn't like anything I said was going to fix things. Not for Ashley. She wanted to see a bias, wanted to blame me for the atrocities of the past, rather than accept that any and every belief could and had been turned into a tool for political gain, somewhere and somewhen. Christianity, Islam, Hinduism, Judaism, even the Greeks and the Romans had used religion to support the status quo to the detriment of others. And the Norse peoples had been no exception.

So I cleared my throat, turning my attention to the rest of the students. "I think that's everything for today. And don't forget, you'll be quizzed on the sagas on Tuesday, so be sure you do the reading and come prepared to defend your interpretations."

Ashley slammed her notebook shut, grabbed her coat and her backpack, and marched out at the head of the rest of the class. I tried not to watch her go, focusing instead on gathering my notes and picking up after myself before the next professor arrived.

There was always going to be a little bit of pushback, I reminded myself. History and our understanding of history changed a little bit more every day as we uncovered more information, did new research. I didn't have anything against Christianity personally, and neither did academia. It was just that we were finally living in an age when we could deconstruct some of the lenses through which the historical narrative had been shaped for the last thousand-plus years. History wasn't being written only from the perspective of the winners anymore. And honestly, it made our understanding of the past a whole hell of a lot richer.

Somehow, though, knowing I hadn't done anything wrong wasn't particularly reassuring.

❦

Ashley's outrage left a sour taste in my mouth. Even though I knew it was just the result of a more well-rounded approach to history—and for the record, I'd offered other theories about Charlemagne as well—it still twisted my gut. The whole drive home I went over it again and again in my head. The idea that my lessons had offended her so deeply upset me. Not because of her accusations, though they certainly hadn't been pleasant, but because I really, genuinely had not meant to offend anyone. Open their eyes a little bit wider, sure, but every professor in the liberal arts always hoped to challenge their students to see things differently, to think critically about what they were being taught.

And it was the critical thinking that was the real lesson, the real gift of the liberal arts. Or at least it had been to me. Learning about other cultures, other faith traditions, seeing the patterns written across history and realizing that this idea of our so-called societal advancement as some invalidation of the faiths of our past was all kinds of bunk. Because here we were in the modern world, making the same mistakes, the same choices on repeat, no matter whether we were Christian or Muslim or Jewish or Hindu or Buddhist or utterly faithless, so why not Heathen or Pagan, too?

I shook my head, my hands still on the steering wheel, my foot still on the brake even though I'd put the car into park. If I was honest with myself, that was what was really bothering me now. When Ashley had sneered at the idea that other gods might have existed—implying that *my* gods couldn't possibly be real—it had cut through me in a way I hadn't expected it ever could. After all, I lived with it every day. Every non-Christian American did, to some degree or another, even in the most liberal places. It wasn't until you broke from the tradition, the culture, that you began to see all the ways Christianity was embedded into the psyche of the western world.

And this area of New Hampshire—my father's home base—wasn't that liberal. Catholics and Methodists and a handful of Baptists, and if you weren't part of one of those churches, engaged with that community, there was a lot of side-eye. We didn't even have a Unitarian Universalist Association nearer than Vermont.

I turned off the car and tipped my head back against the seat, my bronze Mjölnir pendant hanging heavy from my neck. I kept it hidden beneath my shirt in public and tucked in my purse on dates, out of sight of anyone who might question it. The reality was that I could probably pass it off as some kind of nerdy fandom statement, but keeping my faith a secret was exhausting enough without actively lying about its symbols, too. I hated playing it off as nothing serious or real. And I hated that it was necessary. That keeping secrets from the people I loved was part of my everyday life.

But so many of them would react the same way Ashley did, and I just didn't know how to face it—to have them look at me like I was crazy, or worse, humoring me the way they already did with whatever assumptions they'd made about my slow drift away from my Catholic upbringing, like it was just some phase I'd snap out of if they just let me have my way for a few months. As if I'd chosen deliberately to believe in the spiritual experiences I'd had, just to be difficult and inconvenience them somehow. That once the novelty wore off and I'd gotten tired of shocking people, I'd slide back into my predetermined place in the community and start going to church again.

No. There was nothing to be done about it. And it wasn't like it was something I could put on the table this close to the campaign, even if I wanted to come clean. It would have to wait. Maybe forever. And I'd just have to be fine with that.

"Emma?"

I jumped, and the melted nylon edge of the seat belt strap scraped my neck. It was only Alex, looking just slightly rumpled in his suit after a long day, but my heart raced, and I pressed a hand against my chest, slumping back against the seat.

"Sorry," he said, muffled by the glass. I pushed the door open so he'd quit with the shouting, and he caught it, leaning in. "I didn't mean to startle you—you just looked . . ."

"Like I had a rough day?" I asked, offering a weak smile.

He grimaced. "I guess your mother has a sixth sense, huh? She invited me for dinner."

I snorted, unbuckling my seat belt and grabbing my purse. "Of course she did."

"I kind of hoped it would be a pleasant surprise," he teased, stepping back to let me out. "At this rate, you're going to wince every time we cross paths."

"Fortunately for you, today's drama had nothing to do with you or my father's campaign," I promised, bumping my hip against the door to shut it. "Just a student who wasn't happy with how history challenges her personal narrative of the past."

"Ah," he said, falling into step beside me. "Does that happen often?"

I shrugged. "There's always one."

"You don't want to talk about this with me, do you?"

I laughed, suddenly nervous. "It's not that—I'm just still processing, I guess. And it upset me more than it should have." My fingers itched for Mjölnir, for the reassuring warmth of the bronze, but I didn't dare reach for it in front of Alex. "I've never been the professor before. I was always the student, listening, maybe shaking my head. Now I have to actually keep my cool and respond with rational, reasonable argument while under attack."

"And here I thought that was your specialty," he said, nudging me with his elbow.

"We can't all be masters of spin, I suppose," I said, stopping outside the front door of my parents' house. The minute we went inside, it would be all campaign business. Alex and my mother liked to pretend it was a social call, but it wasn't really. It never was during campaign season. And Alex had been at an alarming number of dinners since David and I had broken up three weeks ago.

"If you ever need someone to practice your arguments on, though, I'd be interested to see this mythical rational and reasonable side of Emma."

"Hey!"

"I'm just kidding." He grinned. "About the myth, anyway. Not about the listening. I mean, if you wanted to maybe one day have dinner together *not* with your parents."

I froze, staring at him. "Um?"

"Unless it's too soon, with the whole David thing. I totally understand if you're not ready, or need more time, or just aren't interested at all . . ." He closed his eyes, took a breath. "Sorry. It sounded a lot smoother in my head."

Then my mother opened the door, smiling. "Alexander! Your timing is impeccable as always. And I see you found Emma on your way in. We were just wondering where she'd gotten to."

I opened my mouth, then shut it again and let my mother whisk Alex inside.

Because I wasn't entirely certain, if only because it seemed so improbable, but it sounded like my father's spin doctor had just asked me on a date. And to be honest? I was glad to have a little more time to consider my response.

CHAPTER SEVEN:
AD 998
FREYDÍS

Word came from the North not long after with news of my brother's ship, or so I was told by Thorhall, who had come to fetch me when the messenger arrived. I dropped the milk bucket, not caring whether it spilled, and ran for the house, fear lending speed to my limbs.

I burst through the door into the long main hall in time to hear my father's laugh, as joyful as I might have prayed it could be. "What's happened?" I demanded, gulping a breath. "Why did they not return here directly?"

"Bring the man something warm to drink, and food as well, for his service." My father rose from his chair, not bothering to concern himself with seeing his words turned to action. A servant scrambled in his wake, hurrying to obey, but my gaze remained on my father's face, the broad smile he turned upon me and the sparkle in his eyes that had been missing these last months. "Leave it to your brother to spend the summer being blown about and bewildered upon the waters," he said, cupping my face in his hands for the briefest moment. "He is safe and well, and after so long at sea, the men were not so eager to sail on once they'd found their way home. They'll winter at Thorstein's farm in the North and return to us in the spring, with nothing worse than the bruise upon his pride."

My eyes closed, relief flooding through me so hard and fast I could not help but tremble, my heart pounding in my chest. "They are safe."

"They are safe," he promised, his hands falling to my shoulders, then drawing me into his arms. It was only once he held me that I realized he was shaking, too, as overcome as I was, though he'd never revealed his fear for even a moment during the long summer months. "Thank the gods and all the ancestors."

"Spring cannot come quickly enough," I said, pulling back. "If it were not so near winter, I would brave the ice and ride north tomorrow."

"If it were not so near winter, no doubt he would sail south before long," my father said, laughing. "But the worst is over now. The cloud of uncertainty lifted. Thor kept them safe."

"*God* kept them safe," Thjodhild said, her voice ringing out over the pop and crack of the fire and the low hum of voices. "And if you had any sense at all, you'd be on your way to the church to offer him the thanks he's due."

My father's jaw went tight, a muscle fluttering in spasm just beneath the skin, visible even in the poor light of the hall. He let me go and turned to face his wife. "I'll trust you to offer thanks enough to your god, I think, and I will offer mine where I see fit. Or do you mean to say you have been granted some sight of your god's protection of my sons, that you can speak with such certainty that it was his hand which preserved them?"

Thorvard rose from where he had been seated upon our sleeping bench, one of the many long boards, barely wide enough for two, that lined the walls in the main hall. Only my father had his own room, and that was hardly more than a nook at the far end. A room in which Thjodhild had not joined him for nearly half a year.

"Your gods cannot even bestir themselves to act on your behalf, with all your prayers and offerings. Thorvaldur and Thorstein are good Christian men now, and Gudrid, too, is pious," Thjodhild said, her voice edging toward shrill. "They would have said no prayers to gods who hold no power over their fates, and your gods would have no reason to help them."

"Thor's hammer hung from both their necks," I said, stepping forward to join my father, just as Thorvard pushed his way through to stand at his side. "Thor, for whom they were both named! He would not overlook my father's sons."

"Thor is weak and worthless," Thjodhild snapped. "And you are all three fools to cling to him, fingering a misshapen hammer for protection."

"Enough," my father growled. "I will not suffer your blasphemies uttered so boldly in my hall. Go to your church and give thanks to any god you wish, but you will not speak ill of the gods of our ancestors beneath my roof!"

Thjodhild sniffed, and Leif took his mother's hand. "There will be no reasoning with him," my brother said. "Not until he is dead."

"Even then, you will find me a recalcitrant spirit," my father promised.

"Not after you are buried in the churchyard," Leif said, his blue eyes clear and cutting. "With the proper prayers, even your soul will not stir again."

"Would you truly treat your father so dishonorably?" Thorvard demanded, shocked by my brother's threat.

"I will do what I must to protect our people," Leif said, unashamed. "And you have heard him say himself he will not go peaceably."

My father bared his teeth, his hands hard fists at his sides. "You would do better to consign me to the mound than your churchyard, that we might never meet in your Christian heaven."

"Little fear of that." Leif's smile was brittle. "You're sure to find your way to hell, if you continue on this way. I only mean to ensure you will not trouble us in death as you have in life."

"Trouble *you*?" My father barked a laugh, his face flushed as red as his hair. "Tell me, boy, do you mean the trouble I caused you when I gave you the freedom to worship any god that pleased you? Or when I granted you the right to build your church upon my lands, with my turf and my wood? With my men and my tools!"

"Lands which will be mine," Leif said. "Men and tools which will be mine, and soon enough."

"But not yet," my father said. "And not yours alone."

"Lucky for me, my brothers are good Christian men," Leif said. "Thorvaldur will never stand against me, nor Thorstein while he is married to such a woman as Gudrid."

"And your sister?" I asked. Thorvard's hand closed around mine, lending me support I had not realized I needed. "Do you think me so weak that I will stand by while you betray my father in death, burying him in a manner that will separate him forever from our ancestors? From me?"

Leif laughed. "You, Freydís? No. Once you have your ship, I need not fear you at all. Greenland will be Christian after you've led all the men who resist me to their death. The sea will swallow you all whole, and I will say a prayer of thanksgiving and commend your soul to God for the service you have done me."

It had not ended there, of course, but those were the words that haunted me most as I went about my work, for days and days after. I hated

Thorstein and Thorvaldur for not returning home directly. For allowing Thjodhild to give the credit of their survival to her god and for letting Leif rise unopposed against our father.

And I hated Leif, too. His gleeful pronouncement of my fate would worm its way into the minds of the men, and by the time Thorvard had brought me my ship, I would have no crew to sail her. I would be trapped, then, well and truly. With Leif on the one hand, determined to make my life a misery if I stayed, and Thorvard on the other, who I would have no choice but to spend my life pleasing if I wanted to escape. Three-legged Thorvard, who still had not learned to gentle his touch, and more than once had left me too sore to sit for any length of time. But he had stood with us, as he had promised. Stood with me when it mattered most.

So long as my father lived, I made a valuable wife to him, for more than just the dubious pleasure he could find in my bed. After my father died, he would have a greater value to me as a husband. Thorstein, I knew, would always look kindly upon me, and perhaps he might persuade Thorvaldur to do the same, but Leif never would, and it was Leif who would rule.

But I would not give Leif or Thjodhild the satisfaction of my going to pieces. I would not let them think I had been rattled by their threats. I was the daughter of Erik the Red, after all, and my father still stood tall. He'd even, in full view of Thjodhild, taken one of his slaves to his bed that same night, and we'd all listened to her moans of pleasure as my father took his. Thorvard had grinned at me in the low firelight at the noise they made, eager to have his way, and I'd even pretended loudly to enjoy it, following my father's example of strength. Let Leif and Thjodhild think me indifferent to their words. Let them think they could not trouble me in the slightest.

And that was how the winter found us, tension and resentments growing with every new woman my father brought to his bed, threatening Leif with the possibility of an army of brothers born out of our father's rage. Raised upon it, like Odin's son Váli, to serve only one murderous purpose. I hoped it would be true.

But winter came, cold and fierce and frozen, and went again, and not a single one of the slaves had ripened, making Thjodhild smug.

"God is good," I heard her tell my brother one evening, after Thorvard had taken me to bed. "He has heard our prayers and protected you from this new threat of your father's."

My husband grunted, his eyes narrowing as he looked at me. I couldn't bring myself to meet his gaze and turned my face away. He'd wanted me planted before he sailed, I knew, and he'd certainly worked hard enough to see it done during the long winter nights. If he took Thjodhild's words for explanation—well, at least it would mean he did not find fault in me.

And then it was spring.

⁕

If it had not been for Leif and Thjodhild always nagging at my father, and Thorvard, who I could not risk angering when we had so few allies, I would have saddled the sturdiest of my father's horses and made the long, treacherous ride north to Thorstein's farm with the thaw. Instead, I could only pace the misty shore, shivering in the cold while I waited for my brothers to come home.

"Have you not done enough staring out into the fog yet?" Thorvard asked me. "Would it not serve you better to offer some gift or another to the gods to see them brought home safe?"

"I have done that, too," I said. "Every morning I leave a dish of skyr for the landvættir, and every evening, I give Thor the first sip of my wine and pray for Thorstein's return. What more would you have me do?"

He glanced at me sidelong as I stood there bundled still in my shaggy winter coat, the long threads of wool shedding the water from the mist better than a flat weave. "There are other gods you might appeal to."

"The White Christ?" I asked, lip curling. "You would have me give Leif and Thjodhild the satisfaction? And worse, insult Thor by appealing to another god as if the son of Odin were not capable of bringing my brothers safely home?"

"If Thjodhild's god has the power to keep those women from bearing your father's fruit, and you barren as well, perhaps he is the more powerful."

My face burned, my temper flaring hot. "There is no god in any of the nine worlds who is more powerful than Thor."

"Then how else do you explain it?" Thorvard demanded. "You heard her, Freydís. Her whispering in the dark with Leif. They've placed a curse upon you through their god."

I looked away, hugging myself, and said nothing. There was nothing *to* say in explanation that would not turn his frustration upon me. Because Thorvard wanted me with child, and if he knew I had made offerings begging Thor to keep my stomach flat, he would never forgive it. If I said that I had never caught with child once in the last four years, at least, since I had begun taking men to my bed, he would think me worthless to him all over again. And I could not bear it if he looked on me that way. Perhaps I did not love him, and perhaps he was not the lover I might have wished for, but I thought we'd found some easiness, some peace between us. For his loyalty this last year alone, I had learned to admire him, even to like him. Some part of me wanted him to like me, too.

"If you will not pray to your brother's god, I cannot make you," Thorvard said. "I swore as much to your father when he agreed to give you up. But I never promised I would not pray to the White Christ myself."

I sucked in a breath. "You would betray me? Betray my father?"

"I will do what I must for the sake of our family, Freydís," he said, the words firm. "And if the White Christ is in truth more powerful than the gods of my father, as Leif and Thjodhild claim . . ."

I closed my eyes, hugging myself tighter. We'd spoken of Thjodhild and Leif and their faith before, argued over its merits and laughed at their foolishness, but I had never believed he would be persuaded, no matter how weak he was, or I would not have married him at all. "Go then."

He hesitated at my side, earth and stone crunching under his feet as he shifted nearer and placed his hand upon my shoulder. "I gave you my word that I would support your father, Freydís, and I will. This does not change that."

"You are wrong, Thorvard." I shrugged out from beneath his hand, colder than I had been even in the darkest days of winter. "It changes everything."

CHAPTER EIGHT:
AD 2016
Emma

Dinner was strange, and Alex was clearly uncomfortable, stumbling over his words and losing track of what my father was saying. My mother and father both were too polite to ask, but I found myself hiding my smile in my napkin more than once while we ate. I'd never seen Alex so flustered, but I couldn't deny I kind of liked it. Suddenly he was less the perfect PR guy and more the approachable yet good-looking guy on the street.

You're going to have a hard time finding someone who this isn't going to be an issue for.

I grimaced, Sarah's well-intentioned warning threading through my mind. She didn't understand. Not that it made her wrong—she was probably more right than she realized. And after today's student outburst . . .

Maybe I was crazy to even give Alex the opportunity. If things got serious, he was going to find out the truth. I'd have to tell him eventually. And then what? I knew he shared my parents' beliefs. That he was happy to work for my father's campaign *because* he believed in my father's values.

But he already knew I didn't go to church. That I'd drifted away from my parents' faith and maybe even their values. He knew why David had ended things with me. And he'd still asked me out. Maybe.

Either way, I let him squirm through dinner, through dessert and coffee. If nothing else, it was a fantastic distraction from my own drama, when otherwise I might have been dwelling on my not-so-great classroom experience instead. But when he got up, making excuses about work to finish up and an early morning, with a glance in my direction that was somewhere between hopeful and regretful, I got up with him.

"I should probably call it a night, too. Readings to refresh myself on and papers to grade."

"Of course, Emma," my mother said. "Why don't you walk Alex out, then, and I'll take care of these dessert plates."

"Thanks for dinner, Mamma." I brushed my cheek against hers, then bent to press a kiss to the top of my father's head. "Take it easy, Dad."

"We'll see you for dinner tomorrow?" he asked.

"Um," I said, not letting myself look at Alex. "I'm not entirely sure yet."

"Just let us know, sweetheart," my mother said, dishes already stacked in her hands. "And we'll see you again next week, Alex."

"Of course, Irena. I wouldn't miss it."

"*Bless bless*, Alex!"

I led the way toward the front of the house, letting Alex say a final polite farewell—replying in halting Icelandic to my mother, then far more practiced Italian for my father—and got a head start on jamming my feet back into my ankle boots.

60

"You didn't have to walk me out," Alex said when he joined me.

I pulled his jacket—a beautiful wool peacoat—out of the coat closet and offered him a smile along with it. "Sheep fleece, remember?"

He laughed at my wordplay, taking the coat from my hands and shrugging into it. "Subtle."

"Anyone who can't appreciate a good pun isn't worth sharing a meal with," I said, letting him get the door for me. I slipped outside, then turned to face him as he followed. "With or without my parents."

He froze, the door half-closed behind us and his knuckles white on the knob. I took pity on him—and myself, really—and reached past him to tug it firmly shut. The last thing I wanted was to give my parents the opportunity to eavesdrop.

"If the offer still stands, anyway," I added when he seemed tongue-tied.

Alex made a strangled sound, something that might have been a laugh under ordinary circumstances, finally letting go of the door. "You let me stumble through that entire dinner, agonizing. Thinking I'd screwed everything up and ruined my chances."

"It was kind of endearing, actually," I said. "But it wasn't just to torture you. I wasn't sure if it was the best idea."

"And my fumbling put your mind at ease?"

I twitched a shoulder, not quite able to meet his eyes with Sarah's words still fluttering about, worming their way into the wrinkles of my brain. "It could still end up being a mess."

"Hm." I could feel him studying me, his curiosity a palpable weight. "I'm not sure what to make of that. Whether it means I need to try harder to win you over, or if there's something else."

"It's nothing that won't sort itself out," I said, jumping from the porch to the walk. Just one step. Not much of a risk. "Nothing you need to fight against, anyway. I mean, it'll either work out or it won't, right? We either accept one another for who we are, or we realize it wasn't meant to be."

He ducked his head, catching my eyes. His were brown. Warm and clear, and not so dark that his pupils disappeared in them. He searched my face, and I felt my chin lift in response, in pride and challenge and desperation to hide my fear that Sarah would be right again. That she'd always be right and I'd always be alone.

"I'm not David," he said.

"You can't know for sure that this is going to work out beyond a couple of dates, a few months."

"No," he agreed. "But I'm not ready to anticipate doom before the first date, the first day, the first couple of months. If you don't think there's anything worth exploring here, that's one thing, but if you're just afraid to start because you aren't completely sure it's going to last . . ."

"I know," I said, closing my eyes. "It's totally stupid."

"I wouldn't say that," he said. "I can respect your caution. Especially with the campaign, and the election coming up. If you want to rain-check until after some of the spotlight is off your family, I'll understand that, too."

I shook my head. My father's campaign was the last thing on my mind. And even if it had entered into it at all, Alex was the least likely threat. If things didn't work out, he had too many years of loyalty and hard work wrapped up in the outcome to mess it all up over me.

"I'm free tomorrow night," I said, opening my eyes again and staring into his.

He half smiled. "All right, Odysseus. But if you're not careful, I'm going to start thinking you're just using me to ditch your parents."

"That's Odyssea to you," I said, then frowned. "Or maybe Odysseuaki? Odysseani? Hmph." I waved it away and stepped back, nodding toward his car. "I've got plans for brunch, but any time after that . . ."

"I'll pick you up around seven."

I couldn't help but glance at the house, imagining my parents' response to seeing Alex pull into the driveway to collect me.

Whatever he saw in my face, he laughed. "They'll find out one way or the other. We might as well just get it out of the way."

I wrinkled my nose. "Definitely the downside to dating one of my father's staff members."

"Somehow I don't think they'll mind," he said, pulling open his car door. "Or did you think all these dinners were really just out of the kindness of your mother's heart?"

Before I could answer, he'd gotten in, the door slamming and the engine purring to life.

I didn't miss the grin he flashed me through the window as he drove away. Self-satisfied and confident, with just a little bit of revenge. Because he'd just guaranteed I'd spend the rest of tonight and most of Saturday wondering what he'd meant.

Alex would know better than anyone, after all these evenings at the table together, that the last thing I would do was ask my mother just how many of these dinners she'd orchestrated especially for him.

I wasn't even sure I wanted to know.

"You're going on a date with Alex Stone?" Sarah demanded, loudly enough that the customers at the nearest tables stared. Three of our former classmates, and at least a half dozen church members, who would all probably be judging me for moving on from David so quickly now, thanks to Sarah's enthusiasm. "Are you serious? You can't be serious. Your father's spin doctor?"

"A little louder," I grumbled, shrinking deeper into the booth. We were regulars, and it was usually the same booth every Saturday, but today they'd seated us at a more exposed table, and with Sarah bouncing in her seat, I was really starting to regret it. "I'm not sure they heard you across the street."

"He's *gorgeous*," Sarah gushed. "Tall and dark, and those shoulders. Imagine what your children would look like!"

I winced. "It's just dinner."

"Dinner after you've practically been pre-dating all summer, with these parent-chaperoned dinners."

"Three weeks, Sarah. Not even close to all summer. And trust me that we weren't spending our time getting to know one another. Mostly he was just talking campaign business with Dad."

"And flirting with you, obviously."

I sighed, grabbing the dessert menu and setting it up to shield myself from Mrs. Barberi—one of David's mother's friends—who was not even trying to be subtle about eavesdropping. Because of course. "Hardly. Once in a while, maybe, we teased each other. But it was more . . . brotherly, I guess, than anything else. Or at least that was what I thought, until he asked me to dinner. And even then, I wasn't entirely sure he meant it as a date until he started going on about maybe it being too soon and David."

Sarah's eyes narrowed, but at least she lowered her voice. "You're not second-guessing yourself, are you? I can't believe he put that in your head. Why would he even bring up his name?"

"He was nervous, and he didn't realize what he was doing, I'm sure." I picked at my crepe. Strawberries and cream with strawberry syrup. It was almost too sweet. "Besides, I don't think he was necessarily wrong to be worried about it. I hadn't even accepted before I was already imagining whatever relationship we might have had coming to a screeching halt, because I don't want to go to mass or whatever. Which, thanks a lot, by the way, speaking of putting things in my head."

"That was different," Sarah said. "You were totally deluding yourself with David, and I didn't want you to make the same mistake a second time. But Alex knows why you and David broke up, right?"

"The broad strokes, yeah," I said, pushing my plate away with one crepe still to go. My stomach was sour from the sugar. And jittering over my date.

I'd thought I was doing the right thing last night, agreeing to dinner. I definitely thought Alex was attractive. Smart. Sometimes a little bit too intense, like a dog with a bone. But intensity wasn't necessarily a bad thing if it was pointed in the right direction. Assuming he even believed in pointing anything anywhere before marriage. With my luck, he was a completely celibate virgin and all that intensity was the result of repressed energy.

I hid my face in my hands and groaned. I didn't know anything about the things that were going to matter—the personal, intimate things or how he really felt about *anything* that wasn't directly related to my father's campaign. And he probably thought *I* was a completely celibate virgin.

"I don't think you need to agonize about this," Sarah said. "He already knows you aren't religious if you told him about David. He wouldn't have asked you out if that was a deal breaker."

Except it still could be. It was one thing to think a person didn't really care about going to church—another thing entirely to learn she was worshipping heathen gods. "I should cancel," I moaned into my hands.

"You are *not* canceling," Sarah said. We'd both been freshmen in high school when Alex was a senior, and many an afternoon and evening had been spent giggling together over his butt—among others—in those close-fitting baseball pants. "You are going on this date with Alexander Stone, who I know you've had a crush on since *before* your dad hired him, even if you never wanted to admit it, and you're going to stop overthinking this."

"You're the one who made me *start* overthinking it!"

"I did not," Sarah sniffed. "Alex started it, and he'd better learn quick, or he's going to be in for a world of hurt."

"Ugh." I downed what was left of my water. "He said something else, too. About how all these dinners weren't just out of the kindness of my mother's heart. And I hate the idea that I'm falling right into her hands, if this was really her intention. I mean, if she thinks Alex is good for me, that means she thinks he's going to return me to the fold."

"Please," Sarah said. "It isn't like you up and moved to California like your sister did. You never *left* the fold. You live in the guesthouse. You have dinner with your parents practically every night. I don't think Alex is going to put you any deeper into their pocket."

"Of course he can," I said. "He's a good Catholic boy."

"He's not that Catholic. Even if he supports your father's ideals and positions on things politically, he can't be."

"How do you know?"

Sarah raised both eyebrows, giving me her best *are-you-stupid* look. "If he *were* that Catholic, he wouldn't have asked you out at all. He'd have taken your split with David as a warning and put any thought of it aside."

"Well. Maybe he did. Maybe he's asking me out against his better judgment because he knows it's what my parents want."

"Now you're just being ridiculous," Sarah said. "Your mother might be slightly more manipulative than average, but she's not that extreme, and your father can't love the idea of his PR guy dating his daughter, no matter what Irena might want."

"So you think he just likes me."

"I think he just likes you," Sarah promised. "And I think if you don't tell me *everything*, the minute you get home, I'm never going to forgive you."

CHAPTER NINE:
AD 999
FREYDÍS

Thorvard set sail with his men at the first sign of true spring, a cross hanging from his neck beside Thor's hammer, and I went out to the boulder at the edge of the farm to beg for my brothers' safe return, turning my back upon my husband as he had turned his back upon me. Thjodhild and Leif had crowed about his baptism, of course, but I was determined that my husband would see no benefit from the prayers he made to his new god. Indeed, all Thorvard had accomplished with his acceptance of their Christ was to smother whatever small flame of affection had grown between us, leaving only resentment to fester.

I had carved the runes I required into a small scrap of mountain ash, with Thor's name to seal them, and sewed it into the shift I wore at night. And beneath our blankets and furs, I carved them again while the others were about their chores, and whatever power Thorvard believed the White Christ had, it did not get him a child before he sailed.

Thor had not yet forsaken me, and I devoted myself all the more to my god in return for his protection. I carved his name upon the mountain ash trees wherever they grew and promised him a share of any riches I might find, if he would only keep me safe from my husband still.

"Only bring me my ship," I begged him, sitting beside the boulder after I had made my offering to the landvættir one morning, some days later. "Bring me my ship, keep Thorvard's seed from my womb, and you can have of me what you will."

"Do you not believe the gods will take what they desire, whether you offer it willingly or not?" my father asked, startling me from my prayers.

I had not heard his footsteps, and I flushed at how foolish my words must have sounded to his ears. "How else should we find favor, if we do not gift the gods what we would give to no other?"

My father grunted, sitting down beside me. "For a fortunate few, the gods are friends, to be trusted with promises so broad. For the rest of us, it would be wise to limit our gifts to what we can afford."

"Thor has always protected us, Father. If he is not our friend, what god is?"

"Perhaps none of them are." He stared at his hands, his jaw tight, and dread trickled down my spine to hear him speak so grimly, his voice rough with emotion. "Even Thjodhild's prayers to her god did not bring Thorstein home safe."

My heart seized, clenching tight and hard in my chest between one beat and the next. "No!"

"He was taken by sickness in the North along with most of his men," my father said, the words half-choked in his throat. "Gudrid and Thorvaldur arrived with the tale of it today, along with the dead. Thorstein made her swear to see them all buried properly before he died."

I shook my head, standing up, stumbling away. "It cannot be. He cannot be dead."

But the grief in my father's face said otherwise, no matter how I denied it. "I thought it best if you heard the truth of it from me before you returned. That you might not be caught unaware by Thjodhild and her wailing. She blames our gods, of course. Because Thorvaldur and Gudrid survived, and Thorstein and the others who died all worshipped the White Christ alongside Thor. She and Leif both believe it was a punishment."

I fell to my knees in the dirt and moss, my eyes burning with tears and my heart still too tight, too broken. "I cannot believe it. I cannot believe Thor would let this fall upon him. Thorstein, of all the men!"

"He was the best of them," my father agreed. "The best of my sons."

"It was his summer upon the seas," I said. "He was weak, after being storm tossed. Thor brought him home safe, but with Gudrid and Thorvaldur beside him, he must have turned to their Christ instead of calling upon the god who loved him."

But my father only looked on me with pity. "If Thor loved him, do you truly think a prayer to Christ would have stopped him from acting?"

"If Thorvaldur and Gudrid insulted him, if he believed by helping Thorstein he would only grant more honor and power to Christ, perhaps!" I said. "Would you have me believe instead that he turned his back upon him willfully? Or that their Christ is the more powerful? That when Thor would have granted Thorstein the strength he needed, Christ beat him back?"

He shook his head. "I will not tell you what to believe or which god you ought to pray to. I only worry that you place too much faith in powers outside yourself. After what has become of Thorstein, you cannot blame me. I have no wish to lose my daughter to any god's might."

"You worship the gods, too, Father."

"And our ancestors, and the spirits of these lands, yes. I grant them the honors they deserve, the gifts required to appease them. That is all."

"You named your sons for Thor. You named me for the god Freyr—"

"To please them, I suppose," he admitted. "In the hopes that you might be granted some small measure of their protection. But what good has it done you, truly, Dísa? What good have I done you at all?"

"It is only your grief which makes you say such things," I said, rising. To hear him speak this way twisted my stomach, but I knew it was Thjodhild's work, and Leif's, knotting the strands of his sorrow to their purpose, turning him from the gods he had raised me to love. "Thorstein's fate was woven before you named him, and even Thor would not dare to stand against the Norns. That is all. That is all!"

And then I left him, because I knew if he said another word, everything I believed would unravel, too.

⁂

"I'm so sorry, Freydís," Gudrid said, coming to me when I entered my father's house.

The long pit fire was low, half-banked, and the main room was smoky and dark. Fitting, I supposed, for who could abide the light when they were swallowed by pain and grief? In the dark at least you could pretend it was all a dream.

"I did not leave his side for more than a moment after he took ill, nursing him as best I could. But so many died. So many." Her eyes glistened even in the dim light, and I wanted to hate her for her sorrow. For stealing Thorstein from me. "He fretted for you when the fever rose. He made me promise to do for you what I could, and I give you my vow, Freydís—we will be as sisters. I will stay here with you in Erik's house, if he will let me, that you might have me near."

I stared at her, not understanding. "Here?"

"So you will not be alone," Gudrid said. "So we might support one another while we grieve."

My head ached. "You want to stay in my father's house after your god, your Christ, let my brother die? The Christ you persuaded him to turn to? The god for which he chose to forsake his ancestors, his father, his very name?"

She drew back, her eyes wide. "What?"

"You killed him," I said. "You and Thjodhild and Leif and Thorvaldur. You're the reason my brother is dead."

"Of course." Gudrid's expression softened, her shock turning to pity. "Of course you would see it so. But I had hoped—Thorstein and I had both hoped—you might see reason one day. That you might at least show the same understanding that Erik has."

I laughed, but it was harsh and brought no relief at all to the heaviness in my heart. "You thought I would turn my back upon my ancestors and my father? Upon the gods and land spirits who have never betrayed me?"

"It does not matter," Gudrid said softly, and she caught my hand, pressing warm metal into my palm. "Thorstein wished you to have this, though I cannot imagine what good it will do you, if this is how you feel."

I looked down at the bronze cross. The four hammers welded together that I had gifted him to ensure he had Thor's protection on his journey.

"We need not be enemies, Freydís," Gudrid said when I remained silent. "I am not Leif or Thjodhild, or even Thorvaldur. I would never have married Thorstein if I believed as they did. But perhaps you have more in common with them than you want to know, if you truly think we are the reason Thorstein died."

My hand closed into a fist around the pendant, the edges biting into my palm. "I am *nothing* like them."

"You are stubborn like them," she said, lifting her chin. "Stubborn and blinded by your faith, refusing to see beyond yourself for even a moment. If all that you love is Thor, then how are you any different from Thjodhild, who cares for nothing more than her Christ?"

"You have no right to speak to me this way," I snapped, hating her for the words. For the truth that settled over me like a cloak soaked through with rain, clinging and heavy and cold. "You should have stayed in the North on Thorstein's farm and never come back at all."

She sighed, stepping back. "One day you will realize I only ever wanted to be your friend, Freydís. Your sister. Out of love for your brother, I still do. But even love might crumble if all it is fed is bitterness."

I told myself I was glad when she walked away.

But later, lying upon my bed, my back to the fire and the room, and blankets drawn up in a pretense of sleep, when I opened my fist and looked at the cross, at Thor's cross, my heart ached. Thorstein had sent her to me. My brother, always peacemaking, even in death. Thorstein had sent me his wife and this cross, and I had turned away half his gift.

A breath of cold whispered against the back of my neck with the thought, the bronze suddenly cool in my hand, and I knew. Thorstein was with the ancestors, watching me act the fool. Would he remain with them after Gudrid had seen him buried as a Christian?

I clutched the cross tighter, feeling sick. Was that truly what Thorstein had wanted? To be buried apart from me? From our father and our ancestors? Gudrid and Thorvaldur—they were so Christian, so pious. Why wouldn't they lie, thinking to save his soul, even against his wishes?

I threw off my blankets and ignored the stares of my family as I pulled on my boots and my cloak, grabbed up a cup of wine, and pushed my way out the door.

"Freydís?" my father called, but I ignored him, too. Just like I did Thorvaldur's demand to know where I was going and Thjodhild's sharp comment about wasting good wine on the devil. Gudrid's soft voice rose in response, but I was too far out the door to hear her words by then.

Wine had sloshed over my fingers in my careless hurry, and I licked them clean as I made my way up the path, better worn now, with all the gifts I'd left upon the boulder these last months. And who was Gudrid to tell me what I loved most, besides? Just because I honored the gods, the ancestors, the wights, it didn't mean I was blind to everything else. I'd married Thorvard, hadn't I? To support my father, to do my duty . . .

To protect yourself, to ensure that you would always be free to place your faith in Thor, to love your gods as you wished and sail free of Thjodhild, my thoughts mocked me. In Thorstein's voice, no less. My fool of a brother.

Tears slipped down my cheeks, and I brushed them impatiently away, blinking back the blur from my eyes. "I won't let them take you from me," I said aloud, shouting to be sure he heard me. "Not again."

There was no answer beyond the whisper of cold wind across the grass.

I threw the cup and the wine against the boulder, fell to my knees, and wept.

CHAPTER TEN:
AD 2016
Emma

lex pulled into the driveway at precisely 6:55 p.m. Not *around*
seven, but almost perfectly punctually at seven itself. I'd
anticipated him at least that far—I'd been dressed and ready
since six thirty, seated in the living room with a view of the driveway,
fiddling with some stupid game on my phone that I kept forgetting to
play because I was too busy looking for the flash of his silver car and
debating whether I'd dressed appropriately for whatever dinner plans
he'd made.

Because he *had* made plans. This was Alex we were talking about.
If he hadn't made a reservation, I'd eat my napkin.

I didn't wait for him to come to the door. The minute I saw him
turn into the driveway, I was up, grabbing my purse and fishing out my
keys before dropping my phone into the depths of the main pocket.
I'd regret it later probably, but for now, all I cared about was getting

out the door before my parents saw who was picking me up, and as I pulled the door shut behind me, I could already hear that he'd turned the engine off.

"Don't get out, don't get out," I mumbled, sliding the dead bolt home before I spun.

And there he was, striding toward me over the gravel, looking perfect in a charcoal suit, complete with tie. I was glad I'd opted for my black skirt, the hem falling just below my knee, where my boots took over, and doubly glad I'd gone with the sweater instead of a more casual knit top. But I was beginning to wonder if he ever dressed down at all. Had I ever seen him in jeans? I felt like even at picnics he always wore at least khakis.

"You look beautiful," he said, leaning down to kiss my cheek. "Ready?"

I forced myself to smile instead of glancing guiltily over my shoulder to see if my parents were watching from the main house. "You really didn't have to get out."

He grinned, placing a hand at the small of my back to guide me toward the car. "How did I know you were going to say that?"

"If you knew, then why did you do it anyway?"

"So I could do this." He opened the passenger's-side door for me and stepped back, waiting.

I bit my lip to hide a real smile, refusing to encourage him. "Really?"

"Too old-fashioned?" he asked, watching me get in.

"Just old-fashioned enough," I promised.

His fingers curled around the doorframe, and he leaned down, tucking a fold of my skirt up out of the way. "I aim to please."

Then he shut the door, not so hard that it would slam but firmly enough to latch, and I took a deep breath to steady myself as he half jogged around the front of the car to the driver's side. Because *damn*. He was good.

And I was nervous. The kind of nervous that was likely to make me talk too much and too loudly. I touched the pendant around my neck, tucked safely beneath my sweater, though I probably should have left it in my purse instead, and reminded myself of the things I didn't want to say. No matter how much I liked him. No matter how warm the glow of a potentially successful first date. And no wine at dinner, either, which would only make me flushed and hot.

Alex's door opened and he climbed in. "All set?" he asked.

"Sure, why not?"

As we pulled away, I could have sworn I saw the living room curtain drop, my mother's carefully manicured fingers disappearing behind it. I groaned, tipping my head back against the seat.

"It's going to be fine, Emma," he said, laughter in his voice. "Your parents like me."

"And you're so sure that's a point in your favor."

His hand found mine in my lap, squeezing it lightly. "You like me, too."

I didn't have an argument for that.

The restaurant was nice but not intimidating. Greek food, which was a thoughtful touch, but priced in a range I couldn't really afford, judging by the white tablecloths and the lack of cheese-tastic Greek culture on the walls—excepting a not-so-subtle cross, of course. Everything was clean lines and elegance. Thankfully, Alex really was a traditionalist.

"Dinner's my treat," he told me almost the moment we were seated.

"You mean you don't want to do the post-dinner dance of who gets to pay the bill?" I asked. "I thought that was our generation's dating *thing*."

He laughed. "And here I thought our generation's *thing* was sex on the first date."

I almost dropped my menu. "Alexander Stone, that's the kind of talk that would get you banned from my mother's dinner table."

"What about her daughter's?" he asked.

"As long as you don't think the price of dinner also includes an upgrade into my pants, you can curse like a sailor. I haven't had good Greek food in forever."

"I like the lamb," he said. "But you'll have to tell me how authentic it is. I have no idea how it will compare to the real thing."

"It's been so long since that semester abroad, I don't even think I'll notice." I closed my menu and pushed it toward the side of the table. "Order for me."

He lifted his eyebrows, his own menu dipping. "Pardon?"

"You've been here before, you know what's good. There's nothing on that menu that doesn't sound amazing to me. Order whatever your two favorite dishes are, and we'll go family style. Small side bonus of not making me do the *What are you ordering?* and then choosing something that costs a dollar less so you don't think I'm taking advantage of your first-date generosity."

His eyebrows went higher, which I personally hadn't realized was possible. "Is that really—Do all women . . . ?"

I shrugged. "I can't speak for anyone but me, but I never get anything that's more expensive than what my host is ordering. Doesn't matter if it's a date or a family dinner."

"That's . . . interesting."

"You can't tell me you don't notice when your date orders the prime rib after you asked for a burger. How many times did you ask *them* for a second date?"

He grimaced. "I guess I never really thought about it. I don't think it was ever the dinner order that made or broke the date, though. Usually she just wasn't someone I particularly enjoyed talking to."

"*Talking.*" I swirled my ice around in my water glass, watching him. "Did you know, in the sagas, *talking* is a euphemism? When a woman is described as talking with a man, it means they were carrying on some kind of affair together, more often than not. It took me years to figure out—even with Auntie Anja's *heavily* suggestive readings."

"Well, no wonder *talk* gets a person banned from your mother's dinner table," Alex teased, closing his menu.

I grinned. "Precisely."

"Are you ready to order?" the server asked, appearing at the table. She must have just been watching, waiting for him to set his menu down.

Alex glanced at me. "You're sure?"

"I'm sure," I promised.

He ordered lamb and the chicken kebab, both of which I'd been eyeing, and a bottle of wine, which I now felt a little bit compelled to drink. In moderation, I reminded myself, when he filled my glass. And with plenty of water to balance it out, or I'd regret it all even more tomorrow.

"I don't think I've ever met your auntie Anja," he said once the food was ordered and our drinks were poured. "Or really any of your mother's family."

"They don't exactly fit my father's platform," I said slowly, not sure how I felt about the direction he'd taken. Talking about Auntie Anja and her husband was a little bit too honest for a first date. I clasped my hands in my lap to keep from touching the pendant beneath my sweater. Clutching at it, more like.

"That's right," he said. "Iceland isn't Catholic, is it? Officially."

"Definitely not Catholic," I agreed. But that wasn't the real issue. If they'd been card-carrying members of the National Church, good and proper Lutherans, it wouldn't have mattered at all that they weren't Catholic. It was Auntie Anja's husband, with his claims of being descended from Thor, and Anja's refusal to attend church at all that was the problem. "But Amma—my mother's mother—converted to Catholicism for my grandfather when they married after World War II.

It was so important to him and his family, and she had just come to this strange new country to be his wife and just wanted to belong." I cleared my throat and let myself ask, "Does that kind of thing matter to you?"

He frowned, meeting my eyes. "I'm not David, Emma. I don't expect or need you or your family to be anything you aren't."

It wasn't an answer, not really, and I didn't want to do this again. "But you're Catholic."

"I was raised Catholic, yeah," he agreed. "And what I love most about Catholicism is that there's room for me to follow my own conscience. I don't have to adhere so strictly to doctrine when it conflicts with my conviction of what's right or wrong. But I believe that faith is a personal thing, too. That my beliefs are between me and God, and so are yours."

"That assumes that my beliefs, or lack thereof, involve the same god," I said.

He twitched a shoulder, entirely dismissive. "It isn't my business, either way. There's a reason there are umpteen million denominations of Christianity and a half-dozen major world religions. Everyone finds their own path."

I stared at him, totally baffled by his answer. "But you work on my father's campaign—you believe in the things he believes in, I know you do."

Alex leaned forward. "I believe your father is a good man, Emma. I believe he's the most honest politician we've got regionally. And I trust him to make decisions that benefit more than just himself or his party, to truly represent his constituents. Right now, most of them are Catholic, or at the very least Christian, and that aligns with his values perfectly. When and if that changes . . ." He shrugged openly this time. "I think your father will do the right thing by us, whether that's giving up his seat or changing the way he votes to accommodate the people he represents."

"Wow," I said, sitting back in my seat. "You really are good at your job, aren't you?"

He let out a breath, his eyes darkening with an emotion I couldn't name. "I'm not sure if that's a compliment or not, under the circumstances. I'm not trying to spin things or stay on message. You asked, and I answered."

"I just wasn't expecting that much . . . passion, I guess."

"You don't get into politics unless you're passionate," he said, then grimaced. "Or I guess if you're some kind of sociopath or psychopath. In which case, hopefully I just proved myself a normal, feeling human being. Maybe I should have said, don't get involved with the people in politics who *aren't* passionate."

"Honestly, I never thought I'd be getting involved with anyone in politics at all," I said. "I'm not really my father's daughter, you know?"

He half smiled. "I think you're more your father's daughter than you think you are."

I shook my head. "I don't think I could be as honest about myself to the world as he is. As open about my beliefs or my life. He makes it seem so easy, so natural. For me, it would be utterly terrifying."

"Then why don't you just go to church, like your mother wants?" he asked.

I pressed my lips together. "You'd like that, I'm sure."

"For the campaign's sake, maybe," he said. "But not for you. Not if it isn't real. And even for the campaign, it wouldn't be worth it if it wasn't something you believed in. People would see through the show."

"*Because* Dad is honest," I agreed. "That's exactly what I told my mother when she started in on me again. What good would it do if I started lying to support my father's campaign? If anyone found out, it would just make an even bigger mess. Not to mention the fact that it's morally repugnant."

"And you really don't think you're your father's daughter?" Alex asked, laughing.

I flushed. "I just meant that I'm not political at all."

"The best politicians aren't, either," he said. "But if it makes you feel better, it was the times when you went totally and unapologetically off message that made me want to take you to dinner."

I bit my cheeks, fighting a smile. "You mean the times I made more work for you?"

"I guess I was kind of a captive audience in that regard. But yeah. And knowing that the idea of being open like that terrifies you—it makes me wonder if maybe you're braver than you think. Braver than I ever knew."

"Not brave," I said, looking away. "Not even remotely."

Because if I were, I wouldn't be so afraid right now of telling him the truth. My big stupid secret. My private faith in a god he probably thought was a delusion, no matter how much he talked about everyone finding their own way.

And if there was one thing I knew, one thing that had been proven to me time and again, it was that it was easy to deal with a concept, an idea of something different in theory, but it was something else completely when it was someone you cared about walking a path you thought was misguided or wrong. Even if he understood in theory, it didn't mean it was something he wanted in his life.

I just wasn't ready to face that *look* in his eyes yet. That disappointment or, worse, the expression that said, *Wow, I didn't realize you were that crazy.*

So when our food arrived, I talked about how good it was instead.

CHAPTER ELEVEN:
AD 999
FREYDÍS

When the ship from Norway arrived, I couldn't bring myself to care. My husband wasn't expected back before the following spring, with the ship I'd been promised as a wedding gift, and unless these men had brought my brother back from the dead, they had nothing I could want.

"At least come out to greet them, Freydís," Gudrid said.

She'd been annoyingly persistent in her efforts, determined to have me as her friend. Mostly I avoided her, but I'd found it harder and harder to summon the strength even to leave my bed these last days, and so I could only roll over, pulling the furs up over my head and giving her my back.

Gudrid sighed. "You worry your father, carrying on this way. He thinks some ill spirit has taken hold of you. And you know Thorstein would never have wanted this."

"Thorstein is dead," I said, her words rousing me that far. "Gone and buried like a proper Christian, his spirit trapped by your holy ground. I'll never see him again, not even in death."

"It doesn't have to be that way, Freydís," Gudrid said. "If you were baptized—"

"Enough, Gudrid," Thorvaldur said. "Let her have her grief, and leave off with your talk of baptism. It will not bring him back, and meeting him again in heaven is little comfort when we have need of him now."

I closed my eyes, too tired even to cry anymore, and let out a breath. Perhaps Thorvaldur thought I was a fool for not converting, but at least he understood my grief. At least he realized just how much we had lost with Thorstein's death. Leif and Thjodhild had not let up for even a moment, using Thorstein's death as a cautionary tale. Everyone at Brattahlid, even in Greenland as a whole, had known my brother had worshipped Christ alongside Thor, and now, according to Thjodhild and Leif, they knew it was the reason he had died. Listening to them go on made my head ache, my stomach twist into knots, and my heart pound so hard I could not keep from trembling in rage.

If there had ever been a time when we needed Thorstein more, I could not remember it. And without him, without even the hope of him, there was no peace on the farm at all.

Gudrid patted my shoulder through the blankets, murmuring something that sounded like a prayer before she moved away, and then it was only Thorvaldur looming at my bedside.

"This won't bring him back, either," he said.

I didn't answer. What purpose would it serve? I knew Thorstein was gone. I just didn't know how to go on. Perhaps I didn't want to. Thorstein had been more than just my brother, after all; he had been my friend. And except for our father, the only true support I'd had.

After another moment of heavy silence, Thorvaldur left me, too.

"You've met my sons, Leif and Thorvaldur," my father said, welcoming his guests. "And this is my wife, Thjodhild. I've a daughter as well, Freydís, but she is . . . unwell."

"Sickness?" one of the men asked.

"Grief," my father replied, his tone discouraging any further questions. "You're welcome here as long as you wish to stay, of course. I've storehouses, too, if you wish to keep your goods somewhere more secure than your ship's hold."

"And to show our gratitude, you must take what you desire from our hold," a second man said, as was customary. My father would give them gifts of trade goods as well, when these men departed, in payment for what he took. "We've plenty of food and drink to share."

I snorted, annoyed by the dance of hospitality. Annoyed by the arrival of these men at all. What right did they have to sail the seas? To escape illness and disease? What right did they have to live when my brother had died?

"You have not even looked upon their faces, and already you disapprove," a low voice said, so near it made me jump. "Can no man please you, now you've taken your husband to your bed? Thorvard the Three-Legged, isn't it?"

"Go away," I said, not even turning my head.

The strange man laughed, rich and warm and deep. "I have come a long way, Freydís. Would you truly send me off so unsatisfied?"

"What difference does it make to me if you leave satisfied or not?" I asked, but I turned my head, catching a glimpse of his profile, his size. No wonder his laugh was so deep, as broad as his chest seemed to be. But I refused to roll over to get a better look. He had no business approaching me at all, and I had no intention of encouraging him.

"The difference between a pleasant, fortunate year or a miserable one," he said. "The difference between success upon the seas or bewilderment and starvation."

"You think yourself so fine a sailor as that?"

"You will never meet another so fine," he promised. "But if you would refuse my gifts . . ."

I swallowed and gave in, turning to face him properly and sitting up while I was about it. "Who are you?"

He grinned, a neatly trimmed copper beard framing his smile. "A friend, I promise you that, and happy to know a woman so fierce in her loyalties."

"Your name," I insisted, refusing to be cowed by the size of him, the intensity in his gaze. His arms were banded with rings of silver and gold, and there was no missing the sword on one hip or the odd stub-handled war axe upon the other. A warrior, then, which was certainly strange enough on its own.

He tipped his head, just slightly, part acknowledgment and part censure for my impatience. "Sonnung."

My eyes narrowed. "And what brings you here, Sonnung, to my bedside?"

"I thought you might be lonely," he said. "After hearing what your brothers had to say, I cannot doubt that you must be eager for a friend who shares your faith. You and your father, both."

My fingers found the cross of hammers around my neck, Thorstein's pendant. "You worship Thor?"

"I find him the most amenable," he said, amusement in his voice. "Some say he is a fickle friend, I know, but I've never found him so. Not to those who have shown him true loyalty and honor. Proper respect."

"He has never betrayed me."

"And how could he, when he sees himself reflected in your eyes?"

"I won't have a ship to sail with until the spring."

He shrugged. "Karlsefni has no intention of leaving before then. Not when there is walrus ivory to be had and fine furs to acquire in trade."

I licked my lips, studying him in the firelight. There was nothing small about him. Not his size or his smile or his crooked nose, and certainly not his swagger. I'd never seen a man so confident. "And in the spring, you'll sail with me?"

"In repayment for your hospitality," he agreed.

"Do they call you three-legged, too?" I asked.

His lips quirked, his gaze steady upon mine and his large hand wrapped tight around the pole that supported the roof above. "You won't miss your husband, I can promise you that."

"I don't miss him now," I said, lifting my chin. "Three-legged or not, he hardly knew how to use what he was given, and I don't mean to suffer more of the same while he's away."

"You're a bold woman, Freydís," he said.

"No bolder than you, looming over my bedside and asking for favors as if we've talked before. And nothing to prove your boasts, either, that you sail so well."

"But I can prove myself in your bed easily enough. And even if I've lied about the rest, we could still have a pleasant enough year, you and I."

"Do you think I can forget my grief so easily?" I asked.

His good humor faded, and before my very eyes he seemed to age with sorrow. "Not forever, perhaps, but for a moment here or there, you might. Until you find your fire again. Until you find the will to rise again, and stand alone. For you surely do not serve yourself or the gods lying in that bed, weeping for what you've lost. And I would have you serve me, Freydís, with all the strength you once possessed. I would have you live as a proof to these fool Christians of the power of Thor."

I rolled my eyes and lay back down. "You behave as though you speak for Thor, for the gods themselves."

He offered a strange, strangled laugh. "Are you so sure I don't?"

"There's time enough to learn the truth, one way or the other," I said. "And I am not so great a fool as to be convinced by nothing but boastful words, regardless."

"I could take you by force, if I wished to."

"In my father's hall, and you his guest?" I scoffed. "Even if Thor himself stood at your side, you would not dare."

"And if I were Thor himself?"

"Then you could have me as you pleased." I turned my back upon him, huddling under my furs again. I was too tired to continue, and what interest he'd held was lost now by his bluster. He was nothing but a fool, thinking to use me, and I did not mean to let him. Not simply for his pleasure, and not so easily, in any event. "After you smote the Christians."

"Be careful what you ask of the gods, Freydís," he said. "You may find you do not care for the favor after all."

I only waved him away, dismissing his words just as easily, and closed my eyes. I'd given him too much encouragement already.

But I would have been lying if I'd said I didn't hope he might trouble me again.

Perhaps with fewer boasts and more persuasion.

My father woke me early the next morning, his hand upon my brow as if he feared I might have taken sick in the night. When I stirred beneath his touch, rubbing the crust of sleep from my eyes, he grunted and squeezed my shoulder instead.

"What is it?" I mumbled.

"Get dressed."

I blinked, frowning. "Why?"

"Because unless you are truly ill, there is no reason you should not bathe," he said. "It was one thing to overlook this mourning while we were alone, but I would not have our guests think poorly of us or bring word of our weakness back to Iceland when they set sail again."

"Word already arrived in Iceland with Thorvard, Father, like it or not," I said. "There was not a man among that crew who could not see our weakness plainly, with all the trouble Thjodhild and Leif saw fit to cause."

"All the same," he said. "Dress, and go to the spring to bathe. Make yourself presentable, and receive our guests as you ought."

"I don't see what difference it makes whether it is me or Gudrid who receives them," I grumbled. "She's by far the friendlier of the two of us, and prettier besides."

"You're my daughter, Dísa. That's the difference it makes."

I sniffed, irritated, but threw off my furs all the same. For weeks, my father had asked nothing of me, overlooking the days I spent in bed, carrying on for the both of us in the face of Thjodhild's newfound zeal. Her smug and righteous pleasure that Thorstein had asked for a Christian burial in the end, not to be buried in the mound to join our ancestors.

I had let him suffer alone, a coward in my grief, and if he wished me to bathe and greet his guests, if that was all he desired, I could hardly refuse such a small request.

"Good girl," he said, stepping back to give me room. "And when you're clean and dressed again, and your bedding aired, be sure to see to the gods as well."

"Of course, Father," I said, shoving my feet into my boots and wrapping myself in my longest cloak. It was all I needed to reach the spring, and I had no desire to dirty clean clothes on my grimy skin. I shambled toward the door, stamping my foot to settle it more comfortably inside my boot.

"And Freydís?" I glanced back, meeting his gaze. It was thick with relief, with warmth and affection. "No matter how he was put to rest, he isn't lost to us. Not so long as we honor his memory. We need only remember him as he was."

My throat closed, my eyes burning and dry, but I nodded.

I wanted to believe it, too.

CHAPTER TWELVE:
AD 2016
Emma

I t was strange to be on a first date with a man I knew so much about already, and stranger to feel like I didn't actually know as much as I'd thought I did. When he walked me to the guesthouse door, my stomach turned entirely to butterflies, the heat of his hand burning through my sweater and branding the small of my back. I had no idea what I was supposed to do, how he expected me to act. Should I invite him in? If I did, would he think it meant I wanted to sleep with him? And if he thought I wanted to sleep with him—which I wasn't exactly entirely opposed to, if I was being honest, and it was *not* because I'd had too much wine—would he think I was too easy? What had he meant by that comment at the beginning of dinner about sex on the first date? Or had he not meant anything at all?

And then we were on the small porch, and I didn't even have my keys, too distracted by the million and three questions all knocking around inside my head to even consider the fact that I'd need to unlock my door. I fumbled for them, flushing at my own ridiculousness, and of course they had fallen into the bottom of my purse, forcing me to dig and dig. My cheeks burned hotter with every passing second of delay until he laughed gently and plucked the spare out of the heart of the wind chime hanging from the awning, where my parents had kept it for years.

Alex unlocked the door for me, cracking it open, and tucked the key back where it belonged. But it forced me to duck inside and punch in the code for the alarm before the system decided we were breaking in, and when I turned back, he was standing in the doorway, leaning against the frame.

I dropped my purse on the table in the entryway and took a breath, steadying myself. "Do you want to . . . ?"

He shook his head. "You were pretty clear about what wasn't included with dinner tonight."

I took a step toward him, my hand grasping the interior of the doorframe, level with where his shoulder rested inside the frame itself. His toes, I noticed, glancing down, hadn't crossed the rubber weather stripping into the house.

"I don't think I said anything about dessert."

He smiled but didn't move. "You really aren't the good little Catholic girl your parents want to make you out to be, are you?"

"Holly got all the faith, and I got all the appearance of it," I said. "But if you'd like to preserve *your* virtue, by all means, don't let me be the one to seduce you into sin."

That provoked a snort of laughter. "I'm not quite *that* Catholic, either, thank you."

"Thank God for that," I murmured, letting myself lean against my side of the doorframe. We were only inches apart, and I'd have been lying if I'd said I wasn't a little bit tempted by the sheer warmth of him, with the door open and all the heat escaping my house.

His hand brushed my face, just the backs of his knuckles whispering against my cheek, but my eyes closed, my whole body going hot. His thumb trailed across my bottom lip, his breath tickling my skin. "But I'm still not coming in."

A strangled noise climbed up my throat, and I swallowed hard before it could escape, my eyes fluttering open again. "We could just . . . talk."

"Like in the sagas?" he asked, laughter in his words, in his eyes, and curving his lips.

"If I hadn't told you that story, you'd have come inside," I accused. "Never thinking for a minute I meant anything else."

He laughed again, straightening, and his hand fell away from my face. "I'd have been hoping you meant something else."

I sighed, shivering at the sudden cold now that he no longer blocked the wind quite so effectively. "Not even a single kiss good night?"

"It wouldn't stop at one kiss. I wouldn't *want* to stop at just one kiss."

And just like that, I was too warm all over again. To think I'd been worried beforehand that he wouldn't want to point his intensity in the right direction . . .

"Good night, Emma," he said, brushing his lips against my cheek.

"*Góða nótt,*" I murmured back.

Then he was walking to his car, and I stood rooted in the doorframe, not quite believing that I was watching him drive away.

***

"So?" Sarah asked when she answered her cell, after I finally bothered to look at my phone and saw that she'd sent me more than a dozen texts reminding me to call and give her all the details. Part of me had wanted to make her wait until the next day, let her stew over whatever grist the town rumor mill was grinding, but the other part of me was still trying to figure out what Alex's game was, and if there was anyone who could help me parse the events of my date, it was Sarah. "How was it?"

"Good, I think," I said slowly. "I mean, dinner was good. But after. He wouldn't come in. He wouldn't even kiss me."

"What?" Sarah demanded.

"I don't know. I invited him. And he said he wasn't *that* Catholic, so it seemed like it was going to be fine, and then he leaned in like he was going to kiss me, but instead he just . . . didn't. Like it was just a big tease. And then he said good night, kissed my cheek, and left."

"Did he ask to see you again?"

I shook my head.

"I'm assuming the extensive silence means no."

I sighed. "All signs pointed to yes, but he didn't actually ask. He just said . . . he said he didn't want to kiss me, because he wouldn't want to stop. Which is . . . frustratingly and annoyingly romantic, I guess, but also just kind of—what does that even *mean*? Who does that?"

"An idiot," Sarah said. "That's who. Unless he really *is* that Catholic and was trying to pretend he wasn't."

"If he is, then what is he even doing asking me out at all?" I paced the length of the living room, then the short hall to my bedroom, too, before turning back again. "No. There's no way he was faking. He was pretty clear at dinner about his feelings on religion, and it was all pretty liberal."

"Is it possible that he liked you more than he thought he would?" Sarah asked. "Maybe things got too intense, and it scared him off."

"I was *not* intense," I said. "Nervous with a side of awkward, maybe, but definitely not intense."

"Yeah, but Alex has to face your dad on Monday morning. And you know your mom was spying through the drapes. That's a lot of pressure for a first date."

"He's the one who was saying it didn't matter and telling me not to worry about it!"

"I know," Sarah said. "I know. I get it. But if you guys connected—maybe he wasn't worried about it until he realized he really should be, because it was going to destroy him if it didn't work out."

I moaned, sliding down the wall. "Please don't let that be what's going on. It's going to make it so much worse when I have to tell him how not Catholic I really am."

"You didn't?"

"Of course I didn't! It was our *first date*."

"But you guys talked about religion, you said."

"It was bound to come up," I told her. "But it was mostly just kind of probing to feel out his position on things, not mine. I didn't want to scare him off."

"You should just get it out of the way, Emma. Tell him you're whatever you are, and move on. He'll either understand or he won't, but it's not like you worship Satan."

I tipped my head back against the wall, thumping it once, twice, again. "No, I just worship Thor."

"Right, whatever."

I let out a long breath, forcing myself to ignore the way she dismissed my words. My faith. If someone suggested she was Catholic and not Protestant, she would be offended, but I was just *whatever*. And this was why we didn't talk about my faith. Why even though she knew the truth, I still felt so alone. "You know it isn't going to be that simple."

"Would you rather get all wrapped up in him, let him fall in love with you, and then spring it on him and break both your hearts when he looks at you like you're crazy?" she asked. "Because judging by this conversation, that's where this is headed. And it's going to get there fast."

I closed my eyes, hating that she was right. Hating that she'd looked at me like I was crazy, too, when I'd first told her about my beliefs. That she still to this day couldn't bring herself to say the word *Heathen* without implied subvocal air quotes, when she could bring herself to say it at all. Like it couldn't possibly be as real to me as her faith was to her.

And if Alex responded the same way . . .

We'd been on only one date, but I knew already it would tear me apart.

"Just tell him, Emma," Sarah said. "If you're serious about your faith and it means that much to you, it isn't fair to keep it from him. This is Alex. You already know he can be trusted not to wreck your father's campaign if things go south. Just be honest."

"Yeah," I said, blinking back the tears that pressed behind my eyes.

It was so easy for her to say. For Sarah, for my dad, it was nothing to say they believed in Jesus. People just accepted Christianity as a matter of course, and no one was going to accuse them of being racists or neo-Nazis because of it. No one was going to tell them their god didn't exist in the middle of a history class, or blink if they suggested they'd had some kind of spiritual experience of Christ. And sure, yeah, maybe part of it was that it was a big deal to *me*, and I was making more of it than I needed to because of that, but when the base assumption of everyone around you was that everyone else was monotheist or nonreligious and you weren't either one, it was something that you became a little more acutely aware of.

"Who knows?" I said, forcing all the rest of it away. Forcing myself to keep my voice steady instead of strangled. "Maybe there won't even be a second date."

To be honest, after this, I wasn't sure whether I wanted one.

❧

Around the far side of the guesthouse, I had a tiny brazier—an old brass acorn-shaped ashtray I'd found in a secondhand store—and a small bench made of oak. It was completely unmarked. Unremarkable in every way, really, and tucked out of sight where even the landscapers wouldn't find it. I knelt beside it, ignoring the cold seeping through my jeans, and placed my offerings in the brazier. A small cookie from a batch I'd baked from scratch and a libation of mead poured over it along with a little bit of kindling. Then I lit a match and dropped it carefully on top.

My fingers found the pendant around my neck, clutching it tightly. "Please, Thor, accept these gifts and grant me just the smallest measure of your strength, your bravery, your courage in return."

Some Heathens didn't really believe in the gods, I knew. Or didn't engage with them, necessarily, in the same way I did. Maybe the gods were metaphors, abstracts of natural forces, or just so distant that it didn't make sense to reach out to them first. For them, Heathenry was about honoring their ancestors and the spirits of the land, about living well and honorably within their community, more than anything else. And while I hadn't found a community of my own yet where I really felt like I belonged, I honored my ancestors, too, burning offerings to my grandmother—though I wasn't entirely sure she'd appreciate it—on the anniversary of her death. It gave me comfort to remember her that way. But there was nothing else like the peace that flooded me when I made an offering to Thor. When I reached for him and felt him reach back.

Sometimes, when I closed my eyes, I thought I could feel him at my side, eliciting a shiver down my spine. And just as quickly, the moment would pass, that sense of his presence fading away but leaving stillness and tranquility behind. And right then, I was desperate for a little bit of that steadiness, or I wasn't going to sleep at all.

Maybe none of it was real. God knew I'd asked myself that question before. Over and over and over again, after I had devoured the Eddas and the sagas, and had begun to connect all the dots of my spiritual life, belatedly realizing that none of it pointed toward Jesus Christ. Maybe it wasn't Thor at all, but some land spirit instead, or even one of my ancestors, come to lend me their support. I didn't know what anyone else would make of it, what a community would call what I experienced—who I experienced—but whatever it was, by the time the fire had died and all that was left in the brazier was ash and an *extremely* burnt cookie, I always felt better, no matter what had been troubling me. Because in those all too brief moments, I knew I wasn't alone.

I was so, so tired of being on my own. But I didn't see what other choice I had. Not while I lived at home.

CHAPTER THIRTEEN: AD 999

FREYDÍS

I sank up to my neck in the steaming water of the spring, sighing with pleasure at the warmth before pinching my nose and submerging completely. The water was almost too warm, the heat burning against my eyelids, and I did not like to think of the mess I was making of my hair, dousing it this way, but I used my free hand to loosen it from the thick braid I'd worn to keep it from tangling during the long weeks I had spent in my bed. The cleanliness of my body would be worth little if my hair and scalp still stunk.

My lungs ached, wanting to breathe, but I waited until I was truly desperate before I broke the surface again for air, gasping, then coughing from the sudden cold.

"A daughter of Njǫrd, now, are you?" a man asked, familiar amusement coloring his words. The next moment, he'd slipped into the water with me, all muscle and grace. "I was just beginning to wonder if I shouldn't pull you back out."

I forced myself to meet his gaze, keeping my eyes from his broad chest, scarred and pockmarked from what seemed to me a hundred battles. It was remarkable that he had survived so many wounds at all, never mind with such strength still. "I suppose it shouldn't surprise me that you were watching, eager as you seem to be to spear me through."

He laughed, tipping his copper head back and spreading his arms along the green turf that lined the bank. "You'll find nothing quite so sharp as a spear about my weapon, I promise you that."

"You make far too many promises, Sonnung," I said, looking away. He was every bit as attractive in sunlight as he had been in the dim farmhouse, but I had no interest in giving him the satisfaction of knowing I thought so. "I can't imagine any man capable of keeping them all."

"There are no men like me, Freydís," he said. "You'll see that soon enough."

I sniffed, crossing my arms over my chest beneath the water. "That's what they all say, but once you have your sword sheathed, you'll be just like the others. Panting and heaving above me, dousing me in stink and sweat without a care for my comfort or pleasure."

"Only a fool would crush you beneath him," he said. "And I am no fool. But I won't pretend you'll find anything gentle in my arms. Not if you continue to tease me this way."

"I'm not certain it would matter whether I teased you or not, in that regard," I said, letting my gaze linger briefly on his scarred chest. "What's a fighting man doing among a ship full of traders?"

"Perhaps he's looking for a woman to cool the fire in his blood."

"Then it's Gudrid you want, not me." I rose, not caring what he saw, meaning to haul myself back out of the water. My arms were weak, trembling, and I fell back with a splash, which only made me all the redder, shame flushing my cheeks. I grasped the turf and tried again.

"Freydís." My name on his lips was a prayer. Admiration and desire, awe and naked need.

He was behind me in the water when my arms gave out a second time, but I wasn't so sure it was my strength that had failed me. It was the wash of warmth from my core to my limbs, the quiver in my belly. He had one arm around my waist, his nose behind my ear, and the tickle of his beard, the caress of his very breath upon my neck. I shivered, and he drew me tight against his body, until I felt every inch of his skin against my back. He was so immense, so powerful. Not three-legged, as Thorvard was, but large enough all the same. And hard.

The steaming water was cool against the heat of my skin, of his.

"I don't want Gudrid," he said against my ear. "I want the woman who stands against her. Who fights for the gods she was named for."

"And if I refuse?" I asked, my voice far steadier than I felt.

"I'm not used to being refused," he said, but there was humor there again, lurking beneath his words. Amusement at the game I played, even at his own expense.

"And yet."

He growled, but a moment later, I was standing upon the turf, shivering in the cold. He followed easily, vaulting from the water, and tossed me my cloak before I'd even had time to think of reaching for it.

"Dress before I change my mind," he said.

I covered myself, watching him all the while. His golden skin and copper hair. The smoothness of his stride, and the grace of his every motion. "I wish you'd come before Thorvard."

He looked up from tying his trousers, fighting against the part of him that hadn't accepted my refusal quite yet, and grinned, wolfish and confident again. "I wouldn't have taken you to wife."

"And I never said I wanted you as a husband."

"What *do* you want with me, then?" he asked, stepping nearer. His wool tunic hung loosely from his fingertips, and I knew I had only to whisper and he would drop it and strip us both back to skin.

But I shrugged and stamped my feet into my boots again. "I haven't decided."

His laughter followed me, caressing, as I walked away.

◦⟡◦

Sonnung was everywhere I went after that. Watching me while I ate, his eyes stripping me bare. Leaning against the turf walls of the farmhouse while I shook my bedding out in the open air and spread it on the summer grasses to breathe. He even prowled after me when I carried my gifts to the rock to make my offerings to the landvættir and the gods.

"You were neglecting your duties," he said, circling me while I spread the gifts upon the stone and whispered prayers of long-delayed thanks for the health of our family and our livestock, and the continued prosperity of the farm.

I finished my work and stepped back from the boulder. "First my brother died, and then my father's wife stole his spirit from me. I grieved for him twice over."

"And blamed the gods for your loss."

I shook my head. "Thor protected him while he was at sea, as I asked. And I do not know that there was anything he could do to fight the sickness that swept through Thorstein's crew."

"Thor might have called upon another god to help your brother," Sonnung said. "If he'd been asked."

"And if Thorstein did not see fit to pray to the god he was named for, I cannot blame Thor for spurning him. Not when my brother's final words were for a Christian burial, too." I pressed my lips together, swallowing the bitterness before it bled into my voice. "My father said he is not truly lost to us, no matter how he was buried. But Thjodhild and Leif are so certain he is with their Christ. Why would he choose Christ over his family, his ancestors . . . ?"

"Over you?" Sonnung asked, far too shrewd.

I closed my eyes, tired again and hurting. This was the first time I'd spoken of Thorstein without anger or blame, and it was more exhausting than I wanted to admit. Hate was easier, simpler than acceptance.

"What do you want of me, Sonnung?"

"I should think that would be obvious by now."

"There are other women who might satisfy you," I said. "Women who are not sick with grief for a brother who betrayed them. Women who would welcome your attention without any hesitation at all."

"Women like Gudrid, who have followed Leif and Thjodhild to Christ."

I snorted, dismissive. "What difference does it make once you're inside them?"

"I won't spend my seed on a woman who would raise my child to scorn the gods," he said, all his humor lost now and a fury snapping his words that made my skin turn to gooseflesh. "Surely you can understand that."

My hand drifted to my stomach, pressed against the flatness of my waist. I understood. But if he wanted a child, if that was his hope—"You won't get a child from me."

He stepped before me, catching me by the chin and forcing my face up, my gaze to his. "Would you not welcome it, if I did?"

I swallowed hard and jerked free of his grasp. "You would get me with child and leave me, then? To face my husband with a swollen belly when he returns, having left me barren a year before."

"I would stand by your side, had you need of me," he said. "And claim the child proudly, if it came to that. But you did not answer me, Freydís."

"I am free now," I said. "And with a ship, I'll be all the freer. A child would only chain me, trap me here beneath Thjodhild's eye."

He grunted, his expression shuttering, as if I had offended him. "Would you say the same to Thor, if he stood before you?"

"A child is not a gift," I said, straightening. "It is a burden. And one I've no wish to carry alone, no matter who the father might be."

"You're no Vanir child, that's certain," he said. "No daughter of Freyja would say such a thing. And do you think the goddess is burdened by children? She's a warrior still."

I stared, heat rising to my cheeks again, but it was anger this time, not shame or desire. "You cannot think to compare my life on this farm with all the power that a goddess might possess?"

He flushed, too. "Do you truly believe your life is so ill-fated? That your father would not care for you, your brothers, even your husband?"

"No woman of any wit rests all her hopes upon a man," I snapped. "We know in the end, we face the world alone. Just because no man understands the risks we take, the struggles we face, it does not make them less real. And a child is the greatest risk of all, though it should hardly surprise me that you think it some great gift."

Sonnung drew back as if I'd slapped him, and though I might have been tempted, I'd kept my hands in tight fists at my sides. Just because I spoke boldly did not mean I was a fool, and no man of his size, of his strength, with his scars, would overlook a blow, even from a woman as soft as I had become in these last weeks.

"You should watch your tongue more carefully, Freydís," he said, but I could see the effort it took him to keep his words cool. "You seem not to know what you say, nor do I think you always know to whom you speak. And I promise you, if you keep on this way, it will provoke even the gods who love you to turn away."

"Thor has no grounds to turn from a woman over her temper," I said. "Nor can he possibly condemn bold speech or manner when he is known so well for his."

"Perhaps he does not wish to see himself quite so clearly reflected," Sonnung warned. "Perhaps it is the things he thought he loved most about you which will temper his affections."

"Are you so certain Thor loves me at all?"

His gaze remained steady, clear and sure. "How could he not, when you have shown him such loyalty?"

I let a smile curve my lips, for he could only be teasing me, serious as he pretended to be. Even Thor rarely showed true favor for anyone. He was not like Thjodhild's Christ, who settled somehow in your heart and mind, guiding your hand, even your words.

"If Thor is so pleased with me, then what need could I possibly have of you?" I asked. "He will see me safe upon the seas without your help, surely."

"I thought you knew better than to depend upon a man to see you safe?"

"Thor isn't only a man."

Sonnung sighed like a husband longing to escape the nagging of his wife and nodded to the path before offering me his hand. "He's more of one than you think, Freydís. I promise you that."

I hesitated just a moment, unsure of his mood, of mine. "More promises?"

He twitched one shoulder but turned his gaze away, back to the farm. "Come, I'll help you milk the goats."

CHAPTER FOURTEEN:
AD 2016
Emma

My phone buzzed at ten thirty in the morning on Sunday, just as my parents were heading out for church. I had my books spread over the coffee table, double- and triple-checking my sources on Charlemagne's war with the Saxons, along with everything I had on *The Vinland Sagas*, Gudrid the Far-Traveler, and Freydís, just in case I needed to defend myself again in class on Monday.

I wasn't sure what to think when I unearthed my phone from beneath the mountain of books and papers to find a text from Alex.

Are you free for brunch?

I tapped my pen absently on my notebook, staring at his message for a solid minute before I worked up the nerve to reply.

```
Shouldn't you be at church?
```

He was a lot faster.

```
I have croissants. So fresh they're still
warm from the oven.
```

No one with taste buds could say no to fresh croissants. Unless they had some kind of gluten sensitivity. But even then, I was pretty sure whatever grossness that might follow would be worth it.

I hit the "Call" button, and he picked up on the first ring. "Say yes, Emma."

"Yes," I said. "And you'd better already be in the car."

"Look out your window."

I looked up just as he turned into the driveway. "Texting while driving is against the law, you know."

"Good thing I got one of those fancy cars that texts for me."

"You realize you'll have to actually come into the house in order to have brunch."

He laughed. "I'm prepared to take that risk."

I piled my books as best I could at one end of the table, hoping to make it look at least a little less like a giant mess, and then tripped over my power cord on my way to the door, barely managing to keep my laptop from spinning onto the floor. But I still made it before he had a chance to knock, and just the *smell* of the croissants, already staining the paper bag with their buttery, greasy, full-calorie goodness, made my mouth water. And he'd brought coffee, too, which I took from him before the carefully stacked and balanced cups turned into a big brown stain on the carpet.

"This is a dangerous precedent, Alex."

"Is it?"

I stepped back, letting him inside. "A girl could definitely get used to fresh croissants delivered to her door."

"Maybe that's all part of my plan," he said, smiling. "Once I get you hooked, you'll never hesitate to say yes to Sunday brunch again."

"That was only maybe half hesitation and half that my phone was being used as an impromptu bookmark, actually." I nodded to the pile and made a point this time of stepping over my power cord instead of trying to go through it. "It took me a minute to dig it out."

"What are you researching?"

"A little bit of Charlemagne and some saga stuff. I just want to make sure I've got my facts straight in case last week's issues come back to haunt me this week, you know?"

"You never did give me any details about that," Alex said, accepting my unvoiced chin-jerk of invitation to perch on the edge of the couch.

"It's . . . complicated." I dropped to the cushion next to him and set out the coffee.

Alex, being Alex, produced a handful of paper napkins from his pocket, spreading two out on the table for plates before finally and at last opening up the grease-stained brown paper bag with the croissants. A waft of yeast and butter puffed out, and I groaned, leaning against him to breathe it in.

"You seriously have no idea how much I appreciate you right now."

"If I'd known that croissants were your Achilles' heel, I'd have brought some over weeks ago instead of begging Irena for dinner invitations."

"Please," I said. "Like you'd have to beg. She would have invited you anyway, and you know it."

"Not every week."

"Just every other. Poor you."

"With my luck, you'd have met someone during one of those off weeks, and I'd have missed my opportunity. This way I had Irena to keep me informed."

"Going forward, it would make me feel a lot better if you didn't use my mother as an informant. It makes me cringe even thinking about the kind of information she was feeding you. And the way she was *saying* it."

He laughed. "She only talks that way to you. Whenever you come up in conversation with anyone else, she's all pride and joy, bragging about how well you've done in school and your acceptance to so many prestigious PhD programs."

"Sure," I said. "She can't very well be honest and open about how disappointing I've been to her in every other respect. That would hurt my father's reputation."

"It isn't just the campaign," he said. "She really is proud of you. And even if it doesn't always seem that way, she just wants you to be happy. Whatever that means for you."

"No, I know." I ripped off a piece of my croissant—light and flaky perfection—and popped it into my mouth, where it promptly melted against my tongue in a glory of butter and pastry. "It's just hard coming back. Living here. They keep trying to put me back in that box, you know? The bright little girl who always did as she was told and never caused them any trouble. Perfect for trotting out at campaign events as an example of what good Christian values could produce! But that isn't who I am anymore."

"It isn't who Holly ever was, from what I understand," Alex said, peeling open the lids on the coffee cups. "Your parents cope just fine with that."

"Yeah, but it's different. She was *always* the wild one. But she knew how to skate the line, too. Never went so far over it that she couldn't come back. And then when she *did* come back, forget it. I'll never be able to compete with their prodigal baby girl." And my sister was still Catholic. No matter how many parties she went to or how hungover she was, she always got up for church the next day. She still did, even on the other side of the country. "They expected it from her. Made allowances for her personality from day one. And now she's a youth group coordinator at her church, keeping her parish's teens off the streets with lock-ins and church-sponsored dances, and using her vast experience of ill-advised partying and drug abuse to be hip and approachable, so obviously it was all for a good cause, or part of God's plan, or whatever."

"I can't imagine anything you might do now that would cause them more trouble than Holly did during the height of her teen rebellion, though."

I grimaced, taking a sip of the coffee. A perfect balance against the richness of the croissant. And a convenient excuse not to answer. Holly's rebellion hadn't run very deep. It hadn't been a rejection of the foundation of everything our parents believed. She just liked to have fun—too much sometimes—and now she was getting high off of God instead, which wasn't really something I was in any position to criticize. But it definitely made it hard to talk to her. More difficult, even, than Sarah. Maybe because she was my sister and she didn't get why I couldn't just fulfill my family obligation and go to church to preserve that happy-family image.

Alex took the cup from my hand, ducking his head to catch my eyes. "You know you can talk to me, right? Whatever it is that's been eating you—whatever it is that you think you can't be open about because of the campaign or your parents—I'm not going to judge you, or use it against you. Even if all of this blows up, if we don't make it more than a handful of dates, I'm not going to jerk you or your family around. You know where my loyalties lie."

"No, I know." I closed my eyes so I didn't have to see his earnestness. "It's not that. It's not you. I know I'm making it all into something bigger than it is, probably, but . . ." I sighed, opening my eyes again to meet his gaze, to memorize the kindness, the understanding, the generosity in every line of his face. "I don't want you to see me differently. Or look at me like I'm crazy. I just want to hold on to this beginning of surprise croissants and butterflies in my stomach for a little bit longer."

He studied my face, his lips pressing together. "Just so long as you know that whenever you're ready, I'm here. Whether we're still dating or not. All right?"

I let out a breath and forced myself to smile. "I'm going to go ahead and probably not take you up on that if this doesn't work out. I'm guessing things are going to be weird enough already without adding any uncomfortable confessions to the mix."

He shook his head. "You think that's going to be awkward? Try having to work with your dad when all I can think about is how much I want to despoil his daughter."

"I'm pretty sure the despoiling ship has sailed," I said.

"Is this where you tell me that you slept with an entire frat house of guys during undergrad?"

I snorted. "Hardly."

"Because that's a confession I would definitely be able to make peace with, I'm just saying."

"Two guys," I said. "They were semi-serious relationships. Not 'bring him home to meet the family' serious, but definitely not guys I'd be embarrassed to bring home, either. Like, monogamous, 'this doesn't necessarily have to go anywhere but I like being with you' fun, you know? Two and a half, if you count things that are not actually actual sex in an outburst of repressed Catholic girl at my first party as a freshman, which I *immediately* regretted."

"Were you drunk? Because in instances like that, drunk definitely does not have to count."

"I think that's going to depend on how many times *you* were drunk," I said, popping more croissant in my mouth. Even cold, it was delicious.

"Ah." He cleared his throat. "More than that."

"How much more?"

A blush climbed up his neck, coloring his cheeks and turning his ears bright cherry red. "You really want to know?"

I grinned. "Well, now that you've turned into a tomato, I'm definitely that much more interested."

A muscle along his jaw twitched, and he was suddenly very interested in his coffee cup. "Freshman year, I was trying really hard to make things work long-distance with my high school girlfriend, Jenna, so things were pretty tame at first. But when I came home for Christmas, I found out she'd been cheating on me. We broke up. It was . . . messy." He turned the cup in his hands, rolled it between his palms. "After that, I went a little bit overboard. To compensate, I guess, and prove to the other guys that I wasn't totally wrecked about it, even though I obviously *was*. You know how it is in college. Lots of drinking, lots of hookups. I was done and over it by the end of my sophomore year, but it's not something I'm proud of. Since then, it's only been serious relationships. Stephanie during my junior and senior year, and then Katie, who I think you met at a few of your father's events."

"Wow." I leaned back against the couch, tucking one foot under me and giving him a little bit of space. Giving us both a little bit of space. I didn't know what I'd been expecting when I asked, but it wasn't that. And I remembered Jenna. She'd been the star pitcher on the softball team. I never would have thought she'd cheat. Especially not on someone like Alex. "I'm sorry about what happened with your girlfriend from high school."

He twitched a shoulder. "It was a long time ago. Looking back, it's one of those relationships where you really wonder why you ever thought it was going to work out, you know?"

"I think everyone has a couple of those." I swirled my coffee, thinking about it. There were a couple of boys in high school who I could not for the life of me figure out what I saw in them at the time. And now . . . "Seeing some of the stuff they post online makes me feel like I dodged a bullet, honestly."

"Exactly."

"But it sounds like that was a pretty formative experience."

"I'd be lying if I said I thought cheating was a forgivable event, that's for sure." But he'd relaxed now that he'd made his confession and I hadn't kicked him to the curb, spreading his arm across the back of the couch and shifting to look at me. "What about you?"

"What about me, what?" I asked, settling in a little bit closer to him.

"What's your unforgivable offense?"

I wrinkled my nose, picking at a loose thread on the cuff of my jeans. "I think any kind of betrayal like that is hard to come back from—maybe impossible. But I don't know. I think the worst thing a person can do to you depends on who the person is and the context of the relationship. I don't know what I'd be willing or unwilling to forgive until it happens, you know? Or maybe it's the thing they don't do in the clutch, when you really need them at your side and they don't come through. For whatever reason."

"Did that happen?" he asked gently.

I shook my head. "I don't think I've ever let it."

His hand found mine, our fingers lacing together. I could feel it, the words he wanted to say. The promises he wanted to make, hanging in the air between us. It prickled my skin, giving me goose bumps.

"Don't," I said, before he could give voice to any of it. "I'm not sure that's the kind of promise anyone can really keep. No matter how much they mean it before the time comes."

"That's a rough way to live," he said after another moment. "Never trusting that when it comes down to it, the people you love are going to show up."

"Maybe," I agreed. "But I've never been disappointed, yet, either."

CHAPTER FIFTEEN:
AD 999
FREYDÍS

Sonnung was not so honored a guest that he sat at my father's side, the way Karlsefni did, and for the most part the men and women ate separately, besides, each at their own tables in the long second hall my father had built to host his guests. All throughout the evening meal, I felt Sonnung's gaze upon me, and when we exchanged food and ale for mead and wine, he watched me still, a different kind of hunger in his eyes.

But I was not the only woman being watched. Karlsefni seemed incapable of looking away from our table, from Gudrid at my side. And when he leaned over to my father, jutting his chin in her direction, his lips forming the question, I feared I already knew the result.

"Filthy Icelander," I spat. "He has no respect at all for the dead. And neither do you, if you accept him so soon."

"Hush," Gudrid said. "Karlsefni and his men are your father's guests."

"Thorstein is not a month in his grave!"

She looked at me then, pitying. "He has been dead nearly half a year, Freydís, though you could not have known it. I know the wound is fresh still for you, but Thorvaldur and I had most of winter to grieve."

I slammed my cup down on the table. "You'd take a new husband so quickly? Forget my brother so easily for the first man who looks your way?"

Gudrid sighed. "You would not be happy no matter how long I waited, but you cannot be sure of Karlsefni's intentions, regardless of mine."

"I see the way he looks at you," I said. "And I know the kind of woman you are. You will not be content to wait. You will take him eagerly, afraid you will not be young enough the next time a likely man comes to Greenland, seeking his fortune."

"Is it so wrong to want children? To pray for a family of my own?" she asked quietly. "I cannot live as your father's ward all my life. I will not. And we are not so different, Freydís, you and I. We both want to make our own way in this world, to find our own fortunes. And we will both do what we must to see ourselves made free."

"But I do not betray the memory of the man I loved," I said. "The man who loved *me*."

Gudrid's eyes narrowed. "Only because you would not know love if it bit you. You are too selfish to know it, too selfish to recognize the gift of it when it's given."

"I knew the love of a sister for her brother," I said, rising. "I knew my brother's love, too, before you led him to his death. Perhaps you'll lead Karlsefni to his as well."

"Freydís!" Thjodhild hissed. "Sit down!"

"I've had enough drink," I said. "And enough of all of you."

"Then go," Gudrid said. "Perhaps the fresh air will cool your blood and calm your temper. But hear this, Freydís: Thorstein would not begrudge me happiness, and if he would not, neither should you."

I spun, making my way from the hall and shoving past the men who lingered in the narrower main house, around the long fire and by the door. Even in summer, the night air was cool, and I turned my face to the moon as I gulped it down. Clean and clear but for the warmth of smoke, a familiar sweetness on the back of my tongue.

"That temper of yours is going to get you into trouble one day," Sonnung said, coming to stand beside me. "Just like your father."

I let out a breath. "Gudrid insults my brother's memory."

"Does she?" he asked. "Or does she only recognize that giving herself up to grief will not grant her anything that she desires?"

"She would marry again! As if he had never lived at all, now that he is in the ground. Given his precious Christian burial. So she can put him from her mind and never think of him again, believing him at peace with Christ."

"She wants a family," Sonnung said. "Children. These are things that do not come so easily without a husband, and the longer she waits to begin, the more difficult they will be to find."

"After she stole my brother from me, persuaded him to give up even his gods, maybe she doesn't deserve to have it," I said.

Sonnung grunted, gazing out toward the fjord and the water beyond. "I have no desire for her, that's certain, but Karlsefni is a Christian, too. There are so many in Iceland now. For a time I believed we would overcome them, drive them out . . ."

I did not like where his words led. "My father and I, Thorhall and the handful of others here. Are we so alone as that?"

"Not yet," he said, grim. "But soon, perhaps. Which is why I had hoped—but I would not have my son raised by a woman who does not want him any more than I would have him raised a Christian."

"Then perhaps you should be looking for a wife instead of talking with me," I snapped, starting off into the night, toward the stables and the goat shed. I hadn't asked for his attentions, and I would not let him lay this weight upon me. I would not be made to feel guilty for wanting to be free. If he wanted a child, strong as he was, he would have no trouble finding a willing woman, instead of nagging at me.

He caught me by the elbow, catching me before I'd gone more than half a dozen paces, and I did not have the will to fight, letting him draw me to a stop. Letting him draw me into his arms, his hands soothing away his offense, my irritation and grief.

"What would you have of me?" he asked, his voice low and tender against my ear. "If not my seed, my son to bring glory upon your name and your father's, what gift instead?"

He smelled like smoke and fire, like lightning and rain on parched ground. I closed my eyes, turning my face into his chest and breathing him in. This strange man. Two days I had known him, and barely, but he was everything Thorvard was not. Tall and broad and strong, warrior enough to stand against any threat. And if I could have traded Thorvard and my ship for a life with this man, sailing and fighting at his side—but I had made my choice, and Sonnung did not want me for a wife, even if I hadn't. He wanted a woman who could give him sons. Who wanted to carry them, to devote herself to the raising of them.

"Sail with me," I said. "When Thorvard returns with my ship and I leave for Vinland, I would have you at my side."

"Nothing more?" he asked. "Not gold or riches, freedom or fortune or glory?"

I shook my head. "What there is to be found, we will discover it together."

"Together, then," Sonnung repeated, no more than a murmur. He smoothed my hair and tucked my head beneath his chin. "As you wish."

Sonnung did not press me after that. He did not prowl as he had or follow at my heels. But we met often enough, all the same. Brattahlid was not so large that you could do otherwise, nor was the settlement itself. And every morning when I went to bathe at the spring, Sonnung joined me.

"You are married, Freydís," Thorvaldur chided me one morning after I had returned from washing. "You have no business meeting this man, bathing with him, *talking* with him this way."

"He isn't my lover, Thorvaldur," I said. "Only my friend. And I've a right to friendship, married or not."

"It looks like more," he said. "And as many lovers as you've taken, you cannot expect anyone to believe it is only friendship you share. We all see how he looks at you. How you look at him."

"Do you think I care?" I asked, spinning on him, for he dogged my steps in an irritating manner, and Sonnung had promised to help me milk the goats. "Do you truly think it matters to me what you believe? What anyone believes? My husband is not here, and if he were, he would not dare to act against a man like Sonnung, no matter how often he found us *talking*."

"You are still my sister," he growled. "And Thorstein would hardly have overlooked it, either."

"You're right," I said, lifting my chin. "He wouldn't have overlooked it. He would have laughed with me at all the fool gossip, too pleased to see me happy to care whether Sonnung was more than just my friend. But if you wish to challenge Sonnung, *Brother*, I will do you the favor of begging him for your life. He'd spare you for my sake, Christian or not."

He stiffened. "You think I need your protection?"

"Have you seen Sonnung's scars?" I asked. "Perhaps you should meet him at the spring tomorrow morning and look long before you go about making threats. But if you're so eager to beat someone, perhaps you should turn your gaze to Karlsefni, the way he and Gudrid go on.

If you and Leif join together, perhaps you'll even succeed in frightening him off."

"Watch your tongue, Freydís," Thorvaldur snarled. "Just because that Jotun you've taken to your bed is too strong to threaten doesn't mean I can't beat *you*."

I wrapped my hand around the knife at my belt and straightened. "Try it, and I will cut your balls from your body and stuff them down your throat. Without Sonnung's help."

"What's this?" Gudrid asked, stepping between us with a basket of freshly dyed yarn on her hip.

He glared at me, and I gave the same back, both of us silent, jaws tight.

"Thorvaldur?" Gudrid prodded.

He unclenched his jaw. "A friendly warning, that's all."

"It doesn't look friendly to me," she said. "Or have you forgotten the vows you made?"

Thorvaldur growled again, glaring at Gudrid now instead. "It was in the spirit of the promise I made Thorstein that I spoke at all."

"Nothing Thorstein might have said would cause Freydís to grip her knife that way, imagining it at your throat," Gudrid said tartly. "Get on with your business elsewhere, and leave your sister's doings to Erik to sort."

His gaze flickered, not quite a flinch, at Thorstein's name upon her lips, but near enough that I knew he hated it as much as I did. But he swallowed whatever else he might have said and turned away, unwilling, it seemed, to threaten his brother's widow the way he had threatened me.

Gudrid watched him go, frowning, then sighed and glanced over at me, a furrow still between her brows. "He isn't wrong, you know. Now that the men think you're happy to take a lover while your husband's back is turned, you'll have trouble from them."

"He's not my lover," I said again. "Just my friend."

"Then you'd better hope that as your *friend*, he's willing to use his sword and his fists to protect you while there are so many men at Brattahlid this winter and so few women to go around."

"They wouldn't dare touch me, not while they're guests of my father."

Gudrid lifted one delicately arched brow. "And why wouldn't they, if they think you're willing? Sonnung is the only man who would know for certain otherwise." She shifted the basket, bracing it more firmly against her hip. "Just watch yourself, Freydís, for your father's sake if not your own."

And then she left, too, meeting Karlsefni at the door with a smile.

It was enough to make me wonder, just for a moment, if she cared for him at all.

CHAPTER SIXTEEN:
AD 2016
Emma

F reydís is a monster," Ashley said when I opened the class up to discussion. "She's an awful, horrible, greedy, murderous woman."

I nodded. "But she's also portrayed as brave, too. Braver than the men, who are running away from the skraelings."

"Of course," Ashley said. "I should have known you were going to defend her. Because she isn't Christian."

"Freydís isn't anything," I said, determined to remain calm. Ashley wasn't going to be able to get a rise out of me, no matter how hard she tried. "The sagas never mention her faith at all. In fact, we don't know whether she ever even lived. But whether she lived or she was invented, it's worth discussing what purpose it might have served the authors to illustrate her the way they did. Both as an unrepentant murderess *and* as a woman of remarkable bravery. And yes, that means, sometimes, examining and unpacking the Christian bias that's baked into the story. Just like we did with Charlemagne." I shifted my gaze to a boy with his hand up. "John?"

"She almost seems like a caricature," he said. "Especially compared to Gudrid. Like she's just there to emphasize how good a wife and woman Gudrid is, and how godless the people who weren't Christian could be."

Godless. I turned my grimace into a smile by force of will. "Interesting choice of phrasing, John. But you're right. It does seem like Freydís acts as a foil, just a literary device to further illustrate Gudrid's character by contrast. To put it in context with pop culture, Freydís seems kind of like the Loki to Gudrid's Thor. She can still be brave, slapping the sword against her bare breast to frighten off the skraelings, because that's not really acceptable behavior for a pious and good Christian woman, either, even if it might have been admirable in the more traditional pre-Christian Norse society."

"Can we talk about Karlsefni?" Laura asked from her favorite second-row seat by the window. Even when she was staring outside instead of looking at me, she still always had something insightful to contribute. "Because he seems to be the focus. Even in *The Saga of Erik the Red*, it's all about this random Christian Icelander who shows up, marries Gudrid, and sails off to Vinland."

"Don't forget the children he fathers as her husband," I said. "Gudrid sets a great example of a pious Christian wife, but Karlsefni, as her husband, is the ancestor of those same bishops, too. If the author of *The Saga of Erik the Red* was in fact a descendant of Gudrid and Karlsefni, that makes him just as important to them and their history—far more important than Erik or his family. Even Leif, who appears to have been leading the charge in the conversion of Greenland. Remember that part of what makes Gudrid such a strong example of an ideal woman is likely the very fact that she marries a good Christian man."

"I don't see why that's such a problem," Ashley said. "Or what's so specifically Christian about getting married and having kids. *Everyone* was expected to do that. For thousands of years before Christianity ever came into it."

"That's true, Ashley," I said. "For this period. During Christianity's infancy, that wasn't always the case—but that's a different discussion for a different class, and outside the scope of today's topic, for sure."

"If Gudrid is a good Christian woman because she acts properly as Karlsefni's wife, then what about Thjodhild, who is refusing to sleep with Erik unless he converts?" Laura asked.

"Great question, Laura," I said. "Obedience to God, for Thjodhild, obviously outranked obedience to her husband, and maybe that was seen as more important than fulfilling her traditional responsibilities as his wife. In both sagas, Erik fades out of the picture pretty quickly, and Leif takes over leadership of Greenland—symbolic of, perhaps, the conversion of Greenland and the way in which the old gods, too, were subsumed and overtaken by the new faith. There's a shift in tension, from Charlemagne's problem of converting society as a whole, to the challenges presented by the rarer individual who wasn't interested in taking part in the new community that had been forged. Which is where Thorhall and Freydís come in. One thing these two sagas ignore is the adoption of Christianity alongside the existing pagan gods. Either a character is fully Christian and good, or they just aren't."

"Did it ever occur to you that maybe the people who clung to their old gods, with all the blood sacrifice and murder, might have just been rotten?" Ashley demanded. "There's no reason why someone who was good would hesitate to accept Jesus, but if you thrive on blood and death, then of course you'd want to follow gods who promote it. Just like those creeps in prisons who believe in Odin, and he tells them to murder their cellmates."

"Except that for the Norse, Jesus was a warrior, too, and he won converts by proving his strength over the old gods—allowing men to win battles against pagan foes was a point in his favor," I said, calm and steady still, even though my jaw had gone tight. "But I think it was natural for Christian writers to view themselves and their ancestors as good and justified in their actions, and easy for them to place the blame for the bad things that happened on the people who weren't part of their community. Something we still do today, in fact, even as enlightened as we like to believe we've become."

"Which translates to Christianity is guilty of horrible crimes against the poor innocent pagans, yet again," Ashley said, grabbing her coat and her bag. She'd never even taken her notebook out, I realized—too late. "I don't even know why I bother coming to this class, but I'm dropping it. This is a *history* class, and all you do is talk about how awful Christianity is. You shouldn't be allowed to teach at all."

She stormed out before I could respond. Not that there was anything I could have said, or even wanted to say. She wouldn't have heard me anyway.

So I just took a breath, tried to ignore the way my heart raced, and called on the last student I'd seen with a hand raised. But I had a sinking feeling I wasn't done with Ashley yet.

·◦§§◦·

"It seems like Alex spent quite a bit of time with you yesterday," my mother said when I finally forced myself through her door for dinner. My father was back in Washington this week to vote on a bill to support veterans, an issue he'd been fighting for since he took office, and she was incredibly good at guilt-tripping me into keeping her company so she wasn't "left all alone in such a big house" to eat by herself.

The price of enjoying my mother's home-cooked meals? Just making it through the onslaught of a few prying questions about my personal life. Which was maybe another reason why I'd stuck it out with David as long as I had. We'd had a lot of dinner dates.

"We were just talking."

My mother's eyes narrowed, even as she pressed the salad bowl into my hands to bring out to the table. "*Just* talking or just *talking*?"

"Conversation between two people, addressing a variety of topics," I said, carrying the salad out. Usually I was early enough to set the table, but just the thought of having to endure an interrogation after Ashley's dramatic exit from my class today—I was exhausted, and honestly kind of worried. I was new, and just an adjunct. They didn't have to keep me on to teach next semester if I caused problems for them during this one. Never mind give me a second class like I'd been hoping so I could make a little bit more money.

"He's a good man, Emma," my mother said, setting the pot she carried onto the table next to the salad. "And you know how much your father likes him. If you're not willing to be serious about this, you need to make that clear to him up front."

I rolled my eyes, dropping to a seat. "We've gone to dinner and spent an afternoon talking about our past relationships. You can't expect me to start declaring my undying love quite yet, no matter how many years he's worked with Dad."

"You've known him for years, sweetheart. It's not the same as dating some boy off the Internet."

"Since I've never dated a boy off the Internet, I wouldn't know," I said, serving myself. Lamb stew was one of my mother's best dishes, and I was definitely going to be taking a doggie bag home to stash in my freezer. "And even if I have known him through Dad, it isn't the same. He might as well be a stranger when it comes to the things that matter in a relationship."

My mother sighed. "At least you'll have his maturity and experience to guide you."

"Mamma, please."

"I'm serious, Emma," she said, starting with salad instead of the stew. "You need someone steady, with strong ties to the community you're so eager to neglect now that you're on your own. Someone to keep you grounded and remind you to eat. I saw the way you kept your apartment while you were at school—you lived on those awful micro-waveable dinners and those dehydrated packages of noodles. Look at Holly. She's taking a cooking class in the evenings now and making all her own meals. Even donating her time to the local soup kitchen—"

"I was busy," I said before she could list any more of Holly's virtues. "And poor."

"You know if you'd asked, we'd have sent you something to live on," she said. "You didn't have to be *that* poor. And you're not that busy now, with just your one class."

"I was fine," I said. "I made do, and I will again, once I know for sure what I want to do and where I want to do it."

"You could be more involved, Emma. Come volunteer with us, with the other young women of the parish, even if you don't want to go to mass. There are plenty of young people your age who just do service work, you know, and no one gives them a hard time about going to church."

"After the campaign is over, sure, I'll look into finding some kind of community service something to do. But I'm sorry, I'm not going to tag along on someone else's community event where I don't belong. That's ridiculous."

"So you're just going to leave, then, after starting up with Alexander?" she asked, redirecting us back to my apparently *very* serious relationship. I hadn't realized I'd already made a lifelong commitment by agreeing to one dinner and some croissants. "Abandon him to go off to school who knows how far away?"

"Most of the schools are still in New England. I wouldn't be that far away. And it isn't like you and Dad haven't been the ultimate example of how to make a relationship work even when you're spending half the year apart."

"But it hasn't been easy, Emma. And you can't expect Alex to be willing to make those sacrifices so soon in a relationship. You have to take his feelings into consideration."

I seriously *considered* beating my head against the table, or face-planting into my stew, maybe. Anything to make it stop. "It's been one and a half dates. We might not even be seeing each other next week, never mind next year."

"I don't see why not," my mother said, spearing her salad with a vengeance. "He's practically perfect for you. Smart enough to appreciate your pursuits in academia. Certainly he'd be able to provide for you—he's had other offers, you know. Plenty of people would love to have him on their staff, no matter how dismissive you've been in the past about his performance."

"Dad doesn't ever do anything that would get him in enough trouble to *need* a spin doctor," I mumbled.

"I doubt that Alex would appreciate that kind of comment on his career, Emma. And you know perfectly well that cleaning up publicity messes isn't the main focus of his job."

"Because Dad never *has* publicity messes that *need* cleaning up," I said.

"Because Alexander Stone works closely with your father to be sure he doesn't," my mother snapped. "Honestly! If you think so poorly of him, why did you agree to go to dinner with him at all?"

"I don't—" I stopped myself, taking a deep breath before I dug myself any deeper into this totally manufactured argument. "Listen. Alex and I need to figure this out for ourselves. And we will. When and *if* we've decided whether we even want to be more than just two people who happened to go on a couple of dates, I promise you, I will take his feelings into consideration and incorporate our relationship into my currently nonexistent life plan. All right?"

She sniffed. "I suppose that's the best I can hope for."

I shoved a spoonful of the stew into my mouth to keep myself from responding. *Don't worry,* Alex had said. *Your parents like me,* he'd promised. *It's not going to be a problem,* he'd told me.

I kind of wish I'd recorded dinner so he could have *fully* understood just how wrong he was.

CHAPTER SEVENTEEN:
AD 999
FREYDÍS

They'll be married before the solstice, I'd wager," Sonnung said, clucking at one of the nannies to draw her nearer.

The goats seemed willing to do anything he asked once they knew what it was he wanted. I'd never seen anything like it. And the way he crouched before the goat, taking her head in his large hands and scratching gently behind the ears, around the horns with all the tenderness of a woman for the baby at her breast—

"You're staring, not milking," he said, his lips twitching with amusement.

I grinned to hide the flush creeping up my neck. "It's only that I've never seen a man stroke a goat like he would his lover."

Sonnung's eyes darkened, his gaze trailing from my face to my breasts, to my waist and hips, and down my legs. One long caress, warming me from the inside out. "I'd be happy to put my hands to better use."

"I've no doubt of that," I mumbled, crouching beside the nanny and positioning the pail. I tried to ignore the heat of his body, the nearness of him as he held the goat for me, watching.

Sonnung stared as much as I did, his gaze following me everywhere I went, even while he kept his distance. A reminder that he waited only for me to welcome him, that he spent his days and nights hoping I might change my mind.

I focused instead on the must of goat and hay, the sweetness of fresh milk as it sprayed into the pail. Because it wasn't that I didn't want him. Or even that I hesitated to betray my husband, for he had surely betrayed me already in every way that mattered. I would have gladly taken Sonnung to my bed if I had not known what he wanted of me, and let him pay a fine to my father and Thorvard for the privilege. Certainly I did not fear that my husband would demand my life in punishment—if he did, Sonnung would surely kill him first. But the risk of a child . . .

Perhaps I had been lucky with my pastes and herbs and rune magic, or perhaps it was simply that Thorvard's seed was too weak to take root in my womb. If it was the former, I couldn't count upon my luck lasting, and if the latter, I did not believe for a moment that Sonnung's seed lacked the strength required. Nothing about Sonnung was weak or womanly.

"There are pleasures we might share that risk nothing," he said, as if he knew my mind.

I rested my cheek against the nanny's rough coat, turning my face away. "It will only sharpen your appetite for more."

"And yours?"

I swallowed. "I'm not so certain I would trust even Shining Balder to practice such restraint as you suggest might serve us."

He grunted. "And if our passions led us further, what difference would it truly make? You'd never let a swelling stomach stop you from sailing, and I would be by your side upon the sea."

"Is that what you want for your child? To be raised by a mother who saw him only as a burden, an inconvenience to be ignored while I go about my own business?"

"Everything is either fire or ice through your eyes," he grumbled. "Do you not recognize the spring or the fall, but only bear witness to the dark days of winter and the unsetting sun of summer? Do you truly believe it is so impossible that you might find our child to be a blessing rather than a curse, once you hold him in your arms?"

"I don't want to find out, one way or the other," I snapped, lifting my head to glare at him.

His jaw had gone tight, his eyes hard and flashing. "You would deny even Thor, out of nothing more than sheer stubbornness."

"Thor can take what he's owed, and however he desires it," I said, pulling the pail from beneath the nanny's udders and straightening. "But I'd hardly welcome even his child in my womb with tears of joy and wonder."

He let go of the goat, a cluck of his tongue sending her on her way. But he didn't stand, only looked up at me, his lips pressed thin. "Stubborn and ungrateful, both, that's what you are."

"Perhaps that's so," I said. "But what does that make you, then, so intent upon me when I've told you from the start I had no interest in what you offered?"

"Lies that fall easily off your tongue." He rose then, stepping forward, crowding me against the empty stall at my back, all heat and muscle and lust. "But your eyes say something different, Dísa. With every stolen glance, every look exchanged between us. Even now, you tremble with it."

My head spun with the nearness of him, the warmth of his body, the bulk of his chest, his shoulders, and the unbanked desire in his gaze that threatened to break my resolve.

"Tell me again that you have no interest at all in what I offer," he said, his lips brushing against my ear and the words themselves whispering against my skin, making me shiver.

"It's what comes after that I object to," I forced myself to say, though the words were too breathy, too weak to be at all convincing. I cleared my throat and pressed my free hand to his chest, pushing him back. "The part where you leave me with a babe at my breast and continue on your merry way."

He resisted for a moment, his eyes narrowing. We both knew if it came to a true test of strength I would certainly lose, but if he had wanted me by force, he'd have taken me long before now, not bided his time with sweet words and seduction. And truth be told, I wasn't so sure I'd have fought him if he'd tried. Not hard enough to give him pause, to even make him hesitate. If I hadn't been married, if I'd thought for a moment I might have convinced him to stay beyond his promise of sailing at my side, I'd have let him have me that first day at the spring.

"I'd not abandon my son," he said. "Not wholly."

"No, not your son," I agreed. "But a daughter? And me?"

He stepped back then, his gaze steady and shameless even as he freed me. "If I swore it otherwise, would you believe me?"

"I do not see how you could keep such a vow. Not with Thorvard returning in the spring."

Sonnung snorted. "Thorvard is nothing."

"He is my husband, and the only support my father has left."

"Your father will have Karlsefni's support and friendship once he's married Gudrid. She is loyal enough to ensure that much."

"Gudrid!" My lip curled. "Is that what you'd call her, truly? Loyal! When she'd trade my father's protection, my brother's memory for the first fool with a ship who arrives? When she's betrayed the gods of her ancestors, too!"

"Karlsefni is no fool, Freydís," Sonnung said. "No matter what god he worships. He is shrewd and he is strong, or he would not have his ship and the respect and loyalty of the men who sail with him upon it. And if you think for a moment Gudrid does not consider your father in the choices she makes, you are blinded still by your brother's loss. Karlsefni is not a man Thjodhild will argue with, nor is Leif likely to challenge him."

"And how do you know so much of Gudrid's thoughts and reasoning?" I demanded. "Or does she flirt with you, too, while my back is turned, luring you into her arms and her bed, promising her love if you'll only accept her Christ as well? Will you betray me next, Sonnung? Betray our gods, like the others?"

He growled. "So quick to anger and rage, to foul insults, and you wonder why your father has so few friends, and fewer allies? Why the men look to Leif and would follow him, if it came to it, even with Thjodhild's shrill voice in his ears? You've learned nothing from your father's failings."

"You dare?" I dropped the pail of milk, not caring how it splashed. "You know nothing of my father or me!"

"I know more than you think, Freydís. Much more. You're loyal to the gods, as your father has always been, but that temper you share cuts sharper than any blade, striking down friend and enemy alike. You'd curse the gods, too, and your ancestors, if they spoke to you, whispering words you didn't want to hear, and it's only their silence that's kept you true."

My hands closed into fists at my sides, nails digging deep into my palms. "You have no right to speak to me this way."

His jaw locked, his eyes too bright, too hot. "Do I not?"

My heart raced, fast and wild, and he stared down at me with what felt suddenly like a giant's height, though he had stood before me just as tall a hundred times before, and I'd known no fear. But before he had never seemed to me more than just a man, well made and powerful but a man all the same.

I turned away, cursing my own foolishness as I caught up the pail on my way, still more full than empty in spite of the puddle of milk that had sprayed upon the hard-packed ground. He was nothing but a stray, a swordsman looking for fame, searching for his fate. A man who thought if he found the right words, I'd tumble happily into his bed. But just a man. The days of men descended from gods and Jotuns were far behind us, or the Christians would never have found such fertile ground to plant their seeds of doubt.

"Go to Gudrid then," I called over my shoulder. "Or one of Thjodhild's slaves, and take your pleasure from someone soft instead, if my temper offends you. It makes no difference to me."

But I was not so foolish as to think he did not know that was a lie, too.

I told myself it wasn't shame that kept me away from him after that, ducking behind haystacks and around corners when I saw him coming, and spending my days in the farthest fields or riding my father's sturdy horse along the shore. The long days of summer had turned into the creeping darkness of fall and the coming winter, bringing heavy mist that clung to the coast—another means by which to hide, if I rode into its heart, and at least I wouldn't be lost if I kept to the edge of the waters along the short strip of beach, before the fjord rose up, all stone and steep cliff face.

I told myself it wasn't shame, but it did not stop the flush that climbed up my neck when I thought of the things he'd said, followed just as swiftly by a hot anger reddening my cheeks. Because he hadn't been wrong. About my father or me. About the fact that I wouldn't believe him, no matter what vows he swore. Not when my brother Leif boasted of abandoning his child, a son, and the woman who had birthed him. Not when my own father had abandoned me—left me and my mother both to return to his wife and sons. If she hadn't died and my father had never been exiled from the whole of Iceland that second time, I'd be abandoned still.

"You cannot think to keep on this way once the dark days come," Thorhall said when I returned one evening long after the first stars had shown themselves, riding in at the edge of full night. "Your father won't thank you for losing yourself or one of his beasts, either."

"And I'm to sit inside watching Karlsefni and Gudrid flirt and fawn instead?"

Thorhall shrugged, leading the little horse to his stall and beginning to brush him down. "It's only right that Gudrid should marry again, young as she is. Thorstein wouldn't have wanted her to mourn him too long, besides. Or you, for that matter."

"And who are you to speak for my brother?" I snapped. Thorhall gave me a long hard look over the horse's back, and my face went hot. Thorhall of all people—he'd known Thorstein as well as he knew my father and me. He knew us all. I looked away.

"There's bread and stew still for you," he said. "Kept warm in the firepot, by Gudrid's order and against Thjodhild's wishes. Your father's wife thought you should go hungry, and serves you right for keeping away so long."

By his tone, Thorhall didn't wholly disagree with Thjodhild's sentiments. I ducked my head, accepting the rebuke, for I was honest enough to recognize it was far milder than I deserved after the things I'd said.

"Go on, then," he said. "Be sure you give that girl your thanks, too."

And perhaps I would have, if I hadn't entered the feast hall to find her fair head bent beside Sonnung's as they sat together on one of the long benches that lined the walls. My stomach soured at the sight, anger flaring hot again. Sonnung of all the men, as if taking my brother from me was not insult enough.

"Freydís!" She leapt up, flushing. A moment longer, and I'd have found them doing more than sitting so close, I was sure. "I saved you some—"

I didn't wait for her to finish, leaving the way I'd come, and twice as fast, shoving the men from my path. Ignoring even my father's voice, joining with my sister's call. "Dísa!"

"Freydís, wait."

A hard hand latched onto my arm, jerking me back when I tried to tear myself free. Thorvaldur, and Karlsefni at his side. "Running away to hide?" my brother asked. "Have you not had your fill of this cowardice yet?"

I spit at him, and he threw me back the way I'd come, sending me stumbling into the feasting hall, he and Karlsefni close upon my heels.

"Sit down, Freydís," Sonnung said, steadying me before I fell. His hands upon me were as good as chains, pushing me firmly down onto the bench where he'd been sitting. "Join us while you eat, and hear what Karlsefni has to say before you persuade him to change his mind."

"Karlsefni cannot have anything to say that I wish to hear," I said.

"Not even if it is the offer of a ship?" Karlsefni said, his lips twitching with amusement. Gudrid slipped beneath his arm, and I knew it was her words, her wheedling that had accomplished this, just as her eyes beseeched me now to accept the gift. "Yours alone, if you and Sonnung will sail with me and my new bride to Vinland in the spring."

A bowl of stew was pressed into my hands, and I tore my gaze from Gudrid to Sonnung beside me. Sonnung, whom I had not spoken to for days, for weeks, whom I had gone to such lengths to avoid. Sonnung, who I was not so certain would still wish to sail at my side, no matter what promises he'd made.

"Eat first," he said. "The rest will wait."

CHAPTER EIGHTEEN:
AD 2016
Emma

Tuesday I had office hours, and I spent the entire two hours agonizing over whether I should be making an appointment to talk to my department head or whether I was blowing the whole Ashley situation out of proportion. None of my other students seemed to have any issues with my approach, and I was 99 percent sure that I was in the right on everything I'd said in class—factually.

It wasn't like examining source bias was anything new. In fact, it was absolutely critical for anyone interested in continuing on in history, beyond the survey courses and into academia. Anyone doing research or seriously studying history understood that. My department head would understand it, and I couldn't imagine the administration finding fault in it, either.

I was packing up my notes, getting ready to head home, when someone knocked. My stomach clenched, anxiety wrapping cold fingers around my throat. I swallowed hard, wiped my sweating palms on my pant legs, opened the door . . . and felt my whole body relax at the sight of Alex holding two cups of coffee in his hands.

"Thank God it's just you." I pressed my hand against my chest, my fingers closing around my pendant beneath my shirt, until I realized what I was doing and dropped it again, hoping he didn't notice.

"Not quite the intonation I might have hoped for, but I appreciate the sentiment." His smile melted into a frown, concerned lines forming between his eyebrows. "Everything okay?"

I shook my head, blinking back *stupid* tears. And what was I even crying about? It was totally ridiculous, but I could hardly breathe, my throat was so tight. Relief and fear and everything all spinning together to choke me.

"Hey." Alex glanced behind him, then stepped inside my office, shoving the coffee cups onto the nearest filing cabinet and kicking the door shut at the same time. And then he caught me, his hands gentle on my shoulders, drawing me in, wrapping me up in his arms. "Emma, what's wrong? What happened?"

"Nothing," I managed, my voice broken and garbled against his sweater. "Not yet. It's so stupid. I'm so stupid."

"Shh," he said, tucking my head beneath his chin. "You're not. Whatever's upset you, it's definitely not because you're stupid. That's just crazy talk."

"I don't even know why—" I sobbed, then dragged in a breath, fighting to keep myself from dissolving as I clutched at him. "I'm crying, and it's only been two dates!"

"It's okay," he promised, smoothing back my hair and pulling away to look at me, to let me see his face, his sincerity. "I'm not afraid of a few tears. Whatever you need, I'm here. Whatever happened, we can at least make it sound a lot better than it is. I don't want to brag, but some people think I'm kind of good at that."

It was enough to make me laugh, the absurdity of it all. Of his dorky joke. Damn. Damn, damn, damn, but he was just so *good*. So kind. "I'm just being ridiculous. Really."

"I'm in politics, remember? Ridiculous is what we do."

"You really want to spin doctor for me?"

He smiled, brushing the tears from my cheeks. "Spin doctor, play doctor—whatever you want."

I laughed again, then sniffed. "It's so stupid. I shouldn't even be upset."

"But you are. So let me do that thing where I make myself feel like I'm somehow useful by trying to fix it when that isn't actually what you need from me. It's part of the dating ritual. Like the sex we didn't have on the first date that I'm still kicking myself about."

"And the kissing we're not doing?"

He pressed his forehead to mine. "That too."

I closed my eyes, collecting myself, my thoughts. "It's just—remember last week, that student I was having trouble with?"

"When I found you in your car looking like you'd had a sleepless night."

"It was that bad?"

"You made a good show of playing it cool, if that makes you feel any better."

It didn't, really, but it didn't matter, either. "She stormed out of my class yesterday, furious. Offended. Like, really, really offended."

He drew back again, his gaze sharpening. "By history?"

"By the way I'm teaching it."

"I don't think I quite understand."

I swallowed, looking away. Looking anywhere but at him. I didn't really want to talk about this. It was all too close to the mark, too . . . personal. "One of those coffees was for me, right?"

"Emma." He ducked his head, catching my eyes. "I *want* to understand. Please."

I sighed. "She felt that I was attacking her faith."

"But you're studying the Viking Age, right? Is she some kind of New Agey Wiccan or something?"

"No."

Those concerned lines were back again, and he was studying me. Too closely. But his expression had changed somehow. Focusing in a way that reminded me of that first dinner after David and I had split up. When he'd been grilling me about my future plans. Collecting data for my father's campaign, looking for something he could spin in his favor. "Christian?"

I gave him a tight nod.

"Is this the end of it?"

"I don't know," I said. "My gut says no. That this is the start, not the finish. But I can't—I don't know."

He let out a breath. "Emma, that's . . . something I wish you'd have told us."

Us. Not *him*.

I slipped out of his hold, hugging myself instead. "I didn't think it was going to turn into anything. She was upset on Friday, but it wasn't—there's always one. It's not unusual to have a student who feels challenged when we dig deeper into history, examining source bias. They usually come to terms with it, or the class moves on to the next topic and it gets forgotten."

"Your face on Friday wouldn't have agreed."

I shook my head. "That wasn't what I was so upset about. I mean, it was. But it was personal. A personal thing that was related." I spun away. Nothing was coming out right, and I hated the way he was looking at me. "It didn't have anything to do with the campaign. It was about me."

"Okay," he said, cautious now. "So maybe it wasn't anything then. Or you didn't think it was. But if you're this upset about it *again*— what's changed?"

"I just don't know what to do," I said, frustrated. And there were new tears now, hot behind my eyes. Because I knew what he was thinking. I knew he was looking at me like I was a problem for my father's campaign, a potential mess that might need cleaning up. But what right did I have to expect anything else? After two dates. And he'd said it himself. I knew where his loyalties were. "I didn't do anything wrong. But she's dropping my class. And I don't know. I don't know if she's going to go quietly, or if she files a complaint, if I might . . . get in trouble somehow. Lose my position. Or just not get rehired for next semester."

And boy, would my mother have a field day then, telling me how much time I had on my hands and exactly how she thought I should be filling it: with church-sponsored activities, like my sainted sister. She'd never understand that I couldn't—that doing any of that was feeding into the assumptions people made. Assumptions that were making me more and more uncomfortable by the day. Especially when this Ashley thing was proof positive of the ingrained prejudices I would face.

Alex was silent still, and I turned around, meeting his eyes. He wasn't worried about me anymore. Not the way he had been. I could see it. Like he was calculating percentage points in his head. Phrasing and rephrasing the headline of a press release.

"It could blow up fast," he said softly. "If she decides to make this into something. If the administration comes down on you and the press hears about it."

"You're doing a really shitty job of making me feel better, Alex."

He flushed. "I wasn't exactly expecting this to be a campaign issue."

"Is this how it's going to be?" I asked. "Anything that goes wrong in my life, you immediately start thinking about how you're going to spin it for my father?"

"It's my job, Emma. You know that."

"But *I'm* not," I said. "This . . . whatever this is we're doing. It can't turn into a data mine for you to do your job *better*. How am I supposed to trust you with anything if that's the first place your mind goes?"

He stared at me, his lips pressed thin. Bloodless white lines, disappearing into his face. He didn't even argue. Didn't try to defend himself.

"Maybe you should leave."

"If I do," he said, his words tight, "if I go now, this isn't over."

"That's not something you get to decide."

He reached for me, but I stepped back. "Don't do this, Emma. Don't throw this away before we've even started."

"If you can tell me honestly that you'll be able to compartmentalize, that you won't look at my personal problems as campaign issues you need to spin, as problems for my father first before they're mine, then by all means, do, and we can plan date three right now."

"I just need time," he said.

It was the wrong answer. Even if it was true. Even if I knew it wasn't something he could change in himself overnight. But I just—I couldn't do this. I didn't want everything I shared with him to be . . . *used*. And I was so, so glad I hadn't told him more than this. That I'd held myself back, instead of being up front about my faith. It wouldn't matter now. None of it mattered now.

"Please," I said. "Just go."

Gray-faced and drawn, he did.

He left, and then I was alone again.

But of course when I got home, his car was parked outside the main house. My mother must have invited him for dinner. I dropped my forehead to the steering wheel, gripping my pendant, my Mjölnir. Thor's hammer.

"Lend me strength. Strength and courage and maybe a touch of bluster. I could use all three."

And then I went inside, kicked off my boots, and followed the sounds of spoons scraping pots and pans to the kitchen, where my mother was cooking and Alex was leaning against the counter, his arms crossed, making pleasant small talk.

"Oh, Emma—would you set the table, sweetheart? Alex can help you."

Alex never helped me. My mother never let him lift even the smallest dish. "Alex is a guest, Mom."

"Don't be silly," she said. "He's practically family now."

I ground my teeth, giving him a hard look, but he only gave me a quick headshake in response. Whether it was to ask me not to say anything or to confirm that he obviously hadn't reported our fight to the authority that was my mother, I didn't know. I wasn't sure I cared. He had no business being here at all, as far as I was concerned. But he was. And in the interest of making it through dinner without provoking murderous thoughts, I jerked my chin toward the dining room. "I'll show you where the plates are."

"I'm sorry," he said the minute we were alone in the dining room, our conversation muffled by the open china-cabinet door. Partially, anyway, and I knew my mother had ears like a bat. "I meant to tell you—warn you—when I stopped by with the coffee. And after all of that, I didn't think you'd appreciate it if I said anything to your mother."

"You're not wrong," I grumbled. "But you have no business being here, either."

"If I had canceled, she would have known something was wrong," he said. "And then you would have been on the hook for an explanation, facing the fallout alone."

"That's my problem, not yours."

"You can't really think I was going to hang you out to dry like that?"

No. Of course he wasn't. He was too damn honorable for that. Too good. And it wouldn't help the campaign if my mother and I were at odds. People picked up on that at events and parties. Maybe I was giving him too much credit, maybe that was the only reason he'd come.

"You being here isn't going to make things better for me," I said. "She's just going to use it as more fuel for the fire when she blasts me for messing things up between us." With my luck it would be followed by another chorus of how Holly never would have let someone like Alex get away.

He glanced back toward the kitchen and my mother before taking the plates from my hands. "Maybe. Maybe we just don't tell her anything at all. Pretend like all is right with the world and everything's good between us."

My eyes narrowed. "It isn't going to make it okay. And it isn't like she won't notice when you aren't around."

"It's the last month and a half of your father's campaign. Clutch time. I can make plenty of excuses for why we aren't spending as much time together. She won't be able to argue with any of them. And maybe after all this is over, there won't be anything else standing between us. Just you and me. We could give things another chance."

"And what happens when the next election rolls around, Alex? We take a hiatus, and you magically forget everything I've told you, everything you know that could help or hurt my father?"

"My loyalty will be to you first," he promised. "Supporting you will be second nature for me by then. I'll have had time to . . . to reprogram myself."

"I don't know," I said, closing the cabinet.

"Will you think about it?" he asked. "Just think about it."

"And what are you two whispering about so urgently?" my mother called. "Five minutes before the food is ready, and I don't see any silverware!"

"Please, Emma," he murmured, his hand catching my wrist when I reached for the silverware drawer.

I sighed, dragging the drawer open slowly, staring at his hand—at mine. "I'll consider it."

None of *that* made dinner any less awkward.

CHAPTER NINETEEN:
AD 999
FREYDÍS

If Karlsefni and Gudrid are determined to leave so soon, and to settle, it could be years before we return." Years without Thorvard, unless he chose to follow, I supposed—but with no one to guide him, no crewman who knew the way, he was as likely to be bewildered by the sea as to arrive. And all to the good.

"Let them stay as long as they like," Sonnung said, watching me as I paced before the goats and horses in their stalls. "You could sail back anytime you wished with a ship of your own."

"Thorstein's ship," I said, sinking to a seat upon a low stool. "Gudrid is offering me my brother's ship, though what possesses her, I cannot understand."

"Can it not simply be kindness?" Sonnung asked, leaning against one of the thick wooden posts that supported the crossbeams of the roof.

I shook my head, not in denial so much as confusion. "She might have offered it to me months ago."

"Months ago she was not promised in marriage to Karlsefni," Sonnung replied. "Months ago, that ship, her father's farm, and the share of your brother's in the North were all the wealth she had to see her into old age. Now she will have a husband, a man who has made himself rich enough in trade to support her without Thorstein's ship. And she's been worried for you, Freydís."

I waved the last away. "It is only the promises she made to my brother that concern her. Nothing more."

He snorted, crossing his arms. "Always when it comes to Gudrid, you are blinded."

"If she cared for me truly, for my father, she would not have taken Thorstein from his ancestors and his gods," I said, rising. "You cannot tell me you would forgive her so easily for such an act, were it your family she had helped to divide."

Sonnung looked away, his jaw working, as if he found my words too difficult to swallow without softening them somehow first. "Whether Gudrid has betrayed the gods or not, what matters now is that she offers you her support and friendship, in spite of her faith, in spite of yours. And without condition. Neither Gudrid nor Karlsefni expect you to act as anything but what you are. Giving us a ship to sail and crew as we wish means they need not fear we will do anything upon theirs to offend their Christ and see them sunk by his power in punishment, yes, but it means, too, that we will be free to honor *our* gods as we see fit."

The tight knot around my heart eased. "You'll sail with me, then."

"As I promised you," he agreed, meeting my eyes. He drew himself up, letting his arms fall to his sides, and his hands formed into fists, as if he were gathering his nerve. "If you still wish me by your side."

I dropped his gaze. "The things I said . . ."

He crossed to me, taking my face in his hands, catching my eyes again and holding them, holding me. "You are your father's daughter,

Freydís. That is all. And it is cruel of me to act as if I did not know that from the start. But it seems we both speak foolishly in anger, our tempers flaring hot."

"If Thorvard does not dare to follow, we could have years," I said, covering his hands with mine. "Would you stay so long?"

He dropped his head, our foreheads touching. "You would torture us both for so long as that?"

I closed my eyes, pressing my lips thin. If we had years—if Thorvard might never know, and Sonnung was true to his word, even if my husband followed . . .

"Daughter or son, promise me you'll care for our child, if one comes."

"I would shower them with every blessing, every gift, and see them grow strong and rich," he said. "Daughter or son, I will never turn from them, so long as they honor the gods of their ancestors."

I licked my lips, anticipation and fear mixing in my belly. "And if I am barren?"

Sonnung released a ragged breath, one hand falling from my face to my waist, drawing me tight against him, hard and hot. "There is not a field on this earth I cannot plant, I promise you that."

"Even so."

"Even so, I will share with you every pleasure I know and remain by your side until we are both sated and satisfied. Until we sail back again from this land of wine and grapes and lumber, our fortunes found."

I tipped back my head, my mouth a breath apart from his. "Then I will torture you no longer."

-cϕϕϿ-

His kiss was bruising, his hands burning my skin when they found their way under my tunic first, and then beneath my belt. I pulled his tunic over my head, forcing him to let me go, and he unlaced his trousers, freeing himself before helping me, tugging at lacing and jerking my tunic loose when it tangled in my hair.

He lifted me up after he'd stripped me down, wrapping my thighs around his waist, and then I was pinned against the cold turf wall of the barn, roots and stray grasses scratching against my spine. It had been so long, and his hands had felt so warm, his thick, calloused fingers testing and teasing, stoking me until I burned as hot as he did. But still, in that moment, I stiffened, feeling the length of his hardness pressed between us, anticipating the pain I'd grown too used to in my marriage bed.

Sonnung growled, taking my hand from his bare chest and wrapping it around the root of his need. "Guide me."

Slow and easy, and I was so slick, so ready, there was no pain at all. I buried my face in the curve of his neck, moaning against his skin as he withdrew, only to spear me deeper, filling me *pleasantly* in ways Thorvard never could.

Sonnung's arm tightened around me, his lips finding the nape of my neck, the curve of my shoulder, while his other hand cupped my breast, smoothed over my ribs, stroked my hip, his touch like the tickle of flame, the shock of lightning, making my body hum and my skin prickle.

"More," I breathed.

He groaned, and I could feel him stiffen, growing harder inside me as he drove in again, faster. I shuddered, arching my back, letting him deeper still. Every stroke brought me closer to soaring, my body flushed and my heart racing. My legs locked around his hips, and his fingers dug into my flesh.

And I was there, shivering and shuddering and crying out as I fell into a sea of pleasure and light. A hoarse shout, and he followed, fast and hard, his body going tense, his grasp all the tighter as he spilled inside me, both of us panting and damp.

He held me there a moment longer, his hand a fist in my hair, the scruff of his beard rough against my cheek. He waited for my trembling to stop, my breathing to steady. Held himself inside me, hard enough still that I whimpered at the loss when he finally withdrew.

He chuckled softly against my ear, rough hands hot as flame upon my skin. "You ache for me even now, when I've given you only the smallest taste of what I offer. Just wait, Freydís. Just wait."

It would not be the last time he had me in the barn, even as the days grew colder and the wind more fierce, until I was shivering from more than pleasure beneath him as we lay upon the hay. He was always warm, always burning to the touch, and I knew before the week was out that he had not lied—it had been the smallest taste, the barest measure of what he could give.

But when my bleeding came again as it ought, I welcomed it with more relief than dismay. If even Sonnung's seed could not catch in my womb, Thorvard's surely never would, and I would never have the weight of a child dragging like an anchor, keeping me upon the shore. Whatever disappointment Sonnung might have felt, I chased it from his mind soon after, giving up our game of stealth and welcoming him openly into my bed.

"When Thorvard learns how you've carried on . . . ," Gudrid began the next day, her forehead creased with worried lines and her fingers plucking anxiously at the loom and the heavy, yarn-furred fabric she wove. No doubt a gift for Karlsefni, to keep him warm and dry upon the ship when they sailed.

"I will be gone," I said, dropping the basket of yarn that she'd asked me to bring from the storeroom. "On my way to Vinland with Sonnung and Karlsefni, and if he hears how well Sonnung satisfied me, as he couldn't, all the better."

"And if Sonnung gives you a child?" she asked.

I snorted. "He won't."

"You cannot know that, Freydís. You cannot be certain. And I have seen the way he looks at you, the way he touches you now. He wants you ripened."

"It does not matter what he wants if the gods have already had their say. I am barren, Gudrid, or I'd have had more than one child by now, and even you cannot deny it."

Her eyes softened, pity replacing her fear. "You are young still. And this business with Sonnung has only just begun. There is time yet for a child to come."

I shook my head, stepping back from the looms and jumping down from the platform where she sat—the same raised platform where my father hosted his guests in the evenings while we ate. When the winter days turned into long, oppressive nights, this hall would be full. But while there was light, any at all, the men took advantage of it. We all did, no matter how cold it might have been outside.

"I am not like you, Gudrid, longing for a child, for a family of my own. I've only ever longed for the sea, to find my fortune by it as Leif has, and my father before that. The rest is only ropes and chains, dragging me back."

"Even Sonnung?" she asked. "Even your husband, who stood by your side, by your father's?"

My lip curled. "Thorvard betrayed me and my father both in accepting Christ. Let him feel the sting of the same, suffer my humiliation. It's no more than he deserves, and far less than what I would see done to him if I had my way. If Sonnung and I stayed."

"And what will you do when Sonnung is gone?" she asked, her voice far too gentle, far too kind. "Thorvard might well divorce you, Freydís, or worse, and it does not seem to me that Sonnung has any interest in a wife."

But she did not understand—could not understand. "Fitting, then, since I have no real desire for a husband. If Thorvard had not been my only means for a ship, my path to freedom and fortune, I wouldn't have accepted even him. And now what purpose does he serve? What good does he do me at all, when he listens to the nonsense Thjodhild spouts about her god? If he will forget so easily what he owes his ancestors, he will forget what he owes his wife before long as well."

"Do you truly think so poorly of us, Freydís?" Gudrid asked.

I met her eyes, held her gaze with mine. "I trusted Thorstein when he said he could honor both our gods and yours. If in the end he could betray me, betray all of us, then why should I believe in anyone else?"

"You trust Sonnung," she accused. "A stranger to us all."

"Sonnung honors Thor, and I trust in his faith—but that does not mean I would trust him with my fate or my fortune, no matter what promises he makes. It does not mean I trust in *him*. Not wholly."

Gudrid sniffed and turned her gaze back to her loom, her knuckles white, she gripped the shuttle so hard. "Then have your lonely life, Sister. I can only hope you never realize the cold comfort you have grasped so hard to your breast, for when Sonnung leaves you, you will have nothing else left."

CHAPTER TWENTY:
AD 2016
Emma

The next morning, I had an e-mail from the dean of liberal arts. My stomach sank at the sight of it, and my hand shook as I clicked it open.

In light of a recent complaint, I'd like to meet with you this week at your earliest convenience. As you know, we have a strict policy relating to discrimination in the classroom, and we hope this issue can be resolved as quickly as possible.

Best,
Marianne Marshall
Dean of Liberal Arts

"Shit."

Ashley really had made a complaint against me. Against *me*, alleging discrimination. It was both laughable and horrifying, and Alex was right—it would blow up fast if it went any further. It could blow up fast now, for that matter, if Ashley decided to make it public. And I couldn't leave my father in the dark to be blindsided if she did. But that meant involving Alex, after I'd just ejected him from my life.

"Shit, shit, shit."

I checked the time—just after nine—and then called my father's cell phone instead. He was still in Washington, but the vote had been yesterday. He'd be in his office, not on the floor. It only rang twice before he picked up.

"Emma? Is everything all right?"

"Um." I wasn't surprised that was his response. I never called him while he was in Washington. Almost never called him on his cell phone at all. "I'm not really sure yet."

"Is it your mother? Did something happen at home?"

"No, Dad. No. Nothing like that. I just . . . a student made a complaint against me. And I don't know if it's going to stay quiet. I don't want this to turn into a mess for you in the last six weeks before the election."

He was silent for a heartbeat, then two. "Have you talked to Alexander?"

"Not exactly—yet. It hadn't gone this far, but I have to meet with the dean this week."

"I'm sure it's going to be fine, honey," he said. "Talk to Alex. Let him handle it. I'm sure he'll be thrilled to save the day, prove himself in his field to impress you."

"Dad—"

"Are you in the wrong, Emma?" he asked.

"No, but—"

"If you didn't do anything wrong, then it's all going to be fine. And even if it turns into some kind of story, Alex will put out any fires it might start. That's what we keep him around for. But if that's all, sweetie, I've got to run. I have a meeting at nine thirty."

I sighed. "Yeah. Okay."

"Call Alex," he said again. "He'll let me know how it goes."

"Yeah," I said. "Okay."

"We'll talk about all this over dinner on Friday night, all right?"

"Sure," I agreed. "*Bless bless*, Dad."

"*Bless bless*, sweetheart."

Then there was nothing left to do but call Alex. Who I should have called first anyway, because of course that's what my father would tell me. But calling Alex and admitting I might actually need him to spin *this*? After yesterday?

I would rather have faced down the dean.

So I did, sending a quick e-mail saying I'd be happy to meet anytime this week, outside of my class and office hours, and indicating my general willingness to cooperate. There wasn't really a lot else to say, and it wasn't like I had much of a choice. After that I ran out of things to do to put it off any longer. But I still didn't call. Like the coward I was, I sent a text.

```
Student filed a complaint. Not sure how
serious yet, but meeting with the dean
this week.
```

My phone rang almost immediately in response, and I grimaced, staring at Alex's name and debating shunting it to voice mail for so long that it actually just went to voice mail on its own before I answered. Not that it solved the problem, because Alex just called right back again, starting my phone buzzing a second time.

I bit my lip and answered. "You didn't have to call."

"I did have to call," he said. "But before it goes any further, are you telling me this as the guy you might maybe one day want to date again—please, God—or as your father's spin doctor?"

"Considering my father told me to call and let you handle it?"

"Spin doctor it is," he said. "Are you at home?"

"My class isn't until three, but if the dean schedules this meeting—"

"I'm coming over."

"You *really* don't have to come over."

"I really do. And when I get there, you're going to go through this with me start to finish. I need to know everything, Emma. The whole story. Then we'll decide what you're going to say to the dean."

"When did you become Counselor Stone?"

"Media relations and defense law aren't that different when it comes to presentation. Do you want coffee?"

"Is it really going to take so long that I'll need caffeine to sustain me?"

"I'll bring coffee," he said, grim. "Twenty minutes, Emma, and don't even think about ducking out."

"I'm not twelve, Alex."

"Twenty minutes."

I hung up without saying good-bye. Which was probably what a twelve-year-old would have done, if I was being honest, but . . .

He deserved it.

⸙

"One more time," Alex said, leaning forward to set his empty coffee cup on the table.

"We've been over this three times," I said. "I didn't say or do anything I shouldn't have, unless teaching history and critical thinking has suddenly become some kind of crime. Plenty of academics support my position in regard to Charlemagne; nobody denies the fact that he was waging a religious war and converting by the sword, with the pope's blessing, no less. And I didn't say anything about Christianity in the Viking Age that wasn't true. But Catholicism has evolved so much since then that even if I was criticizing or implying criticism, for all practical purposes, it isn't even the same faith!"

He raked his fingers through his hair, then smoothed it back down again. "Getting angry with me or with this student or with the situation in general is not going to do you any favors when you're in that meeting."

"If the dean doesn't support me on this, she's destroying her own department."

"Or protecting herself by throwing you under the bus," Alex said. "What do you know about this student who filed against you?"

"Not really anything."

"Is she local? From an influential family?"

"I really, honestly have no idea," I said, tipping my head against the back of the couch and closing my eyes. We'd been at this for two hours, and I would have killed for a nap. But I had class still, and the dean hadn't wasted any time. My meeting would take place right afterward. "Her last name is Jones, so it's not like you'd know her from Eve even if you googled her."

"I'm just half wondering if she might have been planted. If this is someone playing politics to give Turner a last-minute boost and steal some of your father's support right out from under him."

My eyes flashed open again, and I lifted my head, staring at him. "You can't be serious."

"It's not outside of the realm of possibility," he said. "Maybe not probable—it's dirty to drag family in like this, even in politics—but definitely possible."

A plant. Meant to sabotage me and my career to get at my dad. That was a whole new world of desperate. "What happens if they succeed? If this really is some mastermind of Turner's team?"

"It'll get messy." He rubbed at his face, his elbows on his knees. "Your father would never throw you to the wolves, but if public support swings toward your student, he's going to have to do some fancy footwork. We'll be treading on integrity and family values pretty hard, and I'm not sure it'll hold."

"I can't even believe this is happening," I said. "I never should have come home at all."

"Don't be that way," he said, nudging my knee with his. "If you hadn't come home, we wouldn't have gotten to not have sex together."

I snorted. "You've got nobody to blame for that but yourself."

"And I've never regretted anything more."

"I can think of at least one thing," I said.

"All right, so I regret one thing more," he admitted. "But Emma, whatever happens, it isn't your fault. From what you've told me, you really didn't do anything wrong. And if they investigate this any deeper, I'd guess that your other students will make that obvious. It'll be a flash in the pan, for both you and your dad."

"And if it isn't?" I asked. "If this loses him the election?"

He reached out, a hand on my knee, squeezing lightly. "*This* isn't going to cost him the election. I won't let it."

"If this is some political game, if they have someone watching me or whatever . . ." I swallowed hard. "What if they find something worse?"

His eyes narrowed slightly, sharpened, and his hand slipped away, leaving me cold. "Is there something worse they could find?"

I pressed my lips together. Looked away. I tried to be discreet, to be careful, but if someone had overheard the wrong brunch conversation with Sarah—

"Emma?"

"How much will it hurt my father if it comes out that I'm not Catholic?"

He let out a breath, almost a huff of laughter. "That's hardly going to be news to anyone in the community. And it's not unusual for young adults to become disaffected. Your mother has already laid plenty of groundwork for presenting it as a phase. It would get us through this election without any problem."

"No," I said, shaking my head. "I mean . . . I mean not *Christian*."

He wasn't amused anymore. "How not Christian?"

I couldn't look at him, so I stared out the window instead. "No-chance-of-coming-back not Christian."

"How would they know?"

"I don't know. Eavesdropping on my conversations with Sarah at the diner, maybe."

"I definitely wouldn't risk more of them," he said. "But it would only be hearsay. Nothing we couldn't handle easily enough."

I wanted to believe him. So much. But . . . "I don't want to lie about who I am, Alex. If someone comes at me directly—I *won't* lie about it."

He smiled faintly. "You really are your father's daughter."

"If I were," I said, "this never would have happened at all. He never would have offended anyone."

"I'm sure that's not true," Alex said. "Anyone who is looking for a reason to be offended is going to find it. And they're going to find it no matter how careful you are. This is just bad luck, that's all. Or, like I said, someone deliberately planning to mess with us."

"Right," I said. "So which do I hope for? That I unintentionally offended someone, or that someone is trying to jerk me around? Both suck for me."

"One sucks a little bit more for your father."

"I guess we'll just see," I said, pinching the bridge of my nose to stave off the headache that was threatening to explode behind my eyes. "Either way, it leads me to this meeting with the dean. And from there, who knows."

"It's going to be okay, Emma," Alex said. "Whatever happens, we'll deal with it."

I had no doubt that he would. I could even believe that no matter how bad it got, he'd find a way to save my father's campaign. He was certainly determined enough. Confident in his own ability. And so was my father. But that didn't mean he could save me.

To be honest, I wasn't sure I even wanted him to try.

CHAPTER TWENTY-ONE:
AD 999
FREYDÍS

I had never known a man like Sonnung. He knew my mind so well, my thoughts, my fears, few though they might have been, and did what he could to soothe them. Perhaps I would not have called him gentle or tender, but he did not force from me what I had no desire to give freely and always saw to my pleasure alongside his own—unlike three-legged Thorvard, who had never learned that a woman required more than a thrusting spear, no matter how thick or how long, to bring her to her own release. If he cared at all.

But Sonnung did. And not even Thjodhild was fool enough to speak against the gods when he stood behind me. She and Leif only sulked and glared, for though my father and brothers knew well enough how to fight, as I did, we were hardly a family of warriors. Erik the Red had found his fate and fortune in farming and trade, not blood, and Leif had done the same, regardless of any stories he might tell of his time at King Olaf's court. Sonnung, however, was a different sort, born and bred to the sword, and however much he spoke of settling to the quiet life, of soothing the fire in his blood and trading his sword for goats and sheep, cows and horses, I didn't believe him for a moment.

Gudrid had not been wrong about the kind of man Sonnung was, only wrong in thinking I did not see the truth of him. For Sonnung might promise to sail with me, to share any fortune and glory we might find, but he did not promise to live by my side beyond that, and I knew better than to ask it. Even when he had sworn not to abandon any child we might have, we both knew it was the child he was concerned with more than me. I had no right to expect anything else, not so long as I was married.

What I meant to him, I was not certain, nor in what he meant to me, but we were happy, Sonnung and I. I was happy, even knowing it would end.

-ᴄᴄᴊᴊᴏ·

"So you will sail with Karlsefni and Gudrid, then," my father said one morning when I was too slow to rise and Sonnung had gone to make offerings to the gods and the landvættir.

Most often, we laid our gifts together upon the boulder, or the steep rocky slope beyond it, but at least once every fortnight he rose before me to perform his own rituals and rites, leaving early and returning late after the evening meal. And always, on those nights, he was hard and hungry, desire and need rolling off him in feral waves. A bloodlust that he could sate no other way.

"I will sail with Sonnung, on Thorstein's ship," I agreed, sitting up when my father settled upon the edge of my sleeping bench.

He snorted, his gaze upon the long central fire, burning low now, with so few of us still inside. Whether the day dawned or not, there were still goats and cows to be milked, and chores to be done.

"Shrewd of her," he said. "But fitting. Thorstein would have been glad to see you set free by such a gift, and whether you care for her or not, it's certainly cooled your resentment. You can hardly be angry with her for marrying Karlsefni when it is that same marriage which has provided you with your ship."

"And Karlsefni's support for you," I said. "Is that not just as true?"

His lips pressed thin, and his hand found mine. His grip was not as strong as it should have been. As it had been. "By the time you return, I fear it will not matter whether I count Karlsefni as my friend, or your Thorvard, either."

"Father—"

But he shook his head, stopping me with a squeeze of his hand. "With a ship of your own, and one you do not owe even to your husband's kindness, you will be free, Freydís. And I pray to the gods, to Thor, to keep you so. I hope when you find this land of wine you all speak of, it will be a good place, with friendly spirits and all the riches you could dream of. If it is, Daughter, find your fortune there. Find wealth and happiness, and give honor to the gods."

"And if it isn't?" I asked, my throat tight. "If what you fear is true, and I return to find you are gone, what would you have me do?"

"Remember me," he said. "Honor me. And for the love of all that is good and right, see that I am sent to the mound, not their fallow churchyard with a cross planted upon my head."

I choked on a laugh and leaned my head against his shoulder. "You are not so old yet that you should think of dying."

"I am not so young, either," he said, pressing a kiss to the top of my head. "And even if I am not dead, this settlement, even this farm— I feel it all slipping from my grasp. Leif and Thjodhild have sown so much distrust, and I am not one of them anymore. Just the old man who fights against their Christ, too stubborn to know his gods are lost, made as old and as weak as he is by their new faith."

"You cannot believe that is true," I said.

"I believe that is how my people see me," he said. "And as to the gods, who can say?"

"Thor is with us," I promised him. "As powerful as ever, and as loyal. The more I speak with Sonnung, the more certain I am that we are not forgotten."

My father grunted. "And who is your Sonnung? I've spoken with Karlsefni, and he swears Sonnung was not among his men when he sailed. Nor is his name familiar to me, to any of us at Brattahlid."

"Karlsefni is mistaken," I said. "For Sonnung arrived with him. He spoke to me while you feasted with the others. And the things he says— he could not know Karlsefni so well if he had not sailed with him."

"Perhaps," my father agreed.

It was not impossible that Sonnung had joined the crew at the last moment, brought aboard by one of the other men and overlooked by Karlsefni while they sailed, though it was certainly unlikely. I could not truly imagine Sonnung of all men hiding in the hold to avoid notice. Or hiding at all.

"Ask your Sonnung his father's name, even so," he said. "If I am to trust him with my daughter upon the sea, I would know that much at the least."

"Trust *me*, Father," I said, dismissing the rest. Sonnung was not my husband, that he might have any say in my fate. "Trust in all you've taught me, and trust in the gods to see me safe again to the shore."

"You have my faith, Dísa, always." He kissed the top of my head again and released me, rising stiffly with a groan. "But I would still know more of the man who has ensnared your heart."

Whatever I had expected him to say, it was not that. I could only stare at him mutely as he walked away, wondering how he had seen what I had refused to admit even to myself. Loving Sonnung—it made no sense at all.

But perhaps . . . perhaps it was not so strange to my father, for he had surely loved another woman once, long ago. Enough to claim her daughter as his own, to bring me here and raise me among his sons.

What a fool I was to forget that even in this, I was my father's daughter still.

I had not expected to see Sonnung until after supper, but he found me in the barn before then, haying the cows and the goats. His eyes on me were hot even in the weak lamplight, making promises I knew that he would keep. He took the pitchfork from my hand, and a growled "Leave us" sent even Thorhall out. Sonnung's body was like stone, the muscles taut, every line, every movement tortured by restraint. He cupped my cheek, searched my face, my eyes. I looked back, holding his gaze, my blood warming already.

"Freydís Thorswoman," he murmured, tossing the pitchfork aside and drawing me tight against him. "Did you know that's what they call you now? My woman, even if it cannot last."

His hand slipped from my face into my hair, his fingers knotting there, and the other became a fist in the heavy wool I wore against the cold. I tipped back my head, offering myself, and his lips found mine, then his teeth, and I opened to him, accepting his kiss as eagerly as I would the rest of him.

Our joining was fierce and fast, his hands rough and his teeth everywhere, marking my skin, mixing pain with pleasure until I cried out, begging, and he drove inside me. I peaked even before he took his second stroke, and then he rode me hard until I found release a second time, waves of pleasure making me shudder, making him groan and sheathe himself deeper still as he followed me over the brink.

"Freydís Thorswoman," he said again, dropping his forehead to my shoulder before his lips found my skin, tasting, teasing. "My woman."

"And who are you?" I asked. "Claiming a woman you believe belongs to such a god?"

I felt his smile against my neck. "Perhaps I am his goði, sent in his stead."

"A warrior and a priest?"

"Is it so difficult to believe?"

"No." His faith ran deep—deep enough that it did not seem strange at all that he might serve Thor as his goði, certainly. And among so many Christians, men like Leif and Karlsefni, and women like Thjodhild and Gudrid, he would have reason for caution, even for deceit. "But is it true?"

"It is not false," he promised. "And it is truth that I wish to sail with you, that I would see this new land through your eyes, and Thorhall's, too. At your sides. We have lost too many, and I would not learn later you had drowned, nor risk being too late to guard you."

I laughed. "You cannot guard me against the sea, nor fate itself. No man can do such a thing, even for his wife."

He sighed, rolling to lay beside me in the hay, propped on one elbow to look at me, and drawing his cloak up to cover us both. "What if the reason you founder is because you have lost your way? If it is not fate but an error that bewilders you? Some small mistake any skilled man or woman might prevent. Or worse, what if the threat comes from your men? We have lost too many already to Christian cruelty, and they cannot know your stubbornness as I do. You'd accept death before baptism, Freydís Thorswoman, and I would not see you forced to choose between the two."

I flushed. "Am I meant to believe you would choose anything else? That if they placed hot coals upon our bellies, you would not make the same choice? And then it would be two of us dead, instead of one."

"No." His fingers brushed the warmth of my cheeks, another smile playing at the corners of his mouth. "You're to believe that my presence upon the ship and at your side in this Vinland would make them hesitate to form such a plan at all."

I slapped his hand away, my pride stung. "I am well able to protect myself, Sonnung."

"Against thirty-five men, or seventy, or a hundred? No man living is so strong as that. But you have seen already how they shy from me, how my very presence in a room will silence them. If they choose to attack us, perhaps we would still lose, but surely we would be better off together than apart. And we could make them pay that much more steeply for the trying."

"Blood for blood," I murmured, for that was what he suggested. I should hardly have been surprised to hear it from a man who lived by his sword, but the thought of killing the men we lived with, worked beside, twisted my stomach.

He smoothed my hair, and I knew he saw my hesitation. "If it is your life they mean to take, you will fight, Freydís, and fiercely. I promise you that."

"It will not come to that," I said, putting it from my mind before it wormed its way any deeper into my thoughts. "Gudrid and Karlsefni would never permit their men to raise swords against us, and those who sail with us will honor Thor, if not alone, at least alongside their Christ. My father will know who we might trust."

"But will you trust in me?"

I rested my cheek upon his shoulder, shifting nearer to his warmth. "Whoever you are."

He spread his hand over my stomach. "Sonnung Svidurson," he said. "Though it will mean little to Erik to hear it. My father does not linger anywhere long enough to be known. Not even by his kings."

"He cannot be an Icelander, then," I said.

Sonnung shook his head. "He's as much and as little an Icelander as he is anything else. But perhaps now you better understand my own wandering, learned at his knee."

As I had learned, too, by my father's struggles, and his father's before him.

"Sonnung Svidurson," I said softly. "And one day, then, you will wander away again."

"Yes." He met my eyes, let me see his own pain at the thought. "But I will come back, Freydís, should you have need of my help, my protection. Keep faith that I will hear you if you call. And in the meantime, love me as I love you."

Strange as it all sounded, I could not help but believe him. I wanted too much for it to be true.

CHAPTER TWENTY-TWO:
AD 2016
Emma

My palms sweating, I sat on a bench outside the dean's office—like some unruly student sent to the principal, I couldn't help but think—and took a deep, supposed-to-be-calming breath, hoping to settle my nerves.

"I'll be right out here, waiting," Alex said.

He'd insisted on coming with me, even though there was no way the dean was going to let him inside. I wouldn't even be allowed a lawyer if there was a formal investigation to go along with the complaint. Not that I wanted one, particularly. I didn't want any of this to be happening at all. Especially not now.

"You're going to be fine, Emma," Alex assured me, his hand on my knee. "And if it all goes sideways, it won't matter. I can spin this if we have to, I promise."

I wasn't sure I really believed that, but I nodded anyway. "Right."

"Ms. Moretti?" I jumped up, half vibrating out of my skin in anticipation. The dean's office assistant smiled one of those completely innocuous, painfully polite smiles that tells you nothing about what's in store for you. "Dean Marshall is ready for you."

"Right," I said again. If I could just get it over with, figure out what I was facing specifically, I knew I'd feel a lot better. It was just the agonizing that was interminable.

Alex stood up beside me, smoothly rebuttoning his suit jacket, and some small part of me was annoyed that he looked nicer than I did in my most professional business suit. It was the tailoring. I hadn't bothered to have mine properly fitted, somehow convincing myself that the days of picture-perfect camera-ready outfits were behind me. *Ha-ha.*

His hand settled at the small of my back, warm and steadying, and the dean's assistant hesitated at the inner office door. "Ah . . . I'm not certain—"

"I'm just providing moral support," Alex assured her, offering a self-deprecating smile.

"Of course," she said, opening the door.

"Ms. Moretti." Dean Marshall rose from behind her desk as I stepped into the room. "Thank you for making yourself available."

As if I'd had much of a choice. She waved me to a chair in front of the desk, and I took it as the door shut behind us. "I'm sure it's just a misunderstanding, but I'd like to get it all straightened out as soon as possible."

"Yes, I'm certain you would," she said. "Unfortunately, that's not entirely within our hands. But for the moment, the complaint is informal, and so long as it remains that way, I think we should be able to handle it discreetly. The last thing either of us wants is press involvement and unfavorable headlines, I'm sure."

"Right," I said, a little more faintly this time. "I would *really* appreciate if it didn't come to that."

"So why don't you tell me a little bit about the class you're teaching, to start. What topics have you been discussing in the last couple of weeks?"

I cleared my throat. "Mostly we've been discussing the early medieval period, from the fall of Rome in the West to Charlemagne's conversion by the sword and the Carolingians generally, and most recently the Viking Age, for which I've assigned some of the Icelandic sagas as reading. As I'm sure you know, the conflict between Christians and pagans is a relevant topic during this period of time, and it's important to examine the role of religion in shaping both the events of those days and our historical narrative today."

"I see," Dean Marshall said, jotting some notes on a yellow pad. "And you've been covering this in class—as a student-led discussion?"

"A combination of discussion of the source material and lecture. I like to begin with some background and context for the source and then open it up to the class to tell me what they're seeing reflected in the text."

"And you're asking your class to consider the biases of the Christian authors in the discussion."

"Of course," I said. "If we don't take into account the context in which our sources are written, we're leaving out an entire layer. Culture and religion inform the ways we see the world, and it's certainly informed the manner in which we record our history. All of that has to be unpacked if we want to understand the past."

"I don't disagree with you, Ms. Moretti," the dean said, studying me over the rim of her glasses. "But surely you can appreciate the difficult position in which this places a devoutly Christian student."

"It isn't even the same faith," I said. "Christians today wouldn't even necessarily recognize the faith of converted Iceland in 1000 AD. It retained so much of the existing pagan structures—"

"I don't think we need to debate the state of Christianity during the Viking Age," she said, smiling. "I'm certain you know far more about it than I do, and we wouldn't have hired you if you hadn't come with exemplary recommendations."

I let out a breath, some of my defensiveness slipping away with it. "The discussions we're having—it isn't even so much a criticism of Christianity as it is how it's been applied by the powers that be. And I understand that there's a desire to see Christianity as some beacon of light in what we still refer to as the Dark Ages, particularly by the faithful, but there has to be room within the historical context to recognize the destruction and suffering it caused, too. That's all I'm trying to do."

The dean lifted her hand, stopping me. "Be that as it may, if your students identify as Christian, and their understanding of the conflicts between Christians and pagans during that time as a narrative of salvation is fundamental to their belief, you're essentially asking them to strip themselves of a foundational element of their identity in order to view history through *your* secular lens."

I pressed my hands flat against my thighs, my fingers itching for the pendant hanging beneath my shirt. "This isn't a religious college, Dean Marshall. It's a public institution. We *should* be studying history from a secular perspective in our classrooms, not reinforcing religious indoctrination—of any kind."

"Are you certain that's what you're truly doing, Ms. Moretti?" she asked. "Or is this all just some misplaced rebellion against your upbringing? Maybe you've swung too far, and rather than presenting history without bias, you've unconsciously brought your own into the classroom."

I stiffened in my chair. "This has absolutely nothing to do with my personal beliefs. In fact, I've been extremely careful to keep my faith entirely to myself. But if my students are challenged to think critically about their own narratives and cultural upbringing, even their faith, then I don't see that as a failing. They *should* be asking questions—we *all* should be."

"Then I assume you don't deny telling your students that—quote—'the gods of the Vikings are as real as Jesus.'"

I flushed. "I don't think those were my exact words, but I did tell them that those gods were as real to the Norse people *then* as Jesus is to Christians *today*, yes. They believed in their gods just as faithfully as we believe in our choice of religion today. I won't deny the people of the past the conviction of their beliefs."

"And you don't see how that statement might have been objectionable?"

"I can see how it might have been misconstrued," I admitted. The phrasing of the quotation had made that more than clear. "But it isn't *wrong*. And it isn't as though I'm suggesting that they walk away from Christianity and start living their life by the tenets of the *Hávamál*. I didn't even assign them anything from either Edda as readings."

"Why not?"

I blinked. "What?"

"Why didn't you assign readings from the body of Norse myth, if you're addressing the conflict between faiths as part of your curriculum?"

My stomach knotted, and my hands had become fists in my lap. "I thought it would be less problematic to discuss *The Vinland Sagas*, and look at their authorship and how it might have influenced the characters—historical and fictional—presented. Having to address the problems inherent in the Eddas as a late representation of the many localized oral traditions of Norse religion at the time seemed a bit too much."

"But those sagas were recorded under the same circumstances, were they not? Belatedly written down to preserve oral family histories."

"Family histories are not as sensitive a subject as what essentially boils down to what's left of a religion," I said. "And to be frank, I didn't want to be accused of teaching the Norse myths but not giving equal time and attention to the Bible by an overzealous student."

The dean winced at that, and I let myself press an open hand against my chest to feel the pressure of the amulet against my skin. The metal was warm, comforting, and I gathered the frayed edges of my temper with the touch.

"I'm sorry," I said. "I just hope . . . I hope you understand that it was never my intention to create a classroom where anyone felt attacked for their faith. I wouldn't wish religious persecution or discrimination on anyone, and I certainly don't want to be the person doing the persecuting."

"It's a tightrope," the dean admitted. "A careful balancing act. And to be fair, I don't believe you intended to create a hostile atmosphere in your classroom. But I do think it's possible that your clear passion for this particular topic might have led you into trouble. We need to be careful, Ms. Moretti, particularly when it comes to faith. I'm surprised that I have to tell *you* that, of all people."

"You don't," I said, irritated by her tone. "That's why I'm not teaching Old Norse religion as part of my course. Why I limited myself to *The Vinland Sagas* and didn't dig any deeper. And everything I've taught has been backed up by other academics. I wasn't going out on any limbs, Dean Marshall. I was just doing the job I was hired to do."

"All of that may be true," she said. "But it may not save you from reprisal. As long as you understand that, I think we're done here for today. I'll be in touch should we need to move things forward in a more formal manner, and in the meantime, I want you to send me your lesson plans for the rest of the semester."

I stared. "My—why?"

"Just to be sure we won't see any more complaints of this kind," the dean said. "And if everything you say is true, I'm certain I won't find any issues, but I'd rather have my bases covered. And I think your father would, too."

Dean Marshall stood before I could manage a response that wasn't pure frustration. I swallowed my outrage and followed her to the door.

"Thank you again for your understanding, Ms. Moretti," she said. "I hope very much we won't need to speak again."

I mumbled an agreement, still seething at the implications, and then it was over, and I was in the outer office, being shepherded back to Alex, who had risen at the opening of the door.

"Everything all right?" he asked.

Such a ridiculous question, and I wasn't sure whether to laugh or to cry. "I guess we'll see."

"Not quite the enthusiastic yes I was hoping for."

I shook my head. There wasn't anything else left to say. Not until we were somewhere safe, anyway. And then maybe I'd beat my head against a wall instead of talking.

Ugh.

Alex led the way back out, and I considered my lesson plans, such as they were, and wondered how I was going to magic them into the detailed outline I was sure the dean expected to land in her in-box.

I'd rather have my bases covered. And I think your father would, too.

It was that last little barb that was rubbing me raw. And the one before it about *misplaced rebellion.* Dean Marshall was Catholic, a member of my parents' church, and while I'd always known my last name had given me an advantage, I was beginning to wonder if Ashley's accusation—that I'd been hired only because of my father—might have been truer than I'd wanted to admit, no matter what the dean said about my references. I got into my car and slammed the door, only to find Alex opening the passenger's-side door to frown at me.

"Are you sure you should be driving?"

I sighed and bounced my head off the back of the seat, staring at the roof. Once, twice, three times . . .

"Emma."

I got out and slammed the door again, hating that he was right.

"Come on," he said, hitting the "Lock" button on his side and closing the door a lot more gently than I would have. "Let's get you home. I'll make you some tea, and whatever happened, we'll talk it through. I'll send one of the interns for your car."

"Right."

"At some point you're going to have to give me something more than one word, you know."

"Sure," I said.

His car beeped, and I pulled open the passenger's-side door. He grabbed it as I started to get in, giving me a tight smile, and I *knew* it was to keep me from slamming his car door like I had mine. Which only made me want to do it more, the mood I was in. But it wasn't like any of this was his fault, and blaming him for it—behaving this way at all—was childish. Utterly childish.

"Sorry," I mumbled.

"Don't worry about it," he said. "Any of it. We're going to get it all sorted out, I promise."

"I'm not sure *we* can solve this one, Alex."

"Maybe not," he admitted. "But if you think you're going to face it alone, you're wrong. I will sit outside your dean's office as the most impotent man alive for days on end while you face whatever inquisitions come next, if I have to."

I laughed a little, some of the stress going with it. "You have more important things to do. We both know that."

"There is nothing more important," he said. "And I think your dad would agree."

I wrinkled my nose. "I wish he didn't need to. I wish he didn't have to concern himself with any of this."

"Then you'd be wishing yourself a different father altogether," Alex said. "Because even if he weren't a congressman worrying about his reelection, he'd still care. The only difference would be that he'd be the one telling you everything was going to be fine in person, and honestly and completely selfishly, I'm kind of glad it's me instead. Otherwise I'm pretty sure you'd still be giving me the cold shoulder, and I'd be screwed."

"Probably," I agreed.

"So you see? It's not so bad."

"For you."

He grinned. "For *us*."

And then he shut the door—gently—and drove me home.

CHAPTER TWENTY-THREE:
AD 1000
FREYDÍS

Mead and wine both flowed from Karlsefni's stores, along with smoked fish and meat and honeyed nuts for our feasting to celebrate both the Yuletide season and his wedding to Gudrid. Father even slaughtered two of his goats, giving portions of both to Thor for his blessing on the match and for health and prosperity in the new year.

"Before you sail, we'll offer another," he promised me. "And ask the gods to keep you safe upon the sea."

But all of this we did in secret, with only Thorhall and Sonnung to help. Like thieves and outlaws, we made our *blót*—the blood sacrifice and ritual by which we honored the gods—and I prayed the gods would not take offense.

Sonnung laughed when I confessed my fears that same night. "The risk you take makes your gifts all the greater. You show loyalty to Thor even when all others turn away, when they demand you do the same. He cannot help but be moved by such devotion."

We'd found a shadowed corner at the back of the long hall, and Sonnung had glowered until those men who were nearest had found another bench on which to rest, granting us a measure of peace and privacy. It was far too early for us to slip away altogether, but that did not stop Sonnung from teasing me with his lips upon my neck, and his roaming hands. Perhaps we'd both had too much of Karlsefni's strong mead.

"Would he not be more pleased if we defied the Christians openly?" I asked. "Would it not show greater honor and respect?"

He grunted. One of his hands had found its way beneath my heavy wool skirt—Gudrid had all but forced me to wear it, and I could not deny the advantages it offered, seated upon Sonnung's lap. "No one defies Leif and Thjodhild more loudly or openly than you, Freydís. And not only for Thor's sake, but to please the spirits of these lands, to honor your ancestors as you ought as well. One quiet sacrifice will not change that. Not when so many will not honor the gods at all."

"When we sail, I would honor the gods properly," I said.

His hand slid up my thigh. "And they will favor you for your boldness, as well as the gifts you offer. Just as they do now. Just as *I* do now."

"What will we do, Sonnung, when we are surrounded by men upon the ship? When we have no privacy at all?"

"We will suffer it, as we suffered for the months while you denied me," he said, nipping at my throat. "And before we go, we will take every opportunity to sate ourselves. But the suffering will make the pleasure we share after all the sweeter, I promise you that."

"So many promises," I teased him.

"And I will keep them all," he said. "For as long as you remember me."

"I will never forget."

He drew back, searching my face. "Perhaps that is so. For good or ill, I do not know."

"For good," I said, smoothing the faint lines of a scowl from his brow. "It will be thoughts of you, of what we shared, which sustain me when I must give myself up to Thorvard again."

Sonnung's eyes hardened, chips of pale-blue ice unmistakable even in the dim light that reached us. "Weak and unworthy fool that he is. A man who cannot value properly what he has been given. And I hope the thought of us together haunts him when he learns of it. Let him be unmanned by the thought of my hands upon your body, my sword sheathed in your core. Let him live with the knowledge that he will never satisfy you as I have."

"With luck, we will escape before he can arrive," I said. "We will have years yet before I must return to his bed."

"And when that day comes, you will return to him with my child," he said. "It will be proof of his weakness, and the weakness of his Christ. Proof of Thor's power, his strength."

I looked away, for even after these last months, my womb had not quickened. I doubted it ever could, and all to the good if it didn't, for I still did not want a child. But I feared that Sonnung would tire of me when he realized the truth—that it was not Thorvard's seed that was weak, but my body. All he wanted of me was a child, a son, and if I could not give him one, what would be left between us?

Sonnung let out a breath, his fingers digging into my thigh—just hard enough to remind me of the pleasures still to come. "You doubt me?"

"Never," I said, and it was true. I had no doubt he could get a child on any other woman in my father's hall. And they would count themselves fortunate to birth so strong a son. And fine daughters, too, with auburn hair, not so bright and hot as mine, but tempered by their mother's blood. Sonnung knew how to leash his temper when there was need, but I was certain that same fire simmered beneath his skin, still, and any child we might have would be a terror, twice cursed by the blood he would share.

"Then what?" Sonnung asked.

But I only shook my head. I had no desire to ruin what we had. He would brush my fear away, at best, too sure of himself and his strength, leaving me frustrated, or find offense in my words, his pride pricked. And I had warned him, I consoled myself after we followed Karlsefni and Gudrid from the feast and Sonnung had brought me to our own bed. I had warned him he would not get a child from me, and he would have no one to blame but himself for the disappointment when he learned I had been right.

"Keep faith, Freydís," he said, as he had so often before. "The gods will not betray us."

It had been a simple thing for Gudrid to persuade Karlsefni to sail west, for with so many men at Brattahlid and little beyond ivory and wool to accept in trade, there was no purpose in his returning to Iceland yet. The ivory was valuable, that was true, and would fetch a fair price, but Iceland had no need of our wool, and coming from Greenland, Karlsefni was uncertain of sailing back to Norway, Christian or not, and risking King Olaf's moods.

"You have never seen such bountiful lands," Leif had boasted early on. "Forests of well-grown trees as far as the eye can see, waiting to be cut and turned to lumber or made into ships, wild-grown vines of grapes and bushes heavy with berries. Even wheat! And plenty of forage and grazing for livestock, too."

"After listening to your brother go on night after night, Karlsefni was eager enough to know the land for himself," Gudrid told me, for we had no choice but to work together in planning the journey, and Karlsefni, Sonnung, and Thorvaldur were often deep in conference upon the topic as well. "And it took only the suggestion to make him consider a settlement. If we prove successful, he could make himself more than just a chieftain. Become a wealthy lord, or perhaps even a king in his own right. Either way, we will have riches aplenty to trade on the return. The lumber alone will make him his fortune, to say nothing of the rest. I never could understand why Leif was so willing to leave it behind."

I snorted. "Distracted by King Olaf's commands, I suppose, and his Christ."

"There is no reason he could not have served Christ with his gold as well as his preaching," Gudrid said, and it was the first time I had ever heard such clear disgust in her tone. "He hides it well enough, as he must, I suppose, but it is fear that stopped him, and nothing else—you can be sure of that."

More than once, I had wondered the same, and my gaze darted to my brother, seated at Thjodhild's right. Leif loved nothing more than lording about the hall after my father had retired to his bed—earlier and earlier these nights, though I did not like to think what it meant.

"Do not let him hear you say it," I warned. "He'll not forgive the insult, no matter how much influence Karlsefni might have. And he will be chieftain sooner than I'd like."

Gudrid's lips pressed thin and white, not looking up from her mending. "Your father is a good man, Freydís, Christian or not, and I am grateful to him for all he's done for me and for my father before that, but Leif is Thjodhild's son more than Erik's, and Thjodhild—Thjodhild is bitter and small. I fear for you when Erik is gone."

"You needn't," I said, my eyes narrowing. I had no use for Gudrid's pity, and I wanted no favors from her. "And if that is the only reason you've asked me to come—"

"Don't be foolish, Freydís," she snapped, then sighed. "If we're to begin a settlement, there must be *some* women to start, and this is what Thorstein would have wanted, besides. You're brave and strong, and desperate enough to sail into a storm, and who knows what dangers your brother's Vinland holds? We have need of you for your own strengths, and if it serves to get you out from beneath Thjodhild's eye, to keep you from trouble here and save your father the heartache that will come when Thorvard arrives and finds you in Sonnung's arms, all the better, for it made it that much more likely you would agree."

I flushed, for though I could hardly admit it to her now, I had not thought of the trouble I would bring my father if Thorvard arrived before we left and learned that I had taken Sonnung to my bed—that I meant to abandon my husband entirely and sail away with my lover, even if it was not for all time. Even if Thorvard arrived after we had gone, he would soon discover the truth all the same.

"Thorvard will not blame my father for the choices I have made," I said, though I was not certain who I wished to convince. "He knows as well as any that I do as I please. And surely if he would blame anyone, it would be Leif and Thorvaldur, who did not do their duty in sending Sonnung away."

Gudrid sniffed, the needle in her fingers faltering as she glanced up at me. "One glimpse of Sonnung, and Thorvard would know there was little they could do—little that anyone could do, for that matter. And it is not as though Erik is as strong and hale even as he was a year ago now. I think Thorvard is honorable enough not to blame your father. But when you return, I do not think he will spare you his anger."

"No," I said. "I don't think he will. But Sonnung will be beside me still." At least I hoped he would. "I won't face him alone."

"I pray Sonnung is as true as you think," Gudrid said. "But if he isn't, Thorvard will know the fear of God if he raises his hand against you. Karlsefni will see to it, since I know too well that your brothers won't."

"Karlsefni owes me nothing, Gudrid. Nor do you."

"We are sisters, Freydís, whether you like it or not, for I swore as much to your brother before his death, and I've no intention of forgetting it. You do not have to like me, or I you, but that's how it is between us, how it will be until my death, and I've made sure my husband knows it."

She said it all so fiercely, I could not bring myself to argue. And perhaps—for the first time—I was not sure I wanted to.

All this time, Gudrid had been much kinder to me than I deserved. Even when I had cursed her for courting Karlsefni and blamed her for Thorstein's death, some part of me had known it, though I could not seem to admit the truth even to myself until now.

"I would not blame you for hating me," I said quietly instead, and I felt Gudrid still beside me in surprise. "But I would have you know I don't dislike you. And—" I cleared my throat, for my voice had gone sharp. "And I am grateful, Gudrid. Even if it has not seemed so."

And then I left her before she could reply.

CHAPTER TWENTY-FOUR:
AD 2016
Emma

S o you're still in suspense," Sarah said after she'd coaxed the story out of me over the phone. It was my second retelling of the day—I'd already had to give Alex the blow by blow, and I was pretty sure round three was going to be dinner with my mother. Joy of joys.

I pressed my lips together and tapped out a correction on my outline. "Yup."

"But you still have your job. You haven't been fired."

"Not yet." I scrolled down, skimming my notes as I went. My lesson plans weren't all that detailed. A rough outline not much more expansive than what I included on the syllabus, and there was no way that was going to be enough to satisfy the dean. "But I'm not holding my breath."

"How are you coping?" Sarah asked.

I shrugged, not even caring that she couldn't see it. "It's fine. I'm sure I'll be fine. Probably won't be pursuing a career in academia by the time this is over, but I was already second-guessing myself on that anyway. I love history, and I love digging into the bits and pieces and perspectives that have been overlooked, but maybe I'm better off doing something else and pursuing that stuff as a hobby."

"What would you do instead?"

"I have no idea," I said. "Some kind of office work? Maybe I could get some kind of job as a research assistant or aide to someone on a relevant subcommittee in Congress. It's not like everything I do doesn't reflect on my father somehow anyway, so I might as well make use of his connections."

"You would *hate* that," Sarah said.

"Yup," I agreed, adding a source to my outline from the stupid Charlemagne lecture that had started it all. Just to cover my butt.

"And what about Alex?"

I leaned back in my chair, stretching out the knot between my shoulder blades. "What about Alex?"

"If you worked as an aide, you'd be moving to DC. Do you really think a long-distance relationship is the best idea?"

"Um." I hit "Save" and refocused on the conversation. "Alex and I aren't exactly . . . I'm not sure that's going to work out regardless, honestly."

"What!"

I winced. "We're kind of taking a break, actually."

"You only just started dating, Emma." I could just imagine her throwing out her arms in exasperation—at the very least, she had to be pacing. "What did you do to mess this up?"

"*I* didn't mess it up, thank you very much," I said, struggling to keep my temper. That she'd even jumped to that conclusion galled me, and it was all I could do to keep from snapping in response. "He's the one who got all worked up about how my personal issue was going to mess with my father's campaign instead of, I don't know, actually caring about how it was affecting me."

Sarah whistled. "Ouch. Really?"

"No," I said, still irritated. "I made it up. Because I'm determined to sabotage everything good in my life."

"I get that you're stressed and upset, Emma, I do, but you don't have to be a bitch about it." Sarah's tone had turned frosty. "I'm on your side, all right?"

I sighed. "Sorry. I know. It's just been a long day. And I still have to fess up to my mom tonight. If she hears about this whole situation thirdhand through Dad, she's going to kill me."

"Do you need me to come?" Sarah asked immediately.

"Thanks," I said, then grimaced. "But apparently Alex already volunteered himself."

"Of course he did." She laughed. "Poor Alex. Did you at least tell him the truth?"

"Nope," I said. "Well. Maybe half of it. But after what happened, I just couldn't stand the thought that he'd look at me and start mentally deducting polling points, you know? I don't want my faith to be a problem he has to solve for my father's sake."

"Just tell him," Sarah said. "I know it's hard and scary—you know how nervous I was when I finally came clean with my family and friends about joining the Alliance church, even, and that wasn't anything close to this—but worst case, it'll make it clear whether he's more invested in you or your dad's career, and you can end things neatly and be done. And no matter what, you'll know where you stand."

"I'll think about it," I promised. And I would. I *had* been. But there was just so much else going on. And maybe I didn't *want* to know for sure where I stood or whether he cared more about my father's campaign than he did me. Not yet. Not when I felt like I might come out on the losing side. Sarah had at least still been worshipping the same god, and minor variations in ritual and doctrine were easier to overlook than the rejection of an entire faith tradition. Nobody around here was going to tell anyone that their Protestant sect wasn't worshipping a *real* god. "Anyway, wish me luck with my mom."

"Good luck," she said. "And let me know how it goes, all right?"

"Saturday, at brunch," I said. "Um—but I think we're going to have to order to go and eat here. The spin doctor says I'm not allowed to discuss my personal issues in public until the campaign is over."

"Ugh."

"Welcome to my life."

And all of this mess with the dean and the campaign was just another reminder of why it wasn't worth doing anything that might potentially make it worse.

⚜

I was only half finished with my new and expanded course outline for the dean when Alex's shiny silver Prius pulled into the driveway, followed by my car, close behind, and then a third to bring the poor intern back home. I only felt a little bit guilty about making use of my father's campaign staff; Alex had already argued successfully that since it was an issue that could impact the campaign and had "required" his involvement, it was technically billable time anyway. But even so, I felt a little bit spoiled.

"Ready for dinner?" Alex called after knocking once and sticking his head in the door.

I groaned, pushing away from my desk and tipping all the way back in my chair. "Can we just pretend I'm not a liability for one more day?"

"Better to get it over with and put it behind you," Alex said, tossing me my keys. "She's got a keen nose, your mom. Especially for fish. And rats. I would prefer to be neither."

"It's the Icelander in her," I grumbled. "They're a blunt people. And they always know when someone else isn't being as straightforward as they could be, I swear. Even as a kid, I never got away with anything."

"So let's not try." Alex filled the doorway, leaning casually against the frame and looking beautiful, as always. The jerk. "Besides, she needs to be prepared in case this breaks out and turns into something. I don't want her blindsided by questions from the press."

"We can't possibly have that, can we?" I closed my laptop and got up, dropping my keys in my purse so I didn't have to look at him. It was uncomfortable to think that the man you might have been dating—wanted to date—would spill your secrets to your parents to make sure they were properly *prepared* for the next press event.

"Emma."

"It's fine, Alex. I called you in as a spin doctor, so you're spinning."

"I wouldn't have breathed a word to her without your permission, Emma. To your dad, either. Even if I was thinking about the campaign, that doesn't mean I would have betrayed your trust."

"It's fine," I said again, grabbing my jacket. "This is your job, and you're not here as the guy I'm dating."

"Except that I am," he said. "Both. At least as far as your mother is concerned. And I'd like to be both to you, too. I just need you to tell me what I have to do to make that happen."

I shook my head. "Honestly, Alex, I'm not really in a place where I can think about that—about anything except how I'm going to deal with all this shit when it hits the fan. So if whatever happens at dinner doesn't convince my mom that we're still in the blissful rose colored–glasses stage of the relationship, at least that will mean one less ball in the air."

He didn't move, just stood in my way at the door, searching my face and keeping his own expression carefully press-conference neutral. "Before we go in there and you decide whatever this is between us isn't a ball worth juggling anymore—"

"Whatever this *was*, Alex—it didn't even have time to start."

And then I pushed past him to face my mother. With any luck, she'd be just as blithely unconcerned as my dad had been.

Except that my dad hadn't worried because he was sure of Alex. Because whatever trouble I got into, he had faith that Alex would get me out of it. Good old Alex. So dependable, so helpful, so good at his job, and practically the son my father had never had.

The whole situation made me want to scream.

My mother's response was everything I should have expected it to be. A long sigh, an exasperated look, and then, "If only you had listened when I suggested it would be good for you to come with us to church."

I counted to ten and kept my gaze firmly fixed to my plate to keep from rolling my eyes. "Somehow I doubt that being demonstrably Catholic would have helped."

"You could have defended yourself," my mother said. "You could have told your dean that you were speaking of your own religious tradition, from a place of respect and deep faith."

"Even if I had been going to mass, that wouldn't have been true," I said. "And the last thing Dad needs is for me to be called out for a lie of that magnitude."

"She's right, Irena," Alex said gently before my mother could argue. "I know it isn't ideal, but it would be worse if she pretended to be something she isn't. It would undermine the entire foundation of our platform and branding."

"Perhaps it could have been true," my mother said, accusing. "If you didn't refuse to come to church. The Holy Spirit might well have moved you, had you only given it the slightest invitation to do so."

"I know," I said. "I'm a horrible disappointment. I get it. But it's too late now. I can't go back in time and march off to mass with you every

Sunday, hoping that God's grace will move me to rededicate myself to the Church."

"Don't be so dramatic, Emma," my mother said. "I'm only saying that you could have saved yourself all this grief if you'd only listened—"

"I'm not Catholic," I said firmly. Maybe I wasn't ready to tell her everything, but this much—this much I was going to be crystal clear about. "I'm never going to be Catholic again. Or Christian, for that matter. Yes, maybe it means I'm going to have a harder time defending myself in this particular instance. Yes, maybe it makes it harder for me when I'm trying to date. And yes, maybe it's a disappointment to you and Dad and Holly, but it's my choice to make. It's *my* faith and *my* beliefs, and I'm not going to lie to an entire community just to make my life or yours a little bit easier."

"Then don't lie. Find something else that gives you a place in this community. Find a faith community you don't *have* to lie to, but don't just give up entirely!"

"Do you really think I'm not *trying*?" I demanded. "Honestly, Mamma. Do you think I wanted this? To feel like I don't fit anywhere anymore? If I could go back to church and pretend I believed and not feel sick inside, I would have done it a long time ago and saved myself a world of hurt and grief."

My mother pursed her lips, giving me a long hard look, and I stared back, refusing to be intimidated. I wasn't a child anymore. I owed my parents a lot, and I was grateful to them for more, but I wasn't going to back down on this. I couldn't change the fact that I'd experienced something else, some*one* else, besides Jesus. I couldn't go back in time and erase Thor's presence, his warmth and comfort and peace, or the laughter I'd heard that night in the thunder and lightning. Thor had reached out when I'd needed a sign, and the very least I could do was to recognize that—to reach back, instead of betraying the gift with stubbornness and denial and lies.

"Well," she said, finally. "If you want to be one of the disaffected youth, I suppose there's nothing I can say to stop you. Maybe it will make your father more relatable somehow. Less perfect."

"It may not come up at all," Alex said. "With any luck, this will all be resolved quietly. And frankly, I can't imagine any reason it wouldn't be, unless someone is trying to fight dirty in the last weeks of the campaign."

My mother's eyes narrowed. "You can't truly believe anyone would stoop to that kind of thing. None of our constituents would condone that kind of behavior in their representative."

"Some might," Alex said. "If they felt threatened. If they thought that Joe might change his position on certain issues because of his family. People are scared, Irena. And they're angry. And this election cycle has been especially . . . difficult, because of the prevailing rhetoric in the presidential race. Joe has been a part of their community for a long time, but you know there were plenty of people who were upset when he spoke out in defense of refugees last year. He knew it was a risk, and we were careful about how we framed his argument, but he broke from what he knew his constituents wanted from him."

"They shouldn't have expected anything else," my mother said. "It isn't as though we've ever hesitated to help those in need before. Between our donations to the local food banks, the time I've spent working as a volunteer, and the drives we run every year to raise money for the shelters."

"I know," Alex said. "And most of our voters do, too. You've both always set a strong example of what one person can do to support and shape their community locally, but now that Joe is working with the Joint Committee on Taxation as chair of Ways and Means, it's about their taxpayer dollars being put on the line for programs they don't necessarily support. Our voters have always been a mixed bag on things like women's health and social programs to support single mothers, to say nothing of the abortion debate. In part *because* of their faith. And

Turner is targeting us on all of those issues. If he can use Emma to make it look like Joe is some kind of false Christian, talking the talk but not walking the walk, it would be a huge advantage to him."

"If this is a political attack on my daughter, Alex, I want everyone to know about it. You find out who is responsible, and Joe's reputation be damned, I will nail them to the wall!"

"Somehow I doubt it's going to be that simple," Alex said. "But I promise you, I'll do everything I can to protect your daughter, no matter who is responsible or whatever their reason is."

My mother smiled, reaching out to cover his hand with hers. "I don't doubt it for a moment, Alex. And neither does Joe. We're so glad she has you now."

That time, I *did* roll my eyes. "Oh please. As if I'm not perfectly capable of taking care of myself."

"Apparently not, Emma, or you wouldn't be in this position to begin with," my mother said. "If you'd done as I asked from the start, just involved yourself so people felt they *knew* this new you, whoever that is—"

"Of course." I shoved back my chair, grabbed my plate, and left the table. "Thanks for dinner, Mom. Sorry I can't stay for dessert."

Turning the water on full blast in the kitchen to rinse my plate effectively drowned out her response, and two minutes later, I had my boots and my coat on and was out the door. If Alex was determined to protect me, he could deal with her by himself. I certainly wasn't going to listen to any more of it.

I hadn't done anything wrong to deserve it. And if Alex was right— if this was just a dirty campaign tactic—it wouldn't have mattered what I'd taught. All of this was about Congressman Moretti, not me.

And it wasn't like I could undo the fact that I was his daughter.

Just like I couldn't and wouldn't turn my back on my faith.

CHAPTER TWENTY-FIVE:
AD 1000
FREYDÍS

I t felt as though the gods chased at winter's heels, for the days grew longer and warmer too quickly for all the work we had left to do before we might set sail, and we were all left scurrying to pack and arrange our supplies. My father had given us one of his precious cows, and a bull, of course, that we might have milk when the calves came, and Sonnung had purchased two goats to be bred for the same. The cattle would travel with Karlsefni, for which I was grateful. Sonnung's goats would be trouble enough.

Anxious as I was, as we all were, to ready our ships, it was no wonder that I lost track of the days.

"Your bleeding has not come," Sonnung said to me while we inspected the caulking of the ship. Thorhall had overseen the work and the scraping of the hull, but Sonnung was not convinced of the other men, and he insisted I must learn what to look for, besides, to keep myself safe should I sail without his sharp eyes.

At his words, I stopped short, watching his hand skim over the planking in a lover's caress. I knew his hands well, knew the pleasure they could give—but surely he could not be right. "It could be nothing."

He glanced at me over his shoulder, and I did not miss his smirk. "Your rhythm is as steady as the moon's, Freydís. Tell me that is not true."

I couldn't deny it, only stared at him like a mute fool, my thoughts spinning too fast and too tight. My throat thickened, a hard swallow doing nothing to soften the lump that had formed.

"Freydís." The humor had left his face, replaced with warmth and concern, and he drew me in, wrapping me in his arms and tucking my head beneath his chin. "I thought you knew and only feared to tell me so soon."

I shook my head. All of me shook. "I cannot be—it cannot be—"

He laughed, low and kind. "It is early yet, and you are not wrong. The babe might still be lost. But it is the start of a child, Freydís, do not doubt that. And if you have quickened now, you will quicken again, should it come to that."

Had it not been for his arms and his strength, I think I might have fallen. My legs felt stuffed with skyr instead of bone, and the trembling had not slowed. "I never thought."

"I know," he said, the words gentle. "I know what you thought. And before me, you might not have been wrong. But surely you see now, this is a gift. Thor's favor made flesh!"

My eyes blurred and I blinked the tears back, hiding my face against his chest while I gathered my strength. A child. A child to burden me, to prove my betrayal to Thorvard, and he wanted me to be glad.

I pushed free of him, stumbling back, but when he reached out to steady me, I slapped his hand away.

"Freydís—"

"No," I said.

He let out a breath, as though I'd cut him. "I cannot help what I feel, Freydís. For you, for the thought of our child. I will not temper it. I will not pretend I wanted none of it. But I thought you had come to trust me in this matter."

"Trust." A sob caught in my throat. "This has nothing to do with trust!"

"Does it not?" he demanded. "When you fear you will be burdened and trapped? That my child will tie you to this farm, shackle you to land? And all because you are so certain you face this alone. Because you do not trust me to care for you both."

"If Gudrid and Karlsefni learn of this, if Thorvaldur or Leif or Thjodhild hear the barest whisper, they will turn the men against me. We will have a ship but no crew with which to sail, and what then, Sonnung? How will trusting you stop it?"

His mouth formed a grim line. "They will not hear of it from me, and should they learn of the child in your womb, seek to stop you from taking ship, I will smuggle you aboard if I must."

"But it is not only that," I said. "It has never been only that. Women die, Sonnung. They are killed by the child they carry when their time comes, and even before. Those who live might still be crippled, but if not, should the gods guard them against the worst threats, they are certainly never the same again, their every thought taken up by the babe at their breast. You do not ask me just to carry your child, to birth it, but also to change. To become someone utterly else than what I am!"

He shook his head. "No."

"I would be softened," I said, the tears spilling from my eyes. I hugged myself, arms wrapped around my stomach. "Made weak and womanly, all my strength drained away to succor your babe. That is what you want, what you ask of me. As if I am unworthy as I am."

He reached for me again, more hesitant now, as though he feared I would swat him away a second time, but I did not have the heart to fight. I didn't want to be rid of him, not truly, not even if it meant I could not escape his child. I hoped only that he might understand, that he would see why a child would always feel to me a curse.

"I do not want you weak," he said, brushing my tears away. "And I would not talk with you at all if I did not think you a worthy match, a woman of strength. Do not doubt it for a moment, Freydís."

And I didn't, when he looked at me that way, when he spoke so fervently. I did not doubt it, but nor was it enough to chase the rest of my fears away.

He seemed to realize it, too, for he drew me in, wrapped me in his arms as if somehow it might protect me. "Death will not touch you, Freydís Thorswoman," he said, his lips against my ear. "And whatever change might be wrought, you will be strong still. I promise you that."

So many promises.

Too many to keep.

Spring followed swiftly after that, and for a second month, I shed no blood. Instead, I was troubled by a sour stomach in the evenings, settled only by a small store of mint Sonnung possessed. "Karlsefni has more in his supplies," he said when I worried there would not be enough to see me through. "And he's agreed to share it for the voyage—there are always a handful of men who need a bit of help calming their stomachs during the first days aboard ship. And once we set sail, your own sickness will be easily explained in the same way."

"Thorvaldur will know I do not suffer seasickness, and Thorhall, too. We sailed together from Iceland, and that trip, storm tossed and troubled as we were along the way, is not one which any of us have forgotten."

"Thorhall is too loyal to give you away, and Thorvaldur will be kept too busy with his own men and ship to concern himself with you."

It would be simpler once we were upon the sea, I knew. For even if the men learned I carried a child, it would be too late to turn back. It made me all the more anxious to shove off, but when we finally hauled the broad ships back into the sea after the long winter, Thorvaldur's took on water, requiring repairs to the hull. A delay we could ill afford.

"It will be a sevenday at most," Sonnung said when he found me pacing along the cliff's edge and glaring down at the ships, two floating gently and the third half-beached while the work was done. "And a good thing it is Thorvaldur's ship and not ours, for I doubt that Leif would be so generous with what is left of his lumber if it were."

But it was not so long a voyage from Iceland to Greenland that seven days would make no difference, if the winds and weather were with a man's ship—and from the height of the cliff it was more than clear that the sea had quieted. Thorvard was coming, and I had no intention of greeting him when he arrived.

"I want our ship ready and waiting, the men prepared to sail at a moment's notice," I said. "Whether Thorvaldur's repairs are finished or not."

"And do you know the way to Vinland, then, to guide us?" Sonnung asked, all practicality and reason in the face of my fear. "We will sail with Karlsefni, and whether Thorvard arrives or not, it will not stop us. It will not stop you."

"Are you so certain?"

"I am," he said. "And if you doubt me, consider that there is Gudrid to contend with. She will not leave you behind willingly."

I sighed. "Perhaps she might, if she knew the truth."

"No," he said. "Not even then. There are too few women sailing with us as it is, and she and Karlsefni both depend upon you."

"Depend upon me?" I snorted. "For what?"

Sonnung's lips curved. "I think you do not realize how terrifying you can be. All the men who sail with us have seen the way you fight. Even if I did not stand beside you, they would shrink at the sight of you with your hand upon a knife. Gudrid will seek you out once we make land, and keep you close, to make the men think twice."

"I will not be left behind to guard the farmhouse," I warned.

"Nor will Gudrid, unless I miss my guess. She has pushed and prodded Karlsefni from the start, and refused more than once to remain behind, though he's suggested it. Do not let her kindness or her faith fool you, Freydís. She is made of iron, same as you, though forged for a different purpose."

"And what is my purpose?" I asked.

He wrapped the long plait of my hair around his wrist, giving it a gentle, teasing tug. "I think you know the answer to that, Freydís Thorswoman."

I could not quite stop my smirk. "I know what you will say, at any rate."

"Do you?"

I turned my head, watching him instead of the ships below. "Love me and keep faith."

"And will you?" he asked, stepping closer. "Even after I have gone, will you remember your purpose?"

"I will honor the gods until my dying breath," I promised. "And not a day will pass that I will not think of you. All the more so if it is your brat upon my hip."

He laughed at my sourness and kissed me, and by the time we returned to my father's hall, not even the quivering of my stomach could keep the smile from my face.

For as long as I had Sonnung, I was certain I would find my way. And I would always have Sonnung. Or at least the memory of his love.

In those days, foolish as I was, it seemed enough.

At last the repairs were made, the supplies loaded, and after inspecting his ship, Thorvaldur's, and mine, Karlsefni told my father we would sail the next day with the tide. We would feast that night, for my father, Sonnung, Thorhall, and I had made blót that morning, sacrificing another goat to Thor, as my father had promised, and asking for our protection in return. In truth, I did not love the feasts, for it meant that Sonnung and I must sit apart, all the men on one side of the hall and the women on the other, and I often found myself far too near to Thjodhild for my comfort. Neither of us liked to be reminded of the other.

But when I returned to the hall from the hot spring, where Sonnung and I had gone to wash the blood from our hands and the sweat from our bodies, to enjoy one another with some small amount of privacy before we were surrounded by thirty-five men and there was nowhere to escape but the sea, Thjodhild was much too pleased at the sight of me.

"Ah, Freydís," she said, smiling widely as I passed her by. Sonnung had gone to check upon the two goats, which still needed loading, for it served no purpose to let them begin shitting and pissing within the hold before morning came, so I was alone, and it was hardly the first time she had taken the opportunity to needle me in his absence. "You've returned, and freshly washed, too. I can only imagine how pleased it will make your husband to find you so."

My cloak slipped through my fingers at her words, falling to the rushes, and I snatched it up again quickly, irritated with myself. I hated letting her know in any small way that she had found her mark. "By the time Thorvard arrives, I'm certain I'll be dirty again."

"Do you mean to find some patch of mud to roll in, then?" she asked. "If so, you'd better hurry, for your father rode out to greet him, and they'll be returning any moment now, I'm sure. Not a day too soon, either. Just think, if he had arrived tomorrow, how sorry he would have been to discover you gone. I prayed that Christ would give him fair winds, that Thorvard would come in time—and now he will know. He will see with his own eyes what you are and all that you've done."

I buckled a belt about my waist, over my long tunic, glad to have my knife close at hand once it was done. But I did not let my fingers stray to the hilt, only forced a smile to my lips, pretending I had no cause for concern. "Did you think I intended to hide it?"

Her face turned blotchy and red, her lip curling in a sneer of disgust. "Do not forget your husband is a Christian now, Freydís. And as such, he is not likely to listen to your father's excuses any longer. It will be up to Leif what becomes of you, and your brother won't look kindly on your whoring."

"As a married woman, what I do and how I behave is none of Leif's concern or yours," I said, but my temper was rising hot, and it took all my self-control not to spit in her face. I wrapped myself back in my cloak and brushed past her instead, eager to find Sonnung and warn him. "But do not worry, Thjodhild," I called back. "I do not forget what my husband has become. And if I have whored, it was done with great purpose—I promise you that."

It wasn't until the damp spring air touched my face that I breathed again, and the full meaning of Thjodhild's words fell on me with a ship's weight. But worse, the sound of hoofbeats drummed against the soft earth, and when I had gathered myself enough to raise my head and look, my heart constricted.

For Thjodhild had not been wrong, and riding toward the hall at my father's side was none other than my husband, Thorvard.

CHAPTER TWENTY-SIX:
AD 2016
Emma

Staring out the window of my office, I dragged the bronze Mjölnir pendant back and forth along its leather cord. I'd finally finished my course outline and sent it to the dean, and now I had nothing left to do but sit for the next twenty minutes, in case a student dropped by. They wouldn't. I could count on one hand how many times anyone had—and all of them during the first week. Students with questions about the syllabus, and a few others who needed exceptions or extra accommodation somehow. I didn't expect to hear from anyone again until mid-November, when they'd stop procrastinating and start actually considering paper topics. And even then, it would be mostly e-mails, not in-person meetings.

Which meant that in reality, for the next twenty minutes, I had nothing to do but worry.

The latest numbers for my father were still tighter than I knew he wanted, and while the dean hadn't called me in for another meeting, she hadn't told me I was in the clear yet, either. If she had to look like she was punishing me to satisfy my student, our meeting the previous day had made it clear she would. But a suspension or administrative leave would definitely draw attention that no one wanted. No one except my father's competition, anyway.

Normally I didn't pay attention to the candidates who ran against my dad. They never won, and I'd sort of tuned it out after twenty years of election cycles. We didn't even watch television during campaign seasons. But I'd finally done some research of my own on Mr. Turner, and the results had made Alex's suspicions seem more legitimate than I'd initially thought possible. Some of the accusations he'd made, the smear ads, were so out there, I couldn't really believe he'd found traction. Suggesting that my dad would support taxing churches if they didn't accept and help refugees, because the pope had made some kind of comment along those lines about church properties in Europe, and my father was such a devout Catholic, for example. On the one hand, it was kind of brilliantly slimy, but on the other . . .

No one could possibly believe that even if legislation of that kind might be proposed, it would ever make it through the House. And even if it did, by some miracle, make it through the House, the Senate would never agree to it, to say nothing of the president signing it into law.

But obviously Turner was gaining support. And whether it was because he'd targeted my father on the refugee issue in this kind of roundabout way, or because he'd directly attacked my father's pro-choice stance and support of women's health issues and funding, or because Dad was being branded as "establishment," just for his length of service, there was really no way of knowing. At least no way for *me* to know. Alex probably had access to a million different metrics and a pretty solid idea of what was doing the most damage. That was part of his job.

I really wondered, though, whether this kind of campaigning would have happened if it hadn't been for the tone set by the presidential primaries and the general election. There'd been so much mud thrown, I shouldn't have been that surprised that families might start getting splattered in the cross fire. And maybe that's why my mother had pressed me about going back to church and getting involved in the community. I was frustrated with her more often than not, but she was smart and savvy, particularly when it came to politics and campaigning. She'd probably seen the writing on the wall, and as much as I hated to admit it, I'd been too stubborn to listen.

But even if I had realized what she'd been trying to say—or why she'd been saying it—I wasn't sure I'd have made a different choice. My fingers closed around Mjölnir, the bronze cool against my palm. My beliefs mattered to me. Just as much as my mother's beliefs mattered to her. The idea of lying—of pretending to be what I wasn't—made me sick to my stomach. It had taken me so long to get here, to understand what it was I believed in, and to reconcile the personal experiences I'd had against the faith I'd been raised on.

Even after spending so much time in the church, as part of the congregation and community, I'd never really had any kind of spiritual experience before Thor. Honestly, I'd wondered more than once what people like Sarah were on when they talked about the joy of welcoming Jesus into their lives and accepting his presence in their hearts. It was so strange to me, so foreign. I knew it was what my mother felt, too, particularly when she volunteered. She said she sensed Jesus and God most clearly in her life when she served others, but I'd never known what that meant. Not really. Not until Thor and the thunderstorm. And after all that, after finally figuring myself out and realizing what I was experiencing was real—if still totally outside of my comfort zone—it obviously wasn't something I wanted to take any steps backward with. I'd fought too hard to win my peace and find my place. Such as it was.

There was a knock on the door, startling me out of my thoughts, and I spun in my chair, hoping I looked like I was some kind of busy and not just twiddling my thumbs. I jogged the mouse, willing the monitor to wake up at faster than a snail's pace, and cleared my throat.

"Come in!"

The door opened a crack, a woman poking her head through. "Professor Moretti?"

She wasn't anyone I recognized—not from my students, or the other faculty and staff. "Yes?"

"I was hoping you might have a moment to speak with me." The door swung wide, revealing a girl with a phone in her hand and an overeager expression on her face. "I'm one of the reporters for the *Hawks Weekly*, and I heard that you were being investigated as part of a complaint of religious discrimination? Since you're the congressman's daughter—"

I stood up and grabbed my coat, my purse, and my bag. "I'm sorry, I'm afraid that's going to be a firm 'no comment.'"

She backed up out of the office as I came toward her. My office hours were close enough to over, and if there was one thing I knew, it was to never ever speak to any kind of press. Whether it was the campus paper or the *New York Times*, it didn't matter.

"I was hoping to write an article in defense of free speech in the classroom," she hurried to say as I passed her and pulled the door shut, making sure it locked. "From what I heard, it sounded like you were being unjustly attacked for not teaching a pro-Christian view of history, and since I'm a Pagan—"

I hesitated at her admission, wishing—but I couldn't. Under other circumstances, I would have liked to talk to her. God knew, it was lonely, and if she was struggling even half as much as I had, questioning everything she'd experienced, everything she felt, everything she was, she could use all the understanding she could get. I wanted to help her, to support her. I would've, but for my father's sake, even for mine, I didn't see how I could risk it.

"I'm sorry," I said again, not meeting her eyes. "No comment."

She skipped a step and got in front of me, walking backward, and glanced down at her phone. "That's not a cross around your neck."

My hand flew to my pendant, which was exposed over the top of my clothes. I hadn't remembered—I thought I'd hidden it in the hurry to look like I was working. My face flushed, and I dropped it down under my sweater. To make this mistake now, after I'd been so careful for so long, and under these circumstances . . . I'd known that I couldn't hide it forever. That I would slip up eventually, but *now* of all times?

"That's Mjölnir," she said. "Thor's hammer. And not some comic book version, either."

"No comment," I said again.

"But if you're a Pagan, too—"

"I'm really sorry," I said, genuinely now. If it weren't for my father, the campaign. If it were just my job on the line and nothing else. But it wasn't. "I can't comment."

And then I ducked down the stairwell and flat out ran for the door. I'd never felt more like a coward in my life.

⁘

I paced my living room, debating with myself. Agonizing over what I needed to do. Of course I knew what I *should* do. But maybe I was being ridiculous. Blowing it all out of proportion. I hadn't answered any of her questions. And so what if she saw my pendant? That didn't necessarily have to mean anything significant. It could be easily explained away with a love for comic book movies, no matter what she thought personally, or even some family heirloom. Most people would buy that.

Unless they were Heathen or Pagan, too.

I wasn't ready for this. That's what it came down to. I didn't want to tell Alex, and I didn't want my father to have to deal with whatever new slimy smear tactics might come with it. If I didn't tell them— if I didn't say anything and this student wrote something about our non-interview—it wouldn't be that bad. And maybe as a Pagan, she would be sensitive enough not to spill something I clearly hadn't wanted spilled . . .

She'd had a phone in her hand. I grasped the hammer, squeezing the warm bronze hard. She'd looked at the phone, and *while* looking at the phone, commented on my pendant.

A smartphone. With a camera.

A camera with a picture?

And I didn't even get her name. I had no idea who she was, so it wasn't like I could call her and ask if she'd taken a picture. If I asked her to delete it, she'd know it was valuable to me. And if it was valuable to me, it could be valuable to someone else. Even if she didn't have a story to run for her own paper, even if the *Hawks Weekly* didn't see the potential, she might just as easily sell it to a paper that *did.*

No, I told myself. No. She was just a kid. And she knew how hard it was. She was Pagan, too. She'd been on my side, sympathetic to my situation. She wouldn't—she couldn't—do that.

Could she?

I swore, staring at my own phone where it sat accusingly on the coffee table.

I couldn't count on her silence, and if I couldn't count on her silence, then I couldn't not tell Alex. I couldn't let my parents be blind-sided by this—not right now. Maybe if it had been earlier in the campaign season, if Election Day weren't a matter of weeks away, that would be one thing. But now?

For all I knew, she could have been lying. She might have been another plant—if anyone had been a plant at all—sent to trip me. How anyone here could know that I was Heathen, I really, honestly, didn't know. But it didn't even have to be that. Maybe it wasn't about getting me to reveal my non-Christianity, just about getting me to say something anti-Christian in relation to history. Something that they could use against me in this discrimination case. Something that would reflect badly on my father's campaign.

I wasn't sure which was worse: a picture of me wearing a hammer in place of a cross, or some thoughtless comment that might have gotten me fired. At this point, I was pretty screwed either way, and unfortunately, my father probably was, too.

My hands were shaking so badly that I fumbled my phone, dropping it on the carpet between my feet before I finally managed to pick it up and compose a message.

```
Student   reporter   found   me   on   campus
today. Might have gotten a compromising
picture. Not sure what to do.
```

And then I hit "Send" before I chickened out.

Because the way Alex was going to look at me when I told him the rest—my heart hurt just thinking about it.

CHAPTER TWENTY-SEVEN: AD 1000

FREYDÍS

I've brought you your ship at last, my love," Thorvard said by way of greeting, grinning broadly as he swung off his horse. "And with time enough to sail her out again, if you wish it, for we had swift winds and kind seas for our journey."

I did not move, my whole body stiff at the sight of him and my gaze straying toward the stables, where Sonnung had just appeared. Sonnung's gaze was hot, and his hand was already upon the hilt of his knife, threat in every line of his body. But I only shook my head, meeting his eyes instead of Thorvard's, begging him to wait. To hold. Only after Sonnung released his knife did I turn my focus back to the man I loathed.

My husband hesitated at my indifference, the smile slipping from his face as he closed the distance between us. I did not miss the silver cross hanging from his neck, nor the absence of Thor's hammer.

"You're still angry with me."

"You're still Christian." I nodded to the cross. "More Christian now than when you left."

"Iceland is Christian," he said, his voice firm. "It will be made law at the Althing this summer. A bloodless conversion!"

"Bloodless but for the men who were tortured by King Olaf in Norway, you mean. The men he killed when they refused to convert."

"Bloodless," Thorvard said again. "For no Icelander killed another. Over Olaf, we had no control."

"Iceland has betrayed their gods and their ancestors, then," I said. "Better if they had all fought and died, for at least then they would have kept their honor."

"If what you say is true, Thorvard, then it is cause for celebration," Leif said. He'd gone to meet my husband as well, it seemed, but I had overlooked him while Sonnung loomed. My brother slapped Thorvard upon the back. "We feast tonight already, to honor our friends, but Gudrid and Karlsefni will be as pleased as I am to hear of this, even if your wife cannot be made to see sense."

"I see a son who would insult his father and his gods by feasting in celebration of their defeat," I said, spitting at their feet. "And I see a man who betrayed his wife because he was too soft and weak to plant her. But we will see what good your Christ's sorcery will do you when you sleep alone, for I will not have a Christian in my bed, husband or no."

And then I walked away, ignoring his sputtering at my back.

"Dísa," my father warned as I passed him, and he turned his horse to follow, for he had not dismounted yet. Too stiff to slip from his saddle so easily as the others, and unwilling to show his weakness before so many. My voice and my insults had carried farther than I'd intended, drawing even the slaves from their work, and Karlsefni's men from the hall. Sonnung stood among them, warmth and pride in his gaze, but I dared not go to him.

"Forgive me, Father," I said, for his ears only now. "But has not Thjodhild already proven I have the right?"

His eyes crinkled at the corners, and I watched him tamp a smile from his lips, bending it into a frown. "No man has the right to force you, that is true enough, but you might reconsider all the same. If only to preserve some small amount of peace beneath my roof before you sail away."

"If Thjodhild has her way, and Thorvard, I doubt I will sail free of my husband now," I said, looking back to see Leif drawing him inside. Thorvard glanced at me, his jaw tight, but allowed himself to be led. The cowardly swine.

"Perhaps you would have a better chance of it if you treated him with kindness instead of scorn," my father said. "I do not know how much longer you can carry on this way. He's as likely to divorce you as not, and what will you do then? Without him, you'll suffer beneath your brother's authority when I am gone."

I sighed, stroking his horse's neck. "If we are successful in Vinland, perhaps I will not return at all."

My father grunted, unhappy with my response. But we had reached the stable, and Thorhall had arrived to help my father down. I looked away, so as not to shame him, focusing instead on holding the mare, keeping her still while he dismounted.

"I do not think Leif will tell him about Sonnung, no matter what Thjodhild might like—the news Thorvard has brought should satisfy her for this night. But he will learn the truth, Dísa."

"And when he does, he will know how I felt when he chose to be baptized," I said. "He will know that he cannot betray me without consequence."

"I am not so certain that will be the lesson he learns," my father said as Thorhall led his horse away. "But I suppose there is little to be done about it, either way."

Leif and Thjodhild succeeded in fouling our feast with their celebration of Iceland's coming conversion, but I bit my tongue and refused to respond to their barbs. My temper had already caused trouble enough for my father, and I was beginning to regret the way I had greeted my husband, if only for my father's sake. But Thorvard seemed happy enough at my father's side, treated as an honored guest after his time away, and I pushed the food around my plate. In an attempt to distract myself from Sonnung's presence when I could not have him, I drank far too much mead—supplied, Gudrid told me, by my husband, who had brought a wealth of provisions along with my new ship.

"I do not expect you to love him, or even to forgive him," Gudrid murmured, sitting beside me at the women's table. "But you might have humiliated Thorvard in private, at the least, rather than create more bad blood between you. He is not so awful of a man as that."

"He is not cruel, I suppose, that is true enough, but do not be fooled into believing he is anything other than a worm," I told her, glaring at him over the rim of my cup, though he did not seem to notice. "If he were kind and good, he would not have converted, for he knew well enough it was because he was not Christian that my father agreed to the marriage at all. Nor is he the slightest bit able to make up for his foolishness with his skill in bed. All he does is grunt and thrust, without even the smallest consideration for my pleasure."

Gudrid grimaced, shifting uncomfortably upon the bench. "And he is truly three-legged?"

"Near enough," I said flatly. "If only he knew how to use his spear, I might have forgiven him much."

"Poor Erik," she sighed. "He tried so hard to protect you and delivered you to your enemy instead."

"I should have listened to Thorstein and Thorvaldur," I said. "I should have refused to marry him altogether, ship or not."

But it was as my father had said—there was little to be done about it now. I could not divorce him. Not as aged as my father had become.

It might have been a different affair if Sonnung had been willing to marry me, but I knew him well enough by now not to dream of an impossibility. And if Thorvard divorced me for my infidelity, it would leave me ruined at the least. Truly, what would have served me best was to be widowed, and I spent the rest of the meal imagining all the ways Thorvard might die while I was gone: thrown from his horse, drowned in a storm at sea, even a fall from one of the steep cliffs would do.

But soon the food was cleared away, the tables taken down, and Karlsefni, after thanking my father with words and gifts for his hospitality, came to reclaim Gudrid, ignoring the hoots and bawdy laughter of his men as he led her from the feasting hall. I had no doubt from the way he looked at her that he thought as Sonnung did, that he should enjoy her while they had a bed and the space to do so, and my gaze strayed again to my wandering warrior.

He saw me watching and rose, invitation in his eyes, holding a single stem of straw, which he dropped to the rushes on his way to the door. My face flushed, for I knew what he wanted—we had used such a sign at the start of our affair, and I had no doubt he meant for me to meet him in the barn—but I dared not follow too close upon his heels with Thorvard still in the hall.

So I went to my husband instead, taking Karlsefni's empty bench. My father had retired, too, leaving Leif to celebrate as he wished. In truth, I doubted my father had the strength to fight him. "We must speak."

Thorvard's lips pressed thin. "I think you have said enough."

I shook my head. "We must speak, for I leave in the morning with the tide, on Thorstein's ship—now mine."

I had his attention then, sudden and fierce, and his cup slammed down so hard against the table that mead splashed over the sides. "What?"

"I've promised Gudrid and Karlsefni, and I will not betray my word simply because you've arrived. I could hardly refuse them after such a generous gift, besides, or risk insulting our new brother."

"I will sail with you, then," Thorvard said. "They cannot object to another ship."

"My father needs you here," I said. "All the more so with Gudrid, Thorvaldur, and me upon the sea." My eyes narrowed. "Unless you would forswear yourself."

His jaw went tight. "I did not promise you I would never become Christian, Freydís, whatever you might think."

"You promised to support my father and me," I snapped. "You promised, and then you followed Leif and Thjodhild to Christ, knowing it is through their faith that they have worked against my father. Now I ask you to remain here, to fulfill the oath you have already broken in spirit if not in truth. Will you do it, or will you prove yourself as false as your worthless god?"

"If you are so concerned for your father, why do you leave at all?" he demanded. "You would abandon him while condemning me for following where you led."

"Gudrid has need of me as her companion, and I knew you would arrive before long," I said, impatient now. "Would you have me make an enemy of Karlsefni?"

"I would have you behave as a proper wife," he said. "Not announce before every man assembled that you will refuse to allow me in your bed. Not sailing off alone, intent upon leaving your husband behind."

I lifted my chin. "I am no less of a proper wife than Thjodhild, if that is how you would measure, for she still refuses my father her favors as a result of her faith. And it is my right to sail, to seek my fortune upon the seas if I wish, just as it has been yours. Or does it make you a poor husband for leaving me behind, for engaging in your trade and travel?"

"I sailed for your sake. For the ship you demanded as a wedding gift," he snarled.

"And did you expect once I had it, I would follow you meekly from shore to shore? Truly, Thorvard, do not tell me you are so great a fool as that."

His face turned red, from his neck to his ears, and I could not stifle my laughter, though I knew it would offend him. I was simply honestly astonished that he might have believed such a thing for even a moment beyond our wedding feast.

Thorvard growled, draining the mead from his cup and slamming it back upon the table for a second time. "Go then," he said. "But I warn you, Freydís, when you return and winter comes, it will be different. You will obey me as you should."

I snorted, rising, for his threat sounded toothless to me. "If you wanted obedience, you'd have done better to marry Gudrid."

And then I left him to find Sonnung in the barn.

CHAPTER TWENTY-EIGHT:
AD 2016
Emma

I'm beginning to think you might be a full-time job," Alex said when I opened the door for him later that afternoon.

He'd tugged the knot of his tie loose, and his hair was a mess. Like he'd been interrupted during a make-out session and hadn't managed to glance in the mirror before he jumped in the car. But more than any of that, he looked tired.

"You didn't have to come," I said. "I'm not—I mean, it could be nothing, really. I just wanted to give you a heads-up, that's all."

He lifted an eyebrow. "Are we going to have to go through this every time?"

I flushed, stepping back to let him in. "I'm not usually this much of a problem child, I swear. And I hate that all of this is falling on you— that I'm just more *work*."

"You're not *just* work," he said, closing the door behind him. "The timing could be better, sure, but on the bright side, it means we're stuck with one another for a little longer. For which I thank the universe."

I rolled my eyes. "Don't confuse my mother's matchmaking with the weaving of the Fates, Alex."

He smiled. "It wasn't just your mother doing the matchmaking, you know. I think she mostly just pitied me. But the dinner invitations might have been my idea initially."

"Then you created a monster, and you have no one to blame but yourself when *you* have to tell her it didn't work out after all," I said.

"It's not going to be an issue," he said.

"It already *is* an issue."

He laughed. "It doesn't *have* to be."

It was exasperating, and the smug confidence in his voice—I didn't know if I wanted to slap him or kiss him. "I didn't text you as part of some game. And believe me, if I'd thought it was something I could get away with never telling you, I wouldn't have texted you at all."

"All right." His gaze softened, and I knew he wanted to argue, to talk more about the relationship we didn't actually have, but he swallowed instead and shifted gears with me. "You said something about a photo?"

I sat down, pressing the heels of my hands against my eyes. Not that it was going to do anything to relieve the pressure behind them. I'd almost made peace with the fact that I was 95 percent sure I was going to cry at some point in the middle of all this. Stupid crying. Why was I always stupid crying in front of Alex?

"I'm not completely sure, but there's a distinct possibility, yes."

He sat down beside me on the couch, the springs creaking. "What of?"

I sat up, drawing the leather cord from around my neck and pulling it over my head. My chest tightened, and I felt cold without the hammer against my skin.

"This."

I forced myself to set it down on the coffee table in front of us and snatched my hands back before I could caress the bronze. I couldn't even look at Alex. It didn't matter that he might not realize what it meant, what any of this meant. I didn't want to see his confusion, either. I was just as tired of blank looks as everything else. It was funny, really. My mother would have known exactly what it was. Anyone on the Icelandic side of my family would have recognized it immediately.

"Okay," he said slowly. "You're going to have to help me out, Emma, because you're acting like this is some kind of bomb that you've just dropped, but so far, I'm not seeing the fuse."

"When I was a little girl, my auntie Anja gave me this," I said. "The pendant, Mjölnir, is the symbol of Thor. The Norse god. I never wore it, of course. My mother and father didn't approve of Auntie Anja's beliefs, and good Catholic girls wear crosses, not hammers. But I brought it with me to college. I didn't know why. It took me a long time to figure out why."

He touched it then, picking it up carefully from the table. "When you said you weren't Christian anymore . . ."

"I'm a Heathen," I said, my throat thick. "I believe in and worship Thor."

Alex let out a long breath, rubbing his thumb over the hammer. I wasn't sure if he was staring at it or me, and I didn't want to know, so I clasped my hands in my lap to keep from grabbing the pendant back and didn't look up.

"What are the odds that this reporter knows what it means? What she has?"

"She said she was Pagan. I don't know if that's true or if she was trying to bait me into revealing my supposed anti-Christian classroom agenda, but she recognized it. She knows what it is and what it means."

"Why didn't you tell me, Emma?" His voice was low, uncertain. Not the spin doctor, but the man who wanted to date me. "We talked about religion that first night over dinner, and you didn't say a word."

"I wasn't sure what you would think," I said, blinking back the tears that were building behind my eyes. "And it's easier to be—to let people think I'm just a lapsed Catholic. Or some kind of agnostic. Even an atheist. The minute you say 'Thor,' people think you're worshipping some fictional comic book character, or that you're some kind of crazy. And I spent so long, Alex, so long fighting that battle already. Trying to decide if I really *was* losing my mind. Because I was talking to a god that couldn't possibly be real, right? That's what we're raised to think. That there are no other gods out there. Just . . . just the devil. Or mental illness, I guess. Those are pretty much the only options." I laughed, harsh and humorless. "Even among Heathens—every community is different, and there are plenty who don't actually believe in the gods. They're just metaphors, or it's just a way of living, not a spirituality. That's fine, I totally respect it, but where does that leave me?"

"When?" he asked. "I mean, for how long? Unless you don't want to—"

I shrugged a shoulder. "Since college. Maybe since before college, but it took me a long time to come to terms with it. To realize, after doing an incredible amount of reading and research, that I couldn't fit what I was experiencing inside the Christian framework I'd been raised with. The last year, maybe, since I've really come to terms with the fact that I'm just not Catholic anymore. That I'll never be Christian again. When you're raised with just one reference point—you've probably never heard the way my father talks about Auntie Anja. She never comes up if he can help it, but he's always been so dismissive. As if it couldn't possibly be real. Like it was all just a joke. And now I'm part of the joke, too."

"That's why you were so upset," he said, gently now. "About this thing with your student. Why you've been so on edge about the whole mess. It wasn't just about the history."

"Nothing I taught them in that class was untrue," I said. "All I did was ask them to consider the sources and the culture of the time, the perspective from which history was written, and take that into account while they were reading. To consider for just a minute the role religion might have played in the conflicts during those periods. That's it."

"I know," he said, setting the pendant back on the tabletop. "I know, Emma—I'm not suggesting anything else. I just didn't realize before how personal it was for you. No matter how long ago it happened. You're standing in front of a classroom and teaching students about the persecution of your own faith—the faith of your ancestors. And then being accused of religious discrimination because of it. That's—I'm so sorry. I'm sorry I didn't get it until now."

I shook my head. "It doesn't matter."

"It does," he said. "I just wish it hadn't taken . . . I wish you were telling me this because you wanted to share it with me, not because someone found you out and you're worried that it's going to wreck your dad's campaign."

I took my hammer back, slipping the leather cord over my head and tucking it beneath my shirt again. "It isn't that I didn't want to tell you, Alex. It's just . . . faith is so personal. And there are so many weird associations. White supremacists and neo-Nazis and Odinists, warping Norse myth to suit their own twisted ideologies. I didn't want you to think—"

"I could never have thought that," he said. "I know you and your family well enough by now that someone would have to show me video evidence before I even started to wonder if it was possible, and even then, I would probably think it was faked somehow."

I half smiled, daring to look up at him for the first time. He was all warmth and concern and longing. "I just didn't want you to look at me like I was losing my mind."

He tucked a strand of my hair behind my ear. "I don't think you're losing your mind. I think you have faith in something bigger than yourself, and however you want to name it—or whatever name it chooses to call itself—that's between you and your god. As long as it's not hurting anyone, I'm not sure it really makes any difference."

"It makes a difference when it comes to children," I said. "When it's time to talk about how you want them raised, and in what tradition."

"Why does it have to be either-or?" Alex asked. "You're living proof that you can raise a kid with all the best intentions, strictly in one particular faith, and they still might end up believing in something else."

I laughed. "That isn't very Catholic of you."

"I thought we already established that I wasn't a very *good* Catholic. What with the skipping church to brunch with you and all."

"You could have gone on Saturday," I said.

"But I didn't. And if I go to hell because I chose you over mass, then that eternity of suffering will be worth it."

I snorted. "You say that now."

"I'll say it forever," he said firmly. "I *like* you, Emma. I've liked you since before you moved back home, and every new challenge you bring me makes me like you more. You're honest and authentic, and even when you keep something like this from me, you don't pretend you're *not* holding something back. I respect that. I respect you. And now that I know your biggest secret, will you please, I'm begging you, give me another shot?"

"How do you know it's my biggest secret?" It was a weak deflection, and I knew it, but I wasn't sure how else to respond.

"Emma."

I let out a breath. "It wasn't—you know this isn't why—"

"I know," he said, and his hand found mine. "I swear to you, Emma, I will never use the word *us* to describe anything other than you and me, together, again."

"Ha."

"I mean it," he said, leaning forward. "Lesson learned, cross my heart. I will never regret anything more than my response to you that day. Never."

"You know what they say about the overuse of the word *never*, Alex."

"I'm pretty confident about my usage right now."

I closed my eyes, pressing my lips together. "I can't ask you to do this. You can't make me a priority in your life right now. As much as I might want that in theory, if my father loses this campaign because you were worrying about sparing my feelings instead of doing what needed to be done, I don't think I could forgive myself."

He laughed. "*Now* I think you're losing your mind."

"I'm serious, Alex," I said, holding his gaze. "It makes me crazy, and maybe it's ruining my life right now, but I'm not going to mess up my dad's career by making you promise not to do your job. These next six weeks are going to suck, and I'm going to just have to deal with that—and support you, and him, until it's over."

"Support me?" he asked, his eyes narrowing.

I nodded.

He grinned. "Does that mean that you're dating me again?"

"It means," I said, pretending exasperation, "that the next time I invite you in after dinner, I'm expecting you to say yes."

That was when he kissed me. His lips on mine, making my heart fly and my whole body flush, even innocent as it was. He pulled back slightly to look at me, asking that silent question that good men ask—waiting for me to answer. To tell him *yes*.

I leaned forward and kissed him back.

And there was nothing innocent about the rest.

CHAPTER TWENTY-NINE:
AD 1000
FREYDÍS

We did not sail the lean fighting ships meant for fast and brutal strikes and war, our hulls far more buxom, made wide and deep to carry heavier loads. We had fewer oars, and the men used their sea chests for benches to leave more room for cargo and supplies. Perhaps we were not so maneuverable or quick as a true dragon ship, but when the wind filled our sail and the *knarr* cut through the sea, it was exhilarating all the same.

"I told the men to stow the oars and stretch their legs and backs while they can," Sonnung said, coming to stand beside me at the bow. After nearly a year on my father's farm, I had forgotten what he looked like with sword and axe belted to his hip, and heavy leather armor atop his mail. He was dressed for war, as richly as any jarl, and I wondered if it was only for the ease of carrying it all on his person or because he had feared some trouble as we left. "Now that the fjords are behind us, and the wind obliging, we should have a quiet day."

"It has been so long since I have been upon the open seas," I said, drinking in the sight of it—slate blue with white foam crests, breaking against the bow. The sky was clear and crisp, spotted by only a handful of birds as Greenland shrank behind us. My first deep breath of sea air and sweat made me feel like a child again, sailing beside my father. Tall and strong and fierce, with ships beyond number at his back, following him upon a grand adventure into new lands. "I have dreamed of this day."

"And the gods have given it to you," Sonnung said, smiling at my pleasure. "I have given it to you."

I laughed, leaning against the rail and studying him now, instead of the sea. Fond memories were all well and good, but it was my adventure now. Mine and Sonnung's. And that made it all the sweeter. "You will offend the gods if you do not grant them their due."

"And who suggested to Gudrid that she might part with Thorstein's ship, now that she would have Karlsefni's wealth alongside her own?" he said. "Who told Karlsefni that you would join him on this journey, if he only asked, and by your presence he might have greater protection for his wife, for you had skill with a blade and a fearsome reputation among Brattahlid's men?"

My cheeks warmed, and though it pricked my pride to know I had required so much of his help, it also softened my heart. "You spoke for me."

"I spoke for you," he agreed. "And I will see you safely to Vinland, too, though I know you think I was only boasting about my skill upon the sea."

But I had watched him from the moment this journey had been decided. I had watched him comb over every inch of the ship, helping to scrape the hull and caulk the planks, to rig the sail and load our supplies. I had seen how his eyes had narrowed as he studied the sky, his hand steady upon the rudder as we rowed our way out of the fjord. He had known the very moment that the sail would catch, and even when he had given up his place at the steerboard to Thorhall, he had given him strict direction first.

"Where did you learn to sail so well?" I asked.

He gave the ship one last glance, assuring himself all was in order, no doubt, before settling beside me against the rail. "My father taught me first, though he much preferred to wander by horse and upon firm land, but when he befriended a child of Njǫrd, my brother and I learned all we could from him as well."

"Was he truly a child of Njǫrd? Or just skilled enough to claim it as a boast?"

Sonnung's lips curved. "He was a true descendant of the god—of that there is no doubt."

"I wonder sometimes if the gods still walk among us," I said. "Or if they have retreated to their shining halls, offended by our foolishness, our cowardice before the invading Christ."

"They are here among us," Sonnung said, confident. "Thor and Odin and Freyr—they will not abandon the men and women who have kept faith, I promise you that. But even Odin can only do so much to thwart fate, and the Norns bind us all, men and god alike, within their threads. We can only do what we are meant to, nothing less and nothing more."

My gaze strayed back toward Greenland, still filling the horizon behind us, and I frowned. "There is nothing to stop Thorvard from following should my father's health fail while we are gone."

Sonnung lifted his arm, and I slipped beneath it, ignoring the pinch of mail and leather, and the poke of his sword's hilt into my ribs. "The gods will keep him from us. And when it is his time, your ancestors will embrace your father, welcoming him proudly to your family's mound. Or, if he is very fortunate, perhaps Thor will honor Erik for his loyalty and welcome him to his great hall in Thrudvang instead. Would he like that, do you suppose? For surely there is no man more deserving of such an honor, for his sheer stubbornness alone."

I smiled at the thought but shook my head. "He would not want to be kept forever apart from his sons, I think. But if he returns to the mound, he will have hope that their spirits might find him still."

"And you, Freydís Thorswoman, would you wish for the same?"

"I do not know," I admitted. "It would be difficult to refuse such an honor, but I am not certain I would wish to leave my father behind a second time."

But when I looked up at Sonnung, his freshly trimmed beard shining copper in the sun, and his eyes even warmer on mine, I thought I might not be unhappy in Thrudvang, so long as he was beside me.

❦

Thorvaldur broke away to sail north in search of walrus, for the ivory and pelts would be valuable in trade, but we stayed near enough to shout to Karlsefni and Gudrid's ship, and Sonnung seemed to always know the swiftest course, finding the currents that would speed us upon our way and avoiding those that might bewilder us once we had left all sight of land behind.

"He is the finest shipmaster I've ever seen," Thorhall said to me after Sonnung had relieved him from the rudder. Sonnung had not worn his mail and leather or his sword beyond that first day, but his axe was still fitted against his hip, the broad head strapped to his belt, half hidden by the leather, and the stub handle hanging down—or perhaps it was not an axe at all. "His sense for sea and sky is unrivaled by any man I have ever known, and at your father's side, I've met a good many."

"The gods favor him," I agreed. "Of that we can have no doubt."

Thorhall's eyes narrowed, and aged as he might have been, I knew his gaze was still sharp, his mind shrewd. "Or perhaps it is something else."

"What else could it possibly be?"

He rolled his lips between his teeth and stood. "Have you seen his axe?"

"Should I have?"

Thorhall grunted and walked away, back down the length of the ship, between the rowing benches made of sea chests, where the men rolled dice and played *tafl*, often cursing the pitch of the deck for a bad roll or upset pieces. We'd had little use for the oars, and clear weather for days. Thorhall bowed his head when he reached Sonnung at the stern, and whatever words were exchanged, they must have been pleasant, for Sonnung tipped his head back and laughed before inviting him to sit and clapping him upon the back.

"Ho!"

I turned my attention across the water, for the shout had come from Karlsefni and Gudrid's ship, and one of his men waved wildly, pointing ahead. I leaned out around the prow to look, and then drew suddenly back as a spout of water erupted from the sea.

"A whale," Sonnung called out to me, grinning. "A shame we have not the means to hunt it, for we would feast upon the meat for weeks to come."

The other men crowded against the rails, and the ship leaned slightly toward the monster, no more than a shadow beneath the water as it swam. Sonnung laughed again, and this time he was beside me, having given up the rudder to Thorhall for the moment.

"Watch," he said, pointing. And as if the whale had heard him, it rolled, one immense eye staring up at us and a long fin slapping against the waves, splashing us all with water. If Sonnung had not braced me, I might have recoiled from the intelligence in the monster's gaze, but a moment later the beast was gone, diving deep enough to all but disappear as it went on its way. I'd seen whales before, of course, but never so near as that.

"They're harmless enough for the most part, if you leave them be," Sonnung said. "But when they've been speared I've seen them turn upon the ship, breaching the water and crashing into the vessel, or coming up beneath to ram it and spill the men into the sea. It is wild and dangerous and thrilling. A true test of courage and strength, even for a god."

"And how did you fare?" I asked him.

His smile was sly. "I lived to tell the tale, as you see, or I could not have come to you."

"What of the whale?"

"The whole village feasted upon its flesh until our bellies were stuffed," he said. "And there was enough still that we were not hungry again the whole winter through."

Then he squeezed my arm, flashed me a blinding smile, and moved away. Back to Thorhall and his rudder, as the sail snapped overhead, the wind propelling us on.

⚜

We met no storms as we sailed, nor were we ever becalmed, which I was certain was due to Sonnung's skill. It was still more than a week before we saw land again, barely a smear beneath the glare of the setting sun, but enough to cause the men to shout and celebrate. We brought our two ships together, tying them bow and stern, and Karlsefni shared the last of his good mead, leaving us with only ale until we found honey enough to ferment our own.

I sipped mine sparingly, for my stomach had gone sour again, and the mint was proving less helpful since we had found the open sea. Our men had thought nothing of my heaving, as Sonnung had suggested, and it mattered less now, regardless. But I was still uneasy when Gudrid found me tucked against the prow of my ship, the wooden cup pressed against my breast and my eyes shut tight against the lurching in my stomach.

"You look ill, Sister," she said, settling beside me on the deck. "Surely you are not displeased that we have found the lands we seek so soon."

I forced a smile to my lips in response to her teasing and took a careful sip of my mead. "You must be eager for solid earth, and Karlsefni, too."

"As eager as you, I'm certain," she said, resting her head against the prow at our backs. "It is one thing to be among so many men upon the farm in winter, when you can still slip away to the barn or the pit house for some quiet, even in the cold and dark. But there is nowhere to go on a ship, no privacy at all. Karlsefni's men are better than most, but I worry already that the lack of women will prove a sore point before long."

There were only five of us, the third a wife of Karlsefni's closest friend, who served as his navigator in part, and I was certain Thjodhild had poisoned her against me, for she had spent the whole winter showing me her back. Not that I cared, then or now, but I imagined it would trouble Gudrid after we were settled if it kept on. The two others sailed upon Thorvaldur's ship, which we had seen no sign of yet.

"We had few enough at Brattahlid to draw from," I said. "Even among the slaves."

"Which is why I worry we will not have long before the trouble starts," Gudrid said. "We'll have to sail to Iceland when we have something to trade, and hope more women will come west. Or at the least, we might bring back a handful of slaves to give the men relief. Before they look to you and me for the purpose."

"Sonnung would kill them first," I said. "And Karlsefni would do the same in your defense."

"Better if it did not come to that," Gudrid said, half smiling. "But I am glad Sonnung is so loyal that he would guard you as he would a wife. I only wish—I wish he would marry you. That you might have this happiness forever."

I looked out over the ships, finding Sonnung easily among the other men, for he towered over even Karlsefni, and the rings on his arms glinted in the last of the sunlight. "It would not be so sweet if it were not stolen. And I think Sonnung has already given more of himself than he is used to, but he could not resist the call of new lands and new fortunes to be made. If we had not sailed this spring, I am not certain he would have stayed even this long."

"I am," Gudrid said. "And I do not believe for a moment it is the promise of Vinland that has kept him at your side. From the moment he arrived, he wanted only you, and these last months, I have never seen a man more content."

I grimaced. "Because I carry his child, Gudrid. That is why he is so pleased."

She stared at me, her eyes wide and bright. "Truly?"

"And why I sit here in the shadows, sipping at my mead and chewing mint leaves to keep from losing my supper," I said, irritated by it all. "From the start, he wanted me. But what he wanted *from* me was a child planted in my womb, raised to love Thor as he does. He knew even before I had realized it myself, he was so intent upon it."

"But Freydís, what will you do? Thorvard will hardly believe it is his—unless you laid with him that last night?"

My lip curled. "I would have rather slept with a goat than welcome him."

"But you might have persuaded him—" Gudrid swallowed the rest, no doubt realizing the futility. And if I had not trusted the promises Sonnung had made, perhaps I would have been desperate enough to confuse the issue in my husband's eyes, but I had come this far on faith, and the thought of betraying Sonnung in such a way had turned my stomach.

"It will be as the Norns weave it, Gudrid, and I will not pretend otherwise. Besides, I could not give Thorvard the satisfaction of thinking

Christ had given his seed the strength to root after all this time. Better he believe himself cuckolded by Thor's power, by far."

She sighed. "I wish you would not see Christ as your enemy."

"I wish your Christ did not command his Christians to make war on me."

"Not all of us believe that is what he wants of us," Gudrid said. "Some of us only want our peace and the freedom to worship as we wish."

"Then you are too few, and too weak," I told her.

And then I leaned over the ship's rail and retched.

CHAPTER THIRTY:
AD 2016
Emma

I hope this isn't going to be another dramatic dinner," my mother said when she met us at the door. Well, she met Alex at the door, anyway, and took his coat, all gracious hostess until she turned her gaze on me.

I'd been avoiding her since the night I walked out, and neither one of us was quite ready to forgive the other completely, but it was Friday, and my father was back from Washington, and it was time to rip off the Band-Aid. Besides, like I'd told Alex after we'd finished the not-so-innocent portion of our evening the day before, the longer I waited, the more likely it was that this would come out and they'd be caught completely off guard. Which wouldn't do anyone any favors, really.

"I'm afraid I'm going to disappoint you," Alex said, smiling. "We're not quite out of the woods yet. But I don't think Emma is going to be making any early escapes this time."

"Ha-ha," I said. "No promises. And you could have said something last time, for the record."

"It's not going to come to that tonight," Alex said, his hand finding the small of my back as we followed my mother through the house. "And if it does devolve into something unconstructive, I'll be leaving with you. In solidarity."

My stomach did a little happy flip, and I felt a smile on my lips, in spite of my dread. "Won't that be a nice change?"

"I think so," he murmured, pressing a swift kiss to my temple before we left the hallway. He'd been right about his lack of self-control. If we hadn't had to worry about my parents seeing his car still in the driveway come morning, he wouldn't have left at all last night. But neither one of us wanted to have this dinner with any more Catholic guilt than absolutely necessary. And that meant at least keeping the illusion of chastity—for the moment.

Of course, if my parents actually believed I was still a virgin, this dinner was going to be that much worse. I hadn't exactly been sneaking around with David, after all, and if they'd ignored *those* signals, then they were really going to be shocked by the whole Heathen thing.

"It's going to be fine, Emma," Alex said.

"You keep saying things like that, but I'm not sure we have the same definition of what *fine* means." Not that it mattered, really. It was my stress level he was talking to—I was practically vibrating—so I forced myself to take a deep, steadying breath, then let it out slowly, willing the tension in my shoulders to slip away.

"Emma!" My father bear-hugged me in the kitchen before drawing back with a grin. "Your mother tells me you and Alex have been spending plenty of time together this last week."

"Only because I've been making him so much work," I said, pressing a kiss to my father's cheek.

He gave Alex a firm handshake and a clap on the shoulder. "At least I know whatever Emma comes up with, we're all in good hands."

"I do my best," Alex said. "But I don't think any of us were quite expecting things to go the way they have."

"And which way is that?" my mother asked. "I assume you're referring to something more than Emma's trouble with work."

I sighed at her tone, grabbing a glass out of the cabinet and filling it with water, even though what I really wanted was something extremely alcoholic. Because seriously—she acted like I'd planned everything to be as inconvenient as possible.

"Emma got caught by a student reporter at the college," Alex said, glancing at me as I leaned against the counter in front of the sink. "And we're concerned there might be some complications. But maybe we'd be better off waiting until we sat down—"

"I'm a Heathen," I said, drawing the hammer out from under my shirt. "And the reporter saw my necklace. I'd been distracted, thinking about the whole situation, and thought I hid it away before the door opened, but apparently I didn't, and she might have gotten a picture. I think she did get a picture. Definitely she recognized it for what it was."

My mother's lips pressed into a thin line, her face going from white to red. "This is Anja's doing, isn't it? All her talk about the Ásatrúarfélagið. And this new husband of hers. Surely you saw the press on that temple of theirs—even the high priest doesn't believe in those gods, not truly, not the way we believe in ours."

I shook my head. "It has nothing to do with Auntie Anja. And definitely nothing to do with the Icelandic Ásatrú fellowship. It's personal. And I wouldn't have even brought it up at all if this thing with the reporter hadn't happened."

"If you hadn't been so *careless*," my mother accused, "and now, of all times, when you know how crucial these last few weeks are!"

"It was an *accident*," I said, crossing my arms over my chest. "If you think I wanted to slip up like this, particularly when I'm being accused of anti-Christian religious discrimination in my classroom—"

"That's enough," my father said. "No one here thinks you did any of this on purpose, Emma."

I stared out the window so I didn't have to see the exhaustion that had settled over him. "I know this must be disappointing to you both."

Alex came to stand beside me, wrapping an arm around my waist. "I think it's brave. It takes a lot of strength to break from what you were raised to believe, to stand by your conviction of something most of the people around you can't, don't, or won't understand."

"Except she wasn't standing by it," my mother said. "She's been slinking about!"

"Because I knew if I told you, this was how you'd respond," I snapped back. "But I never lied to you. I told you up front that I wasn't going to church, and I wasn't going to pretend to be something I wasn't."

"You didn't tell the truth, either," my mother said. "You didn't trust us! And now you've endangered your father's campaign because of it."

"Irena," my father warned. "She has a right to her privacy. We may not agree with it, or with all her actions, but let's not fault her for choosing discretion. I assume, also, that you kept this from David?"

"Of course I kept it from David," I said, stung still by my mother's words—and my father's distinct lack of acceptance. "He only knew I wasn't particularly devoted to *his* faith. And I figured out early on that he wasn't going to be all that tolerant of mine."

"And this student reporter, what did you tell her?"

I rolled my eyes. "I'm not stupid. I didn't tell her anything. The most she got out of me beyond 'No comment' was 'I'm sorry.' But she said she was Pagan, and if it hadn't been for the campaign—I don't want to hide who I am, Dad. If there are pagans on campus, and I could've been honest with her, I might have been able to give her, all of them, some of the support I didn't have in college, when I was trying to figure all of this out for myself."

My father's gaze shifted to Alex before I'd even finished. "What do you think is the best way to handle this, if it leaks?"

"I don't think we should wait for it to leak, honestly," Alex said. "If Emma is willing, I think we should get out in front of this. Take it public ourselves and keep control of the story."

"And what story would that be?"

"That as a Catholic, you don't share your daughter's beliefs, but as a congressman and a father, you support and defend her freedom to believe and worship as she feels called to do," Alex said firmly. "It's a family values issue as much as it is First Amendment."

My father rubbed his forehead. "I need to think about this."

A hard lump rose in my throat. "Dad—"

"I said I need to *think*, Emma," he said. "And so do you. Because if this is just some phase, some belated rebellion . . . This is my reputation on the line, and I don't appreciate being put in this position."

I swallowed, blinking rapidly against the tears I *would not* shed. "The position of being forced to support your daughter?"

His jaw went tight. "I'm going to be forced to make a statement that I'm not sure I believe in order to *support my daughter*. This campaign, my career has been built on honesty."

"You support the Muslim Americans," I said. "You support the Muslim refugees. How is my faith any less worthy of support?"

"That's different," he said.

"How?" I demanded.

"They still believe in God, Emma. In something that *exists*. Not some made-up religion that's spreading through prison systems like poison!"

"That isn't fair," I said.

He sighed. "Maybe it isn't. But that's how other people are going to see this. That's the only frame of reference most of them have. And if I defend you, I'm defending them, too. The racist murderers using Norse mythology to promote their own agendas. And that's not even getting into the connections people draw to Hitler and the Nazis."

"You know none of that is true," my mother said, her cultural pride clearly pricked. My mother always got frosty when anyone slighted her Icelandic side—maybe she'd been absorbed into my father's Italian family, but she would always be an Icelander at heart. Before she'd met my father, she'd been planning to move there with Amma. At least according to Auntie Anja. "Hitler thought of pagans as fools and cowards, to be derided and driven out after he rose to power, and whatever influence Norse mythology might have had on him, it was your American eugenics that provoked him to take things to such an extreme. To blame Ásatrú for that is absurd."

"It doesn't matter if it's true or not," my father said. "Ask Alex if you don't believe me. These are the associations that are going to be made first, and no one in this district is going to look at this as some harmless New Age experimentation. This isn't California or Oregon, with all their hippie-dippie woo-wooing around."

I looked up at Alex, willing him to argue. But his expression was grim, and my stomach sank. "You agree with him?"

He sighed. "He isn't entirely wrong. Which is why I want to take control of this and make sure the initial message that reaches voters isn't some connection to neo-Nazis and white-supremacy groups. If we set ourselves apart from the beginning, we have a much better chance of avoiding that kind of mud sticking."

"So that's it, then," I said. "You're not sure you want to stand by me, because my faith has ugly associations. Because that isn't totally hypocritical or anything, what with every other extremist group of every other more mainstream faith getting a giant pass. We don't judge Christians by the groups who picket the funerals of soldiers and gay weddings, with signs telling them God hates them and they're going to hell, but Heathenry is just a Hitler lovefest, and that's all anyone is ever going to believe, so I might as well just give it up now."

"That is certainly *not* what *we* think," my mother said, turning her formidable glare on my father. "This isn't just a question of freedom of religion or even family values, either, *Congressman*—you're talking about her cultural heritage as well. *My* cultural heritage. And say what you will of Anja's neo-pagan revivalism, there is no denying that your daughter and your wife can both trace our ancestors back all the way to the sagas, and from the men and women of the sagas, in some cases, to those Norse gods you're so intent upon seeing as mud to be wiped from your shoe. This isn't just some made-up nothing she believes in. It's something our *ancestors* believed, too. Or do you intend to imply that my ancestors were all simply deluded fools?"

"Of course not, Irena," my father said, almost scornfully. "But even you have to admit that this is a bit much to swallow."

"It doesn't matter," she said. "I won't stand by and let you insult my family and my culture. Not for your politics. If you won't support your daughter in this because of the associations that may or may not be drawn to Norse mythology, true or false, you're not the man I married or the congressman I believed in."

"You're being ridiculous," my father said. "You both are!"

"And you're losing sight of what makes you a truly good man and a better representative of your district," my mother said. "No matter what her faith is, no matter what mistakes she's made in revealing it at such an inopportune time, the only *right* thing to do is to support her. Just as you've supported the rights of everyone else who may not have shared our beliefs. Emma is right. If you'll spend your political capital to support Muslim refugees, you can damn well spend it on your daughter."

That was the first and only time I had ever heard my mother curse. And she'd sworn at my father in defense of me.

CHAPTER THIRTY-ONE:
AD 1000
FREYDÍS

We sailed south along the coast the following day, searching for any sign of my brother's settlement and drinking in the sight of so much green. And the trees! Rolling woodlands with immense oaks and pines. An entire fleet of ships would not even mark the land, with all the lumber that was waiting. But even with so much wealth before my eyes, I could barely force a smile to my lips.

"More mint leaves?" Sonnung suggested, for I had settled beside him where he steered us carefully, keeping far enough from the land that we would not be tossed against unseen rocks and founder.

I shook my head, leaning against the rail and wrapping my arms around my knees. It was not nausea that troubled me for a change, but pain instead. Far worse than the mild cramping of my monthly courses, but somehow the same.

"You are ill." Sonnung pressed his hand to my forehead, his gaze shifting from me to the shore, surveying the coastline for a safe harbor upon which to land. "And we will have to beach the ships before long, regardless, for long as the days might be here, we are running short on sun. Thorhall!"

My father's servant was never far from us, and Sonnung turned the steerboard over to his steady hand.

"We'll sleep upon land tonight," Sonnung told him, and then turned his full attention to me, stroking my cheek. "I'll be but a moment."

Karlsefni's ship was not far from ours, and Sonnung rose, striding down the length of the deck and calling out. Karlsefni's men slowed their oars, and our men sped up to catch them. Sonnung took up a long length of sealskin rope, knotted with a loop on the end and attached to our own bow, and waited until we were near enough to make the throw. It was a foolish thing, truly, to tie our boats together with the waves battering against our oars, fighting to drive us against the rocks, but after so many days upon the sea, no man aboard would have dared to question Sonnung, and Karlsefni himself caught the rope and tied it fast.

Even so, Sonnung was careful, pulling the ships only close enough together to vault from our deck to Karlsefni's—and I would not have believed such a leap possible for any man, had I not seen it with my own eyes—and then calling back to us to slow again and leave a bit more space.

Gudrid joined her husband once Sonnung had made it across, and after a moment's discussion, her gaze found me, worried lines carving themselves deep into her brow. Then Sonnung and Karlsefni clasped hands, and a shout of command drew the rope taut. Karlsefni grinned, and Sonnung climbed upon the rail, balancing carefully on the balls of his feet and waiting for the oarsmen to lessen the gap.

"All that just to speak of what might have been shouted," I grumbled.

Thorhall snorted beside me. "To give the men a show, I think, more than anything else."

And sure enough, there was a cheer when Sonnung made his leap a second time and landed as lightly as a cat upon our deck. Karlsefni untied the rope and tossed it back, but Gudrid still frowned at me. Clearly Sonnung had told her I was not well.

"Karlsefni agrees," Sonnung said, returning to us then. "We'll beach the ships and give everyone a chance to stretch their legs on dry land. Perhaps even forage for some fresh supplies before we shove off again. A good meal on solid ground will serve you."

I lifted an eyebrow. "And how much fussing will Gudrid do?"

He half smiled, crouching before me, his gaze searching and a touch of concern forming crow's-feet at the corners of his eyes. "If you are ill, you are better ill upon land than trapped aboard this ship, and Gudrid has some small knowledge of herbs and healing, even if she will not invoke the proper gods. I will pray for your sake while she fusses, and make offering, and they will hear me."

I rubbed my stomach absently, massaging the place above my womb, and grimaced. "Just do not let her pray to her Christ. I will not have Thor think I do not trust him with my fate."

Sonnung laughed and rose again. "You need not have any fear of that."

"All the same. I will not share Thorstein's fate."

His humor faded. "You won't, Freydís—I promise you. Not so long as I stand at your side."

It was hard not to believe him when he spoke with such confidence, and after so long at sea, watching him sail, watching him lead, I was just as great a fool as the rest of our crew, for it did not even occur to me to argue.

I was dozing when the ship shuddered, the hull scraping gently over stone and sand, followed quickly by the splash of men jumping into the water and dragging her up until we needn't fear she'd be washed away. I rose and stretched, my own excitement softening some of the dull, squeezing ache in my belly. The men were already shouting and laughing, tossing supplies from the hold into the arms of those below, and Sonnung was among them, carefully lowering one of our precious goats over the ship's side and telling the men to be sure she did not wander, for of course we had no pens.

"Will we stay here long?" I asked him.

"A handful of days, at most," Sonnung said. "Unless one of the men sent to forage finds your brother's longhouse."

"I do not think the gods will be quite that kind," I said. "Not when they've granted us such good fortune upon the sea already."

Sonnung's lips twitched. "It was as though Thor himself sailed with us."

"Perhaps he did," I said, watching the men pile furs and blankets and chests of supplies above the debris of the high tide. "He must be curious, do you not think? The land here is so rich."

"I imagine he is as eager as we are to discover its secrets," Sonnung said. He held out his hand. "Gudrid and Karlsefni are already ashore."

"Waiting for me to join them, I suppose."

He grinned. "A place near their fire waits for both of us, and Gudrid will see that you are fed. She has sworn to me that she will tie you to the nearest tree, if she must, in order to see that you rest."

I took his hand, letting him draw me nearer to the rail. "And where will you be?"

"I will pay our respects to the spirits of these lands and see that the proper offerings are made to the gods in thanks for our safe arrival— but you must promise me you will do as Gudrid bids in my absence." He pressed his palm to my cheek, his smile slipping. "You burn too hot still."

"I am well enough," I said, pushing his hand away. But in truth, I was already tired again and welcomed the thought of sitting quietly at Gudrid's fire for a time. I wanted nothing more than to curl up upon my side beneath a warm blanket and wait for this pain to pass.

"Willow bark," he murmured to himself, seeming to ignore my objection. And then he lifted me up and over the rail, handing me down to another man—Karlsefni, I realized, with Thorhall at his side, standing knee deep in the water.

"I've got her," Karlsefni said, and Sonnung let me go.

"Do not listen if she tells you she does not need to rest," he called down to them. "And do your best to keep her from trouble."

"I'm not a child to be coddled." I struggled in Karlsefni's arms, irritated with Sonnung's words, but he only held me tighter. "You need not treat me as one!"

Karlsefni laughed, sloshing toward the shore. "You must forgive the man for his mothering. At least while you carry his child. If it were Gudrid in your place, I fear I would be just as anxious for her health."

"Gudrid will give you twenty sons and never spill so much as a cup of milk," I grumbled. "Nor suffer any sickness of the stomach, I'm certain, and deliver them all healthy into this world without uttering a cry."

"She will certainly try," Karlsefni agreed. "And it will be my duty to keep her from confusing bravery with foolishness, when her time comes, just as it is Sonnung's now."

He set me down upon the beach on my own two feet, and I looked back toward the ship to see Sonnung lowering the second goat down before leaping over the side himself, a heavy coil of rope over his shoulder, which he slowly unwound. No man could say he did not work himself hard, nor did he ask them to do anything he would not first do himself, from taking a turn upon the oars to steering the rudder for days upon end.

Thorstein's ship may have been mine, but I knew well enough who the men saw as shipmaster, and I could not blame them in the slightest, nor bring myself to resent Sonnung's leadership, either. He had won their loyalty with sweat and skill upon the sea, and he had won mine, too, long before that.

"Come, Freydís," Gudrid called from farther up the beach, at the edge of a deep wood. "Let me see to you before you've made yourself sicker."

I sighed and did as I was asked.

-cᴔᴔᴐ-

It was dark when I woke, gasping from the pain in my womb, with a warm wetness between my thighs. "Sonnung."

The fire cracked, and Gudrid hushed me, half-asleep. "Rest, Freydís. You must rest."

I cried out, my belly knotting. "Sonnung!"

Gudrid sat up then, and her hand found mine, pressed hard against my stomach as I moaned.

"No," she breathed. "Oh no. Karl, wake up. Wake up and send for Sonnung!"

He hovered over me, he and his wife, just shadow and firelight. He shook his head. "He won't be found in time, and I'd likely lose the man in the trying."

"It's the baby," Gudrid said. "His child."

I sobbed, her words sinking like knives into my breast. Sonnung's son. And how could he forgive me this?

"Sonnung, please," I tried to say. "Please."

"Shh," Gudrid said, stroking my hair from my face, helping me to sit up. "There's nothing to be done but to breathe. Just breathe, Freydís, and Sonnung will come—he'll be back by morning, he said, and you won't be alone. You won't grieve alone."

But it wasn't grief I felt through the haze of all that pain, the shock of my blood staining the blanket, slick and hot as it trickled down my legs. Guilt, oh certainly, crashing through me like the thunder that rolled over our heads, and something worse.

Because when it was over, and Gudrid helped me wade into the sea to wash it all away, all I knew was relief.

"Freydís?" Sonnung called.

I turned toward his voice like a flower seeking the sun, but I couldn't meet his eyes. Even in the dark.

He charged forward, water splashing up his thighs, dousing him completely as he took me in his arms, and Gudrid slipped away, murmuring her sympathies as she left.

"Forgive me, Freydís," he breathed against my ear, crushing me against his chest. "I should have stayed. If I had only stayed."

I let him think I cried for the babe.

CHAPTER THIRTY-TWO:
AD 2016
Emma

To say I hadn't expected my mother's response would be an understatement of epic proportion. In fact, I was still kind of dumbstruck after Alex and I had said good night and he had walked me back to the guesthouse after dinner.

"Who knew your mother had so much Icelandic pride," he said.

"I mean, I always knew she took a certain amount of satisfaction in being Icelandic, but I wasn't prepared at all for *that*."

"She came down on your father like a hammer," Alex said.

I snorted. "Inspired by Mjölnir, maybe. I kind of wish she'd gone after him *before* he started dissing Iceland. Not that I don't appreciate that she tagged in, finally—we never would have survived that if she hadn't."

He laughed. "It was something to behold, that's for sure."

"He didn't agree, though," I said, kicking at a stray pile of leaves. "I knew he was going to think it was all nonsense, but I thought—I hoped—he would support me, ultimately. If only because of the First Amendment, if nothing else."

Alex wrapped an arm around me, drawing me against his side. "It's going to be okay, Emma. He'll come around. I suspect if he doesn't, he's going to regret it immensely. Irena clearly isn't going to pull any punches."

"I never thought she'd stand up for me like that," I said.

"I knew she would," he said. "Maybe not the way she did, exactly, but she loves you. Even if you're not living your life the way she might want you to, and she won't miss any opportunity to remind you of it herself, she'd defend to the death your right to make even the stupidest mistakes, if anyone else tried to stop you."

It wasn't that I didn't believe it. Not exactly. And it wasn't that I doubted that my mother loved me in the slightest. I knew she did. Even when she drove me crazy, I knew it was out of love. But somehow, I'd expected my dad would be the one to come to my defense. That it would be him coaxing my mom into acceptance and not the other way around. And I didn't want to admit how much it hurt me to have been so wrong.

"Are you coming in?" I asked Alex, stopping in front of my door.

He smiled, brushing my hair behind my ear and leaning down to press a kiss to my forehead. "I want to."

"I sense a *but*."

His forehead wrinkled, as if it pained him to admit it. "I should probably get to work. Assuming that your dad comes around, and assuming he wants to take the approach I suggested, I need to get some balls rolling in that direction. Or at least get them prepared to roll."

"Alex, if it weren't me—if he were any other congressman and I were some daughter you'd never really met or cared about—would you be giving him the same advice?"

"If he were any other congressman, he wouldn't have necessarily built his platform the way he has," he said slowly. "It wouldn't be real integrity that mattered so much as the appearance of it. And I'm not sure I'd be working for him if that was the case."

"That sounds like a suspiciously long-winded *no*," I said.

"I can't spin anything past you, can I?" He kissed my nose and then brushed his lips across mine.

I caught him by his perfectly knotted tie when he tried to pull away, and kissed him properly. Long and slow and lingering, until I was flushed and we were both panting and a little bit more mussed than when we'd begun.

"You should come in," I insisted, my forehead against his and my eyes still closed. "Just for a little while."

He made a soft noise of objection. "There's no such thing as just for a little while. Not when you're kissing me like that."

"If you don't come in, I'm just going to agonize," I said.

He laughed lightly. "And if I do come in?"

"We won't be talking," I promised. "And once you've distracted me sufficiently and I'm lying naked in my bed, blissed out of my mind, you can sneak away and do whatever work you want."

I loved the way he groaned, gritty and needy and wanting. His hands were already beneath my coat, but he found my skin with his fingertips and pulled me hard against him. "Did you just ask me to fuck you to sleep?"

I grinned at the roughness of his voice, tasting victory. "Is that a problem?"

"Inside," he demanded, reaching for the doorknob and shoving the door open behind me. "Or round one is going to be against the door and in the cold, and I'm not going to regret losing my job in the slightest."

And that was how I successfully talked Alexander Stone into spending (most of) the night.

I probably shouldn't have been sleeping with him. We hadn't been dating all that long, and even though I'd known him for years, it still felt like things were moving fast. Maybe because he *knew*, combined with the fact that I hadn't been able to tell him in my own time. I felt like I was rapidly losing all control of my situation. Like Alex had taken the reins of my crisis, and other than agonizing over whether it would all work out, there wasn't a lot for me to do but sit home and wait.

But whether we'd been dating or not, that still would have been the case, I reminded myself when I woke up the next morning to find that Alex had left and then come back at some point to drop off a fresh croissant in a grease-smeared paper bag. I wrapped it in a paper towel and sank into my armchair, letting each bite melt in my mouth while I considered my circumstances.

Whether we'd been dating or not, if something like this had happened, my father would have had me turn it over to Alex for appropriate handling. And whether we'd been dating or not, I'd still be sitting around in this interminable state of suspended animation, waiting for my father to decide how he wanted to deal with the problems I'd presented, based on the options Alex presented him. And whether we'd been dating or not, it seemed, my father would have looked at me like I was utterly deluded when I told him what I believed. The only difference might have been that Alex wouldn't have walked into that dinner already prepared to support me.

Maybe he wouldn't have supported me at all.

I popped another bite of flaky still-warm croissant into my mouth and chewed absently. Would he have? I wanted to think so. It seemed like he might have. He seemed too fair-minded to have done anything else. And clearly love and affection and family ties didn't stop my father from responding the way he had, so why shouldn't Alex's responses have been genuinely Alex and uninfluenced by whatever relationship we'd been trying to have?

I was still mulling that over, semi-wallowing in my chair, when a knock on my front door was quickly followed by a thump of the door *not* opening and Sarah's curse. "You'd better not still be asleep, Emma!"

While I wasn't guilty of sleeping in too late, I was definitely guilty of forgetting that she was coming with brunch, and there was no pretending otherwise when I leapt up to unlock the door barely dressed in my pajamas. "Sorry! I'm so sorry. I lost track of time."

She lifted an eyebrow, taking me in as she entered, and I shut the door again behind her. "Lost track of the time, or the day of the week?"

"Both, possibly," I said. "Last night was complete insanity."

"What happened?"

I let out a breath, grabbing the coffees from her hand and helping her spread out the rest of the to-go containers on the kitchen table. "I had to tell my parents I was Heathen."

"Oh my God." Sarah stared, the last container suspended halfway to the table. "And Alex?"

"And Alex," I said.

"Oh my God," Sarah said again, sinking into the nearest chair. "What happened? How did that go? Did he understand? What did your parents say? Oh my God, your *mother*—"

"Turns out it was my dad I should have been worrying about the whole time," I said, grabbing a handful of napkins and silverware out of a drawer. "Alex was phenomenal. He didn't care at all, I don't think. Or he did care, but he was most upset about the fact that I hadn't felt like I could tell him. That I hadn't *wanted* to tell him. And I wouldn't have if a student reporter at the college hadn't caught me and snapped a picture."

"Oh my *God*," Sarah said, leaning forward.

"Yup." I grimaced and sat down across from her. "My dad blew a gasket. And my mom was mad that I'd been lying about it, I think, for the most part. I mean, she doesn't want me to be Heathen, for sure, but it was kind of amazing how fast she stomped all over my father for attacking our *cultural heritage*."

"Oh my God," Sarah said, gleeful this time. "I wish I could have been there to see Irena go for the throat. That would have been glorious."

"I would have been happier if she hadn't had to," I said. "I really didn't expect my dad to be so . . ."

"Traditional?"

"Closed-minded, I guess. He's always supported freedom of religion, and you know how hard he's been fighting for the refugees."

"Yeah, but Emma, they're not his daughter. And like it or not, it's never going to be *just* a personal and private disagreement between you two. Not if there's a picture floating around of you fondling Thor's hammer."

"I was not fondling it," I said. "I just forgot to tuck it back inside my collar."

"Whatever," she said, waving that away. "It still means that it's something he's going to have to deal with publicly, and I'm sure that's what's really getting his goat. He's always been prickly about looking foolish in front of the community. Even when we were kids, I remember him losing his temper with Holly after she let slip that he'd gotten a speeding ticket. She was so little I don't think she even understood why he was mad. I don't think *we* understood, either, for that matter."

"I don't think this is the same. You should have heard some of the things he was saying. Talking about how if he defended me, then he was defending neo-Nazis and murderers."

"Exactly," she said. "The politics, not the personal. That was definitely part of what upset my parents, too, when I quit the Church. Having to explain to everyone why their daughter had become Protestant. As if it was something people would hold against them." Sarah rolled her eyes, clearly exasperated just remembering it. "But if you'd told your dad all of this under different circumstances—if it were strictly a private issue—I think he would have responded a lot more reasonably."

I wanted to believe her, but after last night, I didn't trust that my father really had the flexibility required, so I shrugged and opened the Styrofoam to-go box instead.

"So you and Alex are okay?" Sarah asked.

I couldn't quite stop my smile. "We're definitely better than okay."

"Oh my God," she said, slapping the table. "You had *sex* with him!"

"Maybe," I admitted, taking a long sip of my coffee to tease her. "*If* that were true, it might also be possible that it was absolutely mind-blowing."

"I cannot even believe you didn't call me," she said. "And I definitely can't believe you're sleeping with Alexander Stone. It's only been like a week! And I thought you weren't even sure about keeping things going with him at all."

"He made a convincing argument," I said. "And he's *really* attractive."

"Even after you get him out of his suit?"

"Perfect six-pack," I said. "Not too bulky and not too thin. And let's just say that his experience level is not a problem. He knows what he's doing, and it's pretty toe curling."

"I'm jealous."

"You really, really are," I said. "Not that you'd be taking advantage of all his wonders if you had him."

Sarah sighed. "I'm sure my conscience would let me take advantage of *some* of them, at least, but no, you're right. And it's for the best. He'd be too much of a temptation, and if he really is that persuasive, I'd probably have ended up going farther than I wanted to, and then there would have been all the regret and misery that followed. Not worth it."

"He isn't like that," I said. "If I'd told him I wanted to wait, he wouldn't ever have pushed me. But I think we're both glad that isn't the case. And I know I personally am very pleased to learn just how not Catholic he is in bed."

"All right, all right," Sarah said, laughing. "So Alex is perfection in all its physical forms. But what if Irena doesn't change the congressman's mind? What's Alex going to do then?"

My smile faded, and I set down my coffee carefully on the tabletop. It wasn't something I had considered at all, and I didn't like thinking about it now.

"I have no idea."

CHAPTER THIRTY-THREE:
AD 1000
FREYDÍS

We stayed a fortnight, for Karlsefni claimed he wished to send scouts north and south to look for what we might not have seen from the sea, but from the way he and Gudrid watched me, I knew it was not only that.

Between Sonnung, Gudrid, and Thorhall, I was never left alone, and instead of grief, I felt cloaked in shame, so heavy and so thick I could do nothing but stare into the fire's flames. Day after day.

"It is not unnatural," Gudrid assured me. She was always trying to reassure me of something. "Sometimes the babe is too weak, or strangely formed, and it cannot live to be born. I know few women who have *not* suffered a loss such as yours. But you will try again, you and Sonnung. He is man enough. There will be another baby planted before long."

I closed my eyes, exhausted by her need to cheer me. Her assumption that I wanted another child, any child at all.

"I only wish you would speak with me," Gudrid said. "You must know by now that I am your friend. But if not me, then speak to Sonnung at the least. It would do you good to share your grief, and if you would only comfort one another . . ."

She trailed off, and I knew why. I could feel him when he drew near, all warmth and lightning prickling my skin. Sonnung sat down beside me, and I could feel his pain. Not grief, exactly. Not for the child we'd lost, anyway, for he was as certain as Gudrid that he could give me another. Sonnung's pain was the guilt of having left me, of having arrived too late. And I hated myself for letting him feel it at all, but what could I say? How could I tell him that I was glad the child was gone when it was everything he had wanted?

"She is as silent as she was after Thorstein was lost," Gudrid said quietly. "I did not know how to help her then, and she will not let me help her now. But surely there must be something we can do. You brought her out of it before."

Sonnung said nothing, and Gudrid sighed. I heard her gather herself, and a moment later, she left us alone.

"You think I do not know," he said after a long moment. "You think I do not remember that this desire was mine alone."

I swallowed, my throat tight.

"A child was my price," he said. "In exchange for your ship, for keeping Thorvard from your side, for sailing with you now. And it is not in my nature to accept less than the gift that was promised, to forget a debt that is owed. But if you wish to be done with me, Freydís, I will go. I will walk into those trees, and you will never see me again. For I cannot stand to see you broken by my hand."

The breath left my lungs, and I turned to look at him. For the first time in days, I met his gaze. His eyes were dark, his face lined with pain—his own, and what he knew of mine.

"I will give you until morning to decide."

He moved as if to rise, but I grabbed him by the arm. "I tried, Sonnung."

His jaw went tight, his hand covering mine. "But are you willing to risk the same again? Would you resent me, the child—the gods?"

"I—" My mouth was dry, my lips cracked. I pressed them together. "I do not know how to be any other way. I cannot be what I am not."

"I do not ask it of you," he said. "I only ask you to leap with me, to trust in what I have promised you."

"To keep faith," I murmured.

"In me and the gods," he agreed. "Never have they needed it more. And that is the heart of it, Freydís. The seed of my desire for this child— your child. It is for the gods more than it is for me. For their sake. Perhaps for yours."

"Mine?"

He looked away. "A son will grant you support and protection when you are old. He will stand in my place to guard you."

"If he lives and loves the gods, if he honors his ancestors as he should, and is not lured away by Christ."

"No son of mine will become a Christian," Sonnung growled. "He will know his gods and his ancestors, and he will not turn from either."

"My father must have thought the same of us once," I said.

Sonnung shook his head. "It is different, Freydís. You must realize that, even if you do not see the rest."

I slid my fingers through his, staring at our hands. His sun-bronzed skin was darker than mine, the hairs upon his arms bleached to pure white gold. I knew he was different. A great man, and stronger than my father. A strange man, too, who I had seen do amazing things. Uncanny things. And sometimes, the way he spoke to me—it was as though he knew the gods' minds. Certainly he knew mine.

"Think upon it, Thorswoman," he said, leaning down to press a kiss to my brow. "In the morning, I will do as you bid."

That night, long after the sun had set and the moon had risen high, I sat beside the fire, turning his words over in my mind. Dimly, I heard Gudrid sigh, then rise, leaving Karlsefni's side to join me.

"You must rest, Freydís," she said, draping an extra fur across my shoulders. "Or else you will truly fall ill, and what then?"

What then, indeed. "Perhaps I will not live to become old."

"What?" she said, clearly startled, for I had not spoken to her in days.

"Sonnung says a son will support me when I am old, protect me. But perhaps I am meant to die young. Perhaps I will not even live long enough to see Brattahlid again."

"Don't be foolish, Freydís," Gudrid said. "Of course you will see Brattahlid again."

I poked at the fire, breaking the coals to expose the red hearts inside. "If Sonnung sailed with me still, I would feel certain of it."

"But why wouldn't he?"

Because I did not want his child. Because I would have sent him away. Because I was too stubborn to listen, to believe in the promises he made.

"I was glad," I said. "Relieved, when I realized what was happening. When it was over."

"Freydís—"

"I don't want a baby. I am afraid of it, Gudrid. Afraid of how it will change me, soften me into something useless and weak. No man will follow a woman with a child at her breast, and many more would simply laugh if I asked them to sail for me."

"It is a woman's duty, Freydís—what we are meant for," she said. "And men—they only laugh because it frightens them. It is magic they will never understand. Power they cannot begin to grasp. You can be strong still, and a mother, too. And you will prove it, I am certain, if they ever dare to laugh at you."

"Perhaps I do not have your strength, then."

Gudrid snorted. "We have different strengths, but that does not make either one of us weaker. And women—we are able to be strong in more ways than one. Another thing our men will never understand, I think, so fixated on battle prowess and brute force. But listen to me, Freydís. If you love Sonnung, do not let the fear of a child stand in your way. Grasp onto these days, this short time that you have carved for yourselves, and glory in them. Perhaps it will be your love of one another that brings you the fame and fortune that you seek, in the end, or perhaps it will be your undoing instead. But I do not see why you should not enjoy it while it lasts."

I glanced at her in the firelight, surprised by the force behind her words and then by the grief lining her face. "You encourage me because of Thorstein."

"I encourage you because we can never know our fates, and I do not doubt Sonnung's love for you. No one who has watched you these last months can. I am fortunate to have found Karlsefni—to love and be loved a second time—and I would not have you turn from the same." She wrinkled her nose. "Especially not when all you have to console you is Thorvard."

"You liked him once," I said, not quite able to hide my smile.

"That was before I knew him for a fool. And before I realized how he had betrayed you."

"But surely you wished him to be Christian—just as you wish it for me."

Gudrid grasped my hand, holding it tight. "What I wish for you more than anything, Sister, is peace. Nothing less and nothing more. Sonnung, it seems, has granted you some measure of it."

"He did before," I said quietly. "When I had no real fear of a child being born. When I believed I was barren and was glad of it, for it meant I could love him as I liked."

"You can love him still," Gudrid promised. "And if a child comes, he will be a father to it. A husband to you, for as long as we remain here. Perhaps when the time comes that he wishes to leave, that you both do, he will take the boy with him, too."

"And what will I be?" I asked. "What will become of me?"

"You will still be Freydís," she said. "Daughter of Erik the Red, with hair the color of fire and a temper to match. And you will be rich! Rich enough to do as you like and live as you please."

I laughed. "No matter how rich I am, I do not think Thjodhild and Leif will give me any peace so long as I am not Christian."

"Then leave," Gudrid said. "You will have your ship—two ships, truly. Leave Greenland, and follow your fate to its end in another land."

But there were no other lands. Not beyond this one. And Karlsefni's settlement, in the end, would be Christian, too. Rich as I might become, there would be no place left for me to go. Not where I might live free.

Christ's wretched King Olaf had seen to that.

❦

When I woke the next morning, Sonnung was sitting beside me, plucking grass from the earth with anxious fingers and staring out at the sea. He stilled almost at once, every line of his body going taut as a strung bow. How he knew I was awake, I did not know.

"Have you decided?" he asked.

I sat up, studying him in the morning light. His beard was not so neatly trimmed as it had been, and his hair had grown longer since the day we had first met. He wore his mail and leathers, his sword belt not yet wrapped around his hips but near at hand, with a pack of his things.

My heart ached at the sight of him packed and dressed. As if he had already decided I would ask him to go, and did not mean to argue.

"Sonnung . . ."

He took an unsteady breath, seeming to gather himself, and then looked at me. His eyes were clear and flat, the warmth all drained away, but he was ragged and worn about the mouth, his lips too thin. I reached for him, and he flinched from my hand.

"It is morning, Freydís, and you must make your choice."

I sighed. "You are a fool, Sonnung."

His eyes narrowed, a furrow appearing between his brows.

"You are a fool, because you would not have questioned me, nor fought. You would have let me send you away without any argument at all, without any chance to think better of my choice, as I watched you gather your things and my heart broke. If there was ever a time for stubbornness, I'd have thought it would be now."

He stared at me a moment longer, and I stared back. And then he laughed. A short bark and then something deeper, rumbling like thunder from his belly and his chest. I was beneath him a moment later, the breath knocked out of me with the speed of his attack. But I had no wish to escape his arms, to wriggle out from beneath his weight.

"Tell me you do not wish me to go," he said. "That I am not mistaken. That I have not heard only what I longed for you to say."

I smiled against his neck, my hand a fist in his hair. "I do not wish you to go, Sonnung. If I had to, I would beg you to stay."

"You need never beg," he said. "Only love me and keep faith."

That day we sailed, and with my heart, my body healed. So when we found my brother's house nearly a week later, on an island off the coast of the mainland, on that night, I loved Sonnung well.

CHAPTER THIRTY-FOUR:
AD 2016
Emma

Has he made up his mind?" I asked Alex when he dropped by that afternoon. He'd brought us both a late lunch, and I'd barely held myself together while he ate, impatient to know what was going on—if anything. "I mean, we don't have a lot of time to get in front of this, really. He's going to have to make a decision today, won't he?"

"He wants to try keeping the student reporter quiet," Alex said. "I know you didn't get her name, but do you have any idea who she might be? Maybe we can buy the photo from her and have done with it."

I shook my head. "She was a brunette, blue eyes, medium height, and possibly Pagan. That's all I've got. But you can't really be serious about this as a plan."

"It's not my first choice, no," he said. "In fact, it's not even in my top five. But your dad has a friend at the *Courier*, and he's willing to do him a favor."

"Ew."

"He's not—He's in a difficult position. And he doesn't want you dragged through the mud. None of us do."

"Is that how we're spinning it now? Because it didn't sound like that's what he was worried about last night."

"He was upset and caught off guard," Alex said. "Now he's had some time to consider things, and he thinks the best solution is to keep you from being brought into any of this at all. And he isn't wrong, Emma. If the *Courier* will buy the photo and bury it, none of this has to become a bigger issue, and you'll be in a better position with your job, too."

"You're assuming that speculation about my faith isn't already grist for the rumor mill among some of the students," I said. "And you're assuming that just because there's no photo to back it up, accusations won't be made."

"Without the photo, it's her word against ours. And she's just a student. If it goes anywhere, your father will just refuse to comment on unsubstantiated rumors. But I doubt it will reach a level where he'll be forced to say anything at all."

"Yeah, but if it does, that's going to make him look guilty. Like he's trying to hide something."

"He is," Alex said. "And believe it or not, I think he *is* trying to protect you by going about it this way. He knows you won't want to lie and pass it off as something purely cultural, and I think this is his way of trying to keep you from being put in that position."

"I'd rather just come out with it and be done," I said. "I'm so tired of living this way, Alex. Even in college, I didn't feel like I could *talk* about it. And that was when I needed to talk about it most. To test what I was experiencing against the wisdom of the community, you know?"

He half smiled. "Actually, I'm fairly certain I don't know. You haven't really—I don't want to pry, and I don't want you to think I'm only asking because of the campaign. I have a personal interest as well as a professional one. But."

I wrinkled my nose. "But the more you know, the easier it is for you to do your job."

"And maybe talk your dad into coming around," he admitted, apologetic. "But more than that, Emma, honestly, I want you to feel like you can talk to me. Even about this stuff. Even when I really don't have any idea. I'll still listen."

"I know," I said, pushing a piece of lettuce around my container. "I'm just so used to keeping everything to myself. Sarah gets why it's hard for me to come clean, but every time I tried to tell her about the actual experiences I was having, she would get this look in her eyes, like she was scared for me, or of me, or . . . It's a hard habit to break, I guess. And after last night? God. I'm so grateful that you're open and willing to listen, but I wish my parents felt the same way. That Dad didn't feel like I was something he had to hide until someone produced evidence he couldn't ignore. He'll have to address it eventually."

Alex shrugged. "By then, maybe he'll have come to his senses. I know Irena is going to keep working on him. She's already called me to say as much."

"But in the meantime, I have to be his big dirty secret."

I pushed away from the table and dumped my take-out container in the trash. It was getting full after all the packaging from brunch, and I was putting off taking it out. Putting off leaving the guesthouse at all, for that matter. And after everything Alex had said, I wanted to risk facing my parents even less now.

Alex followed me, wrapping his arms around my waist from behind and dropping a kiss behind my ear. "Give it time, Emma."

"It was one thing to be my own secret, but it's another thing entirely to feel like someone else's dirty laundry."

"Let's go out tonight, then," Alex said. "Somewhere fancy. We'll make a spectacle of ourselves, and by the time we're through, you won't feel like anyone's secret."

"Is this more spin?" I turned in his arms, something in his tone raising my hackles. "Are you trying to create some kind of distraction? Make everyone look at the congressman's daughter dating his spin doctor so they won't see what's going on behind the scenes? With my job—with any of the rest?"

His suspiciously blank press face told me I wasn't wrong, and I pushed free.

"Did my dad ask you to do it?"

"Even if he did, whether anything else was going on or not, I'd want to take you out, spend time with you *outside* of the bedroom, where I knew we might have half a chance of talking."

I narrowed my eyes and took a step back. "It was my mother's idea, wasn't it?"

"You can't just hide yourself away in here, Emma. That's going to draw its own kind of attention—especially if this Hail Mary of your father's doesn't work. The best thing you can do is to keep on keeping on. And sure, if it draws attention away from where we don't want people looking, all to the good."

"And if she hadn't *instructed* you, you'd have just said no."

"I didn't say no when you asked whether it was your father's idea."

"Because you knew I'd see the half-truth," I accused. And it was practically my mother's voice coming out of his mouth, telling me to stop hiding myself away. Telling me I needed to be part of the community. Just *engage*. "And I swear to God, Alex, if you don't stop trying to spin me, we're going to have a serious problem."

He raised his hands, all innocence. "It's not about spin. It's about her making a suggestion and my agreeing that it was a good idea—not to mention something I would have wanted to do regardless. Did the thought occur to me that it might garner some positive attention? Of course! It's my job to think of things like that. But I'm not trying to *handle* you, professionally. And frankly, I don't think your mother is, either."

I touched the hammer at my neck, taking a breath. "Are you sure?"

He sighed, dropping his hands and stepping forward. "I promise I won't ever try to spin you purposefully. If it happens by force of habit, I'll do my best to catch myself. That's all I can say."

"All right." I squeezed the bronze until it dug into my fingers and then let go of my pendant. Out on a date wasn't the same as tagging along on a church activity, I reminded myself. And the whole town was going to learn the truth about me soon enough, whether we went out and paraded ourselves around or not. At least when they did, I wouldn't look like I was ashamed of *myself.* "What did you have in mind?"

·⁕·

My father's schedule in the evenings was fairly packed for the next month or so while he was home—the district work weeks having been planned to accommodate the run-up to Election Day, of course—which meant that for the most part, Alex was booked, too. Campaign event after campaign event, half of which I knew my mother expected me to attend. "To show your support." Weekends, though, those we all got off, because my mother and father guarded theirs like gold. And that weekend, with my future at the college still completely up in the air and my secret still a secret, Alex made a point of making our relationship—young as it was—very public.

We went out to a late dinner and then dancing at a club he knew, though I'd never been much for it. Alex had wined me enough that the idea hadn't been completely intolerable, but I still didn't really know what to do with myself on the dance floor.

He laughed and drew me in close, his hands on my hips, helping me find the beat and guiding my movements until I'd loosened up enough to enjoy it. There may have been a couple of extremely potent shots involved in that process, but I was Icelandic enough to know how to hold my liquor, if not my tongue.

I danced, unselfconscious and grinning, teasing Alex more than I might have dared ordinarily, and even happier to realize how successful I was, when Alex spun me around and pulled me back against his chest. Mostly, I suspected, to hide his hard-on. But he didn't leave any room for the Holy Spirit, that was for sure, and the Catholic-school throwback of it all made me laugh.

"So much for taking me out somewhere to *talk*," I shouted over my shoulder. "Or were you going for the saga definition the whole time?"

He chuckled in my ear. "We talked plenty at dinner. This is the making the rest of the male population jealous part."

I laughed again and grabbed his hand, pulling him behind me as I wove through the other dancers on the floor. He'd had plenty of time to show me off, and I was ready to get on to the naked-in-bed part. Alex didn't seem inclined to argue, either, because once he realized I was heading for the exit, he was beside me, his hand on the small of my back, giving me the subtle directional cues I needed not to drunkenly stumble like an idiot through the club.

"Alex?"

We both glanced over our shoulders, but Alex stopped dead, his hand closing into a fist in my shirt to pull me with him. I lifted both eyebrows, slipping in under his arm when a dark-haired woman stepped away from her friends and bounced toward us, all smiles. Her face was familiar, but after the shots, my brain couldn't place her.

"Jenna," Alex said. "I didn't realize you were in town."

Jenna. I squinted slightly, and it clicked. Jenna Ricci. Star softball pitcher and Alex's notorious high school sweetheart. "Oh, shit."

"Only for the weekend. It's my sister's bridal shower." I wasn't sure if she heard me or just ignored it, but at least my presence made her stop short of hugging him. She did still lean in to press a kiss to his cheek, which made Alex go stiff as a board. "It's so good to see you."

"You'll have to give your sister my congratulations," he said, stepping back. "But Emma and I are actually on our way out—"

"Julia said she thought she saw you out with the congressman's daughter," Jenna said, giving me a second, reassessing glance now that she'd gotten our attention. "She said you were being investigated for a discrimination complaint at the college? Your poor father. I can only imagine, especially with how close the race is. He must be mortified. Especially if this is how you're coping—and after everything that happened with your sister, too. Such a shame to see a good family brought so low."

"That's right," I said, before Alex could white-knight. I'd had enough alcohol that I wasn't about to let anyone shame me *or* talk shit about my family—especially not the girl who had broken Alex's heart. "Julia works for the Foreign Languages Department, doesn't she? It's a running joke in the History Department that their office gossips in all six languages. I guess they're not wrong after all."

Alex cleared his throat, but I couldn't tell if it was to keep from laughing or cursing. "Like I said—we really can't stay. Have a great weekend with your sister, Jenna. And give your parents my best."

"Great seeing you, Jenna!" I called over my shoulder as he guided me through the mob by the bar. Alex was shaking, his face visibly red, and I bit my lip, hoping I hadn't gone too far.

I wasn't stupid enough to think that elections weren't won and lost over moments like this one and issues like mine, especially in communities like ours. As much as I didn't want to cost my father his election—if he chose his campaign and his political capital over me? Maybe it was the alcohol, but it felt a little bit unforgivable. It felt like a choice he couldn't really take back.

Just like I couldn't take back my thoughtless snark.

We were out the door and into the cool autumn air within minutes, and I turned once we had some space between us and the line at the door. "I'm so sorry. I shouldn't have said anything—"

He laughed, pulling me in and pressing a kiss to my temple. "As your father's spin doctor, I really shouldn't encourage that kind of behavior."

I let out a breath of relief, smiling. "Then I guess it's a good thing I'm out with my boyfriend."

"Boyfriend, huh?"

"Well, we *are* sleeping together. And I don't think you were ever *not* serious about me."

"Too much?"

I shook my head, wrapping my arm around his waist and resting my head against his shoulder as we walked south toward his car. "Just enough."

CHAPTER THIRTY-FIVE:
AD 1000
FREYDÍS

There is Thorvaldur still to consider," Karlsefni said on the second night after we had found Leif's longhouse.

The roof had needed repair, but the turf and beams still stood strong. Chasing out the animals who had found their way inside over the previous two winters and sweeping out the moldering rushes took a good portion of the morning. But Leif had built the longhouse with a private room on one end, which we shared with Karlsefni and Gudrid, away from the rest of the men, who had fought instead over the sleeping benches that lined the walls outside our small space.

Tomorrow's work would be the start of building a second longhouse to serve those who were not so lucky as to win a bed. We had no shortage of timber for the task, at least, for we'd harvested plenty of oak and pine during the fortnight we'd spent exploring in the North, and turf would be easy enough to come by as well. Leif had chosen a green meadowland for his settlement, bordering an inlet that led out to the sea, but sheltered by the bulk of the island behind us. A very fine place, with no shortage of grass for grazing. The goats and the poor cow and bull Karlsefni had brought would be well contented by the feast.

"I fear for Thorvaldur that he has not arrived," Gudrid said, handing Karlsefni a bowl of fish soup, which stewed inside the iron cauldron that hung on chains over the long pit fire in the larger main room. Sonnung had brought me mine, insisting that I must rest, though the worst of what I had suffered was long behind me.

"He did not have the advantage of Sonnung to steer him right," I said. "Or else the hunting was good in the North, and he has taken his time."

"He might have filled his hold and turned back to trade the ivory," Karlsefni agreed. "Though if he did, I would be surprised."

"He is well enough," Sonnung said. "And having sailed with Leif before, he is sure to find his way. Likely he was only becalmed for a time."

I snorted. "And too stubborn to pray to Thor for good winds to help him on."

Sonnung's lips twitched, but Gudrid only rolled her eyes. "You're hardly one to speak of stubbornness, Freydís."

"I am nothing to Thorvaldur," I told her. "Even you must admit that."

"Shelter for thirty more men would not go amiss, either way," Karlsefni said, his hand finding Gudrid's knee before she could argue against me. "We have only five women, I know, but it is better to have the space for children than not. And who is to say how many we might become?"

My eyes narrowed, for Gudrid had blushed and Karlsefni seemed far too pleased. "You're pregnant?"

Gudrid's face turned a brighter red, and she dropped her gaze to her bowl. "I was not certain, and then after everything you suffered—I did not want you to hear the news as a boast."

I pressed my lips together, unsure of how to respond. Except that it was far from shocking. Of course Gudrid would be pregnant. And she would have no trouble keeping the baby, either, I was sure. Because Gudrid was in everything perfection—from maiden, to wife, to mother, and when she was old, men would travel from far-off lands in search of her wisdom, too.

"The gods have blessed you, and your ancestors surely smile at the news," Sonnung said when I did not offer a response. "I have no doubt that Freydís will join you soon, and all to the good that you will be companions upon such a journey."

"And may our sons live as brothers," Karlsefni said, raising his cup.

"Do not be angry, Freydís," Gudrid said. "I could not bear it if you turned from me now."

I shook my head, but did not meet her eyes. "How could I be angry? You have wanted a child from the start, and no man or woman in my father's house could doubt Karlsefni's determination, either." But all the same, I set aside my bowl and rose. I had no right to my anger, or the pain I felt, for I had not wanted my child, and I did not long for one now, no matter what peace I had made with Sonnung. But I felt it all the same. "I've just remembered, I meant to check the goats."

"Freydís, please—"

I did not linger long enough to hear the rest. Another heartbeat and there would be tears in my eyes, and I could not stand the thought of the men seeing me weep. Already they looked at me differently, some of Karlsefni's men gripping their crosses as I passed, murmuring prayers to their Christ as if my very presence were a threat.

But it was not a proper fear, that I might gut them with an axe or unman them with a knife. It had nothing to do with my strength. It was my weakness that made them afraid.

And once they learned of Gudrid's child, it would be the same foolishness again. Another way in which Christ revealed his power over Thor.

Another way in which I had failed my gods.

Sonnung found me with the goats, as I had claimed, simply lying back in the tall grass and staring at the sky. He loomed over me for a moment, then laid himself down at my side.

"I should not be angry, or upset at all," I said, when he did not speak. "But you know what the men will think, how they will see it as a testament to Christ—and I know well enough what a woman is meant for. If Karlsefni wants a settlement, he ought to have brought a more fertile womb than mine."

Sonnung chuckled softly. "You'll have a child soon enough, Freydís—you needn't worry about that. Sooner than you'd like, I'm certain, and these same men will long for the calm days, before the mother's madness came upon you and you snarled at them like one of Odin's wolves, waiting for an excuse to bite."

"And if I lose your child a second time, what then?"

"You won't," he said, unconcerned.

I pressed a hand to my belly. "If I do."

His shoulder nudged mine in half a shrug. "Then you will birth the next."

But I saw a different future, of one pregnancy lost after another, each more draining than the last, until I had not the strength even to rise and wash the blood from my thighs. I shut my eyes, willing the images away. "They will see it as proof of Thor's weakness and Christ's strength."

"Christ could not have planted a child in you at all to be lost," Sonnung said. "Thorvard is the proof of that, and the men who came before him."

"They were not Christians," I said, stung. I did not like to think how he had learned of them at all. Men talked, gossiped like women in their own way, we all knew. But I hated to consider what they had said of me. "Not then, even if they are now, though perhaps I should have cut off their balls instead of fondling them, all the same, if they went off boasting."

Sonnung laughed again. "It was your brothers' talk, not theirs, that told me."

"The fools," I grumbled, my anger ebbing—but only slightly. "Of course it was. As if they have any right to judge me."

"Does it matter?" he asked. "We are here together, and when Thorvaldur arrives, he will not challenge either one of us, I promise you."

"*When* he arrives." I frowned at the sky. "The last words we exchanged, I threatened to stuff his balls into his face if he dared even to touch me. If Thorstein knew—he would be unhappy to think we had not made peace, but Thorvaldur is so stubborn, so determined to follow Thjodhild and Leif, wherever they would lead. Thorstein was the only bridge between us, and when he died, I lost so much. Not one brother, but three."

Sonnung's hand found mine in the grass, and he shifted nearer, until our arms and shoulders touched. "What do you see, lying here?"

"Shadows and darkness," I said, for I did not lie in the grass to see—rather to be hidden from sight. "Little else."

He squeezed my hand. "I see a vast dome, shaped for us by the gods. And the tireless moon, always racing across the sky. Sometimes I wonder what he thinks of his fate. If on those dark nights when he is lost to our sight, it is fear that has driven him, rather than strength."

"He has reason for fear," I said. "Should the wolves catch him or his sister, it will mean the end of this world."

"Máni is fortunate to know what he faces and what he risks if he fails." Sonnung said. "But we are not all so lucky. Often, we are too blind to see that we are hunted by wolves, never mind knowing their names."

"We are both chased by the same wolf, Sonnung. His name is Christ, and he hunts us all."

"That is not the wolf you fear most," Sonnung said gently. "I am not certain you fear the White Christ at all. Nor do I believe for a moment that he will ever catch you, no matter how many men and women he sets in your path."

I turned my head, studying his profile in the moonlight. "He will never catch you, either."

"No," he agreed. "I will fight with the gods when Ragnarok comes and defeat my enemy on the field that day. And perhaps . . . perhaps it will be Christ who presides after we all lie dead, in place of Shining Balder. If that is the fate the Norns have woven, there is little I can do to stop it."

"But you fight, still."

"I fight to be remembered, even in that golden age beyond the end of things," he said. "And so do you."

I laced my fingers through his and turned my gaze back to the stars. "Perhaps once that was what drove me. And perhaps, one day, it will call to me again. But at this moment, I think I only fight for you. For us, in the time we have carved for ourselves, as Gudrid said once."

"If I swore to you, Thorswoman, that you would not be weakened by me, that the gods will ensure that when you have finished, you will be so fearsome that even Leif in all his righteousness with all the men of Greenland behind him will not dare to act against you—if I made you that promise, what would you have left to fear?"

I shook my head. "It isn't a promise you can make."

I felt his eyes on my face. "What if it is?"

"I would be free of even Leif and Thjodhild? Left to live as I liked?"

"To live and worship and love me," he agreed.

I rolled onto my side, facing him. "But you will be gone."

He grunted. "It is true that I cannot stay, but that does not mean I will be wholly gone. You will not escape the promise you made to the gods, nor will Thor be so easily forsworn."

"He has given me my ship and kept me from my husband's bed," I said. "I asked for nothing more."

"You asked him to keep your husband's seed from your womb," Sonnung said. "If you return to Greenland, to Thorvard, then he is not through."

"Perhaps Thorstein was right from the start," I said, rolling onto my back again. "Perhaps I should divorce him and be done. Now that I have my brother's ship, I do not need his. And once my father is dead, it will hardly matter who my husband is or what support he might give. Leif will have everything he needs without me."

"But Leif would rule your life, with Thjodhild. I have little doubt that he would see you remarried as quickly as possible, and likely to a man more loathsome than Thorvard, eager for your brother's favor."

I groaned, closing my eyes—as if shutting them would change the truth. My brother as chieftain, ruled by his Christian ways. Thorvard was converted wholly, no longer faithful to our gods at all after the seasons he had spent in Iceland. That much had been more than clear. But it had seemed at least that he did not expect the same of me. And so long as he did not betray *that* promise, I was safest as his wife, no matter how little I liked it.

"I must return to Thorvard." The words were bitter in my mouth. "After my father's death it will be all the protection I have left."

"Not the only protection," Sonnung promised. "In Thor's name, I swear it. Nor will you ever carry Thorvard's child so long as you keep faith in the gods. And should you return to Greenland to settle, your fortune made, you will be left in peace."

"How can you be so certain?" I asked.

"Because if it is not so, I will come," he said, still confident and calm. "And I will kill the men and women who have dared to trouble you."

A shiver slipped down my spine at his words, spoken as fact rather than threat. "You are a strange goði, Sonnung, to promise me such a thing so coolly."

"I am a warrior first," he said. "And have no doubt, Freydís—I will protect what is mine."

I believed he meant it.

CHAPTER THIRTY-SIX:
AD 2016
Emma

I'd been extra careful in my classes since the meeting with the dean and our less-than-felicitous run-in with Jenna, not wanting to give the students or the press any more ammunition. Despite my fun and very public weekend with Alex, when I got back to work the following week, I couldn't quite escape the feeling that this was the calm before the storm. And my reckoning was definitely coming.

"Let's go out Thursday night," Alex said, calling me during his lunch break on Monday. We weren't going to see one another outside of campaign events before then. Not even for a quick stolen meal, he was so slammed. "By some miracle my schedule is open, and I know a great place with Thirsty-Thursday teas, if you want to risk it."

"As appealing as that sounds, I think I'm still hungover from Saturday's adventures," I said, leaning back in my chair.

"Then we'll have a quiet evening in," he said. "Just the two of us, no cameras, no press."

"No parents," I added, then sighed. "It *would* be nice."

"I know that sigh. There's a *but* coming, isn't there?"

"I can't," I admitted, wishing he hadn't asked, because Alex was well trained not to accept a soft no. We all were.

He made a soft noise of disappointment, then cleared his throat. "I know you don't have anything campaign related."

"Definitely not campaign related," I agreed.

"Something with Sarah?"

"It's a private thing," I said, hating how uncomfortable it made me. Hating that I felt self-conscious telling him what it was about.

I always tried to mark Thor's day somehow. Not so strictly as a Catholic, because I varied my rituals, but I liked to do something, all the same. Offerings some weeks, meditation others, or maybe just some Norse myth–related reading to center me and remind me that I wasn't alone in that big cosmic spiritual sense. And I needed that little bit of extra peace it would give me more than usual. Especially when my life was on the cusp of blowing up entirely.

"Okay," Alex said slowly. And I knew—*knew*—he wanted to ask. The fact that he hadn't yet was fairly shocking, to be honest. "Well, if you want to talk about whatever or you end up with some free time *after*, I'll be home in front of the television, binge-watching *The West Wing*."

"Nothing you don't mind me interrupting, then," I said, smiling at his dramatic woe-is-me tone—a pathetic attempt to elicit my sympathy for his poor, sad, lonely life. "I'll keep that in mind. But in the meantime, you should get back to work."

He sighed, and the Alex I was dating was replaced by the Alex who managed my father's campaign. "You'll let me know if you hear anything further from the dean or your intrepid student reporter?"

"Cross my heart," I told him. "But would it be so awful, really, if I gave her an interview and just came clean? Let my father make some statement in the aftermath about how I'm an independent adult and make my own life choices, and wash his hands of the whole thing, if he doesn't want to actually support me?"

"With a bonus of making your father look like he doesn't know what's going on in his daughter's life and has lost all control over his family in the lead-up to Election Day, with Turner already pushing hard for a return to the Christian patriarchy?" Alex replied, his tone dry. "No, that doesn't sound awful at all."

"But it would be over. Before anyone else had the opportunity to expose me. You'd have control of the message."

"Your student reporter and her editor would have control of the message," he said. "Not us. And you know exactly how Turner is going to respond. By the next day, you'll be a family of witches controlling your father and all his choices. It will be a thousand times worse than all these stupid accusations he's making about how your father is just blindly following anything that this new 'Antichrist' pope says, without any consideration or concern for his true Christian constituency. And it won't be just you who gets smeared, Emma. It's going to be your mother, too, as the daughter of an immigrant. She'll become an example of how immigrants are destroying our country and our traditional Christian values, literally overnight."

My stomach twisted. "But my mother is Catholic. She's been Catholic her whole life. No one who has known her could ever doubt that."

"They will," Alex said. "That's the kind of campaign that Turner is running, and that's the kind of political season it's been. Anything goes now, Emma. And neither your father nor I want to see you and your mother dragged into this. If we can just hold off until after the election, November ninth, I promise you, we'll put out a statement, and you can come as clean as you want. We've only got a little more than a month to go. Just follow my lead on this until then, all right? Let us at least try to keep this under control."

"Yeah," I agreed, hating the picture he painted all the more because it was one I'd been imagining for years already. My greatest fears spoken in someone else's voice. "You know I will. I just—I hate this, Alex."

"I know," he said, and he wasn't the spin doctor now. "If I could make the world a place where it wasn't like this, where you would never have to worry about any of this—Emma, I promise you, I am going to do everything I can to make this as painless for you and your family as possible. No matter what happens."

I knew he'd try. It was his job, after all, to try. But I still didn't like being the skeleton in my father's closet, and I hated to think what would happen if Alex failed to keep me hidden there like my father wanted. It made everything so much more complicated than it should have been—and the fact that it was my father's choice and not Alex's didn't make me less resentful. Which wasn't fair to anyone but didn't change my feelings in the slightest.

I guessed I'd be spending my Thursday night praying for patience and understanding as well as strength.

As it turned out, I overestimated how long I had before the storm hit in earnest. Monday had been quiet, and Tuesday as well, but Wednesday, I was caught by a cameraman and a reporter on my way into the history building. And not just any reporter, either. Marco Harris. Who, of course, I had graduated with. Because that was life in a small town.

"Emma!" he called, jogging to catch up to me when I hurried past. "How about giving me an interview for old times' sake? For the *Courier*."

I shook my head and kept walking. Marco, of course, wasn't deterred.

"They only gave me this beat because we went to school together, Em. You've got to give me something. Anything."

"Sorry, Marco." And I was, genuinely. But he had to have known I wasn't going to be an easy story.

He slowed, falling back a step. *Please, please, please . . .* And then he skipped to catch up again, crushing my hopes. But this time his easy we're-all-just-old-friends face was gone, replaced by something more determined, more formal, and he had his phone held out, a big red "Recording" button taking up the screen.

"Ms. Moretti, is it true you're being investigated for religious discrimination in your classroom?" We were definitely in on-the-record territory now.

"No comment," I said firmly, shoving through the door in the desperate hope that I might shed him. I was 90 percent sure that Jenna was responsible somehow for *that* particular question, and I hated knowing it was my own fault for baiting her at the bar.

Proving once again that he couldn't take a hint, because some things never changed, Marco followed me into the building. "What about the reports that you've left the Church, that you no longer identify as Christian at all?"

"No comment," I said again, digging my phone out of my pocket. Alex would have warned me if he'd known something like this was coming. Since he hadn't, I just hoped I could warn *him* in time.

"Some say you're not even qualified to be teaching a course on history, that you only got the job because your father pulled some political strings. Is there any response you'd like to make to that?"

I ignored my typos and hit "Send" on a hasty text to Alex before spinning on Marco at the top of the stairs. "No. Comment."

He grinned at my irritation, which I couldn't completely hide. I could already imagine the words on the page. *An agitated Ms. Moretti refused to comment.* "Come on, Emma. I don't have to be your enemy. The *Courier* doesn't want to hurt your father, and I always liked you. I asked you to homecoming two years in a row, remember? All you have to do is tell me the pendant you were wearing in that picture is something sentimental—a family heirloom, passed down on your mother's side. Give me the exclusive, and we'll spin it any way that the congressman wants."

It took everything I had not to grind my teeth, and I could do nothing about the heat that had flooded my face—no doubt all being recorded. I could, however, do my best impression of my mother.

"Marco, Marco, Marco," I said, forcing myself to smile. "While I admire your appeal to high school nostalgia, you know I can't comment."

"Can't or won't, Emma?" Marco asked.

"I don't have any comment about that, either," I said, turning away with what I hoped was grace and poise, not obvious panic. "Have a nice day, Marco."

He didn't immediately follow me up the stairs. The college was technically public property, but I wasn't entirely sure how far he could trespass in the name of the press—or if the rules were something that would stop him, regardless. My phone buzzed in my hand, and I breathed a sigh of relief when I saw it was Alex.

```
Turner  threw  around  accusations  last
night during an event. It all just blew
up—I was just about to warn you.
```

A second message followed almost immediately.

```
Don't  talk  to  Courier  reporter.  Our
friend can't help now. I'll be there
before your class gets out.
```

It wasn't much to go on. And in fact, I wasn't sure it was helpful at all. But if it was Turner who had started it, then at least that made it look less like my teaching was problematic and more like I'd been set up with Ashley. And that meant Turner was hoping for a response, even if that response was just watching us close ranks.

If you come to me, they'll know they have
a story, not just unfounded accusations
and loose talk. Stay there. I'll be okay.

Alex's reply was quick.

Are you sure?

I hesitated, staring at those three small words. A question that told me I wasn't wrong to tell him not to come at all. Because if he thought it would be better for the campaign to be by my side, he wouldn't let me persuade him otherwise. Nothing I said, no assurance I gave would keep him from coming.

So I lied and told him yes.

Because I wasn't sure I would be okay, not really. I *wasn't* okay, and I probably wouldn't be until all of this mess was behind me. But I knew I could do what I had to do for my father's sake. Marco Harris could badger me all the way back to my car, and I wouldn't tell him anything. I wouldn't give him anything.

This wasn't my father's secret, no matter what anyone might say. It was mine. And no one in the press was going to take it from me. No campaign was going to break me open and use me for mud. Not on any terms but my own.

Let them speculate. Let them dog my father. Let them accuse me of whatever they wanted. Until I spoke up, one way or the other, they'd never know. And sure, maybe it would look bad, maybe it would hurt my father, but it was my faith and my life. And I was going to fight for my rights, with or without the congressman's support.

Of course, when I pushed open the door to my classroom, I suddenly realized I hadn't taken all the variables into consideration.

Sitting in the front row, in the place where Ashley used to be, was my Pagan reporter, and lining the walls, it appeared, were her friends.

CHAPTER THIRTY-SEVEN:
AD 1000
FREYDÍS

When Thorvaldur finally arrived, the second longhouse was ready and waiting, and part of me wondered if it had been his intent to avoid the work of building when he chose to sail north first, instead of following us more directly west. But when he leapt from his ship and waded toward us, I was too relieved to care. Perhaps I did not love Thorvaldur as I had Thorstein, and perhaps we fought more than we spoke peaceably, but I was glad to have my brother safe upon land, all the same.

"I was certain you had lost yourself," I said, running into the water to meet him. "Tell me you found ivory enough to make you rich, at least?"

Thorvaldur's eyebrows rose. "You cannot be *happy* to see me, surely?"

"Never gladder," I said. "But only because I would not have wanted to tell Father he had lost another son."

My brother grunted, his good humor blunted by the reminder of Thorstein's loss, but he threw an arm across my shoulders, and though he did not say it, I thought perhaps he was pleased to see me safe as well. "Gudrid and Karlsefni?" he asked.

"Gudrid is pregnant," I told him, not quite able to keep the bitterness from my tone. "But Thor favored us with good sailing, the wind with us the whole way here, and the seas not unduly rough."

"Then you had a better time of it than we did," he said. "My ship needs repair; the hull breached when we struck rock. I was not certain that the work we did on the water would hold to get us here, in truth."

"There is bog iron enough to be smelted," Sonnung said, meeting us when we reached land. "Well met, Thorvaldur."

My brother's jaw tightened, but he nodded. "Sonnung. Did you prove yourself as fine a sailor as you boasted?"

"Better," I said. "You will not trust me, I know, but Karlsefni will agree."

"Karlsefni would know," Thorvaldur admitted, though I knew he did not care to give Sonnung credit of any kind. "You have my gratitude for delivering my sister safe."

It was not friendship between them, nor would it ever be, but they were the kindest words my brother had ever spoken to the man I loved, and I was pleased to hear them. Pleased, too, that Sonnung did not provoke him, only accepted his thanks with a slight dip of his head and waved us both on.

"I'll lend the men my strength in drawing the ship farther up the bank and be along," Sonnung said, squeezing my hand as we passed.

"Have you not tired of one another yet?" Thorvaldur grumbled when we'd left him behind.

I shook my head. "Had he arrived before Thorvard, all Father's arguments could not have persuaded me to marry."

"It cannot last, Freydís," my brother warned. "And I fear the trouble it will cause you later."

"What matters is now," I said. "Who would dare cross him to trouble me, besides?"

"And after he is gone?" Thorvaldur asked.

"Sonnung is worth whatever trouble comes."

My brother grunted again, and any further objections he kept to himself, for we had reached the longhouse and Gudrid came to greet us, her face flushed with happiness. Or the glow of her pregnancy, perhaps. I would not know. The babe I had carried had caused me nothing but misery, while she flitted about, unbothered in the slightest.

"We were so worried," Gudrid said. "But Sonnung promised us you were safe, and if there is any man who knows the temper of the sea even half so well, I have not met him. Come inside and get dry and warm. I'm certain you must be starved for something more than fish after so long on the water."

We had no shortage of game, and more than enough to share with my brother and his hungry men. We ate well on what the men trapped, snared, and hunted, without needing to harvest from the sea. At least throughout the spring and summer, which passed easily and happily after Thorvaldur had finally arrived. For the first time in a long time, all that season and the next, my brother and I laughed together more than we fought.

It wasn't until autumn that we saw the first sign of the others.

Gudrid was heavily pregnant, and I sat with her often during the day, my worry for her greater than my frustration. We'd discussed in the early summer whether she might be better served by returning to Greenland to give birth, but she had insisted that she would stay, and the rest of us women took it in turns to remain at her side, doing the heavier work she would have tried had we not been there to stop her. It had built a peace between us all, though I knew it was for Gudrid's sake more than mine that the three others had come around. Gudrid was difficult to dislike and so easy to love.

"I am *fine*," she said, laughing, when I scolded her for lifting the heavy pot down from the chains on which it hung over the fire. She'd insisted it needed scrubbing, of which I had little doubt, but I didn't think she should be the one to wash it. "Truly, Freydís, I have not had a moment's pain or discomfort. Christ has blessed me with an easy pregnancy, and I am certain it will hold through the birth."

"Sonnung and I have made offerings to the goddesses all the same," I told her, for I did not trust her blithe assurances.

"Do not say so to the others," she told me, clutching at my arm, her expression grim. "Or should anything go wrong, they will blame you both."

"Will *you*?" I asked.

"Of course not," she said at once. "Whatever becomes of me and this child, it will be God's will, regardless, and Karlsefni, too, understands that. But you have enemies enough without adding kindling to the fire."

It was my turn to laugh then. "I have Sonnung, Gudrid. And Thorvaldur, too. Between them and Karlsefni himself, few would dare to act against me, no matter what might come."

"Even so," Gudrid said. "I would not have you take unnecessary risks for my sake."

I carried the cook pot for her, and we settled in the grass outside the longhouse, Gudrid upon a stool and me doing the scrubbing. "Would you have me hide my faith? Live in fear that I am discovered? You heard what Karlsefni said, what Thorvard told him before we left. In Iceland it is forbidden now to worship our own gods and ancestors openly. Would you have me live that way as well? Dishonor myself and my ancestors?"

She sighed, looking away. "I know you chafe with every new restriction, and I do not pretend it is fair—it is only that I worry for you. Sonnung and Thorhall as well, for they share your struggle, though few would dare challenge them, no matter their faith. But we are women, Freydís, and it is different for us. For you."

Because I had let Sonnung into my bed and left my husband behind. Because I did not behave as I ought to in any case, and my father had let me run wild alongside my brothers instead of giving me over to Thjodhild's keeping. Because the rules and laws I had lived my life by were shifting beneath my feet like so much sand with the pull of the tide. My faith was being washed away, one baptism at a time, but still I stood in defiance.

"Here in Vinland, among these men and women, I am safe enough," I said. "But you must know by now I would live as I liked even if I weren't. I will not be made to hide."

Gudrid half smiled. "No, I suppose you won't."

Movement on the water caught my attention, and I narrowed my eyes, lifting a hand to shield them from the glare of the sun. "Do you see that?"

"What?" Gudrid followed my gaze, then rose to her feet for a better view. "Those are not logs, precisely."

"No," I said, abandoning the pot. "I think . . . I think they are boats."

An oar flashed, raised high in signal, though what it meant I was not certain. A handful of the small hide-covered boats ran aground, and strange large-eyed men and women climbed out to dither upon the bank.

"Hello!" Gudrid called out, stepping forward, and I hissed at her to stop, but she only waved me back. "My name is Gudrid."

One of the women stared at us, her head cocked.

"My name is Gudrid," she said again, moving nearer still. "What is yours?"

Our own men had begun to gather by then, and the strangers examined them, moving near enough to touch their cloaks and reaching for the knives and axes they carried. Karlsefni and Thorvaldur were among them; Sonnung had gone to make his offerings and prayers.

"Do not give them your weapons," Karlsefni commanded. "But if they desire to trade, we will offer other goods. Andsvarr, fetch a pail of milk and some of the cheese, and let us offer our guests food and drink."

The woman Gudrid had spoken to now stood before us, having been drawn away from the others by her voice. She peered at the brooches on Gudrid's gown, then studied her face, creeping like a nervous cat nearer and nearer.

"My name is Gudrid," Gudrid said for a third time.

"My name is Gudrid," the woman repeated back.

Andsvarr returned then, and Gudrid stopped him, taking a portion of the cheese before sending him on. She took a bite, making noises of pleasure, and then offered it to our guest.

"It's cheese," she said. "To eat."

The woman took it tentatively, smelling it, then nibbled. Her face broke into a smile with her first taste, and she called something out to the others in a language I did not know.

"It is a wonder we did not see them before now," Gudrid said to me, smiling back and miming bringing the cheese to her own mouth, encouraging the woman to eat more of it.

"They are like landvættir," I said, uneasy. Certainly they seemed somehow too small of stature to be men. "I do not like it, Gudrid. If we have offended the spirits of this land, it will go ill for us this winter."

"They are hardly spirits, Freydís." Gudrid laughed. "Look at them. They're only skraelings."

But I was looking at them. Looking at the way the men circled Andsvarr and Karlsefni, almost prowling as they examined their clothing, reaching hands out to touch the hilts of their knives, the gold and silver of their rings. And they did not look like the skraelings my brothers and the other men had spoken of meeting in the North.

"We should make an offering to appease them," I said. "More than a little milk and cheese."

"Hush now," Gudrid said, unwilling to humor me. "They are men and women, that is all. Seeking trade, no doubt, or perhaps we caught them unaware while they hunted, appearing as if from nowhere the way we have."

But I shivered, wishing that Sonnung were beside me. He would have known for certain whether these people were spirits or men, and what was to be done to appease them.

The woman Gudrid had spoken to ran back to her people, and Karlsefni's men, unconcerned and confident, were offering red-dyed fabric in trade for the fresh skins in the skraelings' boats. No Icelander ever left home without homespun to spend, and the strangers seemed pleased enough to accept it, even while they drank more milk and laughed with one another.

At us, I suspected. At our foolishness.

"I'll set the men to work building a palisade tomorrow," Karlsefni said, though I had not realized he'd joined us. Thorvaldur was with him, watching the trading with sharp eyes. "Better to have it than not, should there be more of them."

"I do not see why they should trouble us," Gudrid said. "It is clear they do not use these lands, or they'd have come upon us long before now."

"Perhaps they did," Thorvaldur said. "Though I agree it is strange we saw no sign of them in all our comings and goings. We've ranged far enough north and south by now that we ought to have glimpsed some indication of a settlement."

"Leif said nothing to me of skraelings, either," Karlsefni said.

"Their presence changes things," Thorvaldur murmured. "If they should prove hostile—"

"We will be cautious in our friendship," Karlsefni said. "It is too late to set sail for Greenland now, besides, even with Sonnung to guide us. We will winter here as we planned. With the palisade wall for protection, we'll be safe enough, regardless."

I met Thorvaldur's eyes, seeing my own doubts reflected in my brother's face. Perhaps we did not agree on many things, but in this, I knew we were of one mind. Skraelings or landvættir, there would be trouble before we were through, no matter how cautious we were.

One of the skraelings groaned, clutching his stomach and falling to his knees in obvious pain. The woman Gudrid had met crouched at his side, shouting at the others gathered about Andsvarr, who was showing off his skill with an axe. One of the men turned on him angrily, grabbing at the haft in his hands, with Andsvarr struggling to keep hold. The skraeling tore it free and spun—

"No!" I shouted.

But it was already too late. The wicked edge of the blade had cleaved another skraeling's skull, dropping him dead.

Thorvaldur cursed, and Karlsefni pushed us toward the longhouse. "Take Gudrid inside. Keep her there, I beg of you."

The other skraelings had bone knives in hand by then, anger written clearly in their faces, and I hesitated. I was as good with a blade as most of the men—better, even, for Sonnung had taught me some of what he knew as well.

"Go, Freydís!" Thorvaldur commanded.

"Thor protect them," I murmured, and grabbed Gudrid by the arm, towing her with me into the longhouse.

"Wait!" Gudrid said, searching for a last glimpse of Karlsefni as he ran toward the trouble, his own axe in hand. "Freydís, please."

"Quickly." I shoved her inside and slammed the wooden door shut behind us, ignoring her objections. "He cannot keep himself safe if he is worrying over you."

Gudrid sank to the bench nearest the door, her fingers knotted together and her face gone white. Then she took a breath and closed her eyes, clutching at her cross instead, her lips moving in silent prayer.

I touched the hammer I wore and did the same. *Protect us all.* There was little else to be done while we waited.

The commotion outside must have startled Karlsefni's bull, for it began to low and then to bellow, so loud we could hear it even through the turf. It was followed at once by hooting and cheers. I rose quickly to peek through a crack in the weathered doorframe, surprised at the change, for the skraelings may not have been many, but there had been enough of them to fight, and they had seemed determined at my last glance.

Thorvaldur was already at the door again, pushing it open and laughing.

"It's safe," he said. "They've gone, and quickly, too! The man who had fallen was ill, the sight of him vomiting caused another to retch as well, and then the bull's bellow frightened them off the rest of the way. We let them take their dead with them, for they gave us no fight at all."

"Yet," I said.

But even my brother seemed unconcerned now. "We need only trot out Karlsefni's bull if they return."

I would have to hope that Sonnung, at least, would not be so foolish when he learned what had occurred.

CHAPTER THIRTY-EIGHT:
AD 2016
Emma

Y ou're not registered for this class," I said, setting my bag down behind the desk.

"Nope," the student reporter said, crossing her arms over her chest.

"If you're not registered for this class, you need to leave," I said, looking beyond her to the friends she'd brought along—most wore pentacles or hammers, and a few even wore valknuts, either around their necks or on their shirts.

No one moved, but most of their gazes flicked to her, watching for cues, I guessed.

"We're here in support and protest," she said. "Because whether you're Pagan or not, it shouldn't matter."

I pinched the bridge of my nose, hoping it would release the tension that was etching itself into my forehead. Whatever I said, it was going to make it all worse. If I kicked them out into the hall and Marco was still loitering, it would just be more incriminating evidence, both against me as a teacher and against my father. If I let them stay in the room, I was creating a divisive or antagonistic atmosphere, which would do nothing to help me professionally.

"While I appreciate your right to exercise the First Amendment, I can't have a group of protesting students disrupting my class. It's not fair to the students who are paying tuition to be here, and it's even less fair to the students who might have felt in any way discriminated against before now."

"But it's my fault," she said, her voice going thin. She swallowed hard, looking away. "If I hadn't come to ask you for an interview, none of this would have happened. I outed you."

And what could I say? If I denied the fact that I'd been outed, I'd be lying—a fact that these students more than any others would remember and be hurt by—but anything other than a denial left room for too much interpretation.

My father was going to kill me. And so was Alex.

"It's fine," I told her. "And not at all your fault."

She let out a breath. "Is it true, then?"

The room was silent, all my students staring, leaning forward, listening with an intensity they had *never* shown for my lectures or class discussions. I pressed my lips together, my gaze sweeping over them—students and protestors alike—and I made my choice. For the dozen Pagan kids who were fighting the same fight, looking for acceptance and struggling to carve out a place for themselves on campus and in the world at large.

It was my story. My faith. And I didn't want to share it with Marco or the press—that was true; I still didn't want it to become fodder for the ugliness of Turner's campaign. But it wasn't just about that now. It wasn't just about me and my family.

"Off the record?" I asked, meeting her eyes again, and she nodded sharply. I turned my attention back to the class at large, all of them still rapt. "I want you all to know that I deeply respect Christianity and its traditions; they're my family's traditions, and I still celebrate them with my parents and loved ones. It has never been my intention to let my own beliefs color or influence my teaching of history in this classroom, and the questions I asked, that I urged *you* to ask as you read the sources I presented, are questions that all academics and historians need to take into consideration when evaluating texts and the historical narrative as it's been passed down to us.

"But the truth is, I'm not Christian. I don't deny that Christ and God exist. I don't think Christianity is a false faith at all. But I . . ." I swallowed, gathering my courage. There was no point in going halfway now that I was doing this. "I worship Thor, and honor both the spirits of the land where I live and my ancestors as part of that faith."

"Whoa," Laura breathed.

I offered what I hoped was an all-business smile. "So now that we have that out of the way, I'd like very much to get on with our class today. Which I'm suddenly wishing I could say has nothing at all to do with the Viking Age, but unfortunately, it's a period which has some far-reaching consequences, so we won't be able to put it behind us entirely. That said, today we're going to turn our attention to the East, to what was left of the Roman Empire, and backtrack to the Code of Justinian, which was rediscovered in the High Middle Ages, around 1070, by the West—just as soon as our guests today head back to wherever they're supposed to be?"

My intrepid student reporter stood up, her eyes shining, and her friends all gathered their things, offering me shy smiles as they filed past. Maybe it wasn't how my father would have preferred me to handle things, and maybe it wasn't the best way to go about it from Alex's perspective, either, but watching them go, seeing them standing a little straighter, with a little more confidence in their steps brought by the knowledge that they weren't alone . . .

Whatever it was, it didn't feel wrong.

⚜

"We have a small problem," I said when Alex answered his phone. I was calling from my office, just after my class ended, though the damage had been done more than forty-five minutes earlier, and I wasn't entirely sure it hadn't already made it to Marco's ears.

"Your tone suggests you're using the word *small* as a euphemism for *large*," Alex said, only half teasing. "But go on. We're already deep in damage-control mode anyway at this point. Even our run-in with Jenna couldn't make this worse."

"That student reporter was in my classroom, with a dozen of her friends, staging a protest in my support."

Alex's beat of utter silence spoke volumes. "Emma, please tell me this doesn't end the way I think it does."

"They asked me directly, Alex. I couldn't lie. Not to them."

He groaned. "What did you say exactly?"

"That I worshipped Thor. That I deeply respected Christianity and its traditions, and shared many of them still, and did *not* believe it was a false faith by any means. I *had* to, Alex. To lie to them like that—I would have been telling them they should hide and slink, that there wasn't a place for them at the table. That the First Amendment was a lie and religious freedom is only for the people who believe in established mainstream world religions. I couldn't do it."

"You realize this forces your father's hand. Emma, he isn't going to like it. Even with your mother's support . . ."

I knew. I'd been turning it over in the back of my mind from the moment the words had left my mouth. "Whether I have his support or not, I am what I am. I don't want to cost him his seat, but you have to understand—it would have meant the world to me to hear someone else say the things I said today. To know I wasn't alone, that I wasn't crazy, and someone else understood. But if it's better for the campaign for him to disown me, or distance himself, or whatever, then just do it."

Alex sighed. "I'll do my best to make sure it doesn't come to that, and I know Irena will, too. I just . . . I just hope you're prepared for what comes next."

"It's going to be what it is," I said. "It was always going to be what it is."

"If your father breaks from you publicly, Emma—there might not be a lot I'll be able to do for you. What happens with the press from that moment on, that's not going to be part of my job anymore. I'll support you personally—you know I do—but professionally, I'm going to be in a difficult position. Do you understand what I'm saying?"

My throat went tight as the implications sank in. He couldn't actively work to control the damage *for me*, because it would be at odds with what he'd been hired to do. At that point, it would be in the campaign's best interests to let me burn. To throw me under the bus. "Yes."

"I don't want this to ruin things," he said softly.

I wished I could promise him that it wouldn't. But the truth was, I'd been trying hard *not* to think about this particular monkey wrench and the consequences it might involve at all. It was going to be almost impossible to separate it from our personal relationship if it came to that, and no matter how much support he gave me privately, it was the public support I was going to need more.

"You have to do your job," I said. "Even if my father doesn't support me, even if he cuts me off entirely, we're still better off with him as congressman than Turner."

"That doesn't mean *you'll* be better off if he wins."

"My father has to do what he thinks is right, and so do I," I told him, crossing to the window and glancing out, looking for loitering journalists and, much to my dismay, finding Marco still in place. "It was only a matter of time, really, before that put us at odds with one another. My only regret is that it has to become news, instead of just a private family matter."

"And you say you aren't your father's daughter," Alex said, some mix of pride and exasperation in his voice. "Just do me a favor and don't talk to the press yet, all right? Let me see what I can talk your father into before you jump off message completely."

"Honestly, I'd just as soon not involve the press at all."

"If only," Alex agreed. "Unfortunately, we won't be able to avoid them for long. And if your father comes out in support, I'm going to need you at his elbow."

"If my father decides to support me, I wouldn't miss the front-row seat," I said.

"But in the meantime—"

"I know, I know. Do not pass *Go*, do not collect two hundred dollars. I'm going straight home, and I'll wait for you to give me the all clear from there."

I just had to get past my old friend Marco from the *Courier* first.

⁓⋘⋙⁓

I took the long way out of the building, leaving through the doors farthest from where Marco had decided to camp out, planning to circle around in hopes that he might not notice me slipping by him from across the quad.

But instead of Marco Harris, I ran into my student reporter, with two coffees in her hands, sitting at the top of the stairs. "Professor Moretti!" She popped to her feet at the sight of me, holding out one of the cups. "I was hoping I'd catch you."

I hesitated, unwilling to accept the coffee she was trying to press on me and the conversation that was likely to follow as part of the exchange. But . . . "I never did get your name."

"Oh." She laughed. "Sorry. I'm Becky Andover."

"Well, Ms. Andover, I appreciate the gesture, but I'm afraid after today's eventful class, I need to head home pretty directly."

"Yeah." She flushed. "I'm sorry—about all of that. About everything."

I shook my head. "It would have come out eventually."

"But maybe not until after the election," Becky said. "Or after the complaint against you had been resolved."

"Or maybe it would have come out while I was under investigation anyway," I said. "That's the trouble with hiding who you are—it can't last forever, and even if it does, it's just as likely to mean you spent your life needlessly or excessively miserable because of it."

"I deleted the picture," she said. "When the *Courier* called, I didn't even have it anymore. I figured there wasn't any point in keeping it, because you'd never agree to an interview anyway."

I let out a breath. "No one else saw it?"

"No," Becky said. "I would never do that to someone. Especially not when I knew it could really mess up their life. It's hard enough without adding something like that on top."

I nodded, glancing down the stairs at the doors. Marco still seemed to be on the opposite end of the building, so I leaned against the railing, giving myself another couple of minutes before running off to hide. "I'm not going to pretend that the timing is great, or that it was necessarily the best way, but I appreciate your support. The intention behind it, anyway."

"I was hoping—" She stopped, cleared her throat, and then met my eyes. "We've been trying to find a faculty adviser for a student organization for pagans. Without a professor to sign off on it, we can't be official, which means we don't get any of the student-government benefits that the other organizations get. I know it isn't ideal timing, but if you're Heathen—would you at least consider it?"

My heart twisted. "I might not even be a professor next semester, never mind next year."

"But once someone signs off, it'll be easier for us to get approval a second time," she said. "And it would be so valuable to all of us. We could start doing outreach, planning events even, like solstice celebrations or Samhain before that. We could have real representation on campus."

I wanted to do it. To say yes. To support her and her friends—to have a community, even if it was just as an adviser, though I would never in a million years admit *that* to my mother. They deserved to have the legitimacy that I still hadn't found. But if I agreed without talking to Alex, without waiting to hear what my father had decided, it would be just as bad as spilling everything to Marco and involving the press.

"I'll need to think about it," I said, hating my own hesitation and the way my father's campaign still controlled me. "But send me your bylaws or whatever you have so far. I'll look them over and see if it's something I feel comfortable with."

"We'd really appreciate it, Ms. Moretti."

"If I do agree to this, it could mean a lot more attention than you want," I said. "And not all of it friendly attention, either. This close to the election, it could get intense."

"But at least people will know we're *here*," she said, fiercely. "We can show them what we are, instead of just being dismissed and ignored and forgotten. We'll be official."

I understood completely. The longing, the determination, the need to be recognized. My mother had spent all those years talking about how important a spiritual community was, but I'd never *gotten* it until I'd become Heathen and found myself suddenly bereft of one. At my small Catholic university, in its even smaller town, I hadn't exactly been in the best position to find like-minded people. But maybe Becky and her friends didn't have to suffer what I had. Maybe *this* town could be just big enough.

"I'll seriously think about it," I promised her.

And whether my father liked it or not, I was leaning hard toward yes.

CHAPTER THIRTY-NINE:
AD 1000
FREYDÍS

We saw nothing of the skraelings for the rest of the season, and Gudrid had not been wrong about the easiness of her pregnancy carrying through the birth, her child born without any trouble at all, much to Karlsefni's delight and my lingering frustration. It had been months, and though Sonnung had assured me a child would come, and remained as confident as ever, my womb did not quicken.

But when winter struck it was hard and cold, even so near to the sea, and I was glad I had no child to worry over. Storm after storm, howling so loud even the thick turf walls could not keep out the sound, and hip-deep snows that trapped us inside. Hunting became almost impossible, and the traps and snares we had set were all buried too deeply to find. The cattle and the goats were brought inside, and we had fodder enough to keep them alive, but none of us had been prepared for a winter this fierce. The men grumbled with so little to occupy their time.

"I mean to take Thorhall and go hunting," Sonnung said some weeks into the season.

The meat had long run out, and no man could live on skyr and cheese alone. Not when they had nothing else at all to grant any kind of satisfaction. Men, I knew, would overlook much so long as they had a woman in their beds, but there were only five of us, and even if we hadn't been married, we were far too few.

"Surely not only Thorhall?" Karlsefni said. "See who else will come with you, and give them purpose—even if they only return cold, wet, and exhausted, it will be better than not."

Sonnung grunted, glancing around the *skali* as if measuring the men. "Choose those in greatest need of exercise and send them to me, then. It will keep them from causing trouble here, I'll grant you, but I will make no promises for the safety of your Christian men."

"It will be as God wills it," Karlsefni agreed. "I'll send them out shortly."

"And what of me?" I asked after Karlsefni had gone to speak to the others. I had no real desire to set out into the snow, nor did I particularly wish to be left behind with Gudrid's wailing baby and men who had been too long from their wives.

"Make your offerings while I am away, Thorswoman," Sonnung said, a wolfish smile upon his face. "To Thor, Njǫrd, and Freyja, and when I return, I promise you, we will feast."

"Do you speak as goði," I murmured, too low for anyone else to hear, "or brag and boast as any other man?"

Sonnung laughed. "Have you not learned by now that I do not make promises I cannot keep?"

And then he kissed me and left, collecting Thorhall on his way. I sighed, watching him go, all self-assurance and strength. He'd been as unconcerned by the skraelings as Thorvaldur and

Karlsefni, though they'd all agreed to the building of the palisade to be safe. But why should Sonnung worry about so small a threat as men with knives and bows when he knew he had the favor of his god? Our god.

We'd found some honey that summer and turned it into mead, though we had too little to do anything but save it for the Yule feast. I felt no guilt at all for pouring a measure to take in offering to the gods, all the same, nor did I hesitate to take a portion of the goat cheese that Sonnung and I had made together. Like the god he served, Sonnung knew all that could be known of his goats and how best to use what they offered, and I was glad to join him at any task, for he made a patient teacher.

With food and drink, and wrapped in my warmest cloak—lined with thick fox fur from animals Sonnung and I had snared—I followed the other hunters from the longhouse and into the snow, unsurprised to see that Sonnung had broken a trail for me to the place we had chosen to make our offerings: a large flat stone that Sonnung had found and placed at the top of a gentle rise, far enough from the longhouse to grant us some small privacy, but near enough to be an easy walk. It was outside of the palisade now, of course, but as deep as the snow had become and as cold as it was, it seemed unlikely that the skraelings would stray far from their hearths.

It was a meager offering, I knew, but there was little to be done, and when I poured my mead in libation to Thor, Njǫrd, and Freyja as Sonnung had asked me to, I promised the goddess also that I would welcome Sonnung to my bed on his return and honor her with our love.

"I know I have spurned you," I said to the goddess, too aware of the conflict in my own heart. "I have prayed and prayed to be spared a child. But I see the way they look at me, Karlsefni's men and even mine. They pity me, and worse, they think it is more proof that you are weak. My empty womb betrays the gods I would honor above all else. So I ask you, please, to bless me, Freyja. Let Sonnung's seed take root."

As I made my way back through the snow to the warmth of the longhouse, I wished only that I had an animal to spare in sacrifice for the fast-approaching Yule.

⁂

"A whale!" Thorhall shouted, bursting into the longhouse with the news and covered in snow and sand. "Fresh upon the shore, and meat enough to sate us all! Sonnung sent me for more men to carry it."

I laughed, grinning at Gudrid. "He promised me we would feast."

"Let it never be said he does not keep his word." She smiled, rising with her little Snorri in her arms to lay him down in his basket near the fire. "You go, Freydís, for I am certain you wish to. Halla will stay with me, and the cook pot will be ready and waiting for the food you'll bring."

"You're certain?"

Gudrid smiled, shooing me away. "Go! Sonnung will be pleased to have you at his side."

I dressed warmly again, wrapping up tightly in my cloak, and went to Thorhall to volunteer myself with the rest of the men, all made eager by the thought of good eating for weeks to come.

"If only you had seen it," Thorhall said to me as we followed the path the hunting party had made in the snow. "Truly, Thor smiles upon us. Lightning struck the beast, and a moment later he had blown it to the shore."

"The gods are good," I agreed, imagining the sight. "And you saw it all?"

"I did," he said. "And helped Sonnung roll it up the shore before it was stolen again by the sea. The others were in the wood, hoping for a deer. But they would not have believed what they saw, I'm certain, or worse, claimed it was Christ."

"Christ is not lord of thunder and the storm," I said. "He does not command lightning from the skies."

"I *saw* it, Freydís," Thorhall said, awe beneath his words. "With my own eyes, I saw his power. Their Christ—he cannot compare to Thor's might."

"I only wish I had stood beside you," I said, and meant it. What I would have given to see the sign of his favor so clearly written in the sky. It could not have been only lightning, for every man had seen that much a thousand times in his life, but must have been something greater to have brought such a brightness to Thorhall's eyes.

"It was our offerings and prayers that pleased him. Yours and mine. The rest of the men have been content enough to ignore their duty to the gods, following where Karlsefni and Thorvaldur lead, but we have proven Thor's strength this day, and they will honor him now, as they should."

"I hope you are right."

"I will tell them what I saw when their bellies are full, and even those who worship Christ will be turned back to the gods of their ancestors again. How can they do otherwise when Thor has fed them and their god has not?"

I murmured something in agreement, but loyal as I was to Thor, to all the gods, I was not certain it would be as easy as that. Thor had already done much to protect us on our journey, and none of Karlsefni's men had so much as thanked him; if they were not grateful to Thor for their very lives, I did not think they would give up their Christ for a feast of whale meat. Thorvaldur surely wouldn't. He was far too stubborn for that.

When we scrambled down to the beach at last, Sonnung and the other men were already at work, carving through the thick hide and blubber to reach the meat inside. The cold weather had become a gift, for while the whale itself was still warm enough from the sea, the carved chunks of meat froze swiftly when packed in snow on makeshift sledges of fabric and saplings.

Sonnung grinned at the sight of me and waved the rest of us down, assigning the men tasks with brisk efficiency before turning back to me, as proud as if he had hunted the beast down himself. "Did I not promise you a feast?"

"You did!" And I laughed. "Thor must have heard your boasts and our prayers, both."

"He will always hear your call, Thorswoman," Sonnung said and tipped my face up to kiss me. "But we have Njǫrd to thank as well, for he drove the beast this way. You made him an offering as I asked?"

"Yes," I said. "And Freyja, too. But even with the whale, we have nothing to offer the gods for Yule."

"A proper offering will come," he said.

"Let us hurry, then, and get the meat back to the longhouse. I am starving already, just at the thought of so much to eat."

"Come." His smile turned to mischief and he let me go, climbing up the whale's bulk and reaching down to help me follow.

The whale's skin was smooth, but not so slick as I imagined. Almost waxy, instead, but when I slipped, Sonnung pulled me up, and atop the great beast, I could see the dark scorch mark down its long back, like a thousand tangled branches of fire, rippling blisters across the thick skin.

"This was truly the god's work," I breathed, kneeling to touch what the lightning had left behind.

"Thor does not forget his people, wherever they may be," Sonnung said.

He drew his knife, driving it through the burned skin. Oily, melted blubber leaked from the cut, but Sonnung was undeterred, carving deeper into the true flesh and offering it to me—not raw and cold, but steaming. Cooked by the lightning that had slain the creature.

"Eat," he said.

"What of the others?"

"They will have their fill soon enough," Sonnung promised. "But Thor meant this for you—and Thorhall, too. For your loyalty, even in this distant land. It is fitting that the first bite should be yours."

Then he leapt down, leaving me upon the whale's back, and shouted at the men to keep the blubber, too, for it would serve us well in the crude lamps we'd fashioned, and the extra light would be a boon when we spent so many hours trapped inside by cold and storms.

I ate the whale meat, staring again at the lightning scorch mark, like the finest knot work, or slender tree branches bared of their leaves and reaching for the sky. I had never seen anything so beautiful, and I touched it again, one last time, hoping to memorize the branching patterns, to keep it always in my mind.

In that moment, it seemed to me the greater gift—to see the beauty in Thor's power with my own eyes, and know with certainty that some small measure of it had been meant for me.

"Thor?" Thorvaldur spat, rising when he heard Thorhall boasting. "Thor is nothing to us here. It is Christ who has fed us, not your blustering god. And if we had needed further proof, we had only to look to the weather. If Thor cared about his people, he would not smite them with these storms and this snow. No! I will not listen to you sing the praises of a false god in my presence. This is not Erik's house, that I must suffer it in silence."

Sonnung and I had been sitting with our men, trading tales and boasting now that our stomachs had been filled, but at my brother's words, I rose, meaning to stand with Thorhall, to speak of what I had seen, too.

"No," Sonnung said, catching my hand and drawing me back down beside him. "I would know which of these men share your brother's mind. I would hear how they dare to speak of the gods."

"We prayed to Christ for food," another man said. "And it is Christ who has delivered it! Christ, who fed five thousand men with only two fish. When has Thor fed even one?"

Thorhall lifted his chin. "He fed his bond servant's family, did he not? He has his goats to feast upon, and shares them with any who travel at his side."

"I found no goat meat upon the shore," Thorvaldur sneered. "Did you, old man?"

"That whale bore Thor's mark," Thorhall said. "You all saw it, burned upon the skin, so deep it cooked the flesh upon the creature's back. You saw, and still you are blind to the gift Thor has given you. Do you not see, even now, he offers you forgiveness, if you will only grant him proper honor and respect?"

"I have no respect for a god who will not bestir himself to fight," Thorvaldur said, and his men mumbled their agreement. "He is not worthy of respect!"

"Sonnung—"

"If they will not believe their own eyes, Freydís, nothing you say will change their minds," he said lowly, his eyes flashing with a fury I had never seen. His gaze shifted to the men who sat around us, with their hammers hanging beside the crosses upon their breasts. "Do you believe as Thorvaldur's men do?"

"No," Arnbjörn said. "It was Thor's mark I saw upon the whale, not the cross. And if Thorhall prayed to his god, I have no doubt that Thor would listen. He could have sent only food enough for the old man, but he didn't. He fed us all, as is his way. Providing for us farmers when the kings and chieftains can't be bothered to do the same."

"Thor fed us," Farulf agreed, and the rest of our men nodded, some touching the hammers they wore and murmuring prayers of thanks.

"That's enough," Karlsefni said, for the argument had risen while we had spoken among ourselves, some of the Christian men threatening Thorhall with violence, and others calling for the meat to be thrown away. They would not accept any gift that was not from their Christ, it seemed, for fear that it would curse them.

"Enough!" Karlsefni roared again, and only then did the longhouse quiet. "Whether the meat has come from Thor or Christ, what matters is that we are fed. Stuff yourselves and be silent, for I will not tolerate your bickering any longer."

Thorvaldur grunted, grabbing his cloak and storming from the room, his men following, and all of them leaving behind what was left of their meal. Karlsefni's men spoke quietly amongst themselves, but I noticed their appetites, too, had faltered. They were not so hungry, it seemed, after all. Not if they owed thanks to Thor for their food.

"Let them choke on it, then," Sonnung murmured.

"They are fools," I said, trying to soothe him. For though he had often come to me in anger, I had never seen him seethe like this over the arguments of other men. More than once, he had dismissed their talk when it had infuriated me. "Pay them no mind."

"Distract me," he said. "Before I do something we'll all regret."

I studied his face, the tightness of his jaw, the bunching of his shoulders, and the tension in his body. Every fortnight he had come to me this way, glorious in his fury and his strength. And every fortnight I had given myself up, accepting the pleasure he offered in exchange for his need and bloodlust. But for the first time, I thought I understood the cause.

"Come, then," I said and rose, drawing him with me. Out of the skali and into our room. Gudrid caught my glance as we passed, and I tipped my head, asking for the privacy we would not have otherwise.

Her lips twitched, but she nodded, and when Sonnung shut the door, I offered him every distraction I knew.

But in the morning, when we rose from our bed and Thorhall told us Thorvaldur's men and those of Karlsefni's who had grumbled about the whale were all ill, I could not help but wonder whether it was Sonnung's anger, not wholly quenched even then, that had brought it down upon them.

CHAPTER FORTY:
AD 2016
Emma

I did manage to avoid Marco on my way home, only to be met by a handful of reporters waiting at the end of our driveway. They'd been camped out in their vans and sliding doors exploded open when I turned onto our street. Men and women with cameras leaped out to record ten seconds of me in the car, turning into the driveway with gravel crunching beneath my tires.

I parked, then took a deep breath to steady myself before I opened the door and winced at the reporters shouting my name and begging for me to respond to accusations that I wasn't Christian.

"Is it true that you split with David Carrara over religious differences?" one of the reporters called out, and I stiffened. *David.* "That he broke up with you when he learned you weren't Christian?"

If he'd spoken to the press . . . Why on earth would he have spoken to the press? I mean, David hadn't been perfect, but he'd at least been discreet and respectful if nothing else. His *grandmother*, though. I could just see her gossiping away—the bridal shower Jenna had mentioned she was in town for had probably been particularly fertile ground after my stupid smart-mouthed response to her insults at the bar—and then the story getting around, and the elder Mrs. Carrara was exactly the sort to be completely self-righteous now about how she'd always known there was something not quite right with me. As if being Heathen was on the same level as being a psychopathic murderer or something.

Though to be fair, to some people it probably was. Unfortunately.

I forced myself to ignore their questions and headed to the main house, where I'd need to go at some point when Alex broke the news to my father and he made up his mind about whether he wanted to close ranks or not. At least this way, I could avoid round two of shouting reporters.

"Mom?" I called, letting myself in.

"Kitchen!" she called back. I should have expected as much, I supposed. With everything going on, she was probably cooking up three storms.

"How long has the press been waiting for me?" I asked when I found her chopping vegetables at the island.

"They arrived just after you left for campus," she said, mincing her onion with a little more fervor than made me entirely comfortable. "Thank goodness for that much."

"They're asking me about David now," I said. "About our religious differences."

My mother sighed, setting her knife aside and looking up at me. "Mrs. Carrara the elder called me herself to give me her encouragements and sympathies, in fact."

"No!"

"She wanted me to know that no one at Saint Anthony's faults me for how you've turned out," she said, her voice icy. "It was all I could do not to bite her head off, and I'm afraid I wasn't particularly gracious."

"I'm so sorry, Mamma," I said softly. "I never meant for any of this—I didn't *choose* it, and I certainly wouldn't have wanted it to come out this way. You have to believe me."

She reached for me, minced onion and all, and I went to her, tears slipping down my cheeks and my throat too tight to continue.

"I know, my love," she said against my ear, hugging me tightly. "I know. And your father does, too, in his heart."

"After today, he's going to be even more furious with me," I half sobbed. "But I couldn't lie, Mamma. I couldn't do it. Not to my students. Not when they asked me directly if it was true. I couldn't betray them that way."

My mother sighed again, stroking my hair with the hand not covered in onion juice. "I can't pretend it won't make things more difficult with your father, but he'll come around, sweetheart. He will. You're his daughter, and no matter what you believe in, it doesn't change that."

I sniffed, pulling back and wiping my tears away with my shirt-sleeve. "Even if I cost him the election?"

"It won't come to that," my mother said, firmly now. "But if it does, it will be the result of his own foolishness, not your faith. He's so high-minded when it comes to everyone else, but if he doesn't prove his words by supporting his daughter—if he won't stand up for his daughter, why should he stand up for anyone else in our community, in the district? No. He'll have made his own bed, Emma. And he'll sleep in it alone, if that's the road he decides to walk."

"You can't mean that," I said.

"Why not?" my mother asked. "If Thjodhild could refuse Erik the Red, your father can learn to sleep on the couch and enjoy every cold comfort for his troubles."

"Mamma—"

"No, Emma," she said, picking her knife back up and starting again on her onions, fast and neat and ruthless. "I didn't marry a coward, and I won't have one in my bed now. Family stands together. Your father used to understand that, and it isn't a lesson I'm willing to let him forget now. Your *amma* would rise up out of her grave if she knew I'd married such a man."

"Somehow I don't think Amma would be terribly pleased to know I'd become Heathen, either."

My mother snorted. "Of course she wouldn't, but she'd never have thought for a minute it was nonsense. She wouldn't hear a word against Anja from Papa when your aunt started wearing a hammer and studying the Eddas."

"I never knew that," I said, though I had no trouble imagining Amma giving Grandpa what for and laying down the law on any subject. She'd come to America and become Catholic for him after World War II, and she wasn't above using those sacrifices for leverage. "I thought Anja didn't get involved in Ásatrú until after she'd gone back to Iceland."

"What we do in private is our own business," my mother said, as if that explained everything. Maybe it did. Anja never had flaunted her faith in public. She'd just . . . stopped going to church.

"But this isn't private anymore," I said. "It's public now, and I honestly can't blame Dad for being angry about that."

"He can be as angry as he likes that his family's private business is being turned into politics and smear attacks," she said. "But it isn't as though you were running all over town shouting poetry to Thor. You've been discreet and considerate, and while I'm not particularly happy about it, either, there are worse choices you could make."

I didn't expect her to understand that it wasn't anything I'd wanted. That it hadn't been a deliberate act but more of a gradual awakening and realization. That one day, after attending a Protestant event with Sarah, I'd realized suddenly why I'd been so uncomfortable with Christianity for so long. And maybe I'd been talking to some other higher power all along, without putting it together. After that, and all the reading and research, I'd still needed the push of the thunderstorm to wake me up.

But I hadn't *invited* Thor into my life, or gone looking for him. He'd just been there, waiting for me to recognize him. And how do you refuse a gift like that from a god?

"If they hadn't changed the mass, I might have been able to pretend a little longer," I told her. "I would have kept pretending. But the new language—it made me feel sick to be there. Like there wasn't room for me anymore." Not when peace was only for people of "goodwill" now. Not while explicit exclusions applied.

She scooped up her minced onions and tossed them into the pot, and then she turned her attention to me, just as focused as she'd been on her knife work a moment before. "I may not believe what you do, Emma, or even agree with it, but you will *always* have a place here. You will always be our daughter, and you will *always* be loved. No matter what."

I felt stupid for ever doubting her. And so, so relieved to hear the words.

But I had a sinking suspicion that my father was going to feel differently—and that my mother was really only speaking for herself.

I helped my mother make a salad, spinning the lettuce excessively—the only outlet I had for my own nervousness and worry. We hadn't heard anything from my father yet, and by now I was sure Alex had broken the news about my little talk in class. I was too afraid to check my e-mail and find out what the dean had to say. It was only a matter of time, I was sure, before she knew about it, too.

"If it were only you, I think your father wouldn't be so anxious," my mother said while I sliced a cucumber, unfortunately with none of her skill. "With Anja in Iceland, it made it easier for him to ignore. And of course no one could have predicted it would come to such a head. This campaign season has been so strange. Any other year, it would have been a minor thing, something easily brushed away and forgotten. But the way Turner has been campaigning . . . It won't take him long to discover that we have more than one Heathen in the family. One is just a fluke, but two, I fear, becomes a pattern."

"Auntie Anja's beliefs have nothing to do with mine," I said. "It isn't as though she went out of her way to convert me."

"I doubt very much anyone is going to give you the chance to say so before they draw their own conclusions," my mother said wryly. "And Anja's situation has always made your father uncomfortable. He's been worried over her for years, though I never understood why, really. Not until now."

I pressed my lips together to stop another apology, focusing my attention on chasing a slice of cucumber before it could roll onto the floor. The only forgiveness my mother thought I should be looking for was from God, and she'd made it more than clear that *that* was my business, and mine alone.

"Alex will see us through," my mother said after another heartbeat. "He'll find a way to turn this in your father's favor, Emma, you'll see. And one day we'll look back on it all and laugh at how worried we were for no reason."

I really wanted to believe it. But . . . "What if Dad doesn't let him?"

"He will," she said.

"But if he doesn't," I insisted.

She banged her spoon on the side of the pot. "If your father puts him in that position and Alex doesn't resign, I'm not sure he deserves you."

I shook my head, scraping the last of the cucumbers into the salad bowl. "We've only been dating a few weeks, Mamma. And I already told him that the campaign should come first."

"Alex hasn't spent the better part of the last decade helping your father to build his brand on family values to see it all thrown away at the first spot of trouble. It isn't just about you, though I think it should be in no small part, of course. It's about all the work he's done and the hours he's put in, and your father choosing either to trust him to do his job after all of that or not. And if your father decides *not* to trust Alex now, of all times, there's absolutely no reason for him to stay. Not one."

The house phone rang, and my mother snatched it from the cradle at the sight of my father's name on the caller ID. "Stir that," she commanded me, her hand covering the receiver, before she disappeared into the laundry room and shut the door.

It was a sign of how serious the situation was that she left dinner in my unsupervised hands for any length of time, to be honest, and I could only hope I didn't screw it up somehow while her back was turned.

Her voice rose briefly, muted by the door and the sound of the exhaust fan over the stove top, and I grimaced. As if I hadn't already screwed up enough.

My cell vibrated, and I fished it from my pocket, unsure whether to be relieved or concerned that it was Alex calling—at the same time that my mother was fighting with my father, no less.

"Is everything all right?" I asked.

"As all right as I can make it for the moment," he said. "I was hoping I might be able to slip away to grab some dinner and stop in to see you, but it doesn't look like I'm going to be able to get out of here before ten. Will you be up?"

"Does that mean you have bad news that you don't want to deliver over the phone?"

"It means I want to see for myself that you're surviving all this and make extra sure you know you've got my support, no matter what your father decides."

"This isn't my first rough campaign season," I told him, forcing a laugh.

"But it's the first campaign in which you've been personally named and attacked. And I saw the footage on the news—the comments they're making about David now. You've been absolute grace under fire, Emma, and I can't tell you how much I appreciate that you've given the press so little today, but I know this isn't easy for you, no matter how brave a face you put on."

My mother's voice rose again, growing sharper, and I swallowed a blithe reassurance. "My mother sounds furious."

"Good," Alex said firmly. "The angrier the better."

"And my dad?"

"I'll tell you everything tonight," he promised.

I didn't like how that sounded, but by his tone I knew he wasn't going to budge. "If you're late, and I'm asleep already, let yourself in and wake me up."

"Are you sure?"

"If you *don't* wake me up, you'll find out that my mother's fury is nothing compared to mine."

Alex laughed. "Then I guess I'd better get back to it. But I'll see you later. Before ten, even, if I can manage it."

I snorted at that. "Not my first campaign season, remember?"

"You underestimate your standing on my list of priorities, Ms. Moretti."

And then he was gone—back to putting out the fires I'd sparked.

I couldn't help but wonder if he was regretting his admission that he liked it when I went off script.

CHAPTER FORTY-ONE:
AD 1001
FREYDÍS

The whale was not the only gift the gods gave that winter, for Freyja, too, took pity upon me at last. Sonnung did not speak of it at first, nor did I, fearing it would tempt the Norns to thwart us a second time, but by spring my stomach had rounded and by summer I was well on my way to ripened. Sonnung, who had always been considerate, became that much more so, and Gudrid, too, often pestered me to rest. It had been a long eight months.

"You did not listen when I said the same to you," I snapped at her one day when she told me to lie down, for I ached all over when I was not weakened by exhaustion instead, and I was far less fortunate than Gudrid in the easiness of my pregnancy. But lying in bed had left me restless, and tired as I was, miserable as this child had made me, I needed something to do.

"I did not have the troubles you do," she said, easing me back down upon the well-stuffed mattress of our sleeping bench before I had managed to get to my feet. "And I have no wish to see you suffer a second loss, either."

I sighed, struggling to find a comfortable position around the awkwardness of my stomach. "I am not so certain it would be the worst thing. Even Sonnung might see reason then, and stop praying for a child I cannot give. Though I would not wish to face the men—and to betray the gods a second time . . ."

Gudrid smoothed back my hair. "I know you are not happy for this child, precisely. That it is not easy, for more reasons than the trouble it might cause you with Thorvard when you return—Sonnung has spoken to me of your fears. But have I changed so much since Snorri's birth? Am I weaker now because of him?"

"You are different, Gudrid," I said, shutting my eyes against her reason. "You have always been what you are, and strong because of it. If you were less of a woman, less of a wife or a mother, that would make you weak. But that has never been the source of *my* strength, and I do not know that I could change that now."

"You'll learn to find strength in whatever role you are given," Gudrid said. "Of that I have no doubt, and nor should you."

"Gudrid!" Karlsefni called urgently into the longhouse. "My sword, and quickly!"

I struggled upright, alarmed by his tone, and Gudrid frowned, digging through his ship chest where it had been buried beneath cloaks and winter wear.

We had little use for weapons that were not meant for hunting. Even during the depths of the cold, the snow drifting high enough to block the door and the men sick and short-tempered, there had been few fights—not that those few had not been brutal. Thorhall had come to us in the spring, in fact, begging us to leave these Christians behind and sail home again to Greenland, but knowing of the babe I carried, Sonnung had refused him.

I found Sonnung's short sword easily enough, for he kept it at the ready—perhaps because most often when threats were made, they were made against those of us who worshipped in the old way—along with a simple round shield he'd made, and followed Gudrid from the room, ignoring the ache of my feet and the burning in my chest. If Karlsefni had need of his sword, Sonnung would, too, but I was not fool enough to think I could carry his longer, far heavier blade.

"What is it?" Gudrid asked her husband, handing him the blade.

Karlsefni glanced at me, then looked quickly away. "Skraelings."

"I told you they would come back," I said, pushing past him through the door. "We were fools to think they were no threat. That we could carry on after what happened. Would you have ignored it if you thought they'd poisoned us? If one of your men had died instead?"

"You cannot think to fight," Gudrid said to me. "You waddle more than you walk!"

I straightened, not caring for the twinge it gave me at the small of my back, but with a few swings of Sonnung's short sword, the muscles had loosened enough. "I would see the trouble for myself and be certain Sonnung is not left defenseless at the least."

Karlsefni grunted but had not the time to argue. "Gudrid, keep Snorri safe in the longhouse until I return. Sonnung will see to Freydís."

The men had gathered outside the palisade, attempting to count the small brown boats and the skraelings who guided them, paddles splashing and angry shouts floating over the water. Sonnung stood in the heart of the assembled men, surrounded by those who had sailed with us. He held a long-handled axe in one hand, the other, stub-handled, still hanging from his belt.

"Sonnung!" Karlsefni called.

At the sight of me at Karlsefni's side, he laughed. "I ought to have known you would not stay put."

"I am not so near to bursting that I cannot fight," I said, daring him to say otherwise.

He grinned. "Nor would I refuse you the right. Our son will learn from his mother's strength, just as he will mine."

Room was made for me among our men, and Sonnung nodded now and again at some comment from them. Neither our men, Thorvaldur's, nor Karlsefni's were warriors, but Sonnung was clearly spoiling for the fight.

"I see now why you thought them landvættir, small and strange as they are," Sonnung said as the skraelings drew nearer. "But I promise you, they will bleed and die like men."

Thorvaldur and Karlsefni joined us then. "Should we not return behind the palisade?" my brother asked.

"Hide, you mean?" Sonnung said, his lip curling. Ever since that winter night after the whale had been found, they had avoided one another at all costs, and it seemed Sonnung had not forgiven Thorvaldur yet. "You are so keen to claim your Christ is a warrior, more powerful than even Thor. Surely he can lend you some small measure of courage to face this threat."

Thorvaldur's face flushed. "It is the stronger position."

"If we had bows for every man, perhaps," Sonnung said. "But unless you wish them to surround us, to cut us down one by one when we are driven out for food or water, we dare not retreat now."

"We are only farmers and traders, Sonnung," Karlsefni said. "Without even shields enough to form a wall. You ask these men to fight, but they are ill-equipped for such a battle."

"Nor are we prepared for a siege," Sonnung replied. "Even if the palisade might hold—and I do not think these men are so foolish that they will not realize fire will do the work of destroying it for them— there are no springs inside the walls, no wells. You will die miserable and pathetic deaths for lack of water."

"Listen to him if you wish, Karl," Thorvaldur said. "But remember he is a stranger to us all—just because he wears a sword and speaks of war, it does not mean he is the warrior he would have us think."

"Sonnung has proved himself time and again," I said. "You have seen it with your own eyes."

"I have seen him seduce my sister into betrayal of her husband and her kin," Thorvaldur said. "I have seen his influence over you grow. You who never wanted a child, now carrying his devil spawn, and gladly, if it will keep him at your side. When did you become so weak, Sister?"

Sonnung's sword pressed against my brother's throat before he realized my intent, and I stepped forward after that to crowd him, forcing him back. "I am not the one looking for excuse to hide, Brother. And if you think I have done what I have done in service of anyone or anything but the gods—Thorstein would have understood."

"Where was Thor, then, when Thorstein sickened?" Thorvaldur demanded. "Where has he been since, to defend himself against the march of Christ?"

Sonnung growled, the sound low and deep as thunder. "Thorstein did not ask *Thor* for his help. He called out to Christ and *died*. Do you think it was not Thor who smote you this winter after you had cursed his gift? That he has not seen everything you have done? Why should he fight at all for men so foolish they cannot see the truth when it stands before them?"

"Enough," Karlsefni said, his hand closing about my wrist, urging me to drop the sword that still pressed against Thorvaldur's throat. "We have no time for this squabbling while our true enemies are in sight."

I lowered my blade, my other hand upon Sonnung's chest, steadying him, if not holding him back. Karlsefni was not wrong. And Thorvaldur's words were only talk and bluster to disguise his own fear. "Sonnung and I will stand and fight. Any who wish to join us are welcome to remain. But if you are afraid, if you would rather hide behind the palisade, then go. Better to have just twenty men of courage than one hundred who will break and run."

There were more than twenty in the end who stood with us. Thorhall, of course, and the majority of the men who had sailed under Sonnung, and Karlsefni, who knew what it meant to lead and would not risk any appearance of weakness, though he spoke quietly to his men, and many of them returned behind the wall. Thorvaldur, too, remained, with a small number of his crew, for after accusing me of weakness, he could hardly turn away.

The skraelings beached their small boats and leapt from them, armed with axes and bone knives, with bows and arrows.

"Now!" Sonnung roared, and we charged against them, for it served us not at all to stand back.

The few men who carried proper wooden shields toppled the smaller skraelings, but there were so many of them, too many for us to overcome with brute strength alone. I slashed my sword, shoved with my shield, and slashed again, catching flesh and jarring against bone. But the skraelings fell, and it was as Sonnung said—they bled like men.

When the next wave came running toward us, and men to my left and right began to fall from the arrows that flew with precise and steady aim, our line broke almost at once. "Why do you flee?" I snarled at their backs. "Men like you, capable of killing them like sheep!"

"Freydís!" Sonnung's axe sank into a skraeling I had not seen, knocking the enemy away before his knife reached my stomach, and I realized we were alone, the rest of our men having fallen back. Cowards, one and all.

I raised my sword and screamed, slapping the flat of the blade against my breast. "Fight! Fight with me! Fight for Thor!"

At our backs, there was a bellow and then a shout. The skraelings' eyes went wide with fear, and Sonnung grabbed me, pulling us both out of the way as Karlsefni's bull charged wildly, driven by two of our men.

The skraelings scrambled out of his path, many of them turning away, running back to their small boats. Another cheer and the cow followed—less deadly without the bull's sharp horns, but no less intimidating as she trampled man after man.

Our enemies shouted among themselves in their strange tongue, and it was clear from the pitch that their leader had called a retreat.

By the grace of the gods, we had won. I laughed with relief, Sonnung grinning down at me as he held me close and safe, and then something inside me tightened, my belly hard and rippling with a breath-stealing cramp of pure agony.

My knees gave beneath me, hot liquid leaking between my thighs, and I screamed again.

Perhaps I had been too ripe to fight after all.

-cǝǝ-

My labor was fierce and terrifying, despite all Gudrid's soothing and encouragements, but it went quickly after Sonnung carried me into the longhouse and gave me over to her care. Quickly, but painfully. When Sonnung had retreated to make offerings and pray, I did not stifle my screams or my tears any longer, either.

But in the end, when I was exhausted and weak, Gudrid placed a small wailing boy in my arms.

Sonnung's son. Perfect and unblemished but for one strange mark. A pattern I had seen before, upon the whale's blistered skin.

The twisting, beautiful branches of a lightning strike, just over his heart.

-cǝǝ-

"My brave Thorswoman." Sonnung's rough knuckles brushed against my cheek, warm and dry and drawing me from sleep. "I am sorry to wake you, Freydís, truly, for you have earned your rest. But I fear you wouldn't forgive me if I left you asleep."

"What is it?" I frowned, catching his hand and holding it to my face. Even half-awake as I was, I could see his distress, and I struggled to sit up, my stomach protesting at once. I cursed the pain. To be confined to my bed again—I hated it.

"Thorvaldur," Sonnung said.

His tone told me everything, and tears pressed against my eyes as I fought again to rise. Sonnung helped me, wrapping a cloak around my nakedness and then lifting me up. He nodded once to Gudrid, who hovered nervously nearby, my newborn baby in her arms.

"Do not let her exhaust herself," she said. "And do not keep her long, no matter what she says."

"He does not have long," Sonnung replied and carried me out into the skali.

The wounded had been brought inside and given beds nearest to the fire. Aesa tended to my brother, pressing a damp cloth to his brow, and at the sight of me, her eyes went dark and angry. "Are you happy now?" she spat. "You and your man have killed him. You killed them all."

"Hush," Karlsefni said, rising from where he sat in vigil nearby. "Thorvaldur made his own choices, and he dies with honor. All our men did."

Sonnung jerked his chin at Aesa, and she huffed but moved away, giving up her stool to us. But even sitting took more strength than I had left in my stomach and back, and I grasped at Sonnung to keep my balance, leaning forward against Thorvaldur's sleeping bench. He'd been wounded in the stomach—by arrow or knife or axe, I did not know—and the bandaging was wet and foul smelling.

"Brother?"

Thorvaldur stirred, just a slow blink and the barest turn of his head. "Freydís."

"Brother, forgive me," I said, pressing my face against his hand. "I should not have questioned you—should not have shamed you. If you had been inside the palisade—"

He coughed, his fingers twitching against my skin. "Tell them. Tell them I died with a joke upon my lips. That I died well."

Hot tears slipped down my cheeks. "Of course," I promised. "Of course I will."

"Be brave, Freydís," he said to me, his voice barely more than a breath. "Be strong."

My brother's last words.

Two ragged, weak breaths later, he was dead, and Sonnung carried me, protesting, back to bed.

"We cannot remain," Karlsefni said several days later.

The four of us were alone in our small bedroom, Gudrid and I nursing our sons. Sonnung doted on the boy, gentle and affectionate, eager to love his son and lavish me with praise for my mothering.

"You cannot mean to leave so soon," I said, a chill in my blood at his words. "We cannot go back, Karl. We have barely even begun to settle!"

His gaze slipped away from our small family—a family he knew he would divide if we left—and settled upon Gudrid and little Snorri instead. "With Thorvaldur dead, and so many others lost, there are too many who want only to return home. Perhaps the land is not so bountiful in Greenland or Iceland, but at least they would not live in fear of attack."

Sonnung grunted. "It is not only that."

"No," Karlsefni agreed, meeting his eyes. "There is the fighting to consider, too. There are those who would blame you and Freydís for Thorvaldur's death and all the other ills that have befallen us. Much as I would like to think we might live peaceably here, regardless of our faiths, it is a wound that has been festering for too long already, and it will only become more poisonous, not less."

"You do not realize what you ask of me," I said, my heart aching. "You do not realize what you are saying."

"We do," Gudrid said. "We do, Freydís, and it hurts me to know the pain it will cause you, but I fear what another winter like the last will bring."

"The seas will not be with us if we leave so late in the season," Sonnung said. "Unless you wish us all to drown, we have no choice but to wait until spring."

"You are certain?" Karlsefni asked.

Sonnung's hand found mine. "As certain as the sunrise."

"Then we will tell the men that we leave in the spring, as soon as the seas will permit us, and perhaps that will be enough."

"Karl—"

"I am sorry, Freydís, truly, but I see no other way. You and Sonnung—you must make the most of the time you have left."

"It will be an easy winter," Sonnung said by way of reassurance, as if it could console me in the slightest. "I can promise you that."

"No one but Thor can promise such a thing," I said, turning my face away that he would not see my heartbreak.

He caught my chin and turned my face back to his. "I do not make promises I cannot keep, Freydís Thorswoman. By now, you of all women should know that."

CHAPTER FORTY-TWO:
AD 2016
Emma

It was nearer to eleven than ten when Alex finally knocked on my door, but I wasn't even close to asleep. Not when I'd come home to another e-mail from the dean waiting for me, and another meeting—which I was sure would decide my fate as a professor—scheduled and hanging over my head. It was almost a relief to let Alex in, for whatever distraction he'd brought with him.

"Sorry I'm so late," he said, barely waiting for the door to shut behind him before he kissed me, stroking my cheek and drawing me close. "You have no idea how crazy it's made me, not being able to come to you. I've been agonizing since you texted me about the reporter from the *Courier*."

I laughed a little at that, burrowing deeper into his arms and pressing my face into the curve of his neck. His collar smelled like Chinese food, but his mouth had been all cool mint. "You really didn't have to worry. It was only Marco, and even if it hadn't been, I know how to handle myself."

"It's not that," he said, smoothing my hair. "I wasn't worried about you slipping. I was worried about *you*."

"I'm fine, Alex," I promised. "Really."

"Maybe you can fool the press and your students, Emma, but it's hard for me to forget how difficult this was for you to share with your parents—with me."

I shook my head, stepping back. "That's only because I cared what you thought. But everyone else? If it hadn't been for my father's campaign, I'd have already been more open about all this with the wider world, hoping I could connect with people who shared my experiences. Looking for a community of my own. Sure, maybe the timing could have been better for work, but aside from that, I don't particularly care what strangers think of me."

"They're going to think a lot of awful things before Turner is done," Alex said, studying me. No doubt looking for the lie beneath my words.

But there wasn't one. "I care about what my father thinks and about how much damage I've done to his campaign. And I care about you and my mother and Holly and Sarah. Beyond that—I mean, of course I'd like people to know what Heathenry is actually about, but what the rest of the world thinks of *me* isn't something I'm going to waste my time worrying about, Alex, honestly."

Even then, I wasn't sure he believed me completely, but he let it drop with nothing more than a small frown. "I wish I could bring you better news on the campaign front, then, at least."

I'd left my parents' house after dinner, before my father had come home. Maybe it had been cowardly of me to slink out, but my mother had encouraged it. Knowing how late Alex was going to be, I could be fairly certain Dad wouldn't be home much earlier, and even if I hadn't been able to make out the words, I'd still heard enough of my mother's argument with him over the phone to know he wasn't completely Team Emma yet. No matter what reassurances my mother had offered.

"Tell me," I said, pulling him with me to the couch.

Alex sighed, tugging the knot of his tie loose and pulling it free from his collar. "He's determined not to address this at all. No matter what Turner says or anyone else, and Turner's already got idiots lining up to talk at length about how Ásatrú in America is nothing but racist garbage. On the one hand, I understand your father's position. It's a private matter relating to his family, and to dignify it with a response is only going to encourage more attacks along the same lines in the future. But it puts us—the campaign, I mean—in a difficult position. And you most of all."

"My father can't take me into consideration when he makes his decisions on this," I said. "Neither can you."

"I know that's what you've said, Emma, and I appreciate it—so would your father, under any other circumstances—but this isn't something that offers a stark black-and-white dividing line. Your father has built his reputation on his family values and, in no small part, the idea that he's the patriarch of a good Catholic family. Holly's rebellions were one thing; drinking and partying aren't necessarily diametrically opposed to Christian values. Plus, she's put that all behind her now. But . . ."

"But rejecting Christianity completely to worship a different set of gods altogether obviously is," I finished for him. "And I'm not the easily excusable teenager acting out, like Holly was, either."

He twitched one shoulder, tossing his tie down onto the coffee table and letting himself sink into the couch cushions. There were lines around his eyes, and deeper shadows than I liked beneath them. "The people who like him will think he's refusing to be drawn in and lower the tone of his campaign. They'll believe he's protecting your privacy. But the people who are looking for a reason to vote elsewhere might think he's betraying his values by not defending his daughter."

"Those are the same people who will vote against him if he *does* defend me, though," I said. "He's not going to win with them no matter what he does."

"Maybe not," Alex admitted. "But if his silence has shaken even *my* faith in him as a congressman, what do you think it's doing to the rest of his voter base?"

"You can't make that comparison," I said, pulling my feet up under me for warmth. "You have personal stakes in this. If I were just some girl you didn't know and hadn't been romantically interested in, you'd see it differently."

"I don't know that I would," he said, staring blankly at the table-top. "At its heart, this is about the First Amendment. And I'd seriously wonder why your father was willing to lend vocal support to one non-Christian faith but not another. Just because there are fewer potential voters to glean from it? Because he's only really willing to support people who believe generally in his same God? And I don't think I'd be the only person asking those questions, either. If he doesn't support his own daughter as a Heathen, would he support unrelated atheists? Agnostics? Hindus?"

"Of course he would."

Alex lifted an eyebrow. "This isn't a very good proof of it, Emma."

"How could it be?" I asked, as surprised as Alex probably was to hear myself defending my dad. But the things Sarah had said, the things Alex had told me, too—it made sense to me. And not just because I wanted to think the best of my father. Really, it was why I hadn't wanted to tell him at all. "It's far easier to support a stranger who believes differently than it is to accept that division in your own family. I'm basically rejecting everything he raised me to believe. All the values he takes such pride in and thought he'd instilled in me. Not to mention the afterlife element. Even if my father was a saint, he'd still be upset."

"But you can say that because you know him. You know *him*. His voters don't have the inside scoop. They don't know that this *isn't* representative of his real beliefs. And maybe—" He stopped himself, shook his head. "I want to believe that you're right about this. That it's just because it's his own daughter and his own family and that no matter what non-Catholic or non-Christian faith tradition you'd chosen, he'd have responded exactly the same way. But the longer this goes on, the more he hems and haws and makes excuses for not getting out in front of it, the less sure I am that's really the case."

"You're spinning yourself inside out," I said, lacing my fingers through his. It was so strange to find myself in this position, to be reassuring him, instead of the other way around. Up until now, Alex had been my father's staunchest supporter, his greatest defender. "You know who my father is, Alex. And you wouldn't be working for him if you thought he didn't believe the First Amendment was for everyone. It isn't like he's forbidding me from believing what I believe, or trying to pass laws to limit my rights or anyone else's."

If he wasn't responding to any of the accusations and comments Turner was making about me, it meant he wasn't sacrificing me for his campaign. Which was something I could live with, even if it wasn't what I'd hoped for. But honestly, I wasn't sure he'd ever come completely around to acceptance. Maybe I'd never thought he would. Maybe that was the real reason I'd been so willing to let him think what he wanted to think about my faith, or lack thereof, for so long.

Alex squeezed my hand, staring at our fingers twined together between us. "I'm supposed to tell you not to talk to the press. To ignore all of this and keep pretending you're his disaffected Catholic daughter. He's hoping your slip with your students will stay quiet, I suppose."

I stared. "But it wasn't a slip. He knows that, right? You know that."

"I know. I told him."

"He wants me to lie."

"Not lie, exactly," Alex said, clearly uncomfortable being the messenger. "Just keep being discreet."

I drooped back against the cushions, too tired and disheartened to fight. "Maybe he'll get lucky and none of this will matter after tomorrow."

"What's happening tomorrow?"

I rubbed my too-dry eyes and shrugged. "I have another meeting with the dean. And with everything that's come out—it's like you said. I'm already being accused of anti-Christian discrimination. Now that they know I'm a Heathen, too, I'm guessing I've got no better than a fifty-fifty chance of still having a job by the time I walk back out."

Alex lifted his arm, a silent invitation, and I slipped under it. "I'm so sorry, Emma."

But whether it was because there wasn't anything he could do to help me or because he wished he could have done more to protect me all the way around, I wasn't sure. I just knew it meant I was on my own.

My father had seen to that.

⸙

Alex had his hands more than full with the campaign and deflecting media requests the next day—the calls had started as early as six in the morning, the nonstop buzz of his phone waking me up while he made himself coffee and did his best to sneak out without disturbing me.

"Sorry, I hoped I wouldn't wake you," he said, dropping a kiss on my forehead when he realized I was awake. He only half buttoned his shirt before throwing his jacket on and stuffing his tie in his pocket. "Go back to sleep. And call me after your meeting, all right?"

"For the campaign's sake or for yours?" I grumbled, pulling my blanket up over my head.

He tugged it back down, his eyes serious. "Mine first, Emma. Always."

I caught his hand when he turned away and squeezed, hoping he knew I understood.

⸙

When my own phone started ringing at nine, after I'd finally managed to get back to sleep, I wasn't any happier of a camper. Especially not when I realized the caller ID said "Holly."

"What do you think you're *doing*, Emma?" she demanded before I'd even finished my half-awake hello. "Marco Harris called me at five in the morning for some article he was writing for the *Courier*. About *you*. Asking if I had any reason to believe you were secretly racist, or if you had any neo-Nazi friends."

I groaned, holding the phone slightly away from my ear to keep the level of shrillness to a minimum. "What did you tell him?"

"What do you *think* I told him?" My sister's voice went even sharper, and I knew she was offended that I'd even asked. "No comment, of *course*. And then I called Mom, only to find out that you're being outed as a Heathen and investigated by the college for religious discrimination in the one stupid class you're teaching. During an election year. During *the last month* before the election!"

"Right," I said, my brain still playing catch-up. "That."

"Just tell them you're Catholic and be *done*, Emma. I don't understand how you even let this happen. Would it really kill you to go to mass and pretend you're not completely ridiculous for five more weeks?"

"I'm so glad you called, Holly. No, I'm coping with all of this just fine, thanks for asking. It isn't like I'm waiting to find out if I lose my job in addition to losing Dad the election or anything. Obviously everything is going totally to plan in my life. I did all of this on purpose just to sabotage the family, because I just couldn't stand the thought of letting a whacked-out antifeminist religious extremist lose a seat in the House of Representatives. New Hampshire really needs that kind of representation."

"This isn't funny, Emma," Holly hissed. "You've been home for less than six months, and you've totally destroyed Dad's career."

"Well, we can't all be prodigal daughters and give up partying too hard for mentoring teens at church," I snapped. "And for the record, I'm not laughing. I can't help who I am or what I believe, and correct me if I'm wrong, but isn't one of your commandments 'Thou shalt not lie'? How do you think God punishes jerks who pretend to be Christian but are really just using it as a disguise to get ahead politically?"

"If you're not Christian anymore, what difference does it make? It isn't like any of that applies to you."

"No, but do you know what Heathens believe? We are our deeds. Honor and human decency still matter, Holly. I'm not lying for your convenience, and I'm not going to hide my beliefs as if they're something to be ashamed of. They're not."

"And what does your faith say about hurting your family and friends? About doing harm to your community?" Holly asked. "Does that all get a pass in the name of honesty? Or are you counting that as human decency now?"

I sighed, wishing I'd never answered the phone at all. "I'm doing the best I can. Trying to balance what's right with what's least harmful. And it would've been nice if my own sister could take five minutes to recognize that instead of jumping down my throat before I even had a chance to explain myself. But it's fine. Whatever. Consider your opinions duly noted. I have to get ready for a meeting that's going to decide my academic fate, but I'm sure Mom will keep you up to date on anything we didn't already cover."

And then I hung up. I didn't have the bandwidth to hold my sister's hand while she figured out all the ways in which her approach had been completely awful and worked her way toward an apology. Because she would apologize eventually. Holly didn't always think things through, but she usually got there, and even on this topic, I didn't think it would be any different. Or at least, I wanted to believe it wouldn't be.

Maybe I'd just hung up so I wouldn't find out I was wrong.

CHAPTER FORTY-THREE:
AD 1002
FREYDÍS

The winter was mild, just as Sonnung had promised, and we spent every moment together that we could, he and I and our son, whom we named Vingthor for the god we both loved. And while I still did not know how to be a mother, it came more easily than I had thought—perhaps because I had watched and helped Gudrid do so much.

But every day was bittersweet, one more day lost and one day nearer to parting. And what was I to do with our son?

"He'll be old enough for weaning by the time we sail," Sonnung told me. "If you fear your husband's treatment of you or the boy, I will take him with me when I go. He can be fostered somewhere safe until he is old enough to look after himself and guard you."

"You would have me give him up altogether?"

He smiled, taking my face in his hands. "Not because I doubt you, Freydís. Because I promised you my child would not be your burden to bear alone. To me, our child is a gift, but for you—even now, with Gudrid's help and mine, I can see how he might limit you. If you desire your freedom, I will not begrudge it."

"Let me think upon it," I said, unsure if I was relieved or hurt. And guilt-ridden, too, because I did not refuse at once.

But Sonnung understood. He saw that I was not Gudrid, who could be mother, wife, and mistress of the farm all at once. He saw that in my heart, I did not *want* to always worry for a child—or even my husband. I only wanted to be free to do as I pleased, and from the start Sonnung had been what pleased me most.

And so I pleased myself and him with every moment we had left.

Spring came sooner than I wished it to, and Karlsefni wasted no time in setting the men to work upon the ships. Sonnung oversaw our own, as he had done before, and with Karlsefni, he shared the added load of Thorvaldur's. I tried not to look at my brother's ship while it was readied. Despite the good weather, his men had glared at me all winter, grumbling and muttering amongst themselves. Karlsefni did what he could to quiet them, but it was little use.

As his sister, and because he had no wife, his belongings had come to me. Except for the pendant I had made for him, the match to the one I already wore of Thorstein's, I kept nothing, giving it back to his men to share instead, that they might not accuse me of killing him out of greed. They did not realize how much it hurt me, how much I dreaded returning home to deliver such news. If my father still lived, learning of Thorvaldur's death would kill him, and that would be upon my head, too.

While the ships were readied, Gudrid and I packed our belongings, filling our sea chests to bursting. The cattle would be slaughtered before we left—there was no purpose in sailing Karlsefni's ill-tempered bull back across the sea—but Sonnung had insisted on keeping his goats, so they would share the hold with our lumber, furs, and foodstuffs. Thorhall had found grapes when he traveled farther south the previous spring, and we meant to go south again before we sailed east, to gather more to bring back.

Vingthor played happily upon the bed while we worked, pestering Snorri, who wanted nothing more than to wander now that he'd learned to walk. "Be kind, little monster," Gudrid chided her son. "Vingthor is your brother in all but blood."

"They'll hardly remember one another when they're grown," I said, removing Sonnung's sword from their limited reach and hanging it back upon the wall. "Not if you truly mean to move to Iceland."

"It is Karlsefni's home," Gudrid said. "If things had been different here, this land empty, perhaps it would be otherwise. But I cannot ask him to remain in Greenland."

"And what will you do with your father's farm? Or Thorstein's share in the North?"

"My father's farm I will sell back to Erik, or Leif, I suppose. But I thought I might give Thorstein's half to you. Just in case."

I pressed my lips together, hearing the words she did not say. *Just in case Thorvard divorces you.* Perhaps I wished he would, except for what it would cost me, thrusting me back beneath my brother's thumb. I would be worthless, too—no man of worth would want an adulteress after her husband had cast her off, and Sonnung would not stay, even then. Could not, I was beginning to suspect, though I shied from the thoughts.

"Have you made up your mind what you will do with Vingthor?" Gudrid asked. "If you will send him with Sonnung to be fostered or not?"

"I fear I must," I said. "For his sake as much as mine. Unless the gods are good and I arrive to find my husband dead."

"You should not say such things," Gudrid said in the same chiding tone she had offered to her son. "Not even in jest."

"Even so," I said.

She sighed, studying me. "Karlsefni and I have spoken and agreed: if it would comfort you, we would foster Vingthor for you. In Iceland, no one need know he is not our true son, and he would be well cared for—of that you can have no doubt."

"It is kind of you to offer," I told her slowly. "But in Iceland, as your son, he would be raised a Christian."

"But he would be safe and loved, even spoiled," Gudrid said. "Surely that is what matters most."

I shook my head. "I did not carry Sonnung's child and birth him only to give him up to Christ."

"If you are worried that Sonnung will object—"

"No, Gudrid," I said. "Sonnung chose me because I worshipped Thor. Because I promised Thor he could have anything he wanted, if he would only provide me with my ship and guard my womb from my husband. Vingthor belongs to the gods more than me, and I will not betray them. Not when Thor has given me so much."

"You would truly rather let him be raised by a stranger?"

"Do you have so little faith in Sonnung, after all these months?" I asked her. "He dotes upon his son. Whatever home he finds for him, Vingthor will be well loved."

Gudrid spared me a doubtful look, though she did not voice any further concerns, and I ignored it.

Sonnung *always* kept his word.

The air was still crisp when we set sail at last, but it warmed as we went south, hunting and gathering as we saw fit. We took our time, following the coastline, and only when all three ships were filled to bursting did we finally turn east.

I watched the sunset on that last night in Vinland, Sonnung beside me and Vingthor tucked between us, and struggled to hide my fears.

"You must remember what I have told you," Sonnung said, his voice low. And he opened his hand to show me a silver hammer, offering it as a gift. "You need only call for me, and I will hear. Wherever I am, I will find my way back to your side."

I let out a breath and took it from him, looping the leather cord over my head. "And our son?"

"When it is safe and you are ready, I will return him home to his mother."

I leaned into his warmth, and he wrapped his arms around me, tucking my head beneath his chin. "It will feel as though I've lost a limb."

"Not for always," he promised. "In time you will find your strength again, and all of this will be a pleasant dream of memory. A source of comfort in the dark."

"If I had not married Thorvard . . . ?"

Sonnung sighed. "If you had not married Thorvard, you would not have bargained with the gods. We may never have met at all. And if by some trick of the Norns we arrive in Greenland to find your husband dead, I would still have no choice but to leave you."

"Because you serve Thor," I said, though not quite as a question.

"Because I am what I am," he answered. "And I have no wish to give you less than you deserve."

"What do I deserve?" I asked, brushing impatient tears away. "What do I wish for that you cannot give me wherever you go?"

"Do not ask me to take your freedom, Freydís. Even in exchange for love, you would resent the trade before long."

Much as I hated to admit it then, I knew in my heart that he was right. But that night after the sun had set, we loved one another well, and I wished, just for a moment, that I was more like Gudrid.

I wished that I saw freedom in love.

⁂

We sailed on, Sonnung at the rudder guiding us over calm seas, the wind filling our sail and pushing us on with greater speed. It was as easy a journey home as it had been to leave, but when we caught sight of the great bulk of Greenland at last, it brought me no relief.

My gaze turned to Sonnung instead, my heart aching in anticipation. He would stay only long enough to see that Thorvard did not mistreat me, and then travel on, taking ship with Gudrid and Karlsefni for Iceland, and I knew not where beyond.

I would be left behind.

⁂

"We did not think to see you for some time yet," Leif said after greeting Gudrid and Karlsefni warmly and declaring a feast in celebration of their return. "Did you not find the land as rich as I had promised?"

"Richer still," Karlsefni said. "But we fell afoul of the skraelings. And I fear we bring ill news to Brattahlid."

"Where is Father?" I asked, stepping forward then so Leif could not continue to ignore me.

My brother's face grew lined, but he met my eyes, and I knew. I swallowed hard against the pain. My father had known his time was coming and said as much, but I had hoped that he was wrong.

"When?"

"The first winter after you left," Leif said, and to his credit, he seemed no happier to share the news than I was to hear it. "Thjodhild and I buried him in the churchyard, in the hopes that in death, at least, he might repent."

"He did not want that," I said. "He would never have wanted that."

"He would have wanted to be with his sons," Leif said. "That much I think we can both agree upon."

My eyes narrowed, for though it was true, I knew he had not wanted it like this. My husband, sworn to support my father, ought to have stopped it. If he had been a man of honor . . . "Where is Thorvard?"

Leif's gaze flicked to Sonnung behind me, Vingthor in his arms. "Inside. Why should he hurry to greet a wife who left him for another man?"

"He should hurry to explain why he betrayed my father," I snapped. "Or he will wish he had no wife at all."

"Freydís," Gudrid chided, ever the peacemaker since Thorstein's death. "You do not know what has happened yet."

"I know," I said. "It is more of the same. Leif and Thjodhild doing as they like, and my husband following like a fool wherever they lead. Can anyone wonder why I left?"

"Careful, Sister," Leif said. "I am your chieftain and lawmaker now that Father is dead, and you will treat me with respect."

"When you have earned my respect, *Brother*, you will have it. Not before."

Leif stiffened, but his gaze faltered, slipping to Sonnung again, and though my brother fingered the hilt of his knife, he did not dare draw it. Even with a child in his arms, no one could want Sonnung for an enemy.

"Were I less a Christian," Leif growled, "I would let Thorvard take your life for your adulterous behavior."

"He might try," I said, pretending not to hear Gudrid's exasperated sigh. "He wouldn't succeed. And then what would you do? Kill me yourself?"

"I have assured Thorvard that it would not happen again," Leif said, bulling onward as if I hadn't spoken and addressing himself to Sonnung instead. "My father's indulgence ended with his death, and Freydís will behave as she ought from this day on."

"What Freydís does or does not do is hers to decide," Sonnung said. "But I will warn you now, Leif the Lucky, that should any harm befall her by your hands or by your willful ignorance toward those who would mistreat her, your good fortune will come to a swift end. By Thor's name, I swear it."

Leif clutched the cross he wore. "I'm not afraid of Thor."

Sonnung bared his teeth. "Perhaps you should be."

And then we both left my brother behind. For I had much to say to Thorvard still, and I saw no reason why I should wait. Let Karlsefni and Gudrid share the news of Thorvaldur's death, and perhaps then my brother might show some small measure of regret for his words.

I had no desire to learn whether or not I was wrong. For even as much as I disliked him, as foolish as I thought he was, and as unkind, he was the only brother I had left.

CHAPTER FORTY-FOUR:
AD 2016
Emma

We'd gone over it more than once the night before, and in theory, I totally understood the whys of what kept him away, but sitting around waiting for the dean, anxiety clawing its way up my throat with special thanks to Holly for the bright start to my day, I definitely (and unfairly) resented Alex's absence that afternoon.

"Emma?"

The dean stood in her open door, watching me as I rose, smoothed the wrinkles out of my skirt, and fought to walk confidently across the outer office toward her. I wasn't going to behave like a wayward student; I hadn't done anything wrong. So I gave her a tight smile, straightened my shoulders, and after she waved me to a seat, made sure not to slouch.

"I had hoped we could leave things as they were," the dean said without any preamble, sitting down across from me behind her desk. "Even that this might all blow over, with nothing worse than an informal complaint on your record. But I'm afraid that with the additional media attention brought by the campaign, we're now in a very different and very difficult position."

"Has Ashley decided to make her complaint formal?" I asked.

The dean's lips thinned, and she gave a small flick of her fingers, neither confirming nor denying the name of my student accuser. "After your little speech in class yesterday, she doesn't need to. You've handed her all the proof she needs to support her claims, and at this point, it's clear to me that you've brought your personal bias into the classroom—knowingly or not."

I'd been expecting it, of course, but it was still a punch to the gut. My hands balled into fists, but I was careful to keep my voice level. "Would you say the same thing to a Christian professor teaching medieval history without criticizing the Church?"

"I don't think that's particularly relevant, Ms. Moretti."

"If that's what you expected me to do, then I think it is. I wasn't hired to teach history with a pro-Christian spin, and I never taught it with an anti-Christian agenda, either. I just asked my students to consider and evaluate their sources and the biases of their authors. A critical skill for their continued study in the field."

"From what I've heard, Emma, you opened your class yesterday by confessing that you worshipped the Norse gods. If that isn't bringing your personal beliefs into the classroom, I don't know what is."

"Because I was asked directly," I said. "Because there were a dozen *non-Christian* students in that room, and I wasn't going to stand there and lie to them—leave them thinking that there's no place for them on this campus, in our community. Maybe lying would have made things neater and cleaner, but it would have encouraged the marginalization I promise you they already feel.

Should I have created an atmosphere where they didn't feel they had a right to their beliefs instead? Would I be sitting here in your office now if I had?"

"That isn't—" The dean took a breath, catching herself. "Whatever your reasons for bringing your personal faith into your classroom, it isn't something I can overlook in light of the recent complaints."

I snorted. "Of course."

"I'd like to give you the opportunity to resign. You're a bright young woman, and I don't want your future to be hobbled by this kind of . . . youthful indiscretion."

Indiscretion. Just like Alex had referred to it as a *slip.* Except it hadn't been either. I'd made a very deliberate choice to support the students in that classroom who likely *did* suffer discrimination. Maybe not in my classroom, but in others, every time someone treated Christianity as a legitimate faith tradition and then turned around and dismissed theirs as so much superstition.

"I don't think so," I said.

The dean's jaw went tight. "What exactly are you saying, Ms. Moretti?"

I swallowed, leaning forward. "I'm saying that I'm not going to go quietly if it means the only thing those kids learn is that admitting to being non-Christian will get them fired. I'm saying that you're absolutely not going to avoid the media attention that you don't want pointed at this department. And I'm saying that if you *do* fire me, I'll sue for wrongful termination. And the timing of this meeting is going to make it very difficult for you to prove that the exposure of my faith and beliefs by my father's opponents had nothing to do with it."

Then I rose, forcing another smile to my lips and hoping she didn't see the way my hands were shaking. "I'll look forward to hearing from you when you've made your decision, one way or the other."

There was really nothing else to be said about any of it. So I went ahead and showed myself out.

But what I'd just done—what I'd just declared my intention to do—was going to bring the storm crashing hard and fast over my head. And probably my father's, too, in the worst way.

I touched the pendant at my throat, my tucked-away Mjölnir, and was that much gladder my god was the god of thunder.

❧

Becky was waiting for me at my office, which I suppose I should have expected. Just like I should have expected the reporters still hanging around at the end of our driveway when I'd left for my meeting, and good old reliable Marco still lurking outside the building for the *Courier* when I arrived. I'd studiously ignored them, but I hadn't made Alex any promises when it came to conversations with the non-press. I hadn't exactly intended to go as far as I had today, though, and maybe I wouldn't have if Holly hadn't called and started in on me. But either way, I owed Alex at least a text before I got distracted by anything else.

"Come on in," I said to Becky, unlocking the door and waving her through ahead of me. "I just need to send a quick note, and I'm all yours."

"Are you sure?" she asked.

I lifted my eyebrows. "I don't see a line of desperate students behind you, so I think you're fine."

She smiled at that and allowed herself to perch on the edge of the chair across from my desk while I dropped my purse, hung up my jacket, and then tapped out a quick message to Alex, outlining my *dramatic* meeting with the dean so he wouldn't be caught completely off guard. Honestly, I hoped she didn't fire me, because I wasn't sure how I was going to pay for the lawsuit I'd threatened—or if I even had a case. But it couldn't be a bluff. I had to be prepared to take action, and I couldn't count on my father's support or money if it came to that.

Or even Alex.

I pushed the thought away and set my phone facedown on the desk, turning my attention to Becky. "What can I do for you?"

"I was wondering if you'd had time to think about signing off on our student organization as an adviser?"

I forced myself to smile instead of grimace, because I had thought about it and I knew what I wanted to do, but my talks with Alex last night and Holly this morning had left me a little muddled. Not that it changed what I wanted, just that it was going to alienate my father even further than he was already, not to mention potentially doing more damage to his campaign. And how much of *that* responsibility was I ready to take on? How right was Holly about how much harm I was doing to my family?

"If you don't want to—"

"It isn't about what I want," I said carefully. "None of this has been. And I don't want you to think that you don't have my full support. I think a student org for pagans is a great idea, and honestly, I wish I'd had one when I was in school. It would have been great to get together and involved with students who understood what I was going through in breaking away from Christianity and finding my own faith, even if we weren't worshipping the same way or the same gods."

"Then I don't understand," she said. "What more is there to think about?"

I chewed the inside of my cheek. Loyalty to my father and my family felt like too personal a concern to share. And I didn't like what it implied. That I had to choose one or the other. That I couldn't be a Heathen supporting other non-Christians *and* support my father with his campaign. It wasn't the world I wanted to live in, and it definitely wasn't the world I wanted for anyone else. My faith shouldn't reflect poorly on my father one way or the other—it shouldn't have become political fodder at all.

But it had. And now I had to decide whether I was going to embrace it completely or play it safe for whatever good it might do my father. I'd already taken a larger step down the first road than I'd meant to, but at least my threatening to sue would stay relatively private for the moment. Becoming faculty adviser for Becky—that was going to make a much bigger and much more public splash.

"I just need to consider whether or not this is the right thing for me to do. Or whether I'd really be doing everyone more harm than good. But no matter what happens, Becky, you should know *you're* doing the right thing, a great thing, in building a community for yourselves. Don't let what anyone says about me or any of this discourage you from moving forward."

"We *can't* move forward without an adviser," she said, rising. Her shoulders had slumped, the vibrance gone now. "That's the problem."

I sighed. "Just give me until tomorrow, okay? And if I can't do this, I'll help you find another faculty member who will."

She nodded and left, and I watched her go, hating myself for not just saying yes. But if I had—I gripped Mjölnir again, drawing the warm bronze out from under my shirt and letting the hard edges dig into my palm—what if it was the straw that broke the camel's back?

I needed to talk to my father. Not through my mother or Alex, but directly. I needed to know if doing what I thought was right was going to destroy any chance of his acceptance.

Because if I was honest with myself, that was the only thing holding me back.

⁘

I prayed first. Made a libation of mead to Thor and left a dish of milk for the land wights on the small patio out back. It didn't matter so much anymore if anyone found my makeshift altar or the offerings I left on it, so I didn't tuck it all away when I was done the way I usually did, but for the first time looked at the space around me and thought of where I might leave it permanently instead. Beneath one of the oaks that shaded the guesthouse, maybe. The landscapers could mow around it, and if I marked it off with some stones, they'd know it was a purposeful space. It was entirely possible they wouldn't even realize that it was anything other than a new garden bed of some kind.

I'd been so afraid for so long, so anxious about anyone finding out the truth, that I hadn't realized until that moment how much of myself I'd devoted to hiding. How small these things were that I'd been so terrified would be discovered. Of course no one would care about a little altar beneath an oak tree. It didn't mean anything by itself. Just like my pendant didn't. Just like the dish of milk left at the back door could just be for a stray cat. These small ritual things that meant so much to me, that I thought spoke so loudly of my faith—but no one who didn't know what to look for would really think anything of them. And who had ever been looking? No one. Not until Turner and this campaign. And even that—I wasn't convinced he'd known what he was looking for, so much as he was looking for *anything*.

A tickle of warmth and electricity shivered down my spine, and for the first time in months, I felt like I could breathe without the weight of fear and anxiety and frustration. Just deep, clear breaths of clean air. I thanked Thor for the gift, the wellspring of strength that seemed to burble up from my heart, and then thanked my ancestors, too, with another small libation beneath the tree I'd chosen.

Because whatever happened, whatever came next, I didn't have to hide anymore or pretend to be anything that I wasn't. I'd been imagining every terrible thing for so long—the silent judgments of others, and the festering self-judgments that followed—that it was a relief now to *only* face reality. To know that the reality could never have been as awful as I'd imagined it and built it up to be. And even if the timing could have been better—everything with Ashley and the college, Turner and the campaign and the smearing—it had brought me here, to this place and this realization.

I was free.

And it was glorious.

CHAPTER FORTY-FIVE:
AD 1002
FREYDÍS

Every morning in Brattahlid after Gudrid and Karlsefni had left and taken Sonnung and Vingthor with them, I wished I had never come back. I woke up alone, going through the motions of living, but never truly feeling alive. I made offerings to the gods, cared for Sonnung's goats, and considered traveling north to the farm Gudrid had gifted me a share of. Considered, but did not go.

Thorvard and I argued. First over my father's burial—I had dug him up in the dark of night and buried him a second time beneath the mound as he had desired—and then over Sonnung and our child. Again and again the same fight, the same fury and resentments, and then he grew angrier still when I told him flatly, at last, that I did not care.

"I have heard the women talk since I returned," I said. "And I know you did not keep an empty bed while I was gone, nor even while you were in Iceland, before Sonnung and I had ever started. So I do not see why you should feel so wronged."

He laughed bitterly, kicking at an empty pail and startling the horses. "Do you not? When you have made me look the greatest fool? And still you will not let me in your bed!"

"Is that all that troubles you?" I asked, crossing to my father's stallion and stroking his long nose until he calmed. "That everyone knows I will not spread my legs for my husband? You good Christian men thought well enough of Thjodhild for the same."

"Thjodhild served God," Thorvard snapped.

"And I serve mine," I said calmly. I hated that he had followed me to the barn. It was the only place where I felt that Sonnung was still with me, that he might return at any moment to sweep me into his arms again, helping me to laugh away my sorrows. "But that is the trouble, truly, isn't it? I will not follow you to Christ like a good wife ought."

He growled and looked away. "I would not care if you were Christian or not if you would only *obey*."

"You should have chosen a different wife if that was what you wanted, for I surely made no promises of that nature, and neither would my father."

"And if you were not so frigid, perhaps I would have reason to overlook it," he spat.

At that, I laughed, for I'd had enough men between my legs to know the trouble in our bed had little to do with me. "Is that the best you can come up with, Thorvard? Better to have accused me of barrenness than complain I did not respond to you as I should. Do you never wonder *why*, after so many others had found me everything warm and delightful, you found me so cold a wife? Did it never occur to you that the fault might be yours?"

"No other woman has ever complained," he mumbled, clearly stung. "For some I have been too large, but you were no untried maiden being pierced for the first time."

"That does not mean it did not *hurt*," I said. "And if you had shown even the smallest interest in my pleasure alongside yours, *I* might have seen fit to overlook *that*."

He fell silent then, his face drained of color. "Freydís . . . I swear, I did not—I never meant—"

"I know." I turned my face into the stallion's neck, irritated that I had let him draw me into such an argument at all. "I know you never meant it."

"Was the rest of it—was it only because I had hurt you?"

"No," I said. Then I let out a breath, realizing the truth. Perhaps not the pain he had caused me in bed alone, but he had hurt me, too, and deeply, when he had chosen Christ. I might not have loved him, but I had trusted him until then. Trusted that there was something in him that my father had seen, for which I might find some small affection. "Yes."

"If I had treated you more gently—"

I shook my head, then pushed away from the horse and faced him. "I do not know what I would have done or what we would be now. Perhaps I would have pleased you enough that you would not have chosen Christ. Perhaps I would have been content enough to overlook it if you had. But none of that matters, Thorvard. We both made our choices, and they have brought us here. I cannot change who I am. I *will* not change who I am only to please you."

"Let me in your bed again," he said. "To sleep, if nothing else. Give me that much, and perhaps . . . perhaps we can begin again."

It was a small request. Nothing more than a balm for his pride and a means by which he might regain some measure of respect. And if it meant an end to his sniping, to all the arguments and the fighting, what harm in that?

"Only to sleep," I agreed. "But for any good it might do, you may tell the others whatever you please."

If I had not been Erik's daughter and Leif's sister, and as wealthy as I now was—if I had not been fearsome in my own right, as well—I was certain Thorvard would have divorced me long before and been well within his rights. But if my husband did not exactly warm to me at once after so long at odds with one another, neither did he make things more difficult after that day. Slowly, pretended courtesy became something more, something real instead, and if we would never love one another, we at least found a way to live.

But for me, living beneath my brother's roof was still a misery.

"What are you doing, Freydís?" Thjodhild demanded, finding me in the storeroom, where I was preparing an offering to carry out to the land spirits and the gods.

I made offerings to my father's spirit, too, every month, and often Thorhall joined me for that, but the rest of the men who had sailed with us, worshipping Thor alongside Christ, looked away now when I passed. When Leif and Thjodhild spoke against the gods, they said nothing. And every sunrise, they followed my brother to his church, honoring Christ instead of Thor.

"You know what I'm doing," I told her. "It is the duty you have neglected all this time. The work of protecting our people and our livestock, of ensuring good harvests and fine wool."

"You will not take food or drink from these stores to give to your foul gods," she said, wrenching the dish of milk from my hand. "Brattahlid is Christian now, and before long, the rest of Greenland will follow. There will be no more offerings of this kind."

I stared at her, disbelieving. "You cannot truly mean this?"

"We have tolerated your nonsense long enough," Thjodhild said. "Now that Leif has taken your father's place, it is time for you to learn yours."

My emptied hands balled into fists. "Will you forbid me, too, from honoring my father?"

"Better if he is greeted by silence than the tales you will spin, no doubt urging him to cause us trouble and grief. Until you returned he rested quietly. Now there is spoiled milk, and the ewes will not let their lambs near enough to suckle."

I snorted. "You've offended the landvættir, then, and it is no fault of mine, and certainly not my father's. Perhaps if you made an offering to them instead of traipsing out to your church, you would not be so troubled."

"We have no need of their kindness," Thjodhild said. "We have Christ to see us through."

"And yet your milk is still spoiled."

Thjodhild slapped me, then dumped the dish of milk I'd prepared over my head. "Erik might have loved you, Freydís, letting you have your way in everything, but I will not, nor will your brother. You have heard what I have said, and you will do as I bid from now on."

I drew the knife from my belt and slammed her against the wall, pressing the blade to her throat. "Tell me now, Thjodhild, how much do you trust in your Christ?"

"Freydís!" Thorvard grabbed my arm, hauling me back. How much he had seen or heard, I did not know, but he looked at me with pity in his eyes. "What did you intend, truly? Do you honestly believe that Leif will overlook it if you slit the throat of his mother?"

I spat at her feet as he pulled me away. "Remember this, Thjodhild. Remember that I am not afraid."

But she smiled, stepping close now that Thorvard had stolen the knife from my hand. "You will do as I have bid," she said again. "And that will be the end of it."

Thorvard caught me up again when I tried to lunge, dragging me back when I would have tackled her to the ground. "What good do you think it will do you?" he hissed. "What do you hope to prove by attacking an old woman?"

"She insulted me, my gods, my father!"

When Thjodhild was well away, he let me go, and I collapsed onto the cold ground. "And she will do worse to rile you, if you let her. She will keep at it until you are driven to rage and murder, and then blame it upon your gods, claim it is proof of their evil. The few who still pray to Thor will be persuaded to give him up, and she will be rid of you, too, when you are outcast and exiled for your crimes. You do not realize, Freydís, how much your father protected you."

I lifted my gaze, looking up into my husband's face. "You were meant to do the same. To free me from this. You swore I would not be made to become a Christian."

"And I will speak to Leif on your behalf," he said, his expression grim. "But there will be little I can do or say if you keep giving Thjodhild the trouble she wants."

I closed my eyes, the sour stink of milk filling my nose. Thorstein had warned me often of the dangers of my pride, and Sonnung, too, had told me my temper would do me more harm than good. But I could not help but think that if I had been a man, and Thjodhild one, too, no one would have held me back.

"Go wash," Thorvard said, more gently now. "While you are gone, I will do what I can."

In the end, I was not wholly forbidden from making offerings to the gods. Thorvard had argued that Thjodhild had no right to tell me what I might do with what was mine. If I chose to leave dishes of goat milk for the landvættir or to sacrifice one of my own goats or hens to Thor, I was free to do so, but I was still forbidden from offering anything that had been made part of the farm's stores. Even the milk that had come from Sonnung's goats since our return from Vinland.

To his credit, Thorvard did not begrudge me when I traded furs and lumber for more livestock in response. And Thorhall joined me in making a fine sacrifice of goat, sheep, and blood to the gods in protest. My father might have wished to keep the peace by making his offerings in private, but I saw no reason to do the same. What was mine, I would give, and I would do so boldly. I only hoped it would shame the other men into doing the same.

But Thjodhild continued as Thorvard had predicted, always needling me for one thing or another and encouraging the other men and women to slight me. As the months passed and winter drove us all into closer quarters than we liked, it became clear I could not remain at Brattahlid, not if I wished to be free, and Thorvard was not so blind that he dared disagree. But it was not until the spring, when the Icelanders arrived—two brothers who had heard of Karlsefni's journey to Vinland and wanted to do the same—that I saw my escape.

"I know the way," I told Helgi. "For I sailed with Karlsefni, too. If you wish to go to Vinland, I would travel with you."

"We," Thorvard said, overhearing my offer. "If you sail to Vinland again, you will sail with me."

"Have you a ship?" Finnbogi asked, his attention caught, but he addressed Thorvard rather than me. "It would be better, surely, to have a few more men if the skraelings are as hostile as Karlsefni warned."

"Two ships," I told him, irritated.

"But we can crew only one," Thorvard said.

"We have thirty men." Helgi's gaze flicked between us before settling on my husband, as his brother's had. "And if you will bring thirty more, we should not be too few to discourage attack. We would not wish to settle, mind you, as Karlsefni attempted. It's the lumber we're after, and the furs, should we have time."

"Likely you will wish to winter there, still," I suggested.

"Perhaps," Finnbogi agreed, shrugging. "But with sixty men, we ought to be able to fell enough trees before the sea turns wholly against us."

"Can you ready your ship in time?" Helgi asked.

I looked to Thorvard then, for much as it galled me, he had more experience at sea.

"It is readied even now," he said, meeting my eyes. "We need only take on fresh supplies for the journey, and we can be on our way—it seemed prudent after the winter we've had. But speak to your brother, Freydís, and perhaps he will grant us the use of his house."

I glanced at Helgi and Finnbogi, who looked more at my chest than my face, and rose to find my brother as Thorvard suggested. The two brothers and their men could make do in the house we'd built for Thorvaldur's men, but they would not share mine.

If I had not been so desperate to escape, if Thjodhild had not made my life so difficult at Brattahlid, perhaps I would have thought twice about sailing at all. But in that moment, I wanted only to be free. And it seemed to me that Vinland was the only place I might find any kind of peace.

At the very least, those lands to the west were filled with fond memories, not crowded with pain and frustration, as Brattahlid had become. In Vinland, perhaps I might dream again of Sonnung, and it would be as he had said before he'd left—not a reason for sorrow, but a source of comfort in the dark.

CHAPTER FORTY-SIX:
AD 2016
Emma

My father came home for dinner that night, leaving Alex to handle damage control at headquarters, and I sat down in my usual spot at the table, pretending not to notice the tension. He was so tightly wound, I was sure he'd snap completely the minute I started talking. So I waited, prudently, until we'd all served ourselves and my mother wasn't flitting back and forth in and out of the kitchen. And then I waited a little bit longer, while my father complimented my mother on the meal—a goulash with ground beef that his mother used to make and my mother had managed to learn without altering it beyond recognition or taking away the nostalgia factor.

When his mouth was full, I cleared my throat. "There's a group of pagan students on campus who are trying to form an official student organization, and in light of—well, everything, I guess, they've asked me if I'd be willing to sign off as their faculty adviser."

My father stopped chewing, his spoon clacking against the ceramic bowl.

"I warned them that it might attract some negative attention to their organization if I agreed, but they don't seem to be able to find an alternate faculty member who is willing to sign off, and honestly, as someone who knows what it's like to be facing that transition from a more traditionally acceptable faith to something completely nontraditional, I think the only right thing to do is to support them."

"This includes the student who took the picture? The supposed reporter?" my father asked.

"She deleted it after the *Courier* approached her and she realized it could make things difficult for me," I said. "And I have no reason to think she's anything but sincere in both her faith and her desire to build a community for herself and other students who share her nontraditional beliefs. You and Mamma both have always been adamant about the importance of community in—"

"The girl who started all this trouble for us," he insisted, interrupting me.

"I don't think that's fair," I said, keeping my voice even. "I think if anyone deserves the blame for starting anything, it's Turner, and if anyone helped him, it was probably the student who lodged the complaint against me with the dean, accusing me of religious discrimination."

"At the college you've now threatened to sue," my father snapped. "After you were given the option to resign quietly. To keep all of this quiet."

Of course Alex had told him *that*.

"It wouldn't have stayed quiet, Dad," I said, meeting his eyes. "Even if I had accepted Dean Marshall's offer and turned in my resignation, it would have been public record, and Turner would have cited it as proof that I *was* discriminating against Christians. It would have been an admission of guilt. And like I told you from the start, I didn't do anything wrong. I'm not going to let the college punish me for not being Christian or for being a target of your opponent's campaign rhetoric. Not without a fight."

"Think of the message it would send to those students if she let the dean force her out, Joe," my mother said. "Emma's right to fight this, and if it were any other cause, you'd have already given her your support. This is the person we raised her to be."

"It certainly is *not* the person we raised her to be," my father growled. "The person we raised her to be wouldn't have found herself in this position at all."

"Whether I was Christian or not, I'd still have taught that history class the same way," I said. "I'd still have been trained to look for and examine source bias. Being Heathen has nothing to do with that."

"And if you were Catholic and attending mass every Sunday and engaged to David, with his mother on the parish council and his father on the Catholic school board, you'd have been above reproach—you'd have had a defense against this!"

I shook my head, stunned at his implications. "So it would have been okay for me to stand up against embedded historical and contemporary discrimination of non-Christian faiths, but only if I were your good little Catholic girl still?"

"That isn't what I said." He pushed his bowl away. "But I'm inclined to believe you would have had the sense not to get involved in this kind of trouble this close to an election, at least! Maybe David would have had some kind of stabilizing influence on you, since it's clear you don't care in the slightest about the position you've placed your family in, and for a man who should be able to handle you with his eyes closed, Alex has been completely useless in keeping you on message."

"First of all, David and I wouldn't be engaged," I said, struggling to keep my jaw from clenching at the fact that he'd brought both David and Alex into this. "We probably wouldn't have still been dating at all except that I knew I couldn't make a scene in *September* during an election year. And second of all, nothing about *me* changed when I became a Heathen. I'm still the person I was. I just found a faith that fit who that person is! And for you to sit there and act like I don't care about the family just because I believe in something different than you do, or think standing up for people whose struggle I'm not blinded to anymore is the right thing to do—"

"Nobody thinks you don't care about your family, Emma," my mother assured me, glowering at my father. "And to be perfectly frank, after the way David's grandmother has responded to all of this, and his mother, too, I'm glad to think we won't have to see more of his family than absolutely necessary. He'd never have understood about Anja."

"Anja!" My father ground her name between his teeth, his face flushed. "If it weren't for Anja, there wouldn't *be* anything for anyone to have to understand."

"You will *not* blame any of this on my sister," my mother said. "But if you insist on blaming someone, had you acknowledged her faith publicly years ago, we wouldn't be facing this issue now. There wouldn't be a scandal of any kind, and your constituents would realize that Emma is simply embracing a different element of her culture, rather than rejecting your sacred campaign of family values."

"Listen," I said, banging the serving spoon on the rim of the pot to stop them. Because I wasn't trying to break up my parents—I didn't want them fighting about this, about me. "Just please, listen," I said again after they'd both turned to scowl at me.

"I'm closer to thirty than I am to twenty," I said. "Which makes me an adult no matter what definition you want to use. And as an adult, I'm the only one responsible for my decisions. Just. Me. Not Auntie Anja, not either of you, and definitely not some boyfriend. If those decisions make you unhappy or feel like a rejection of the beliefs you hoped to instill in me as a child, I'm sorry. But you *did* raise me to do the right thing. To stand up for others and support people who don't have the same advantages I do. So I'm going to keep doing that, even if I'm not doing it as a Christian. Even if you won't always agree with me on what the *right thing* is. Taking part in my community, contributing, and helping others in my community—that's not just a Christian idea. It's part of Heathenry, too."

My father rolled his eyes and shoved his chair back from the table. "Maybe when the Vikings raided the coasts of England and France their religion was real, but if you expect me to believe that this is some calling, some found *truth* for you, you can forget it. This neo-pagan heathenry garbage is nothing but a made-up faith used as an excuse by too many people to justify racism and bigotry in the United States. And maybe right now it conveniently supports your *Christian* ideals of community service, but I guarantee you'll change your tune when the *right thing* is something that doesn't serve your own self-interest. So do whatever you'd like, Emma. That's all your so-called faith stands for, anyway."

And then he left, his goulash only half finished and my mother staring at him with her mouth agape, and I had the answers I'd been looking for.

The answers I'd never expected in a million years.

"Thanks for dinner, Mamma," I said softly. "I'm sorry I ruined it."

She sighed. "I'll pack up the leftovers for you to keep in the freezer."

Which was my mother's way of saying that if I didn't want to have dinner with my parents for a while, she'd understand. And maybe it would be for the best, while my father cooled down.

Except I wasn't sure he would. Not about this. No matter how much pressure she put on him, he'd already made up his mind about me. And I'd made up mine, too.

The guesthouse was dark and empty when I stuffed my leftovers in the freezer, and I'd only been there five minutes before I realized I had no interest in spending the night alone; all I'd do was listen to my father's accusations on repeat until I fell asleep, if I was lucky enough to fall asleep at all. So I grabbed pajamas, some clean clothes, and my toiletry bag, tossing it all together into my backpack and slipping out again. Alex had told me he'd be at home catching up on television, and I didn't think he'd mind if I surprised him.

Or at least I hoped. By the time I'd parked my car outside his modest little house and turned off the engine, I was second-guessing myself enough to eye my phone and think about texting him. Before I'd finished typing my overly apologetic and explanatory message, the front door opened and Alex came out, dressed in a pair of red athletic shorts and one of his all-purpose white undershirts. He knocked on my car window and I flushed, feeling even more awkward that I'd been caught outside his house, and rolled it down.

"Were you going to sit out here all night?"

I held up my phone as proof that I'd been about to text him. "I was going to wait until you invited me."

Alex laughed, taking the phone from my hand without even glancing at the message. "You don't need an invitation, Emma. And if you did, you already had it anyway. Come on inside."

He pulled back from the window, and I rolled it up while he jogged around the front of the car, opening up the back door to grab my bag and then waiting for me, when I was still a little bit slow to follow. We hadn't been dating that long, really. Even if I counted those uncomfortable dinners with my parents before I'd realized his intentions, it hadn't been even a month and a half. And here I was, showing up at his house uninvited after a fight with my father. My fingers tightened around the steering wheel.

He pulled the driver's-side door open for me, and I pushed everything else away, unbuckling my seat belt, grabbing my purse, and climbing out. Alex shut the door and caught my hand, tugging me back toward him for a kiss. Soft and quick, but promising more once we got inside.

"I thought you said you were going to be busy tonight," he said after he'd let me go, and I slipped beneath his arm instead, walking with him back toward the house. Funny to think I'd never been inside, when he'd spent so much time at my place—he knew his way around my parents' house like he'd been raised there, practically.

"It's Thursday," I said, not sure suddenly why I hadn't just come out with it before now.

"Has been all day," he agreed, laughing again. The entry hall light wasn't too bright, but warm, and he shut the door behind us before dropping my backpack at the bottom of the stairs opposite.

"*Thor's* day," I said, poking my head around the doorway to the right—snooping, really, if I was being honest. The television hummed, casting a glow over what looked like a cozy living room. Whatever he'd been watching was frozen mid close-up by my arrival, some kind of procedural, I thought. "I treat Thursday like a Sunday. But I finished earlier than I thought I would, and the idea of hanging out alone for the rest of the night sounded pretty miserable after the *awesome* dinner I had with my parents."

Alex made a soft noise—not quite a snort, but more than a sigh, and I looked up to find him leaning against the doorframe next to me. "You should have told me."

"Which part?" I asked.

He half smiled, taking my purse from my hand and setting that down on a small sideboard table tucked beside the stairwell and covered in a mess of mail. I liked that there was one part of his life that wasn't quite so orderly; the living room was strangely tidy for a man living alone.

"Even if you had other things you needed to do, I would have gone to dinner with you. Lent whatever support I could and then left, if that's what you needed."

"I know."

"But?"

I shrugged. "I guess I felt like I needed to do this by myself. Talk to him father to daughter. And if you'd been there, it would have been more of both of us talking through you instead."

"And the Thor's day part?"

I wrinkled my nose. "I'm just a little self-conscious still."

"I wish you wouldn't be," he said softly, holding my gaze.

"I know that, too," I promised.

He made another of those small noises and then tipped his head toward the doorway. "Want a tour?"

I let out a breath, relieved that he didn't seem inclined to push me. That he was willing to wait until I was ready to talk. That in that moment, he was more interested in me—in us—than the drama I might cause the campaign, either by fighting with my father or by worshipping a Norse god.

"I'd like that a lot."

We didn't make it beyond the bedroom. A stroke of genius on his part, or just a happy accident—I wasn't sure it mattered.

※

Alex had asked me to wait. To hold off until after the election, for his sake if not my father's. But I knew I couldn't. That if I did, it would be an act of cowardice and feed this idea that there wasn't room for me to be Heathen. That the pagan students on campus should hide their faith and pretend to be Christian if they wanted to get anywhere in life. That everyone should just keep their heads down and fly under the Christian radar. But there were plenty of people who didn't have that luxury, and I hated the idea that I was saving myself at their expense—at anyone's.

And in the end, Alex had only sighed, admiration mixing with aggravation for the storm that we both knew was coming. "You have to do what you think is right," he'd agreed. "I shouldn't be surprised, and no matter what kind of headache it gives me professionally, I'll support you. And so will your mother."

We'd left my father's most likely response unsaid. But honestly, if he'd made up his mind, I'd made up mine just as stubbornly, and at least I knew Holly had come by her own unreasonableness naturally. Whatever happened between us—all of us—I'd face it as it came. Just like I'd face the fallout of my decisions, alone if necessary. Because as much as Alex's personal and private support meant to me, as long as he worked for my father and my father's campaign, the reality was he wouldn't be able to hold my hand or stand next to me in front of the press when it all went public.

And it would. Turner wouldn't waste the opportunity I was giving him. Alex and I had both agreed on that, too. But I wasn't going to keep on living in fear of how much worse things could get. Not when saving myself meant sacrificing the potential for something better for those students. Not if the message I was sending them was that they should live in fear, in secret, too.

I was just glad that Alex understood. David and his family? They never would have.

But Becky was ecstatic when I spoke to her after my class, and she hugged the signed form to her chest. "Thank you so much, Professor Moretti."

"Emma," I said, her response enough to ease the last of my lingering doubts. She needed this more than I needed to be safe. Far more. "Just Emma is fine."

"Emma!" Her eyes were bright and glossy. "You don't know how much this means to us."

"You might regret it still," I warned her. "Things are going to get worse before they get better, with all of this coming out and the campaign. And I still don't know if I'll be here beyond the end of the semester, which means you might be hunting for a new adviser come January."

"But right *now* we can have our own student org. And it's only October. That gives us two months and then some to start raising awareness and plan activities. Maybe by the time we're done, some of the other professors won't be as afraid to sign off, if we need them."

"I hope so," I told her, pulling my coat on. "And if you need anything from me, you have my e-mail. But I'd get that in before the storm hits, just to be safe."

"I'm going straight to the student org office," she promised.

And I knew she meant it, so I smiled and locked my office door behind us both. Becky took off down the hall at a run, shouting for one of her friends, who had been loitering by the stairs. A muffled screech of excitement followed, and they both skipped down the stairwell and out of sight. I lingered by my office door for another minute, giving them plenty of time to clear out and hoping—praying—that Marco wasn't waiting for me outside. I hadn't seen him on my way in, at least, and it wasn't entirely beyond the realm of possibility that he might have given up on the idea of getting any kind of story from me. Particularly with the way my father and Holly had chosen *not* to respond.

There was a chance, after all, that Turner might not find out. That no one would realize the significance of my name on that particular form and report it to potentially interested parties. Alex, I knew, wasn't betting on it, and I understood why he was anticipating doomsday. But me? The longer this stayed quiet, the longer I was likely to keep my job, and while I was less and less sure that I wanted to make academia my home in the long term, I did still want to see the semester through.

Even the year, if I could wrangle it. For Becky and her friends more than for myself, maybe. But either way, I had a better chance if no one started pointing fingers at the dean and accusing her of not doing her job because of me.

Or worse. Whatever that might be.

CHAPTER FORTY-SEVEN:
AD 1003
FREYDÍS

Leif was glad to see the back of me and more than happy to loan me the use of his house for as long as I wished to remain in Vinland. But as eager as I had been to leave, almost from the moment Helgi and Finnbogi arrived at our camp in Vinland, I wished I had not agreed to sail with them at all.

"You said we would share the house," Helgi said, annoyed, when he found that we had taken my brother's longhouse for ourselves and our men.

"We built the second longhouse just as soundly," I said. "You'll have room enough and then some, and Karlsefni will not begrudge my lending its use after my men helped his to build it."

"And I suppose you will tell me you did not realize you violated the other agreement we made," Finnbogi accused, his gaze upon the men who were coming and going, unloading our supplies from the ship. "Instead of thirty men, as we agreed, I count thirty-five."

His resentment surprised me, and I frowned in response. "But you brought thirty-five as well."

"Thirty men," he said. "As we agreed."

"And five women," I said, nodding to them where they huddled together.

He sneered. "Women count for nothing."

My jaw tightened. "Then why did you bring them at all?"

"To please our men—and you might have done the same. Or do you mean to see to all their needs, in addition to your husband's?"

My hand closed around the hilt of my knife. "Thorvard is the only man I sleep beside."

"But not the only man you've slept with," Helgi said. "Perhaps we might come to an arrangement while we are here. To share the use of you with him, and leave the five slave women for the rest of the men. Better just the three of us than thirty-five, yes?"

I spat at Helgi's feet. "I am not a whore to be *shared*, nor would I shame my husband by so much as *talking* with two men so beneath him. See to your men and your boats, and I will forget you suggested it at all, but insult either one of us again in such a way, and I will slice your tongue from your mouth and ram it up your brother's backside."

Finnbogi laughed and clapped his brother upon the shoulder. "The cat has claws and teeth, my brother. But only wait long enough, and she will purr for us both. When she is ready, and not before."

"Or scratch our eyes out," Helgi said, letting himself be drawn away. He glanced back, his lips twitching. "Still, it might be worth the trouble."

I growled, wondering if cutting their throats would be worth the trouble it would cause me. But I did not have my sword at my hip—another gift from Sonnung before he left—and while I knew I possessed no small amount of skill with a knife, they would have the advantage of brute strength and longer reach. One of them, perhaps, I could gut, but the other would be on me before I had finished, and I doubted they would hesitate to take my life.

"Do not let them goad you," Thorhall said, coming to stand at my side. Of all the men, he alone had remained loyal to me, refusing to swear himself to my brother when he had learned of my father's death and ignoring Thorvard's commands as if my husband had never spoken at all. But he was growing older with every passing month, aged by his grief and the respect we had both lost. In a fight, the most he could do for me was die first and well, and we both knew it. "They're not fools enough to touch you without your welcome, no matter how brave their talk."

"It's the talk that worries me more," I said, remembering Sonnung's warnings when we sailed before. His worry that the men might turn against me and I would stand alone in my defense. "The two of them are nothing, and Thorvard would fight at my side if it came to it, I think, but what if the next time it is ten men, or twenty, and they believe the things Finnbogi's said? That I am just another whore to be passed around among the men."

"Thor will guard you," Thorhall said. "He will guard us both, as he has before."

Love me and keep faith. That was what Sonnung had always said when I'd fret. And this was not the first time I'd wondered what those words had truly meant—if I had loved more than just a man.

I pushed the thought away and offered Thorhall a smile instead. "Let us make Thor an offering, then, for our safe arrival, so he knows we have not forgotten him while we sailed."

At least in Vinland there was no Thjodhild to scowl while we honored the gods.

It would have to be consolation enough.

Helgi and Finnbogi did not linger at our camp, and chose to sail first north, then south to explore the land. It suited me well enough to be rid of them, and Thorvard and I stayed near the camp instead, hunting and trapping for furs and food, and traveling inland for lumber. We kept a guard, always, against the return of the skraelings, but we saw nothing of them and were glad to be left alone.

"Are you so sure of Thor?" my husband asked me one day while we checked and reset our snares. "Do you not ever wonder whether Christ's power might serve you just as faithfully?"

"I do not know Christ," I said, and though I had fought against Leif and Thjodhild fiercely, I found I had little interest in arguing with Thorvard on the matter. He had made his choice, and I had made mine, and now that we had come to terms again, I did not wish to ruin what small peace we had managed to find. "And it was not Christ who kept me fed, who guarded me in battle and upon the seas. All I know of Christ is the death he has brought to my brothers. The pain and betrayal he has brought me."

"Christ has kept me safe," he said. "Every time I have sailed, he has delivered me again to shore, and when I have prayed for fairer winds, he has brought them."

"Then I am glad for you," I said, crouching down to free a squirrel from one of the snares, still alive. It was not worth the trouble of skinning him, and we had better game for eating.

"He gave me a son, too," he said, less confident now. "On one of the slaves, while you were away. I thought to claim him, but I was not certain—Erik counseled me to wait until you returned and speak to you first. He said it was his greatest regret, not asking Thjodhild to take you in, but only telling her she must. He had no wish to see the same troubles repeated any more than they were already."

I fussed with the snare long after I had reset it, pretending more work than it needed while I gathered my thoughts. He had kept this from me for a year, and I wondered that I had not heard whispers before now. Or perhaps the men had whispered, and I had been too preoccupied with my own troubles to hear.

"I thought you were barren," he went on, as if it was a fair excuse. "Thjodhild said you must be. But then you returned with Sonnung's son."

"Vingthor belongs to Thor," I said, more irritated with Thjodhild than my husband. Always she involved herself, as if she could not rest until she knew I suffered. "It was by Thor's power he was born, and Thor's alone."

"You do not deny it," he said softly.

I rose but did not meet his gaze. "If I might have paid the god another way, even now, I think I would have. But Vingthor was the price for the favors I asked for, the gift the gods required. I love him, more than I ever thought I could, but I never wanted a child, and I do not believe the gods will give me another."

He was silent for a long moment as we continued on, and I left him to his thoughts, for my own spun as well. I had always known my father regretted that Thjodhild and I had never come to terms, but I was not certain his asking her to care for me would have changed our relationship at all. I would always still have been the proof of his disloyalty while he had lived in exile, a daily reminder of his faithlessness, when she had believed he loved and wanted only her. Often, growing up, I had thought she must have been a very young, very foolish bride.

But I was not so young, even if some would say I had acted foolishly. *If you are shrewd,* my father had said, when he had proposed my marriage to Thorvard. And blinded by love, I had forgotten for a time, too caught up in Sonnung.

"If I love your son as my own," I began, choosing my words with care, "in exchange, will you love mine?"

Thorvard stopped, and I stopped with him, looking up at him now, my breath held. He worked his jaw, his eyes fixed upon the trees, the sky, the leaves—anywhere but me. "Is that all you would ask? That I treat Sonnung's son as mine?"

"Look away when his father comes back, should he ever return at all. But for that . . . for that I would promise you my loyalty as well. You need never fear I will give myself to another man but for Sonnung, nor would we shame you again so publicly. Not if you love our son."

"And what of me?" he asked. "Will you be like Thjodhild, forever bitter and angry, punishing the women I take to my bed?"

"What right would I have to resent them?" I snorted. "No, Thorvard. If you wish for a bed slave or a lover, take one. So long as they bear me no malice as your wife and remember their place, I do not see why you should not." I half smiled, almost apologetic. "It is not as though we married for love."

"No," he said. "No one could ever accuse us of that."

"But perhaps—going forward—we might at least be friends?"

Thorvard searched my face, what remained of his bitterness seeming to melt away. "Friends, then," he agreed. "But you must know—I would have given you more, if you had let me."

I dropped my gaze again, fiddling with a spare bit of string. "Perhaps if things had been different, I might have done so, too."

As it was, neither of us would ever be the same, but I could not bring myself to regret the choices I had made. I would never regret my loyalty to the gods and my ancestors, nor those too-brief years with Sonnung. And the more I thought of it all, the more it seemed to me to be just one unruly mass of wool, stuck altogether and not meant to come undone. My fate, it seemed, was less a weaving and more a confusion of knots.

Even so, in that moment, I knew I had found some small measure of peace.

Helgi and Finnbogi returned some weeks later and continued on as they had begun, slighting me at every opportunity and insulting me when they bothered to acknowledge me at all. I did my best to follow Thorhall's advice, and Sonnung's and Thorstein's before, refusing to let my pride or my temper lead me into trouble.

It was easier in some ways to ignore their jibes. They did not have Thjodhild's knack for cutting words, though their men laughed all the same. I would hear them holding court around a fire pit they'd dug outside their longhouse, boasting and bragging and drinking too much mead and wine. But I was not so foolish as to join them, and Thorvard, too, thought it prudent to keep our men from mixing much with theirs.

Perhaps if we had sent our men to drink with them, we might have left that much sooner, whether we had enough lumber and cargo or not. But then we still thought we might winter in Vinland and wait to sail again until spring.

"Where are you off to?" one of Helgi's men asked, rising as I passed him with a bowl of wine. I'd left my goats at Brattahlid, so wine and mead from our supplies were all I had to offer. "A woman alone, venturing beyond the palisade, when there are skraelings to worry about."

"I have my sword," I said. "And I know better how to use it than you do, I'd wager."

He grinned in such a way that my skin prickled in warning, and he skipped a step to keep up. "Why don't you teach me how to use mine to best advantage, then, eh?"

Another man had joined us now, following at my back, and a third leaned upon an axe ahead. One was just a nuisance, nothing I could not handle with Sonnung's sword on my hip. Two was more trouble than I wanted, but trouble I could dispatch, all the same. But three—three was a growing concern, if they were fools.

Unfortunately, as far as I could tell, all Helgi and Finnbogi's men were fools.

"Nothing to say?" he asked when I didn't answer. "Think because you're a chieftain's daughter, you're too good for the likes of me? Everyone knows even your husband won't have you, since you whored yourself to that sell-sword. By all rights, you should be begging me to take you."

I stopped short at his words, still inside the palisade, and sighed. This was Helgi and Finnbogi's doing—I had no doubt of that, though whether they had meant it to come to this, realized the seeds they had sown, I was less certain.

"You're wrong," I said, setting the wine upon a stump nearby. I closed my fingers around the hilt of my sword instead, drawing it swiftly from the leather scabbard and pointing it at his throat. "No matter how long it had been since I had known the pleasure of my husband's sword between my legs, I still would not want an unwashed, lice-ridden, horse-faced whoreson like you."

His eyes had gone wide, and when I stepped forward, he lifted his hands, palms out and empty, falling back. "Helgi said—"

"I do not care what Helgi said," I told him. And when his gaze shifted to the man who had been behind me, now at my left instead, I drew my knife, too, giving him a warning glance. "I do not care what you think I have done or what you have heard. I am Freydís Thorswoman, daughter of Erik the Red, and that sell-sword you believe I whored for taught me to gut a man in the time it takes him to blink. It's been some time, I'll admit, but I'd be more than happy to practice on the three of you."

The two men confirmed my guess when they exchanged a look with their friend, holding his axe now as a threat rather than a walking stick. And if he chose to rush me, swinging it, I was not sure what I would do. But these men did not need to know my doubts.

"No," the first man said at once, stepping back again. "We just wanted a little fun, that's all—not swords and blood."

"I'm sure you can find it somewhere else, then," I said, letting my blade slip to point at his breast instead of his neck. "With one of the bed slaves Helgi brought you, or whatever livestock you can find."

He flushed again, more insulted than embarrassed now. "There's no cause for that! We're Christian men, not pagan goat lovers like you."

I sneered, lifting my sword again. "Shall I slit you open navel to nose, or nose to navel, then? Better yet, perhaps I'll begin with your balls . . ."

He swallowed and jerked his head at his companions. "That Frankish whore Finnbogi bought will have us all for a silver coin, I heard Runi say. I prefer my women more willing, anyway."

I didn't sheathe my sword or my knife until all three of them were well on their way, sauntering off as if they'd won and arguing over who would have her first. My hands shook so violently, it took me three tries.

Three men.

How long until it was four? Or five? Or ten? Some months yet, maybe, but after the first snows fell, if winter came hard and the men had nothing but drink and women on their minds, it would be only a matter of time.

Thor, protect me.

Much as I loved Vinland, much as I wished to keep out from beneath Leif's and Thjodhild's eyes, perhaps it would be wiser to go.

At the first hint of dawn the next morning, I rose, intent upon speaking to Helgi and Finnbogi before they went about losing themselves in the woods. Thorvard still snored, undisturbed, and I left him there, for he'd come late to bed, drunk, after celebrating a successful bear hunt with his men. He had earned his rest and his glory—for between the lumber and the furs and foodstuffs we'd gathered already, we would have more than enough to recover what we had spent in coming, even if we left tomorrow.

In fact, after looking over what we'd collected the day before, all the meat we'd dried and wood we'd cut in anticipation of winter's worst snows, I feared we had too much to haul.

I did not bother with my sword or boots, only threw Thorvard's cloak over the linen dress I had slept in, eager to be done with it all and return to my bed for the sleep that had eluded me all night. Helgi and Finnbogi had the larger ship, and if they would trade, even if it cost me a handful of silver pieces in addition, it would be worth the price.

The rest of our men slept as soundly as Thorvard, and I did my best not to wake them on my way out. In the fresh air outside the longhouse, my steps slowed, my hand reaching for the knife I had left behind. But it was early, and so few were awake . . .

I ought to have turned back. That is what I told myself later, over and over again, after all of it was done. I ought to have turned back for my sword and my knife, perhaps shaken Thorhall awake as well.

I ought to have done many things, but instead, I continued on. Too sure of myself, too determined to arrange our return home, that we might be on our way that much sooner.

Too eager to leave these fools behind.

CHAPTER FORTY-EIGHT: AD 2016
Emma

I went to Alex's place instead of going home, at his gracious (and, I suspected, partially self-serving) invitation. No Marco from the *Courier* or any other reporters hanging around the end of the driveway. I was glad for the quiet, even if it was a little bit strange to be in his house alone. He hadn't even finished his tour, interrupted so completely the night before, and I wasn't sure what he'd really meant for me to do with myself. But he couldn't have imagined I'd just sit, waiting.

Generally speaking, I preferred to avoid the television, and I didn't have the password to his wireless network, to stream anything on my own laptop, stuffed in my backpack and abandoned beneath the table beside the stairs. So after poking around in his fridge—and finding it alarmingly well maintained, without a single festering leftover to be found, and nary a stain on any of the shelves where a spill might not have been wiped up as immediately as it should have been—I got myself a glass of water, leaned against his kitchen counter (honestly, I was only surprised they weren't granite, considering the immaculate and tasteful state of everything else), and frowned at my very tidy surroundings.

How had I never realized he was *this* clean? And how had he been managing in the guesthouse, with my "I will balance every piece of recycling I can in the top of this bin and only empty it when the stack finally topples and recyclables have spilled across my floor" approach to life?

Cradling my water glass against my chest for fear of leaving a ring on any surface—Alex had to be a coaster man, judging by the place mats on his breakfast table—I fished my phone out of my pocket and dialed Sarah, one-handed.

"You know some of us work from nine to five, right?" she said, skipping right over a hello.

"I'm in Alex Stone's house, and even my *mother* does not keep her kitchen this clean."

"Oh," Sarah said, and I could practically hear her eyes roll. "So it's clearly an *emergency*, then."

"It's four thirty," I told her. "You're mentally checked out anyway, and if you'd really been busy, you wouldn't have answered the phone."

She didn't argue. Not really. Sarah didn't exactly love her job. *Program administrator* didn't sound exciting to me, either—and no matter how many times she tried to tell me what program she was administrating, I still wasn't completely clear. Something to do with the county and subcontracting. "With everything they're saying on the news, I wasn't sure you didn't need something serious."

"Oh," I said. "That."

"They even interviewed David," she said, her voice dropping to a slightly more furtive tone. One of her coworkers had probably just walked by her office door. "He played it up as all betrayal and outrage to have been kept in the dark. You'd think you were making animal sacrifices behind his back or something, with the way he was going on. It was the most ridiculous performance I've ever seen in my life."

I snorted, wishing I felt any kind of surprise at all. "I guess I was dating David because he reminded me of my father, then, or something. I'm sure he's desperate to distance himself from me, for his own sake or because his parents are pushing him to it." And I wasn't sure it mattered which. Either way, he wouldn't have been a good match for me. "I should have broken it off with him six months ago."

"Well, what are you going to do now?" Sarah asked. "I mean with all this speculation and the things Turner is saying—and now Julia Ricci is accusing you of coming to campus drunk or hungover, and heavily implying some kind of substance-abuse problem, dredging up all those old stories about Holly's high school escapades. Turner's suggesting your dad's been bribing officials all over town to cover up the fact that you've both been out of control from day one, and someone at the *Courier* has come forward to say your dad has asked them to bury stories before— and again with this religious-discrimination complaint. He can't keep ignoring it forever."

"That'll be news to him," I said, not quite able to smother my bitterness. Julia Ricci. Of course she did. Probably with Jenna's encouragement—payback for dating Alex and because I hadn't let her passive-aggressive comments slide. And so much for Dad's "friend" at the *Courier*. "Because he's definitely planning on it. And I'm apparently supposed to do the same."

"Oh, honey." Sarah sighed. "I'm so sorry, Emma."

"Today I agreed to act as faculty adviser to a group of pagans who want their own student org on campus," I said. "And yesterday I threatened to sue the college for wrongful termination if they fired me. After the dean asked me for my resignation and I refused."

"No!"

"Yes," I said. "Which is why I'm here, at Alex's, and not at home. My mom gave me like a gallon of goulash last night after I told my father, and you know what that means."

"You've been uninvited to dinner for the rest of the weekend?"

"At least," I agreed.

"And I'm guessing you're still not allowed to brunch out."

I grimaced. "To be honest, I hadn't even thought about that, but even if my father was encouraging me to speak up, I don't think I'd want to put myself in that position. And the *Courier* has been particularly insistent. You remember Marco Harris? He's been all over me on campus, trying to get an interview. He even called Holly in California."

"Marco can't-take-a-hint Harris? You've got to be kidding. But please tell me this means I'm going to get to see this mythically spotless kitchen and officially meet your mythically understanding and supportive boyfriend."

I laughed. "I'm not sure we're at the 'invite my friends over to his place without asking' stage yet. This is only the second time I've ever been here. And you've met Alex at least half a dozen times."

"When he was your dad's spin doctor. Not as your *boyfriend*."

"I'll ask him and text you later," I said. "But no promises."

"We can't *not* have brunch," Sarah said. "Especially now."

My throat went tight, and I swallowed hard, so relieved that she wanted to be with me. That she was ready to weather the storm. But if I said any of that, I really would break down. "When you see this kitchen, you're going to understand completely why I called you," I told her instead. "I'm afraid to put my water glass down. And the living room is like one of those everything-just-so museum-quality rooms where you know you're not really supposed to *touch* anything. Except that there's a couch and the television, and he was streaming some police procedural last night, so he obviously does use it somehow. But without making it look like he uses it. It's totally bizarre, Sarah, I'm telling you."

"You'll break him in," she said, letting me change the subject and laughing along. "I have faith."

Truthfully? I kind of did, too.

-cΩΩo-

The insistent buzzing of Alex's phone woke us up the next morning, two full hours before I'd set my alarm. I groaned and pulled the pillow over my head. Alex hadn't gotten home until late, and we'd lost more sleep after that for the most obvious reason, which meant I'd really *needed* that extra two hours if I was going to drag myself to Sarah's for brunch, and I was cursing myself for chickening out about asking Alex if he'd mind me inviting her over instead.

But Alex's swearing—*that* I wasn't expecting to hear through the heavy down pillow (pristinely packed away just for guests). And I wasn't expecting him to touch my shoulder after, shaking me gently the rest of the way awake. Before, he'd just silenced his phone, glanced at the message, and either got up as quietly as possible to let me sleep or snuggled back down next to me under the blankets.

"Turner's calling a press conference," he said, his voice strained. "He's going to call for your father to drop out of the race."

I pulled the pillow off my head and stared at him, absorbing the words. "What?"

"Why don't you call Sarah and see if she'd be willing to have brunch with you here? That way we can all watch it together, and nobody is going to catch you by surprise coming or going."

"Don't you have to go in to the office?"

"There's only one reason why he'd make a move like this, Emma," Alex said softly.

"To force my father's hand about me," I said. "Which is why you should probably be with my dad."

"There will be plenty of time for me to get to the office or to your dad afterward," Alex said. "And if it comes to that, honestly, your mother might be glad to have you with her at the house. But if you don't want to be there, then I'd rather you were here. With Sarah."

With a friend, because whatever else was in that text message, he was worried that the things Turner would say were going to be hurtful for me to hear. Hurtful *to* me.

"I can handle this, Alex," I told him. "I promise, I'm going to be fine."

"Humor me?"

I grabbed my phone, texting Sarah, who was probably already up and done with her morning yoga routine by now. How I'd become best friends with a morning person, I still wasn't sure, but I could definitely count on her rolling with the punches on this one with a minimum of fuss, whereas I would have been scrambling and half-asleep.

"You think it's going to be that bad?" I asked him after I hit "Send" and set my phone back on the bedside table.

He shook his head. "There isn't any way this ends well."

Alex was on the phone when Sarah arrived with a brunch buffet of primarily breakfast pastries. But he smiled appreciatively and took the box of croissants and danishes out of her hands, heading back to the kitchen while dictating instructions to some poor intern on the other end of the line.

"I didn't think we'd really have a lot of attention for the actual eating part of things," she said, hugging me. "Are you okay?"

"I'm fine," I said. "Honestly, you and Alex. There's nothing that Turner can say that I haven't been imagining worse for years now."

"Even so," she said, searching my face. "I'm glad Alex is worried about you. But are you sure you wouldn't rather be at home with your parents?"

"I'm sure that my face is the last one my father is going to want to see when all of this is going down." I shrugged, leading her through the living room from the entry as we followed Alex to the kitchen. "It's fine. We're here. Alex is plugged into headquarters by phone and Internet already, crafting a plethora of responses ranging from condemnation to bland dismissal to righteous indignation and defense—I think he's just waiting for the details and quotations at this point to drive things home. And in between calls with the campaign team, he's been updating my dad. It's all very well organized."

"Much like his kitchen, it seems," she said, her gaze traveling over the spotless, completely bare counters and fingerprint-free stainless steel appliances. "Wow."

"I know," I agreed, slipping my hand into my sleeve to open the fridge and pull out the water pitcher and a bottle of orange juice. I was not going to be leaving *my* fingerprints where they didn't belong, either. At least not this early in the relationship.

"And that living room?"

"He didn't know I was coming on Thursday night, and it was just as clean then," I told her.

"The whole house is like this?"

"The. Whole. House."

"Sorry about that," Alex said, slipping his phone into his back pocket. "I'm so glad you didn't mind the change of plans on such short notice, Sarah. Feel free to make yourself at home."

"Um," she said, giving the kitchen another pointed sweep. "I'm almost afraid to touch anything."

Alex laughed, taking the orange juice from my hands. "It's a little bit extreme, I know. But if I don't keep things hyperclean, it's a *rapid* decline into chaos. I'm kind of an all-or-nothing guy."

"Do you cook?" she asked, flicking her fingers at the empty dish rack.

"Ah." He cleared his throat. "Not . . . often."

Sarah nodded, tossing me a triumphant grin. "Well, that explains it. It's a lot easier to keep a kitchen immaculate when you're not actually using it."

"It's not like he has a lot of time to slave over the stove," I said, giving her a gentle push toward the breakfast nook with a look I hoped she interpreted as *Don't you dare give him a hard time for not cooking.*

"I'm not criticizing," she said, lifting both hands, palms out. "I'm just saying."

Alex offered a self-conscious smile. "She isn't *wrong*. Mostly I just have to wipe down the counters and dust everything once a week. The dishwasher loads are mostly just glasses and silverware. But I know *how* to cook, I promise."

"If you didn't, I'm sure Irena would teach you everything you never knew you wanted to know and then some," Sarah said. "If it came to that."

That meaning Alex and me forming a more permanent relationship. Not Sarah's most subtle approach.

"I'm really more worried about being too messy for you than whether or not one of us is going to get stuck doing all the cooking," I reassured him before Sarah could needle him any further.

Alex shook his head, his hand slipping into mine. "I'll be happy to cook *and* clean for you, for as long as you'll let me."

"Clean up *after*," Sarah corrected.

I threw a napkin at her face, and Alex laughed. But neither one of us denied it. And while I picked at my croissant, and Alex found us juice glasses and coasters and dessert plates to catch our crumbs more effectively than napkins, I thought about what he'd said. About being an all-or-nothing kind of guy.

It had only been a couple of weeks, and it was completely crazy to think about it, but I was pretty sure he was all in with me. And even after just a couple of weeks . . .

Well, I was done holding myself back when it came to more than just my faith. If Alex accepted me as I came, I wasn't going to drive him away.

"Congressman Moretti's blatant abuse of his power to secure his pagan daughter a position which allows her to influence young and impressionable minds, and then protect her job over the objections of her own students, who have called her out for what she is, is just the latest example of his corruption by the establishment politics of Washington!" Turner said, his face red with the passion of his speech. He wasn't leaving anything unembroidered, that was for sure.

"We can no longer sit idly by, trusting him to represent us—trusting in his bland reassurances of traditional family values and his show of Christian faith—or our interests any longer. And if he had any shame, any *respect* for us at all, he'd have dropped out of the race long before now. Retired gracefully from public service and addressed the concerns we've raised honestly, like the man he claims to be! Congressman Moretti of ten, fifteen years ago seemed to be a man we could believe in. But what we know now about his family, about how he's used his influence in the media to keep the truth from us for *decades*, what his silence has told us in this last week, has made it clearer than ever that the man we trusted may well have never existed.

"Which is why I'm calling on you—all of you—to speak up. If we cannot demand Congressman Moretti's resignation, we can at least demand that he address the concerns that have been raised. And if he won't, then we can *certainly* demand that he drop out of this race for reelection."

I pressed my tongue hard against the back of my teeth, fighting to keep my outrage at bay. But I couldn't just sit there and watch him behind that podium, slandering my father's good name with virtually no proof that he'd ever done anything even remotely wrong. Turner was using some earmarked education funds that had ended up supporting the liberal arts programs at colleges and universities across the state to suggest that my father had bribed the dean into hiring me, which made absolutely no sense at all, and then accusing him of never having been Christian, just because I'd been outed as a Heathen.

Instead I paced behind the couch, back and forth, while I listened to him continue on. Repeating the same nothing points. Going on and on about how my father had knowingly planted me at the college in order to corrupt our youth and work to supplant the good Christian morals of our state. And he obviously had more than one person at the college feeding him information, because he was waving a copy of the form I'd signed off on when I'd agreed to act as faculty adviser to Becky's student organization, like it was some kind of proof of this completely fabricated plot.

"First Congressman Moretti insisted we welcome *terrorists* into our country, voting over and over again to allow a flood of refugees within our borders, unchecked. And now he wants us to ignore the fact that his daughter is bringing neo-Nazi ideology onto our own college campus, where she's *advising* your children! But it stops here," Turner said, bringing his hand down on the rostrum. "With *your* help and support, with your voice raised alongside mine, we can stamp out this corruption! We can remove false Christians like Joseph Moretti from positions of influence and reclaim our country for Jesus Christ!"

"No one can possibly believe this," Sarah said. "Your mom and dad—they've never been anything but sincere in their faith, and they've done so many good works. All those volunteer hours your mom has put in at the food banks, all the donations she and your father have raised. They've never ducked a single obligation to their community. And this total BS about you being a neo-Nazi? He has no proof of anything!"

"He doesn't need them to believe it, and he definitely doesn't need proof," Alex said. "He only needs to shake their faith. But with any luck, Turner's shown his hand too early. We've got weeks to earn back their trust—to show Joe in the community, participating in church activities, doing the same volunteer work he's been doing for the last three decades."

"It's not going to matter if he doesn't address this head-on," I said. "Turner's pushing hard on this idea that my dad isn't doing his duty to his constituents by maintaining his radio silence about me, to say nothing of the burrowing worm of suggestion that he's been using the *Courier* to lie to them for years. And you know how people are. It's salacious gossip, and they want to hear all the juicy details."

"They're not going to get them," Alex said. "Even if he addresses Turner's accusations, your father's not going to give them any personal details. It'll be the barest bones he can get away with."

"And then Turner will just come out with another speech like this, accusing him of dishonesty," I said.

Alex sighed, turning the volume down a few bars now that Turner had wrapped up. "I know."

"He has to face this," I said. "He *has* to."

"I know," Alex agreed, rubbing his forehead. "And that's what I'm planning on telling him—again. But to be honest, I don't think it's going to change his mind, no matter how many times I repeat myself."

I hugged myself, my gaze shifting from Alex, who looked exhausted and drained at even the thought of retreading this ground with my father, to the television and Turner's smug yet deeply concerned talking head. Like he cared about anything except winning.

"I'm coming with you back to the house," I said. "He won't listen to me, either, but I have to try."

"What can I do?" Sarah asked.

"Come along for the ride," Alex told her. "I'll feel better knowing Emma has a friend after I have to take off."

I rolled my eyes. "I'm fine, Alex."

"I know you are," he said, covering my hand, which was resting on the back of his couch. "But it doesn't hurt to have a little bit of extra support. And it definitely doesn't hurt to let people see that your best friend is sticking by you and your family."

Sarah snorted. "I see how it is. Does that spin-doctor brain of yours ever turn off?"

Alex half shrugged, not denying it—but then, I already knew it didn't. Not really. The weirder part was that I was starting to get used to it.

"Will you do it?" he asked her.

"Yeah," Sarah said. "I'll do it."

He was right. It did feel good knowing my friend wasn't going anywhere. That I wasn't alone in this and I had her support. That she was even willing to be used by Alex to spin things for me.

Me. Not the campaign. But me.

His phone buzzed and he answered, squeezing my hand and getting up from the couch to excuse himself from the room while he barked more orders to the staff and corrected wording on press releases. Every contingency prepared for. I chewed my lip, watching him pace beyond the kitchen doorway. He'd said he'd be heading in to the office with my father, but I wondered if my mother hadn't been right after all. Loyal as Alex had always been, I could see the fractures, the frustration, the wear . . .

"Looks, brains, and a clean gene, plus he's obviously completely in love with you," Sarah said. "Does he have any warts?"

"Workaholic neat freak doesn't count?"

"I feel like you're going to find out."

I just hoped I wasn't going to cost him his job in the process.

CHAPTER FORTY-NINE:
AD 1003
FREYDÍS

I stumbled, cursing, back into the room I shared with Thorvard, my lip still bleeding and my ears ringing from the hard blow to the side of my head. My husband did not so much as stir until, shivering and shaking, I slipped beneath the furs.

In the years before I was married, I'd taken my share of lovers, and then there had been Sonnung, after, but never in my life had I ever suffered what these men had forced upon me. Never had I been treated with so little respect or such cruelty. Even the discomfort Thorvard gave me was wrought only of ignorance, not malice and unkindness. But these men—these men had left me feeling hollow and abused.

Thorvard grunted as my cold feet brushed against his legs, the rest of me just as frozen as he gathered me against his side. Then he stiffened and pushed me away instead. "You're cold as a winter's wind," he accused, his breath still heavy with wine. "Where have you been?"

I said nothing, my teeth chattering. Warm as the nights had been that summer, I should not have been so cold, but I could not stop shuddering with a bone-deep chill.

"Slipping off to meet some lover?" Thorvard demanded, sitting up to get a better look at me. I curled into a tighter ball beneath the furs, but he grabbed my face, turning it toward him, and even in the firelight, I could see the suspicion in his eyes, the distrust. Knowing it was the wine that talked more than my husband did not make it hurt less.

I jerked free and turned away from him. "I swore to you that you'd have my loyalty, that I would take no other lovers but for Sonnung. As you well know."

"You stink as though you've come from some man's bed, and what I *know* for certain is that it is not my seed spent inside you."

"I thought to speak to Helgi and Finnbogi, to ask them if we might take their larger ship back to Greenland and leave this wretched place behind."

"And used more than words to persuade them, it seems." Thorvard pushed me from the bed, and I rolled out of it, rising stiffly instead of falling. "Do you think I am so dim that I would not notice?"

I lifted my chin. "Does it truly look to you as though I seduced them, even drunk as you still are? A split lip and bruises upon my body, and that is what you accuse me of?"

"Every man at Brattahlid knows Sonnung was not always gentle—that you enjoyed it even when he wasn't."

"*Sonnung* loved me," I spat. "Helgi and Finnbogi *attacked* me."

He swung his legs over the edge of the sleeping bench, sitting up and staring at me hard. "Is that true?"

I grasped the silver hammer Sonnung had given me. "I swear it upon Mjölnir—may Thor strike me down where I stand if I lie."

His eyes narrowed, but even fogged by drink, he knew not to question such a vow. "They raped you?"

"As good as," I said.

Thorvard looked away, his gaze upon the door—as if he could see through the wood and the turf to the other longhouse. "And then they simply let you go."

I sank to a seat upon the bench opposite, where Sonnung and I had once sat together—slept together—still clutching my hammer against my breast. "They said no one would believe me, least of all you."

"Why?" Thorvard asked, and I was uncertain still whether he trusted my words. "Why would they do this?"

I shook my head, shivering again. "It was my unwillingness that enraged them. They thought . . . they thought I believed myself their better. All Leif and Thjodhild's sneering. They said I insulted them by refusing. That I never hesitated to take a man who wanted me."

Thorvard cursed and rose, pacing the small room. "Why did you not leave? Why did you not come to wake me?"

"I tried!"

"You would have me believe they took you by force? You! Freydís Thorswoman, of all women!"

"I had no weapon with which to defend myself," I said. "Finnbogi slipped between me and the door before I realized what they were about. Helgi grabbed me by the arm when I tried to run, twisted it up behind my back. Thorvard, they must not go unpunished. We must not let them!"

He snorted, reaching for his trousers. "And if I refuse to act against them, you will accuse me of being weak. Harp at me until I am driven into madness. Yes. Yes, *I* must see them punished. *I* must act in your defense. Your fool of a husband. And once again, you have brought me nothing but dishonor and shame."

"They dishonored *me!*"

"Because they believe I am too weak to act against them. That they need not fear me in the slightest. That I am only your soft little puppy, easy enough to kick away should I nip at their heels." He belted his pants, shoved his feet into his boots, and grabbed up his axe, glowering. "Because of you."

I flushed. "You were weak and soft before you ever met and married me, Thorvard. And everyone knew it."

"Rouse the rest of the men." His grip on the axe tightened. "They will all know differently before long."

Still barefooted and dressed in only my shift and my husband's cloak, I shoved bodies awake in the main room, urging them up. Thorvard was already outside, bellowing for Helgi and Finnbogi, and the men in our longhouse were reaching for knives and swords, if they had them, fumbling to dress through the fog of sleep.

"Hurry!" I said. "Before that fool Thorvard gets himself killed!"

We had thirty-five men to their thirty, but there were the women, too, to consider. Helgi and Finnbogi kept them close, using their favors as particularly sweet rewards when their men earned one—no doubt to keep their gold and silver for themselves. Stupid women who had watched while the two brothers had all but torn my arm from my shoulder and forced themselves upon me.

One of the men, quicker than the rest to wake, ran off to the pit house to rouse the men who slept inside, for we did not have room enough for everyone in the main house, and the others, still bleary-eyed and confused, but dressed and armed and ready enough to fight, followed me, spilling from the longhouse to stand beside Thorvard.

"Face me!" Thorvard roared. "Face me like men!"

I worried my hammer, skimming it back and forth on its leather cord. If only Sonnung had been with me still, Helgi and Finnbogi would never have dared to touch me. Nor even to think of me with desire. And five men more or not, I was not certain how this would end.

Thor, protect us. Grant us your strength.

Finally, Finnbogi and Helgi pushed their door open, armed with swords and dressed in leather. I could only be grateful that they had no mail. But that made me think of Sonnung again, and I blinked back futile tears. *Sonnung, if only you were here.*

His absence had been a hole in my heart, like the loss of a limb after three joyful years together. And I was glad, suddenly, that he'd taken our son with him. That I had not brought Vingthor here to witness this, though I had not liked letting him go when I did not know how long it would be before I saw him again.

Before I saw either one of them again.

"What troubles you, Thorvard?" Helgi asked.

"You rape my wife, and you ask me that?"

"Rape?" Finnbogi's eyebrows rose, all surprise and laughter. "I think you misunderstand, my friend. Freydís came to us—offered to trade. A little pleasure in exchange for our ship, that she might sail home with more lumber, that's all. It is hardly rape if the woman is so willing."

"Liar!" I shouted.

"We all know what she is," Helgi said, ignoring me. "Though why you've kept a pagan whore as your wife, we all wonder."

"Filthy Icelandic *dogs*." I lurched forward, knife in my hand, but one of Thorvard's men caught me, his fingers, hard as iron, wrapping around my arm.

"We have witnesses," Finnbogi called out, raising his voice to be heard by all. And a snap of his fingers brought the women out. All five, their heads held high. "Tell these men what you saw."

"She seduced them," the black-haired girl said, taller than the others, with a wooden cross hanging from her neck. Her words were accented strangely. Not Icelandic, Norse, or even Dane. The Frank, perhaps? "Slipping into the longhouse before dawn, dressed in nothing, and asking if she might arrange a trade. Finnbogi refused, of course. Why would he trade his larger ship for a smaller one? It was their own fault they'd brought too many men and had not room enough for all the cargo they wished to carry. But she only smiled and let her cloak fall away, persuading them with the favors of her body to do as she asked."

"I'd rather take a goat to my bed than give myself up to a Christian," I spat, struggling against the men who held me. "And you saw! You saw what they did to me!"

"Either way," Thorvard said coolly, as if he cared not at all for the truth—or perhaps he even believed them. "You've taken what's mine. And I will not be made a fool a second time."

"Kill them!" a voice called out from behind me. A voice I knew so well. A voice I had dreamed of for more than a year. I tore free of the hands that grasped at me, searching the faces of our men. *Sonnung.* "Kill them both!"

Finnbogi shifted uncomfortably and tossed a small purse to the ground at my husband's feet, coins clinking inside. "She is not worth so much as that, but we offer it freely, to buy peace for ourselves and our men."

"Another insult to your honor, Thorvard," Sonnung shouted over the noise of the others—from where, I could not determine, though I searched desperately for some glimpse of him. "Do you not see they think this all some joke? They think you weak! Toothless!"

Thorvard made no move to pick up the purse, nor did he so much as look at it, his expression worn and grim. Tired. "I'm afraid if I accept your payment, generous though it may be, it will do nothing to prevent another man from thinking as you have. Whatever else she might be, Freydís *is* my wife, and I am sworn to her protection."

"Kill them all," Sonnung called, and the rest of Thorvard's men murmured agreement. "Kill them, and no man will ever dare to stand against you. Kill them, and you will have both fame and respect!"

Helgi bared his teeth. "You cannot be serious. She is nothing, Thorvard. Certainly not worth this."

"Worth my reputation?" my husband asked. "If because of this, I am remembered, then perhaps she has been worth every insult I've suffered. Finally and at last, she will be good for something."

And then he swung his axe, cleaving it into Helgi's shoulder before he even thought to raise his sword. Thorvard stole the blade from his nerveless fingers and swung that, too, slicing Finnbogi across the throat. Blood sprayed over him, painting his face and his bare chest with steaming red, and for a moment, we all stood and stared, disbelieving.

One heartbeat, then another, and behind me, Thorvard's men roared. They surged forward while I stood frozen, still, and Helgi and Finnbogi's men, who had been slower to rise—not called for at once and roused to arms as ours had been—fell back.

⁂

"I made you a promise, did I not?" Sonnung said, low against my ear. "I swore to you, before you were done here, no man would dare to raise a hand against you."

I let out a breath, afraid to turn—afraid he was not truly there to look upon. How he had come—I did not know how he had come so far, so fast. Or perhaps I did not want to know. Not when knowing meant he must leave me again.

"Not fast enough," he objected, as if he'd read my thoughts. "You must forgive me for not arriving in time to stop them. But you will be safe now, Freydís. I swear it."

"Protected by Thorvard's reputation," I said. "Not my own."

Sonnung grunted, and sidelong, I saw him. His shadow blending with mine upon the ground and my body prickling with his nearness. "That much will be your choice. If you wish to be feared, the means to become so is at hand. But I cannot promise it will bring you happiness. The men and women who tell your story, who remember it, may well revile you, and there is Thorvard to consider, too."

I found my husband among his men, their shouts and the screams of the dying drowned out by the rumble of thunder overhead. A constant low growl, until it was all I could hear but for Sonnung's voice.

"If you claim this fate, Freydís, he will be remembered as nothing more than your husband. Weak and unworthy. If you show mercy instead, he will be known in his own right. He'll forgive you for every imagined slight, sure of his own strength, and perhaps—perhaps you will find happiness with him, too. But you will be remembered only as his wife, your father's daughter, and little else."

They dragged the men who were still sleeping from their beds and out into the grass, killing them before they could rise, not giving them even the chance to fight. The bodies of Helgi and Finnbogi's men littered the meadow, and Thorvard had begun to count them rather than rooting out the few who had escaped, kicking them faceup and stripping them of armbands and rings as he went.

The women huddled together against the longhouse, weeping and moaning, arms wrapped around one another and heads bent together, faces turned away. The women who had watched and done nothing when Helgi and Finnbogi had dragged me behind that curtained end of the longhouse. The women who had lied.

I crossed the field, stepping carefully around the bodies, but unable to avoid completely the pools and puddles of blood turning the earth to mud. Sonnung did not follow, but I felt his gaze upon me. I knew he watched.

"Why?" I demanded when I reached them.

The black-haired woman who had witnessed looked up at my voice, her lip curling and her eyes narrowing in spite. "Why what?"

"Why did you lie?"

She rose, tall and proud, staring at me with open disgust. "Thjodhild told me of you. Of your foul pagan ways. She told me, too, that you should have been killed for what you'd done. Carrying on in your adultery so openly, thinking yourself above the law."

"Thjodhild." My fingers tightened around the knife in my hand. "Of course."

"You should be dead now, too. You! And then we would be free of your curse, free of the taint of your gods upon these lands. Greenland would be cleansed of your pagan rot, your husband set free to take a good Christian wife."

And the way her eyes glinted—I knew. She was the slave who had given my husband his son. "When did Thjodhild tell you all this?"

"While you were away," she said. "When you abandoned your husband to live here with your lover. I was Thjodhild's then. A gift from Thorvard. Until she sold me to Helgi and Finnbogi."

"And you thought Thorvard would marry you if I was dead?"

She lifted her chin again, unashamed of her presumption. "Why not, when I had mothered his son? There are few enough women for him to choose from, and he knew me. He desired me."

"If you had not lied, you might have had him," I said, a coldness fingering its way through my veins. "If you had spoken in my defense, I might even have been glad to overlook it if he brought you to our bed."

She sneered. "I'd have brought a knife to repay your gratitude, and slit your throat before sharing him with you."

"Then I suppose it does not matter either way," I agreed and grabbed her by the wrist, tearing her away from the other four women and throwing her down upon Helgi's bloody corpse. "Kill the women, too!" I called. "Kill them all, and let us have done with it. Should anyone ask, we need only say the skraelings took them all."

Thorvard strode forward, the other men pausing in their work of collecting the dead, their sudden silence roaring in my ears. "They are women, Freydís."

"They were Helgi's and Finnbogi's slaves," I said. "And they lied."

"Of course they lied," Thorvard said. "Do you think for a moment they would have lived if they had not said what Finnbogi wished to hear?"

"They die with the rest of the men," I commanded, raising my voice above Thorvard's reason.

But none of his men moved from their positions, all of them looking away, pretending not to hear, not to see.

"No, Freydís," Thorvard said, his voice low but firm. To protect his son's mother? But surely he would not have given her up if he cared for her at all. "It is not done to murder women this way. It is not Christian."

I tore the axe from his hand and spit in the dirt at his feet, and then I grabbed the woman by her black hair, twisting it around my fist. Her throat was the first I cut, hot blood spilling over my fingers, but not the last. All five of them, one by one, were killed by my hand.

Because I was not a Christian.

Because these Christians would have been happy to see me dead.

CHAPTER FIFTY:
AD 2016
Emma

Y ou."

That was how my father greeted me when I stepped out from behind Alex into the living room. It made me glad we'd left Sarah at the guesthouse, to handle this confrontation in relative privacy. *You.* By which he of course meant, *Author of all my troubles.* Maybe that wasn't entirely fair of me—I was sure he didn't blame me for everything Turner was throwing at him. Probably just the latest round of awful. And maybe I deserved it, at least in part. I wasn't going to pretend innocence.

And I wasn't going to bother with small talk, either. "Dad, you have to make a statement. A real one. And address this. I know it's personal and it's the principle of the thing at this point, but if it's my privacy you're really trying to protect, and not just your own butt, then I give you full permission. Just do it. Tell them everything. Tell them you don't agree with my beliefs and throw me under the bus. I don't care. But address this, or Turner is going to win."

"You don't get to tell me how to run my campaign, Emma," he said, his face flushed. "Especially not after you threw the grenade that blew it up."

"Joe!" My mother's voice was sharp and angry, but she hadn't moved from her position in the doorway, her arms crossed and her face paler than I liked. "You know that isn't fair."

He grunted, looking away. As good an apology as I was going to get, probably.

"I'm sorry that I messed things up for you," I said. "I'm sorry that I gave Turner any kind of ammunition at all. I can't do anything about it that isn't entirely dishonest, and at this point, it would do more harm than good. But you can do something. You can confront his accusations and *address* them."

"I don't answer to him," my father said, hitting the power button on the remote. The television went black, and he gathered his notes, his phone, his keys, and his glasses, dropping each into its assigned pocket and patting his jacket to reassure himself it was all there. "I'm certainly not going to start now."

"Joe, please," Alex said. "I've been saying it from the beginning, but Emma is right. If you don't get out in front of this, it's going to cost us the election. You've seen the numbers. They were already falling before this. I can call a press conference—I can get the press here within the hour, if you'll just talk to them. With Emma and Irena behind you, the three of you standing together as a united front. We can turn this around."

"And say what?" my father demanded. "Lie about how I'm happy to support my daughter's freedom to worship however she likes? Admit to them that I've failed her as a father and as a Christian? Because that's what this is, Alex. That's what you're asking me to do."

"You don't have to say any of that," Alex said. "You know I can spin this. I can make you look good without forcing you to say anything that isn't true. That's what you pay me for. That's why you've kept me on all these years. But you've got to let me do my job if you're going to win this."

I closed my eyes when I heard the pleading note in his voice. The frustration that underlay it all. *Let me do my job.* When I opened them again, I couldn't help but glance at my mother. She was watching Alex, white-lipped, her mouth a thin and anxious line. And I knew this was it. The moment she'd been waiting for. The breaking point between my father and the boy he'd taken under his wing, treated like a son—but he'd already given up on me. Why shouldn't he let Alex down, too?

"You know my feelings on this, Alex," my father said. "This stunt of Turner's doesn't change anything. My mind is made up."

Alex swallowed. Nodded once. "Vincent has a selection of releases for you. I went over them before Turner's press conference, and all you'll need to do is approve the final language. He'll be happy to see you through the rest of the campaign, and while he's still a little rough around the edges, I think he'll shape up nicely as a replacement if you win."

My father froze, staring at Alex. Then his gaze slid to me. "This is your doing?"

I shook my head, mute. I couldn't even breathe.

"You're going to lose this election, Joe," Alex said. "And it isn't going to be because of Emma or because of this manufactured scandal that Turner has cooked up. If you had let me do my job from the beginning—if you'd even let me do it *now*—we could have stopped this free fall, mitigated the losses, and rebuilt. There's time, still, to do the work that needs to be done. To save your seat. But I'm not going to stand by and watch you sink your own ship, hurting your family and yourself in the process, for no better reason than sheer pride and stubbornness. I won't be part of that. Not anymore."

"Alex—" But I didn't know what to say. I didn't know how to finish.

My father stared at us both for another long moment, his jaw working. "You're resigning. Now."

"Effective immediately," Alex said. "It's the only card I have left to play, Joe. You've got to see that. I wouldn't be doing this if I didn't believe it was the right thing. The only thing that could possibly shock you into doing what needs to be done."

My father shook his head. That was all. Just shook his head and walked out of the room—out of the house altogether, the door slamming hard behind him. And beside me, Alex deflated at the sound, visibly wilting.

"Alex." I took his hand, drew him with me to the couch. Dropped my head to his shoulder and hoped he could feel what I didn't have the words to say. "I'm so sorry."

"It was the right thing," my mother said. "You did the right thing, Alex, and don't let anyone ever tell you otherwise. He needed to realize the consequences. Maybe he won't lose me or Emma, but he deserved to lose you, just like he's lost his voters. I'm only surprised you lasted as long as you did."

Alex let out a breath. "I had hoped he would rethink—"

"I know," my mother said. "But we can only do what we can do. And now you're free to protect Emma, at least, if nothing else."

I squeezed Alex's hand. "I don't want you to do anything for me that's going to cause you any more trouble than this. If it's going to hurt your prospects, then forget it. You have to take care of yourself first. I can take care of me."

He pressed a kiss to the top of my head. "Don't worry. I'm fairly limited in my resources without the campaign. But at least I can stand next to you and hold your hand without worrying about the mixed signals it sends."

My mother snorted. "Don't be foolishly modest, Alex. You still have the reach of your contacts in the press, even if you don't have the money. And they'll still come when you call."

I sat up, staring at my mother, then at Alex. "What if we did?"

He lifted both eyebrows. "What?"

"What if *we* called the press and I talked to them? I have a right to address the accusations he's made. Really, I could probably sue him for defamation of character if I could dream of affording it. But at the very least I can defend myself. Just because Dad refuses to talk to them doesn't mean I can't. And it might help. With just a little bit of spin, to cover his butt for him."

"He won't like it," Alex said. "He'll hate it."

"Let him hate it," I said. "He's still a good congressman, even if he doesn't know how to deal with me. This idea that he's failed as a father, failed me and his family—it's blinding him. But it won't stop him from doing a better job than Turner."

Alex studied me for a long moment, then looked to my mother. "If you're willing to stand with her, to support her—and we'd have Sarah, too. And me. Obviously it would be better if we had Joe in the background, but I think we could make it work without him. Even if we've lost some trust with Turner's accusations about burying stories, with enough outlets, we can mitigate some of that. And Turner wouldn't expect it. Not the way Emma has been avoiding the press so far."

"Because you told me to," I grumbled.

"Because it was what your father wanted," Alex said.

"But maybe if we *show* him that people will understand—that they won't see this as his failure or whatever he's worried about it looking like—maybe he'll come around, too."

My mother sighed, catching the leather cord of my pendant and pulling it out from under my shirt to rest on top instead, openly. Her fingers lingered on the bronze, just for a heartbeat, and then she met my eyes.

"I don't know that it will help your father come to terms with your faith. But if this is what you want to do, and if Alex thinks it will help save your father from himself so we can keep that weasel Turner out of the House, then I'll do whatever you need me to do."

My mother wasn't wrong about Alex's reach. And after Turner's inflammatory accusations that morning, the press was more than happy to finally get a response, if not from the congressman himself, then from his family. And who better, really, to counter Turner's claims about my faith than me?

Marco Harris was front and center in the mob. We'd chosen to host my pseudo press conference outside the guesthouse, and my mother had ordered pizza and doughnuts and sent Sarah and Alex out for a variety of drinks and some veggie platters for the gluten- and dairy-free outliers. Marco, with his notepad open and a cameraman at his shoulder, had a celery stick hanging out of his mouth like a cigar.

"Always feed them well," my mother had said to me while we'd watched them descend like locusts. "That way they're happy and comfortable before you start talking and predisposed to give you the benefit of the doubt. A full stomach is the completely legal next best thing to a bribe."

When I took my position on the stoop, just high enough to make me more visible, with Sarah and my mother on either side, and Alex stepping forward to introduce me and give the press an idea of what I'd be talking about—and what I wouldn't be—I hoped she was right. I'd sketched out what I was going to say with Alex, and I flexed the note cards in my hands anxiously, snapping them back and forth, not even hearing Alex over the roar of my own nerves.

I touched the hammer hanging over my shirt, the bronze cool to the touch, and then dropped my hand self-consciously when a camera flashed. My mother caught my hand and squeezed it, then pushed me forward gently as Alex stepped aside—but not back. When I looked at him, I knew he meant to stay right there by my side.

"Thank you all so much for coming," I said, my voice breaking halfway through.

I cleared my throat, took a breath, and forced myself to stop fidgeting with my cards, resting them gently on the banister instead and pressing them flat with my damp palms.

"I know I'm not exactly the person you might have been hoping to hear from, but since Mr. Turner seems so interested in me and my faith, I hope you'll allow me the opportunity to set a few things straight."

Alex's hand found the small of my back, and I straightened, somehow feeling stronger for the contact, the reassurance of his presence, and the knowledge that if he weathered this with me, it seemed pretty unlikely that anything else was going to scare him off.

"I *am* a Heathen," I said. "I can't and won't speak today for all Heathens, because their experiences and beliefs might not be the same as mine. But what being Heathen means to me is that I believe in and worship the Norse gods, and Thor particularly; I honor my ancestors in prayer; and I believe in doing what I can to support my community."

I gave them a minute, letting that sink in and glancing down at my cards briefly to make sure I was on track before going on. "Mostly all that just means that sometimes I pour mead or wine into the grass underneath the nearest oak or rowan tree and pray that Thor and my ancestors will lend me the strength, courage, and support to help me get through whatever personal or professional challenge I'm facing that day. I talk to him the way most of you probably talk to Jesus, and for me, he's just as real or unreal as any other god being worshipped today.

"But these last weeks, it's also meant standing up for other pagans in our community. Being there for them as a resource and faculty adviser while they navigate their way through finding their own beliefs and faith. It's meant revealing my faith so that other people might feel safer about theirs. Because I believe, honestly and wholeheartedly, that we are not a community of people who judge one another based on what god we worship, but rather on the strengths of our characters.

"And the strengths of *my* character come in large part from my father, your congressman, who taught me to stand up for and support others, to embrace the differences between us and to celebrate them. To put others before myself and, above all, to do the right and moral thing, even if it isn't always the easiest path to walk."

I swallowed, searching for any kind of understanding—but of course it wasn't the understanding of the press I was really looking for. It was the understanding of the community, the voters who would mean the difference between my father winning or losing.

"My father didn't want to respond to Mr. Turner's accusations, because he felt doing so would invite an invasion of my privacy and the privacy of our family. As far back as I can remember, he was always trying to shield and protect my sister and me from the campaign season and the political machine. I can't speak to the lengths he might or might not have gone to do so—but I imagine it wasn't anything more or less than what any other father would do for his daughters. And maybe he's right in keeping silent now. Maybe standing up here today and addressing you directly about my faith and Mr. Turner's concerns about it isn't the right thing to do politically. But I wanted you all to know who I am. I wanted you to know that I'm still my father's daughter and my spiritual experiences are no reflection on his faith or his abilities as a father, and certainly have no bearing at all on his capability to represent you as a congressman. He is still the same man who has stood for you and your interests in Washington for the last twenty-some years, and whatever life I lead, it doesn't change that."

I shuffled my cards, slipping the ones I'd covered to the back of the pile. Almost done. Almost done and then the chips would fall, one way or another. But at least I'd know I'd done everything I could, either way.

"I didn't choose this," I said. "Not any more than any of you might have chosen to experience your god's love. And my experiences, they don't make me believe for a minute that yours aren't just as real and honest and authentic. In fact, experiencing what I have—it's made me understand more completely the passion that other people carry in their hearts for their own god. Passion that, until I found Heathenry, I had never felt in church or in prayer, that maybe I'd been more willing to dismiss or doubt.

"My faith has made me more able to accept the things I couldn't before, to understand and accept the people in my community and the experiences they've had. And I can only hope that by speaking to you today, I've allowed you to understand me a little bit more easily. That I've shown you that even though I'm not a Christian anymore, I'm still the girl you've watched all these years trailing after her father at campaign events. I'm still a person who lives her life by the same ideals that our community has always valued. And despite what Mr. Turner would like you to believe, my dad is, too.

"I hope you'll let him continue to represent you. Thank you."

I stepped back, and Alex stepped forward, shielding me from the shouted questions and fielding a few of them confidently. I hadn't realized until that moment, I think, how *very* good he was at his job. A laugh and a smile here, a lighthearted remark there, and even though they hadn't gotten much more information than they'd started with, the reporters seemed happy with his responses.

"I'm sorry," he said when they'd calmed down. "I can't speak on behalf of Congressman Moretti or his campaign at this time. But I'm sure you'll have a statement from them shortly."

And then he turned, waving us into the guesthouse because there was no way we'd be able to make it to the main house until the majority of the press had cleared out of the driveway. Once the door was closed, he swept me up into a bear hug, spinning me around.

"You did great, Emma. Absolutely perfect!"

I hugged him back and let out a shaky laugh. When he put me down, my legs were shaking—I was shaking. "Do you think it will help?"

"I think it will be huge," Alex said. "And the way you talked about your faith—you made it completely accessible and understandable. There will be people who won't like that you compared Thor to Jesus, of course, but that's going to be their issue, not yours. If you didn't win your father back the lead, I don't know that anything will."

I stumbled, reaching out for my mother, and she hugged me, too, her eyes bright. "I didn't know," she said into my hair. "I didn't realize."

"It's okay," I said. "I never told you. How could you know if I never told you?"

She hugged me tighter, then let me go. "If your father doesn't come around—he'll come around. After that, I don't see how he could do anything else."

Alex's phone was buzzing, with text messages or phone calls, I didn't know, because mine was blowing up, too, and Sarah was in tears, hugging me in turn and promising that she'd never try to talk me into going to church with her again, even though I couldn't imagine that even a third of what I'd said was anything she hadn't heard before. Or maybe she just hadn't listened until now, too sure of her own rightness to hear what I was saying and understand it.

"Emma?" my mother said, and when the house line had started ringing, I wasn't sure, but she held out the handset to me, and I knew from her expression—I *knew*—that it was Dad. Sooner than I'd expected. Sooner than I was ready for. But it had to be good. It had to be good or he wouldn't have called at all. And maybe—even if I hadn't saved his election—maybe, like Sarah, he'd finally heard me, too. Maybe we'd still won. But something bigger. Something more important. Though to be honest, after listening to Turner speak, hearing how casually he was willing to throw all pagans under the bus as malcontents and problems to be solved, beating him was still a pretty big priority in my life.

I took a breath and reached for Alex, who nodded, and then I took the phone from my mother's hand.

"Hello?"

CHAPTER FIFTY-ONE:
AD 1003
FREYDÍS

After I was finished, with Thorvard still shocked and gaping, and the other men eager to be as far from me as they could manage, I stumbled away. One foot after another, after another, after another, rubbing my hands together to flake the drying blood from my skin, until I tripped over a hillock and fell to my knees in the waist-high grass.

My stomach heaved, bile climbing up my throat, making my mouth water, and I retched, tears spilling down my cheeks and the sour, bitter taste of vomit coating my tongue. I wiped my mouth on the back of my hand, unable to stop myself from sobbing. Strong arms caught me up, and Sonnung dragged me against his broad chest, rocking me back and forth, murmuring gentle words of reassurance that I did not truly hear, only knew by their tone, their comfort as I cried into his shoulder.

"Hush," he said when my sobs had softened into hiccups. "It is done, Freydís. Your choice made and your fate claimed. It is done now."

I shook my head—my whole body shook. "They lied. They lied, and she would have killed me if I hadn't."

He stroked my hair, both of us upon our knees, hidden by the tall grass. "Perhaps."

"You could have stopped me." I shuddered again. "You could have held me back."

"It was your choice to make," he said in firm rebuke. "A choice you had every right to make. Did I not tell you once before, Freydís, that you would fight fiercely for your life? If it had not been today, it would have been another."

"But the other four might have lived," I said. "I might have spared them."

"You would have learned before long that Thjodhild's poison had found them, too," he said. "Though perhaps you are right. I am not certain any of the rest would have been bold enough to act upon it. Certainly they would not have been encouraged by Thorvard."

"And now?"

"Now you are free."

It was a small comfort.

Too small, I feared, to balance against the weight in my chest.

"You have done what you must, Freydís," Sonnung said. "It is finished now."

Though Sonnung lent me some measure of his strength by coming at all, he did not linger. Once I had calmed, and Thorvard began to call for me, he slipped away—disappearing between one blink and the next, though the meadow stretched open and clear. I wished I could have followed, but I rose and began my long walk back to the settlement, burying the horror that had driven me away. I would not show Thorvard any glimpse of doubt or regret. I would not let the men see that I had wept.

"I've sent the men to begin loading the ship," he told me, unable to look at me when I returned to our small room. "We'll sail as soon as it is done. With both ships filled, we need never return."

"Then we will settle in Greenland," I said. "On that farm of yours. Far from my brother and Thjodhild. We'll be left alone."

"If that's what you wish," Thorvard said.

"Where else is there to go?"

His lips pressed thin. "The farm is near enough to a sandy shore that it will hardly matter, I suppose."

So he could sail and ply his trade as he pleased, I understood. So he need not remain trapped upon a farm with me.

I nodded once, though I knew he did not see it, for he kept his gaze trained upon the knife in his hand, running it against the strop. There was no blood left on the blade, but my hands and clothes were still stained.

"I must wash," I murmured.

And then I slipped away. From the room and then the longhouse, ignoring the stares of Thorvard's men. Sonnung had understood my choice, had not looked on me with anything but compassion, and I did not care for the way the men crossed themselves or kissed the heavy crosses hanging from their necks as I passed. Even Thorhall looked away.

Sonnung had warned me—if only I had listened. Only too late did I realize it was respect I longed for—not their fear. But there was little to be done about it now.

I washed in the river, pushing away the memories of what I had done as the blood sloughed from my skin, and thinking instead of Sonnung. When he had promised me he would come, I had not dreamed he meant this. That I might summon him with a thought and a prayer. And how he had arrived—or gone again—I still did not understand.

But perhaps I did not have to. He had made a promise, and he had kept it—as he had kept every promise he had made before.

Perhaps, as he had said so often, I need only keep faith.

If that was so, why should I worry about the rest?

⁂

It was a long journey back. Not because storm or sea turned against us, for the sailing was easy, and we were never becalmed or bewildered or swept up by a strange current. Rather, it was the silence of the men, their uneasiness when they looked my way. Even Thorvard did not crowd me, leaving me to my thoughts where I sat tucked against the ship's prow, fingering the silver hammer hanging round my neck.

If only Gudrid had come, and Karlsefni, things might have been so different, my fate set upon a different course. But they would be settled in Iceland by now, at Karlsefni's farm, where I dared not follow. I would not live anywhere that I must be baptized and made Christian, and in Greenland at least I would have my freedom in that regard. Begrudgingly granted, perhaps, for my faith in Thor would always be a thorn in my brother's side, but freedom still, if Leif valued his life.

I had not believed Sonnung so long ago, when he had said the words. Never did I dream for a moment that I would be driven to kill in such a manner. Even when we had faced the skraelings, I had not wanted to see them dead. I had stood against them boldly, strong with Sonnung at my back, but it had not been a personal attack.

The splash of the water against the hull turned to a gurgle of blood from the black-haired slave's throat, and I hugged my knees to my chest, warding off the chill that followed and the sourness on my tongue.

They did not call me Thorswoman anymore—that was certain. The word they whispered when I passed was foul and accusing. *Murderess.* And that was not all, perhaps not even the worst, for I knew what they believed, no matter how determinedly Thorvard had tried to silence such thoughts.

"She killed them to keep the poor women from telling Thorvard what they saw," one of his men had murmured, thinking his voice too low to be heard. "To save herself from being punished for adultery, now that it's her Christian brother who gives the law instead of Erik. Everyone knows she ought to have been killed for all she did before, but her father wouldn't hear of it. That Sonnung only paid his fine, and money for any child he might get on her, and it was settled before Thorvard even knew what was done."

Before even I knew, if what the man had said was true. Certainly I'd had no part in any meeting between my father and Sonnung related to our affair, but the more I heard people speak of Sonnung, the stranger he seemed. Not that it would have been odd, exactly, if he had approached my father directly to settle things before trouble began. I only thought I would have known that he intended it. Or that I might have been included, if not by Sonnung, then by my father at the least.

But I had known nothing, save for Thorvard's sullen acceptance, and I wondered how much gold and silver it had taken to mend the wound to my husband's pride. A much larger sum than Helgi and Finnbogi had offered, to be sure, and no wonder Thorvard had refused to be bought a second time.

I rested my head against the curving wood of the prow and sighed. If Thorvard realized that I had stolen his fame, I did not think he would forgive it. But it had not been fame or reputation, nor even my fate that I had been thinking of when I acted. I'd been blinded by anger, betrayal, and rage.

And perhaps if I had been a man, Christian or not, that would have been excuse enough. Certainly my father had recovered from the deaths he had wrought. But for a pagan woman living among Christians—and an adulteress, besides?

These rumors and whisperings were only the start, and it would be just as Sonnung had warned me. I would be reviled.

But better alive and hated than dead.

Better remembered as a whoring murderess than forgotten as a Christian.

CHAPTER FIFTY-TWO:
AD 2016
Emma

Auntie Anja!" My sister didn't even wait for her to put down her bags before she was hugging our aunt and blocking the hall entirely. Holly had always been exuberant. Or maybe *passionate* was the better word. Never afraid to take risks—never doubting herself or her convictions. If Holly had been the Heathen in our family, the world would have known on day one, and no one would have dared to question her, either. As it was, I was glad to settle for grudging acceptance with a side of argument regarding my attendance at Christmas Eve mass.

"Let her in the house, Holly," my mother called. "And don't leave poor Björn standing in the cold."

"You call this cold?" Björn called out, shaking the snow out of his red-gold hair and stomping his boots to keep from tracking it inside. "You have been away too long, Irena, if this is what you call winter."

The weather had been unseasonably mild and consistently strange, and I didn't envy my father his job when it came to arguing the truth of climate change with his fellow congressmen. Warm winters were hell on the towns that survived on winter tourist sports like skiing and snowboarding, and even the people who didn't believe entirely that climate change was of our own making still supported measures that might possibly keep things from getting worse.

"We're so glad you could join us for the holidays this year," my mother said, giving Auntie Anja a perfunctory kiss on the cheek before welcoming her husband warmly. "You haven't met the girls, of course—Holly is the one who has no manners, and that's Emma, lurking in the doorway, giving you a chance to take off your boots before she bombards you. And her fiancé, Alexander, just over her shoulder."

"If you want, I can take your bags," Alex offered when Auntie Anja had made it into the kitchen proper.

"Fiancé and bellhop. What service." Anja relinquished her backpack and the extended handle of her suitcase with a smile before catching me up in a hug as fierce as Holly's had been. "I wish I could have come sooner, sweetheart. I wish you had told me when all this began!"

I hugged her back, sinking into her warmth, her understanding. "I wish I had. But I wasn't sure. Not really. And I didn't know if you'd understand, after all the press on the temple. I thought you'd think I was crazy, too. Then it all kind of exploded before I had the chance."

"Björn, come meet my Emma and her Alex," Anja said, drawing back to beam at me. She touched the hammer over my breast. "Did your mother tell you this was your amma's Mjölnir? And her mother's before that. To think if Holly had been older, I would have given it to her instead. And then where would we be?"

I laughed, grasping the hammer tightly. "I'm glad you gave it to me."

"It was meant to be yours, that much is clear," Björn said, giving Alex a nod of greeting before returning his full attention to me. "Keep faith and love Thor, and you will have all the strength you need to face any challenge—I promise you that."

"Don't encourage her," my father said, but it was warm and teasing as he extended his hand to Björn. "She's already got more than enough strength in her to conquer the world. Courage and stubbornness, too."

"The stubbornness she gets from her father, not her god," Anja said, sniffing. "And don't think I've forgiven you so easily, Congressman. Putting your daughter through all that grief for nothing more than your pride. When Irena told me what was happening, I had half a mind to fly over here myself and give you a piece of *my* mind. You're lucky that Emma had the grace and the courage to do what you wouldn't."

My father wrapped his arm around my shoulders. "And I count myself lucky every day—don't you doubt it for a moment."

Things weren't perfect yet between us, but we'd come a long way. If he still worried more than I wished he would about what other people thought of me and my faith, or Anja and Björn's—well, at least I knew it was because he wanted to protect me. Not because he didn't understand me or refused to accept my beliefs.

Having the election won and behind us had helped a lot. But mostly, I think it was that after my speech, he'd realized that just because I'd rejected Catholicism, it didn't mean I was rejecting everything else he'd taught me.

"If you'll follow me up, Björn?" Alex said. "I can show you which room you're in."

"And then the mead," Björn said, kissing Anja's cheek as he passed her by with his own luggage. "You and I and Emma will pour an offering of thanks for our safe travels, and we will share the rest."

I wasn't sure really what to make of Auntie Anja's husband. He laughed loudly and often, drank a little more than I thought anyone should—but cheerfully, at least—and seemed to wear his faith far more openly and unashamedly than anyone I'd ever known. But he loved Anja. No one could doubt it, the way he looked at her and the way she looked back, and if I hadn't had Alex, I might have been a little bit jealous of how utterly happy they seemed to be.

"Björn's family is descended from Erik the Red," Auntie Anja told us one night—boasting, I thought, really. "They were Greenlanders who came back to Iceland half a dozen generations later."

"We like to say we're Freydís's bastards," he said. "The story goes that she carried on an affair with a stranger who traveled to Greenland with Karlsefni and his crew. In my family, we believe he was Thor, and that was why she refused to become Christian. Because she had known the love of her god and could not bear the thought of betraying him. But of course none of that was written in the sagas—just family lore, passed down from mother to daughter and father to son."

"Is that what brought you to Heathenry?" I asked. "That story?"

He shrugged. "I'm not certain I was ever anything but Ásatrú. All my life, Thor was with me, I think. Just out of sight. Waiting for me to recognize him. But when I was ready, not before."

My breath caught, my throat closing at how easily he'd captured my own feeling, my own experience. "Yes."

His gaze found mine, and I felt that familiar shiver—electricity shimmying down my spine. "We need only keep faith. As Freydís did, so long ago."

"Poor Freydís," I said softly. "I wonder if she realized what it would mean. If she would have made the same choices or followed Gudrid to God instead, to be remembered with fondness instead of turned into a villainess."

"Would you?" Björn asked.

Alex shifted beside me on the couch, his hand on my knee, and I knew he was listening, wondering what my answer would be. I covered his hand and laced my fingers through his.

"It would have been easier, maybe, but I would have felt . . . empty."

Björn nodded, as if that was all the answer he needed. "More than likely, Freydís would have been forgotten altogether, I think, if she had accepted Christ. It is because she fights that we remember her. Because of her stubbornness and her violence, because she refused to live her life on any terms but her own, no matter what her family wanted of her or what was expected by her society. May we all rise to the challenges of our time with her ferocity of spirit."

"Didn't you hear?" Alex said, a smile in his voice. "Emma already has."

Björn laughed at my flush and leaned forward, raising his cup in salute. "Perhaps there is a little Freydís in your blood, too."

"Don't be ridiculous," Anja said, saving me. "*Our* family is descended from Snorri Sturluson. Though whether that's something to be proud of or ashamed of, I still haven't made up my mind."

"I think that's the better explanation for Emma's brilliance, personally," my mother said. "No one but a poet could have pulled that speech out of thin air."

"Alex helped," I said.

"Hardly," he said. "And even if I'd written it start to finish, it was your heart that sold it."

I leaned back, lifting up his arm to snuggle beneath it. "I'm just glad we both got to keep our jobs."

"And what *are* you planning on doing after your year of teaching is up?" Alex asked, teasing me now. "If you had some kind of five-year plan I could spin for the illusion of momentum and success . . ."

I *momentumed* a pillow right into his face, and it wasn't long after that we made our escape back to the guesthouse and some small amount of privacy among the half-packed boxes of my belongings. Björn had already offered to help with some of the heavy lifting of my move, and Alex and I meant to make the most of it.

But that night, I was glad to still have a bed nearby.

And tomorrow, I'd have to remember to thank Snorri with some mead.

CHAPTER FIFTY-THREE:
AD 1004
FREYDÍS

I had not doubted for a moment that Leif would come. My husband's men were not so loyal to me, too Christian to lie for my sake to my brother's face for long. And Leif was the only family I had left, but for the son Sonnung had given me, and Thorvard, who would not look me in the eye. There was little satisfaction in the freedom his fear had bought me. Not until Sonnung came again to return our son to my side and Thorvard left us in peace, and not when Leif rode up the barely worn path to our modest longhouse, his expression set and grim.

"You came a long way for nothing," I told him, gesturing for one of Thorvard's slaves to see to my brother's horse. In truth, I had expected him months ago, but perhaps I had overestimated his courage. "And I am surprised the chieftain of Brattahlid would come so far at all."

Leif's face was red from the wind and his riding, and there were lines around his mouth and eyes that had not been there before. But that, and the filth of his clothes, were to be expected when he must have spent days upon his horse, sleeping rough along the way. "You know why I've come, Freydís."

"To make a show of your power," I agreed. "And that is why you did not summon me to Brattahlid but came here alone, and by horse instead of sailing. So that your men would not see how weak you are after all."

His jaw went tight, a muscle jumping near his temple. "You should be exiled for what you've done, outlawed."

"Should I?" I asked. "For defending myself?"

"You murdered five women with your own hands!"

I swallowed, grasping the hammer at my throat. "Slaves. Of the men who attacked and dishonored me. Women who watched what was done to me and lied, because I was not Christian. Because I was a pagan who deserved what I had suffered, who they had hoped would die. If I killed them, it was my right. And if they died, it is because your god was weak and mine was strong."

My brother looked away, doubt and fear creeping like shadow across his face. "If your gods are so powerful, why have they done nothing to stop Christ's rise?"

On the ship and since our return, I'd had long quiet days to think on this. To consider what it meant that Sonnung had come, and how he had protected me. How Thor had protected me. And now I had no doubts.

"Why should they defend men and women who are so weak? So eager to see them replaced? The gods reward us for our honor, our loyalty, our strength, and our faith. Perhaps they were glad to see the back of you, if you could be so easily swayed. Perhaps they watched you slink off to hide behind your Christ and sneered."

"You think yourself so much better, Freydís, simply because you are too foolish and stubborn to accept Christ. No one else in Greenland has refused baptism, even if they worship the old gods alongside the new. No one but you!"

There was Thorhall, too, but for his loyalty and friendship, I had given him Finnbogi and Helgi's ship, and he had left. My actions were too much even for him to excuse. Only Sonnung understood.

I lifted my chin. "Then I alone have been loyal. I have honored the gods and our ancestors as they should be honored, and the spirits of the land. In turn, Thor has honored me. And I promise you, Brother, if you raise a hand against me now, seek to punish me for acting in my own defense, you will learn quickly, too, whose god is the stronger warrior. I will stand, and you will fall."

My brother stared at me, his jaw working and his hand upon the pommel of his sword. I did not have to touch my knife—I was so certain of myself, of Thor's protection and strength. A shame Leif could not say the same, his hesitation shouting the truth of his god's weakness and my brother's own doubts. I smiled, wild and ready, and he flushed, dropping his hand.

"You are my sister," he said, as if he had always been fond of me. As if he had ever loved me as Thorstein or even Thorvaldur had. As if it were not fear that stayed his hand. "I have no desire to do you harm. Wherever you place your faith, it is between you and the gods. Whatever crimes you committed elsewhere—they, too, are between you and the gods."

I snorted at his pretended compassion. "The laws of Greenland do not reach across the sea. You are no king, and the king you served, who might have supported you, is long dead now. As I said before, you have come a long way for nothing. I have no need of your pardon or your protection."

He glared at me, but if he had expected gratitude, he was an even greater fool than I had believed. "When the day comes that you no longer live under the protection of your god, be certain that I will remember your words."

And then he climbed upon his horse again and started back the way he had come.

But I only laughed at his toothless threat, pleased to see his back stiffen at the sound.

After all, I was still Freydís Thorswoman, though I doubted anyone would remember me by that name, and after everything I had seen and done, I was certain of one thing if nothing else: so long as I honored the gods and raised my son to love them as I had promised, I would be free.

I might be loathed, scorned and hated by the Christians, but I would still keep faith.

And Thor would never abandon me.

AUTHOR'S NOTE

S adly, I am not an Icelander. For that reason, I must humbly beg forgiveness for taking liberties with the narratives of *The Saga of Erik the Red* and *The Saga of the Greenlanders*. Together they make up what we call *The Vinland Sagas*, and from them I teased out the tale of Freydís, the very problematic and sometimes outright villainous daughter of Erik the Red. My only defense is that these sagas are not, by their nature, true accountings of what happened, but rather the oral tradition belatedly recorded hundreds of years after the events took place.

Much like in Homer's *Iliad*, there is little we can be absolutely certain of. But what we *do* know is this: At some point around the year 1000, some intrepid Norsemen sailed across the Atlantic to North America, settling eventually in Newfoundland in Canada for some unknown period of time. We found the remains of their longhouses at L'Anse aux Meadows, along with evidence of ironwork of some kind, and detritus that suggests they sailed at least as far south as the Saint Lawrence River. And as far as what we can know for certain goes—that's about it.

The sagas tell us a little bit more—that Leif Eriksson, the most famous son of Erik the Red, was the first European to set foot on these newly discovered (but already occupied) lands, one portion of which he named Vinland. After he returned to Greenland, boasting of his find, an Icelander named Thorfinn Karlsefni, at the urging of his wife, Gudrid, chose to sail to Vinland to explore it more properly—even, perhaps, to found a colony, if he could. In between these two adventures, it's possible that Thorvaldur and Thorstein, Leif's brothers, ventured across the sea at least once, and after Karlsefni's attempt at a settlement failed (for what reason we'll never actually know—nor can we be certain that a permanent settlement was actually his intention), it's possible that Freydís led a journey of her own. There is not, however, any mention of a man named Sonnung in those sagas, and his romance with Freydís is entirely my own invention—though to those of you familiar with my writing as Amalia Dillin, he is perhaps not entirely unexpected in his appearance.

The actual order of the events recorded in the sagas and the actual accomplishments of the individuals involved are impossible to know for sure, but it's likely that the journeys documented in the preserved accounts weren't the last or only trips across the Davis Strait. The Greenlanders had no significant source of lumber of their own and depended upon trade, primarily with Norway, to supply it—and while Erik the Red might have had a temper and/or an incredible run of bad luck, I doubt very much he raised his children to be fools. Why waste hard-won walrus ivory trading for wood if it can be gotten elsewhere for free? Leif was generally considered to be a strong leader and a good man, upstanding and honorable in every way—which is to say, perhaps not the coward Gudrid and Freydís accuse him of being in *this* book, though from his glancing interactions with his sister in the sagas, I have no trouble believing that he saw Freydís as a problem he wasn't at all sure how to solve. Whether that was because she was pagan and he was commissioned to convert Greenland to Christianity by King

Olaf of Norway (who was in fact determined to convert both Norway and Iceland as well, and not above resorting to the torture and murder of pagans to see it done), or because she took after their father as an unpredictable and ill-tempered murderess—well, I'm obviously inclined to believe the answer might be both. But the truth is, we don't even know whether Freydís lived, or whether she was an invention of the saga authors to serve as a foil to the pious Gudrid.

Finally, because we just aren't sure which communities the Norsemen were interacting with as they explored the now-Canadian coast, I think it's incredibly important to note that I portrayed the indigenous peoples of North America as they were recorded in the sagas. The archaeological evidence we have is extremely limited, as is Freydís's perspective, and as a result, so is the illustration of the First Peoples in this book. *Skraeling* is an unflattering Old Norse word that indicated an othering of the native peoples it describes, and the term almost certainly referred to more than one community. The sagas include an account of Thorvaldur's adventures and death at the hands of so-called skraelings (along with the reported deaths of several of the native people at the hands of the Norse) in an area well outside the bounds of the settlement in Newfoundland, for instance, and this same word was also used to refer to ancestors of Inuits in northern Greenland.

I absolutely recommend reading these sagas for yourselves to learn more about the details (and variations) of the events I've explored in this book—they're both relatively short, with translations available to read for free online, and well worth the time! In addition, I found *The Far Traveler* by Nancy Marie Brown to be a very readable nonacademic survey of what we *think* we know about Gudrid and *The Vinland Sagas* today. And if, like me, you're fascinated by the pre-Christian religious traditions of the Norse people, which were highly localized and variable in their time but by the nature of their preservation have become viewed as far more monolithic than they ever were in reality, definitely get a copy of *Nordic Religions in the Viking Age* by Thomas A. Dubois, which covers not only pagan traditions but the coming of and adoption of Christianity, and addresses how these faiths might have influenced one another. (Spoiler: they influenced one another a *lot*.)

For more information on the Viking Age generally, Iceland, and its settlement and culture, you might find *Viking Age Iceland* by Jesse L. Byock interesting, as well as *The Vikings: A History* by Robert Ferguson, from whom, in part, Emma gets her less than flattering portrayal of Charlemagne's campaigns. I also encourage you to explore *The Norse Mythology Blog* by Dr. Karl E. H. Seigfried (who also inspired Emma's discussion of Charlemagne) at www.norsemyth.org, which contains an incredible wealth of resources. Lastly, www.hurstwic.org and www. vikinganswerlady.com shouldn't be overlooked for quick and often in-depth reference.

In the contemporary timeline, while Emma's town and district in New Hampshire are pure invention, her faith and beliefs as a Heathen are true to life in that modern Heathenry, particularly within the United States, takes many forms. Her spiritual experiences and particular beliefs in regard to her gods should not necessarily be considered typical, because there is no typical. And like the religion of the Norse peoples over a thousand years ago, every individual community of modern Heathens has a slightly (or sometimes wildly) different take on what their faith and beliefs entail. While it's likely that all of them relate to the gods of the historical Norse peoples and their way of living to some degree, *how* they relate to those gods or what they believe those gods to be is highly localized and variable. For some Heathens, the myths are purely metaphor. For others, the gods are very real presences, if not in their lives, at least within the world itself. And for the rest, a thousand shades in between.

Most Heathens of my acquaintance will agree that (1) community is essential to the Heathen way of life, (2) veneration and honoring of ancestors and land spirits should never be overlooked, and (3) personal relationships with the Norse gods are very unusual and/or share little in the way of similarity with the kind of personal relationship with Jesus familiar to Christians. Generally speaking, that relationship with the divine (and other spirits), if it exists at all, is dependent on reciprocal gift giving, which is why Emma makes offerings of libations and food items to the gods as part of her rituals and prayers—to solicit the blessings she's looking for in exchange.

Even writing this book as a Heathen myself, I am certain my portrayal is flawed. There is no way to really be comprehensive, to address every variation of Heathenry that exists, in one narrative following one person in one town, and Emma's lack of faith community is one glaring issue in her representation, which I hope is recognized by fellow Heathens as part of the conflict and struggle of her character.

If you'd like to learn more about modern Heathenry, *Óðrœrir: The Heathen Journal* (odroerirjournal.com) is a fantastic resource where you'll find links to translations of the lore, and articles discussing what we've learned about how the Norse peoples worshipped and how that's applied today in our modern world to reconstruct their faith.

It's my greatest hope that in this book you'll recognize a spectrum of spirituality, faith, and belief on both the Pagan and Christian side, with neither faith tradition given more or less legitimacy than the other, except through the eyes of the characters themselves. Because Emma and Freydís both believe in the Norse gods, for example, it's natural that they would see Thor's power at work. But I hope very much that their perspective is not read as a denial of the reality of Christianity or the divinity of Jesus for Christians. I believe in the depths of my soul that religion and spirituality are very personal experiences, and while Christianity may not fit Freydís or Emma, that doesn't mean it's less legitimate in any way, shape, or form.

There is no doubt in my mind that Emma is fortunate to live in the modern world, in a land where her freedoms are legally protected. Perhaps, like Freydís, she still sacrifices some portion of her reputation and standing in her community to worship freely, but thanks to the

First Amendment and the support of influential members of her community, she won't live in fear of conversion by the sword. She will never be forced to choose between her life or her faith. Even her ability to reject the faith community in which she was raised and choose another that fits her more naturally is an incredible privilege.

But what is true for Emma, a woman of high standing and privilege in her community, is not always true for all people today—even in the United States. If she simply felt called by her god to cover her hair, she might have faced a much more dangerous backlash. She might have been told outright she doesn't belong in her community, sneered at as a terrorist, harassed, and even physically attacked. In short, if she did not have the advantage of *appearing* to fit in with the prevailing faith and culture of her community, she might just as easily have faced difficulties not entirely dissimilar to those of pagans like Freydís living in Iceland or Greenland a thousand years ago.

I hope and pray that it will not be another thousand years before we can finally put this kind of prejudice firmly behind us, but in the meantime, hopefully the stories of Emma and Freydís might at least contribute positively in some small way to getting us there.

ACKNOWLEDGMENTS

I have to quickly thank the friends and family who supported me in writing this far too personal book—Karen, Diana Paz, Mia, Mattias, and Emi. This was a rough one, I know, and I appreciate all your encouragement and patience while I slew the beast.

Also, I want to thank my editors Jodi, Kelli, and Tegan not just for letting me write this book, but for helping me to write it well. I still can't really believe it's happening. I'm sure I'll be kind of wishing it weren't before we're through, but I can't tell you how much it means to me to see this manuscript, with Emma as I wrote her, become a book.

Thanks also to Aunt Debbie and Uncle Johnny for sending me the right tools at the right times so that I had them when I needed them while writing this incredibly difficult story. Those runes became a lifeline.

And last, but never least, thanks so much to Adam, who gifted me my bronze Mjölnir pendant even before he realized I was Heathen, and accepted my unexpected conversion with incredible understanding, love, support, and every reassurance I could ever have hoped for. I couldn't be me without you. <3

ABOUT THE AUTHOR

Amalia Carosella began as a biology major before taking Latin and falling in love with old heroes and older gods. After that, she couldn't stop writing about them, with the occasional break for more contemporary subjects. She graduated with a BA in classical studies as well as English from the University of North Dakota. A former bookseller and an avid reader, she is fascinated by the Age of Heroes and Bronze Age Greece, though anything Viking Age or earlier is likely to capture her attention. She maintains a blog relating to classical mythology and the Bronze Age at www.amaliacarosella.com and can also be found writing fantasy under the name Amalia Dillin at www.amaliadillin.com. Today, she lives with her husband in Upstate New York and dreams of the day she will own goats (and maybe even a horse, too).